Heidi Swain lives in Norfolk with her husband, two allegedly grown-up children and a mischievous black cat called Storm. She is passionate about gardening, the countryside and collects vintage paraphernalia. *Mince Pies and Mistletoe at the Christmas Market* is her third novel.

You can follow Heidi on Twitter @Heidi_Swain or visit her blog: http://www.heidiswain.blogspot.co.uk/

Also by Heidi Swain

The Cherry Tree Café
Summer at Skylark Farm

Heidi Swain

Mince Pies and Mistletoe at The Christmas Market

**SIMON &
SCHUSTER**

London · New York · Sydney · Toronto · New Delhi

A CBS COMPANY

First published in Great Britain by Simon & Schuster UK Ltd, 2016
A CBS COMPANY

Copyright © Heidi-Jo Swain, 2016

1 3 5 7 9 10 8 6 4 2

Simon & Schuster UK Ltd
1st Floor
222 Gray's Inn Road
London WC1X 8HB

www.simonandschuster.co.uk

Simon & Schuster Australia, Sydney
Simon & Schuster India, New Delhi

A CIP catalogue record for this book
is available from the British Library

Paperback ISBN: 978-1-4711-6876-5
eBook ISBN: 978-1-4711-4727-2

Typeset in Bembo by M Rules
Printed and bound by CPI Group (UK) Ltd, Croydon, CR0 4YY

Simon & Schuster UK Ltd are committed to sourcing paper
that is made from wood grown in sustainable forests and support the Forest
Stewardship Council, the leading international forest certification organisation.
Our books displaying the FSC logo are printed on FSC certified paper.

To Amelia
Merry Christmas my darling girl

Chapter 1

As I stood in the chilly kitchen of the poky student flat I had called home for the last three years, waiting for the kettle to boil, I couldn't help wishing I had dropped out of university before the temperature had plummeted from autumnal to arctic. I still wasn't really looking forward to moving back in with Mum and Dad, but at least in my childhood home the frost was firmly fixed to the outside of the windows and my bed was always aired and warm.

There could be no denying that Dad was disappointed that I had abandoned studying my Masters and the associated opportunities he had been so keen for me to grasp, but at least now, thanks to Lizzie and Jemma and The Cherry Tree Café, I had an alternative to placate him with, not to mention an opportunity to swell the savings for my far-flung travel plans.

Running a cake and craft themed market stall in the run

up to Christmas might not have been what Dad had in mind for my first-class graduate status, but at least it would show him that I was prepared to enter the world of work and wasn't expecting him to pick up the tab as he so generously had for the last three and a bit years.

I finally had a 'life plan' of sorts mapped out, and as well as adding to the money I had squirrelled away, courtesy of my part-time hours spent waitressing and working in bars, I was desperate for the chance to get back into Dad's good books. I was worried about him and didn't feel at all comfortable about how increasingly preoccupied Mum said he was by his work at the council. Going home to Wynbridge would give me a chance to put lots of things in my life back on an even keel and you never know, I might even find a way to finally get over Steve Dempster, the boy who had broken my heart and whom I had never really stopped loving.

'So you *really* are sure you want to do this?' said Lizzie from the cosy sitting room of her flat above The Cherry Tree Café for what felt like the hundredth time. 'Because I'd hate for us to be the cause of even more friction between you and your dad.'

'It'll be fine,' I reassured her, cradling the phone against my ear whilst scrunching up my frozen toes and absentmindedly stirring a heaped teaspoon of sugar into my coffee. 'Like

I said, the extra money will boost the travel savings and my willingness to dive into work is bound to put me back in favour with Dad. This is actually the perfect opportunity for me to rebuild some bridges,' I added, thinking not just of my father.

'Well, I know it's selfish,' said Lizzie, who sounded far from sorry, 'but I for one will be delighted to see you, even though the circumstances could be better, and I know Bea will be thrilled, as will Jemma.' She lowered her tone to a confidential whisper. 'She's still trying to find ways to do everything herself as usual, but it's impossible and she's absolutely exhausted.'

'Still no holiday booked then?' I asked, taking a sip of the bitter, cheap coffee and mentally counting off the hours until I could treat myself to a cup of the café's finest blend.

'Nope,' Lizzie sighed resignedly. 'I honestly don't know how she does it.'

Given that I had only recently turned twenty-two, was single and for the most part carefree, I didn't know how she did it either. Since Jemma had opened the café, she had only taken two weeks off and that was after the birth of her son Noah. Somehow she managed to juggle the business, two small children and a husband who worked all hours. Even the mere thought of her hectic work–life balance was exhausting to me!

'I try and do as much as I can,' Lizzie continued, 'however,

3

on top of everything else this market stall idea is just too much for the pair of us, even though we're desperate to see it succeed.'

'Of course,' I told her, 'I totally understand.'

'And we're really up against it time-wise now,' she carried on regardless, 'we're almost halfway through November already for goodness' sake!'

'Look,' I said, tipping the rest of the coffee down the sink and rinsing out the mug, 'don't worry about it. Just get everything as prepared as you can and I'll take care of the rest. I'll be with you in a couple of days. By this time next week everything will be up and running like clockwork. I guarantee it.'

Lizzie didn't answer immediately and I knew exactly what she was working herself up to say.

'And you're sure it won't be a problem if you run into . . .'

Her words trailed off and I took a deep breath before answering.

'Oh Lizzie,' I said, in as blasé a tone as I could muster, 'Steve Dempster and I haven't been an item for over three years, and I haven't clapped eyes on him for the last two. I think we're both grown up enough to be able to live and work in the same town, and besides,' I added with a shrug she couldn't see, 'for all I know he could be married with a couple of kids by now.'

'Well, as long as you're sure,' said Lizzie with concern.

I could all too easily imagine her chewing her lip and frowning.

'I am,' I said again, wishing I could find a way to truly convince both her and myself. 'I really am.'

'But what we're asking you to do will mean your paths are bound to cross practically every day,' Lizzie went relentlessly on. 'Odds are you'll end up working right next to him. The Dempster family fruit and veg empire dominates that market. You know full well that theirs is the biggest stall by far.'

'Yes, I do know,' I cut in. 'Believe me, Lizzie, I have thought about all that.'

I'd thought of little else during the last few days. In fact, I'd thought about it so much I'd gone and spent the last of my ready cash having my eyebrows threaded and my thick dark hair pampered with a lavish hot oil treatment, but I didn't tell Lizzie that because I didn't want her to get the wrong idea. After all, there was no harm in a girl taking care of herself, was there?

'Fair enough,' she finally relented, 'oh and by the way . . .'

'Hmm?'

'He isn't married and he certainly doesn't have any kids.'

I wasn't sure if that made me feel better or worse. I really had been head over heels in love with Steve Dempster when he dumped me just before we were due to leave together for university. Had it not been for the untimely death of his older

5

brother and Steve's insistence that he needed to stay and help with the family business, I was sure we would have gone, but given the tragic circumstances, our relationship simply wasn't meant to be.

Of course I'd never managed to muster the emotion to *really* hate him for picking the family grocery firm over me because the whole situation was just too sad and I knew the heart-wrenching decision had been born out of duty. It was a totally selfless act and one that, in some ways, made me feel inconveniently even fonder of him.

'Well, whatever,' I said, quickly dismissing all thoughts of my former beau and thinking that 'dumping' was really too harsh a word to describe what had happened. 'As I said before, I'm looking forward to doing this for you and Jemma. Just have everything ready and leave the rest to me.'

'I can't wait,' said Lizzie again, a noticeable edge of excitement creeping back into her voice. 'See you Monday!'

I might have been moving back to Wynbridge, but there was one thing I was sure of – I was definitely *not* going to 'do a Lizzie Dixon'. She had returned to our hometown when I was an A level student, fallen hook, line and sinker for Ben Fletcher and her crafting business at The Cherry Tree Café, and never left. My own plans really couldn't have been further from hers, but I was grateful for the lifeline that she and Jemma had thrown me nonetheless.

Thanks to them, I finally had my way forward all figured

out. I was going to repair my relationship with Dad, find a way to get over Steve Dempster, have fun with my best friend Bea, earn myself some extra money and then head straight to the travel agent's and book a ticket to somewhere hot, exotic and exciting.

'Here you are at last!' said Mum, rushing down the path to meet me and pulling me into a tight hug. 'I was beginning to get worried.'

'I told you I wouldn't be here before three,' I laughed, breathing in the comforting scent of her familiar Estée Lauder perfume. 'Why do you always halve the time I tell you a journey will take?'

'Because I can't wait to see you, of course,' Mum smiled, taking my face in her warm hands and kissing my rosy cheeks. 'And if you're such a clever clogs then why don't you just double the time you tell me you'll take to get here?'

That was actually a very good point.

'Come on,' she said, finally releasing me and walking back up the path, 'let's get you inside. It's freezing out here.'

'But what about my stuff?'

'We'll get it in a bit.'

She knew as well as I did that I was putting off the moment of going inside and facing Dad.

'Oh come on,' she said, reaching for my hand. 'You'll feel better once you've seen him.'

Personally I wasn't so sure, but I knew I couldn't put it off forever.

'She's here!' Mum called through the hall before I had a chance to head up the stairs to the sanctuary of my room and together we walked to the kitchen.

Dad was sitting at the table with the local newspaper spread out in front of him and a yellow highlighter poised over the page. Marking up all the gaffes in the weekly paper was one of his favourite pastimes and I felt my lips curve into a smile as I realised that even though his little hobby used to annoy the hell out of me it was comforting to know that some things hadn't changed.

'Ruby,' he said, pushing back his chair and jumping up to give me a hug.

I was completely undone by his demonstrative welcome and wrapped my arms around his familiar bulk. He was almost ten years older than Mum, but in that moment he struck me as even older. The feel of his arms around me reminded me of his father, a wholly different man, and I was grateful for the warm and uplifting embrace that I had missed on more than one occasion since I left for university.

'I'm so sorry about it all, Dad,' I said into his chest, 'I know I probably should have been able to stick it out, but I'd just had enough.'

'Hey now,' he said, kissing the top of my head. 'Don't worry about it. I understand.'

'Do you?' I asked, pulling away a little and looking up at him and wondering if perhaps rebuilding our relationship was going to be easier than I thought. Perhaps being away from home and stewing over everything in such minute detail had meant I'd actually got his opinion on my decision to leave university out of all proportion. 'Do you really?'

'Of course I do,' he said reassuringly, rubbing my back, 'I'm not a complete ogre, you know!'

'I know,' I laughed, blowing my nose on the kitchen roll Mum handed me and shaking my head. 'I'm sorry,' I sniffed.

'I'm just pleased to have you home,' he said, pulling out a chair for me and sitting himself down at the table again. 'You shouldn't be working in bars and living in that damp old house. You know your mum and I have only ever wanted the best for you and if you felt that leaving university was the right thing to do then so be it. I'm just grateful that you've decided to come back here to us. This is where you should be now, shouldn't she, love?'

'Well, yes,' said Mum, an edge of doubt creeping into her tone. 'But only as long as this is where she wants to be, of course . . .'

'This is where she belongs.' Dad beamed.

Mum opened her mouth to say something else, but I cut her off.

'But you do know that this is just for a few weeks, just for the holidays really, don't you, Dad?' I said gently. 'Like

9

I explained to Mum on the phone, I'm still planning to go travelling abroad in the New Year.'

'Absolutely,' he nodded agreeably, 'and that sounds wonderful. To tell you the truth, I wish I'd seen a bit more of the world when I was your age.'

I began to relax again, relieved that he really did understand.

'But why don't you consider hanging on for a bit?' he went on, fixing me with a meaningful stare. 'Why not wait and see what the New Year in Wynbridge has to offer?'

'What do you mean?'

'Well,' he said. 'You'll need money for your travels, won't you, and there are always vacancies at the council in January. Vacancies for good jobs, Ruby, that would give you something worthwhile to add to your CV before you jet off. I hate the thought of you selling yourself short, especially after all the hard work you've put into your academic career during the last three years.'

'But the people doing the hiring these days are happy for prospective employees to have seen a bit of the world,' I insisted. 'They like their interviewees to have lived a little and gained some life experience.'

Just because Dad loved his work at the council and had always been a passionate ambassador for the little town, he seemed to live in the hope that one day I would want to follow in his footsteps and he was clearly not above using my rather thin CV to manipulate me into changing my plans. This new argument was little more than an upgraded variation on ones we had had before and they had always ended with me knowing he would, at some point, try again to tether me to the town which would always mean more to him than me.

'And they'll have wonderful salaries,' he carried on as if I hadn't said a word, 'especially for someone with a first-class degree! I'm not suggesting for one second that you don't go travelling at all, but why not spend a few months working first? That way, as well as enhancing your future prospects, you'll be able to put away even more money and travel in style instead of slumming it on one of those hazardous all-in backpacker deals.'

'Absolutely not,' I sniffed, feeling annoyed that I'd been lulled into believing that my homecoming was going to be easier than I initially thought. 'Thank you for thinking of me,' I said as graciously as I could manage, 'but the answer is definitely no.'

'Well, it was just an idea,' he smiled amicably. 'But you really do need to give some serious thought as to what you'll do for money,' he reminded me. 'How do you expect to fund these far-flung globetrotting dreams of yours? I know you've told Mum you've been saving as much as you can but plane tickets aren't cheap and you'll need at least a few hundred pounds in a contingency account just in case anything goes wrong. You really do need to be thinking about some sort of job, Ruby.'

'I have,' I told him, proudly thrusting out my chin and thanking my lucky stars that I really had got it all sorted. 'I start work on Monday.'

'Oh, that's wonderful,' said Mum, as she filled the teapot with steaming water from the kettle. 'Isn't that wonderful, Robert?'

'What job?' Dad pounced, his eyes narrowed slightly as if he wasn't altogether sure he believed me.

'I'm going to work for Jemma and Lizzie at The Cherry Tree Café again.'

'Waiting on tables?' he said, raising his eyebrows.

'Well, she does have the experience,' Mum kindly stepped in.

'No,' I said, 'not waitressing, actually. They're taking on a market stall until Christmas Eve and I'm going to be running that. Lizzie wants me to sell her Christmassy crafting bits and pieces and Jemma has come up with some special seasonal bakes.'

My admission was met with a stony silence.

'I'm going to be working on the market selling mince pies and mistletoe, Dad. How does that sound?'

'Oh no,' he said sternly, his affable attitude heading right out of the door. 'That's completely out of the question. Those wretched market traders have been nothing but trouble during the last few months and the last thing I want is you joining forces with them. Did you know about this job before you decided to drop out of university?' he added sharply.

'Of course not,' I gasped, furious that he thought I had been scheming behind his back. 'I just didn't want to study any more and if you'd been listening to a word I'd said when I graduated last year you would have realised that before you encouraged me to enrol for my Masters.'

'Sorry,' he said when he saw how hurt I was by his accusation. 'I shouldn't have said that.'

'No,' Mum tutted. 'You shouldn't have.'

'But I don't care what you say,' he went on. 'A job at the council with me will be far better for you than working with that lot. I'm not having you out in all weathers in that market square.'

'Well, it isn't up to you,' I told him, trying not to let him see how upset I was. 'Everything's arranged. Apparently trade in the town has been a bit slack and this is Jemma and Lizzie's way of trying to help out for a few weeks and I haven't got any intention, as you put it, of joining forces with anyone. I'm just looking to earn some extra money.'

Dad's expression was unfathomable and part of me was expecting him to insist that if I wasn't prepared to back down then I should promise to consider a position at the council after the stall closed on Christmas Eve.

'I thought you'd be pleased,' I said, still keen to clear the air and win him round. 'I thought you'd be proud that I'd managed to sort something out on my own before I got here.'

He didn't say anything else, just stood up, walked out of the kitchen, slamming the door behind him and leaving me nursing a giant slab of heartache and an uncomfortable sense of foreboding. I had had such high hopes for a reconciliatory reunion but now I couldn't help thinking that perhaps Mum's concerns about his behaviour were justified. Where had the reasonable Dad I loved so much disappeared to, I wondered, and more importantly, was it going to be possible to find him again before I left town?

Chapter 2

During the next twenty-four hours Dad surreptitiously tried every trick in the book to talk me out of taking up Jemma and Lizzie's proposition. He even offered to cash in one of his ISAs to fund my dreams of travelling the world out of his own pocket.

'But I thought you had that money earmarked for a new conservatory,' I reminded him just before bedtime on Saturday night. 'When you and Mum came to my graduation ceremony you said that you'd had a couple of local chaps in to measure up and that you were already thinking about designs that would complement the garden!'

'Yes,' he said, neatly folding his highlighted paper and setting it aside, 'well, that was before I knew what you were planning.'

I had known when I accepted Lizzie's offer that he was going to think the job was beneath me, but I hadn't bargained on him having had trouble with the traders as well. I had based my decision to push ahead in part on the fact that the market was, and always had been, an important part of the town and as such, given Dad's usually fierce local pride, I hoped he would be happy to see me working amongst the tight-knit community.

'Could you just clarify,' I asked, as another idea suddenly occurred to me, 'are you not happy that I'm going to be working on the market, or are you pissed off that I'll be rubbing shoulders with the Dempster family?'

Steve's dad, Chris, and my dad had hated each other for as long as I could remember. It had been a nightmare when Steve and I were dating, but Steve's mum, Marie, had always been kindness itself and my mum welcomed Steve with open arms, as long as Dad was out of the house, of course.

Neither Steve nor I had ever known the real reason behind our fathers' feud, but it went back years and for us was a complete pain in the backside. The men were both born and raised in the town and as such should have been firm friends, but they couldn't stand the sight of each other and I'd never bothered to try to get to the bottom of why. Perhaps now was the ideal time to start investigating.

'For a start,' Dad frowned, 'I will not tolerate that kind of language under my roof and secondly, this has nothing to do with the Dempster family. This is about you, Ruby. You need to be stretching yourself and looking for a position that matches your level of education and intelligence. How do you think "seasonal market trader" is going to look on your CV?'

'Considering jobs are so hard to come by in a small town at this time of year, industrious and adaptable, I hope,' I said cheekily, before slipping out of the room and up to bed.

Unfortunately he was still on a roll as we sat down to eat Mum's legendary Sunday roast beef dinner, and for that I begrudged him all the more. I had been craving her thick, rich gravy and crispy roast potatoes since the moment I decided I was first coming home and I resented the fact he wouldn't let the argument drop even long enough to let me clear my plate. His increasingly dogged attitude left me in no doubt about what Mum had had to put up with in the run up to my return.

'"He won't be that bad"!' I hissed in her ear as together we loaded the dishwasher after we'd finally cleared away our plates. 'Those were your exact words when we spoke on the phone, "I think he's coming round to the idea of you coming home early."'

'I know,' said Mum, biting her lip. 'He does seem a bit wound up, doesn't he?'

'A bit!' I frowned. 'He ruined dinner for me and I've been craving your Yorkshire puddings for weeks.'

Mum shook her head and set the machine to start.

'I can't believe,' I went on when she didn't say anything

else, 'that after all your years of being married to him you read him so wrong!'

'Well, if you'd told me about this market stall plan before you arrived,' she said sagely, 'I could have been working him round to the idea of that as well, couldn't I? How was I to know you had that little twist tucked up your sleeve?'

'I'm sorry,' I said, rubbing her arm and feeling guilty for expecting her to shoulder the responsibility for what I'd set in motion. 'I just didn't think it would be such a big deal. To tell you the truth, I thought he'd be pleased that I'd got something lined up and that I wouldn't be cluttering up the place watching TV all day.'

'You thought, that with your wonderful degree, he'd be pleased you were moving back home to be a Wynbridge market trader?' Mum said doubtfully.

'Oh God,' I sighed, wrinkling my nose. 'I really didn't think this through properly, did I?'

'No,' said Mum, 'you didn't, but then I suppose you were too busy thinking about . . .'

'Don't say it,' I warned her. 'Lizzie and I have already been through it and I've told her it's all fine.'

'What are you two whispering about in there?' Dad called through from the dining room.

'Nothing!' we chorused.

'We're just finishing the dishes,' Mum added.

'Well when you've done, come and look at this, Ruby,'

he called again. 'I've found a vacancy in last week's job supplement that you might be interested in: great salary and benefits, and before you say anything, it's only a temporary contract, six months at the most. It would be the perfect position and far better for you than risking frostbite every day.'

Mum and I looked at each other and rolled our eyes.

'Are you there?'

'No!' shouted Mum, switching to stealth mode and quickly steering me towards the utility room. 'She's just popped out to stretch her legs.'

I looked at her, open-mouthed.

'Oh go on,' she urged, 'take my coat and go and get some fresh air for goodness' sake.'

It was freezing outside and already getting dark, but the atmosphere was considerably more relaxed than the one I'd just left behind. I rammed Mum's woolly gardening hat on my head, grabbed her battered old wax coat and set off, thinking how ironic it was that I had planned to make my first appearance in public looking polished and pristine and here I was, wind-blasted with pinched features and frozen digits. I set off at a brisk pace, deciding to stick to the outskirts of the town, and wishing I had thought to pick up my purse so I could treat myself to a hot drink should I come across anywhere that was open.

I skirted the edge of the park which, thanks to the brisk

northerly breeze, was all but deserted. Only the most determined dog walkers were out, rushing along, heads bent, with no time or inclination to admire the dramatic silhouette of bare branches or the ragged clouds which scurried across the darkening sky.

I stopped for a second to look at the bandstand and remembered how it had been the focal point of so many clandestine teenage meetings. I had endured my first, and last, taste of a cigarette under its roof and enjoyed many, many lingering kisses. Giving myself a little shake I set off again, only now wondering if I had perhaps underestimated the impact that the thought of seeing Steve again had had on my decision to accept Lizzie and Jemma's timely invitation.

It didn't seem to matter how fast I walked or how far, I simply couldn't get warm and just a little further on I realised I could barely feel my toes. Gratefully I ducked through the gate of St Mary's Church with the intention of thawing off a little in the covered porch before heading back home. I forced myself not to think about how Steve had promised that one day this was where we would be married and have our children christened or how, just weeks later, his brother's funeral had snatched away all those youthful fantasies.

I had barely set foot on the hallowed ground when I spotted the man himself crouched over his brother's headstone tenderly arranging the flowers that I knew were replaced every week come rain or shine. Rooted to the spot, I stared at his bent head, my heart beating wildly in my chest and the chill of the wind suddenly no longer an issue. If anything I was grateful for its cooling impact on my blazing cheeks.

My first instinct was to turn tail and run, but I fended it off and instead raised my eyes to the heavens, threw up a quick prayer and continued along the path towards him. Why wait for our first meeting in the packed market square when I could get it over and done with in the relative privacy of the churchyard?

'Steve!' I called, my voice catching in my throat and the wind carrying it off and away.

I took another step closer and tried again.

'Steve!' It sounded odd, hearing my voice calling his name after all this time.

He twisted round, a frown firmly etched on his handsome face and the expression in his dark, heavily lashed eyes unfathomable from that distance. He stared at me for what felt like minutes but was actually only seconds, then stood up and walked to meet me on the path.

'Ruby?' he mouthed, evidently still not really sure that it was me.

'Hey,' I said, only just remembering the hat.

I pulled it off and quickly stuffed it in my coat pocket, then gave a silly, self-conscious little bob and a wave.

'Ruby Smith,' he said again, the frown now banished and

21

a tentative smile stepping up to take its place. 'My God, what are you doing here?'

For a second I couldn't supply him with an answer. I stared dumbstruck at the familiar but different face of the boy who had now become a man, and a stunning specimen of a man at that. His thick dark hair was worn longer than I remembered and the stubble was a little darker, but the deep brown smiling eyes and slightly crooked nose courtesy of the rugby pitch were familiar enough. He was broader than I remembered too, and taller. I realised with a jolt that the boy I had fallen in love with was all grown up and I can't deny there was a fleeting, but very definite flicker of disappointment that I no longer had a claim on his heart.

'I'm back for Christmas,' I said eventually and somewhat huskily. 'I've come back to see Mum and Dad.'

'My God,' he said, shaking his head as he devoured me with his eyes and his complexion flushed deep enough to match my own, 'I can't believe you're actually here.'

He seemed so genuinely pleased to see me that it was impossible not to wonder why he had let me go in the first place. I had begged him to give our relationship a chance to work long-distance but he had been adamant that a clean break was the only option and the best choice for both of us.

'Crikey,' he said, scratching his head and scuffing at the path with the toe of his boot, 'I don't know what to say. It's been so long.'

'I know,' I swallowed, 'I almost ran in the opposite direction when I spotted you.'

'Well, I'm glad you didn't,' he said, 'I can't tell you how many times I've wanted to get in touch and see how you're getting on.'

My heart was off and running again, like a steam train at full stretch and I couldn't help wishing I'd plucked up the courage to talk to him the last time I'd seen him instead of turning away and melting into the background.

'So why haven't you?' I asked, knowing full well that I hadn't been any braver.

'Because I couldn't think of what to say or text,' he admitted, 'and I was pretty sure your dad wouldn't be particularly thrilled if I just turned up on his doorstep. I can't imagine he would have welcomed me with open arms, can you?'

'No,' I said, biting my lip, 'I guess not.'

It was nice to know that he had been thinking about me, but I couldn't help wishing he'd acted on his feelings.

'So what are you up to these days?' he asked, rubbing his hands together before thrusting them deep in his coat pockets. 'Are you still at uni? You must have finished your degree by now.'

I opened my mouth to try and form some sort of response but was fortunately saved from having to explain that I would be working practically side by side with him for the next few weeks. Truth be told, I suddenly wasn't quite so sure that my heart and stomach could stand seeing him all day every day, especially if their current behaviour was anything to go by.

'Steve! Are you nearly done? I'm freezing. That bloody church is as cold as a morgue!' A tall slim figure with cascading blonde hair that, I couldn't help noticing, seemed to be behaving beautifully despite the breeze, stepped around the corner. 'Oh hello,' she said, looking me up and down before quickly linking arms with my former heart's desire. 'Who are you?'

'This is Ruby,' said Steve before I had a chance to introduce myself. 'She's an old friend,' he continued. 'We go way back.'

'Oh do you now?' said the woman, sounding less than impressed as she readjusted the collar of her immaculate red woollen coat.

'Ruby, this is Mia,' Steve went on, 'she's . . .'

'Freezing?' I interjected.

I had no desire to have the intricacies of their relationship spelled out. Given the proprietorial grasp Mia had on Steve's arm it was pretty obvious that she was his current other half. Now my heart felt like lead in my chest and had slackened its pace to merely ticking over.

'Well,' I said, pulling Mum's hat out of my pocket and ramming it back over my now less than glossy locks whilst trying to sound jolly and carefree, 'don't let me hold you up. It's about time I was getting back anyway.'

I had almost made it as far as the church gate before the tears came and Steve shouted after me.

'Hey, Ruby Sue!' he hollered. 'It's really good to see you again!'

He was the only person in the world who ever called me that. He had assigned me the nickname after one of the characters from *National Lampoon's Christmas Vacation*. We had been snuggled under his duvet one snowy Sunday in December enjoying a festive film marathon when he first said it and it had just stuck. His unexpected utterance of it again did nothing to stem the flow of tears as I hurried home.

The one good thing that came out of Steve's surprising use of my nickname was that it got me off the hook with my best friend Bea. So busy with packing and planning, I hadn't found the time to even tell her I was moving back home, let alone that I would be working on the market, and I had all my fingers crossed that furnishing her with a blow by blow account of my churchyard meeting would put her in a forgiving mood.

Bea had been my closest pal ever since we met. I had been studying for my A levels at college and she was working in her family's holistic health centre and attending college part-time. Ordinarily our paths probably wouldn't have crossed but Bea had a fondness for cake, anything sweet in fact, and more often than not it was me who ended up waiting on her table at The Cherry Tree Café during my time working there. Consequently we soon began to chat when we spotted each other at college and struck up a friendship that had stuck.

There had only been one awkward time in our relationship and that was when she started dating Steve's best friend, Sam. Fortunately however, I was immersed in university life by the time they got together and knowing how crazy she was about him I knew I had no right to make a fuss. I might have only been in my late teens but I recognised true love when I saw it.

'You know you really should have told me you'd decided to come back,' Bea pouted when I phoned her later that day and explained what I was planning to do. 'The last time I heard from you, you were staying in your seedy student pad for Christmas. I can't believe you've made all these decisions without me. I thought I was supposed to be your best friend!'

A heartfelt apology furnished with all the juicy details of my reacquaintance with Steve (excluding the unsatisfactory reaction of my heart) had, as I hoped, proved enough to gain Bea's forgiveness. I have to admit it was rather nice having a clandestine phone conversation about boys hidden under the duvet, hopefully out of earshot of my disapproving dad. I think we both felt about seventeen again.

'And he actually called you Ruby Sue?' Bea gasped when I told her how my little church visit had ended.

'Yep,' I confirmed, 'shouted it loud enough for the whole world to hear.'

'The cheeky bugger.'

'I know,' I said, biting my lip and feeling grateful that she was on the end of the phone line and not standing in front of me, because the way my eyes filled up again would have been a dead giveaway about how I was really feeling about what had happened.

I still couldn't believe he'd said it, especially not with the beautiful Mia clasped to his side. Initially he'd seemed awkward and a bit tongue-tied when he saw me but he'd obviously gotten over it pretty sharpish. Evidently he still had the cheek of the devil tucked away in his seductive armour.

'So what about you and Sam,' I enquired, knowing that nothing pleased Bea more than the opportunity to talk about her hunky firefighter boyfriend, who was coincidentally still Steve's best buddy. 'How are things going?'

Unusually she sounded less than certain.

'All right,' she said dully. 'I guess.'

'Just all right,' I frowned. 'That doesn't sound like you two. Normally when I ask about him you're tripping over yourself to tell me all about his latest grand romantic gesture.'

'Yes,' she said, 'well. There haven't been quite so many of those lately.'

'Oh,' I said. 'I'm sorry to hear that.'

'So am I,' she said sulkily. 'I really thought he was the

27

one, Ruby, but my dream Christmas proposal feels like it's slipping further out of my reach every day.'

'Oh Bea,' I sympathised, now wishing we were together so I could give her a comforting hug.

I knew there was nothing in the whole world that she wanted more than to live her life as if it had been lifted straight from the pages of a romance novel and ever since she had started dating Sam she had been hoping that he was the one who would deliver her heart's desire, along with her fantasy festive wedding proposal.

'Oh never mind,' she said briskly, 'tell me some more about what Mia was wearing.'

'No,' I said, unwilling to go back over it all again even though I knew she needed cheering up. 'I've already told you everything I can remember. God,' I sighed, 'can you imagine if *they* got engaged at Christmas?'

'Not likely,' sniffed Bea, 'I didn't even know they were dating and Sam tells me *everything* about Steve's love life. Sometimes I can't help thinking he envies his best friend's freedom to pick and choose a different woman every week.'

I can't deny I felt more than a little uncomfortable with the idea of Steve dating women on a weekly rotational basis.

Chapter 3

I've never been a fan of early starts, especially in the depths of winter when there is more dark than light crammed into the day, so the alarm buzzing away at six a.m. the next morning was less than welcome. I had spent the night tossing, turning and thinking about how different my life would have been if Steve's brother's motorbike had made it round the sharp right-hand bend at Hecate's Rest. It was shocking to think that at twenty-two I had already lived more of a life than Sean Dempster had ever had a chance to.

Unbearably for Steve and his parents there had never been any solid evidence to explain what had caused Sean to clip the trees that bordered the crossroads that night. Excessive speed was suggested, although everyone who knew him thought it unlikely. A deer in the road, or the involvement of another vehicle hadn't been ruled out either, but the plain truth was that no one knew and the family, along with their friends, had to come to terms with the fact that they never would.

'You all set then?' smiled Mum, setting down a steaming mug of tea and a glass of orange juice in front of me as I slumped at the kitchen table and twisted my hair up into a loose knot. 'You don't exactly look full of the joys.'

'I hate getting up in the dark,' I yawned. 'You know that.'

'Well, you'll just have to get used to it,' said Dad unhelpfully as he walked into the kitchen dressed, shaved and sickeningly prepared to face his working day. 'Market traders keep ungodly hours. Earlier than this actually,' he added glancing at the clock. 'Oh dear, you're running late already, Ruby!'

'Actually,' I snapped, snatching up the mug of tea, 'I'm early. We're just getting everything ready today. This time tomorrow I'll be setting up.'

My insides groaned at the thought, but I wasn't going to let Dad know how much I was suddenly dreading the early, frosty starts.

I skirted around the edges of my fellow traders in the market square. They all looked as though they had almost finished setting up and were ready to begin selling. I shuddered nervously at the thought that tomorrow I would be joining them, and made for The Cherry Tree Café. My sagging spirits soared as I pushed open the door, the rich aroma of the much-anticipated coffee sweeping over me, and the little bell announcing my arrival tinkling excitedly overhead. I had never been able to put my finger on exactly what it was that made the café so perfect, but the enthusiastic and warm welcome that enveloped me definitely went some way to explaining it.

'Ruby!' shouted Ella, Jemma's daughter, as she darted around the tables and chairs. 'You're here!'

'I am,' I beamed, 'and my goodness, look at you! However much have you grown?'

'Too much,' said Jemma, appearing from behind the counter, 'she's already outgrown the school shoes she had in September!'

'Jemma,' I said rushing towards her, 'gosh, it's good to see you.'

'And it's good to see you! I can't tell you what a relief it was when Lizzie said you were thinking about helping out with this market stall idea.'

'Well I'm not thinking any more,' I told her, 'it's happening. In fact, I can't wait to get started!'

If it wasn't for the absurdly early starts, I really would have been as enthusiastic as I pretended to be, but I wasn't about to say anything that would wipe the smile off Jemma's pretty face.

'Wait 'til you see what you're going to be selling,' said Ella dreamily. 'Everything Lizzie has made is so sparkly and pretty. I've already put loads of things on my Christmas list!'

'Christmas list,' I teased. 'Ella, it's the middle of November! Surely you can't be thinking about Christmas already?'

'Of course I can,' she said witheringly, 'it's my way of helping Mummy and Daddy spread the cost.'

Jemma looked at me and rolled her eyes.

'She's all heart, this one!' she laughed. 'Come and grab a coffee. Tom will be here with Noah in a minute. He's ferrying the kids about today so we'll have a few minutes to chat and look through the stock before we get busy.'

She slid a mug across the counter and I reverently cradled it in my hands, closed my eyes and breathed deeply.

'You're supposed to drink it,' said Lizzie as she pushed her way through the beaded curtain that separated her flat above the café from her work, 'not inhale it!'

'Oh I know,' I said, 'and I will, but first I just want to savour the moment.'

'Student overdrafts and waitressing wages don't run to finest blend then, I take it?' she asked, tying her pretty cupcake-patterned apron around her waist.

'Afraid not,' I sighed, 'but believe me,' I confirmed as I took my first sip, 'this has been totally worth the wait!'

A sudden rush of chilly air announced the arrival of Tom with Ella's curly haired little brother Noah and just after that Angela, the third member of the Cherry Tree workforce, joined the throng and the place descended into momentary chaos.

'So,' said Tom, helping himself to coffee as Angela made sure Noah was comfortable in his buggy and Jemma frantically checked that Ella had remembered to put her homework in her school book bag. 'How did your dad take the news?'

'Well, obviously he was overjoyed that I've decided not to finish my Masters,' I nodded.

'Oh Ruby,' he said impatiently. 'You know that's not what I'm talking about. I haven't dared mention anything about this stall idea when I've seen him at work. He's like a bear with a sore head at the best of times these days as it is.'

'Is he?' I frowned. 'Why's that then?'

That didn't sound like Dad at all. He was usually in his element at work. Even happier than when he was at home sometimes.

'I'm not really sure,' shrugged Tom, 'but I can't help feeling there's something a bit off going on that I don't know about and that your dad is at the centre of it.'

'Well, that doesn't sound right to me,' I told him, 'I think you're letting your imagination run away with you, Tom. You know as well as I do that Dad runs a very tight ship. He simply wouldn't allow anything untoward to be "going on" as you put it.'

'Well,' he sighed, 'I hope you're right and I'm sure time will tell but one thing I am sure of is that if he gets wind of the fact that I knew you were planning to help the girls run the stall, my life wouldn't be worth living.'

'Don't worry,' I told him, 'your name hasn't come up at home so if I were you, I'd deny all knowledge. Blame it on us girls.'

'You could even make out you aren't happy about the idea,' Angela suggested as she swept by, planting a perfunctory kiss on my cheek. 'I have something for you, Ruby,' she whispered.

I was just as thrilled to see Angela as Jemma and Lizzie. She had initially taken over my few hours when Dad made me give up the job to focus on revising for my A levels and she had been an instant hit. She was the perfect fit for the place and from what I could recall it wasn't long before she was spending as many hours as Jemma in the kitchen. Initially she had taken the job to see her through a rough time after the death of her husband, but now no one could imagine the place without her. Her daughter had moved to Australia a long time ago and I was sure both Lizzie and Jemma thought of her as an extra mum.

'Actually,' said Tom, raising his voice loud enough for Jemma to hear, 'to tell you the truth, I'm not all that sure I am pleased about it. Jemma has enough on her plate at the moment without having all this extra baking for the stall to worry about, even if it is just for a few weeks.'

'Don't start,' warned Jemma, pointing at the clock on the

wall, 'there's no time and anyway, Ruby's here to save the day. Everything's going to be fine now.'

'Was it not fine before then?' I said to Angela as she reappeared from the kitchen.

'Don't ask,' she whispered, spinning me around to tie my own apron in place. 'Just don't ask. There now,' she grinned, 'I think Jemma always hoped she'd see you wearing this again!'

I smoothed down the prettily patterned fabric and smiled at the sea of faces before me. It felt good to be part of the Cherry Tree family again.

With Tom, Ella and Noah finally out of the door we grabbed the opportunity to sit in the area of the café designated for the crafting courses Lizzie ran, and looked through the plans and products that she and Jemma had come up with for the market stall.

'Don't hurry through it all,' insisted Angela, as she refilled my mug and handed fresh cups to Jemma and Lizzie. 'There's plenty of time.'

'OK,' sighed Jemma, as she pulled out a notebook and pen from her apron pocket. 'Thank you, Angela. Now Ruby, as you may or may not know, trade at the market has taken a bit of a tumble in the last few months.'

'Yes,' I nodded, 'I do know a bit about the situation. Lizzie has been keeping me up to speed.'

'And so,' she continued, 'with that in mind, initially just in the run up to Christmas, there are going to be a couple of extra stalls to try and help draw the shoppers back in.'

'So I'm not going to be the only newbie then?' I asked, delighted by the unexpected revelation. At least I wouldn't be the only one who hadn't run a stall before.

'Well, new sellers haven't exactly been queuing up for the pitches,' Lizzie admitted. 'So far the extra spots have been filled by us, a roasted chestnut vendor and a couple called Simon and Jude who sell vintage stuff.'

'But the whole retro vibe is ridiculously popular right now,' nodded Jemma, 'and from what I've seen their stock is top shelf so hopefully people will like what they have on offer and be tempted to look at the rest of the market.'

'And what exactly am I going to be selling?' I questioned. 'I know Ella was pretty excited by what you've been making, Lizzie.'

'I'll go and get you some bits and pieces to look through while Jemma runs you through the list of what she has come up with,' she said, pushing back her chair and standing up. 'I can't risk eating or even hearing about any more of these festive sweet treats. At this rate I'm going to be the size of a house!'

'Oh,' I said, rubbing my hands together in anticipation, 'that good, eh?'

'That good!' confirmed Lizzie and she wasn't wrong.

'I love the sound of the star-topped mince pies and the iced and spiced buns,' I said a few minutes later, 'and the cinnamon and cranberry tray bake slice.'

'Not to mention the sticky toffee, toffee apples and the bags of marshmallow-filled rocky road,' drooled Lizzie, picking up the thread as she dumped another box on the table.

'And the mini gingerbread family complete with the dog,' I added for good measure. 'But how on earth are you going to keep up with demand, Jemma?'

'Do you know,' she said, biting her lip, 'at the moment I have absolutely no idea, but we'll manage. I keep telling Tom I can cope, so I'm going to have to find a way.'

'And I'll help, of course,' said Angela as she bustled by to turn the café sign from 'Closed' to 'Open'. 'We'll all chip in.'

By the time I had finished looking through all the things Lizzie had made to sell I really couldn't wait to get started and I could totally understand why Ella had such a gargantuan Christmas list already.

'These advent calendars are so pretty,' I told Lizzie, 'and the idea of supplying so many things in kit form is inspired!' I picked up one of the bags, thinking about how the demand for homemade and homespun seemed to be increasing all the while. 'People don't always have the time to make things from scratch so these kits are the perfect compromise.'

'Well, I'm pleased you think so,' smiled Lizzie. 'It's good

to know Jemma, Angela and I aren't the only ones who like them.'

'Love them,' I corrected.

The calendars were made up of twenty-four numbered drawstring bags in various colours and patterns which would be strung up using little pegs along a piece of wire or a length of gingham ribbon.

'These must have taken you ages to make,' I said, taking a closer look.

'Not really,' she shrugged, as if her clever efforts were nothing. 'Once you get a production line going, you'd be surprised.'

'And I love these stockings,' I gushed on, 'and this festive bunting.'

'And what about these gingerbread decorations for the tree,' Jemma cut in. 'How sweet is he with his little gingham bow tie?'

'He's adorable,' I nodded, 'but I think these are my absolute favourite,' I said, reaching for one of the mason jars which contained a little snowy scene complete with a tiny deer and a couple of fir trees.

Out of the corner of my eye I spotted Jemma and Lizzie exchanging a quick smile.

'You know,' I said, looking back at the table which was laden with Lizzie's festive makes, 'I think this stall is only going to be open for business for a week, two at best.'

'What?' cried Lizzie. She sounded utterly outraged and I couldn't help but laugh as her complexion turned as red as her head of unruly curls. 'Why?'

'Because,' I said, shaking my head, 'I can't possibly see how you can have enough stock to last until Christmas!'

Lizzie looked relieved and started to laugh with me.

'Oh she has,' said Jemma, pointing at the cupboards that ran along the length of the crafting area, 'believe me, it will be a miracle if she sells out!'

'Well,' I said, 'prepare to be amazed, ladies, because I reckon this stuff is going to fly off the stall.'

'All we need now,' said Jemma chewing the end of her pen, 'is a name for the venture.'

'Oh I've been thinking about that,' I cut in. 'How about, Makes and Bakes from The Cherry Tree Café?'

'Oh yes,' clapped Jemma, 'I love it!'

'I'll paint up a banner this afternoon!' joined in Lizzie, grabbing Jemma's notebook and pen.

Chapter 4

By lunchtime I had sorted through and re-packed Lizzie's pretty Christmas crafts, helped her make the banner to hang across the front of the stall and worked out with Jemma rough numbers for her batch baking of biscuits and buns. Lizzie's plans, of course, were far simpler because her products didn't have an expiration date and, as I watched Jemma rushing around working things out, I began to understand what Lizzie had been trying to explain when we'd spoken on the phone. Seeing Jemma working flat-out I could also understand why Tom still wasn't sold on the idea of the stall, but hopefully his opinion would change when it was up and running and we'd established a routine.

'Time for a quick sandwich and a chat?' said a familiar voice next to my ear.

'Bea!' I squealed, jumping up and pulling her into a hug. 'I didn't expect to see you today! I thought you were at work!'

'I am,' she said, 'but my next client isn't booked until one, so Mum suggested I come over and surprise you. Surprise!' she laughed.

'Oh wow,' I grinned. 'It's so good to see you.'

Bea's family business was conveniently located on the opposite side of the market square to The Cherry Tree Café and therefore perfectly positioned for popping over to stock up on coffee and pastries.

'Come on,' she said, tugging at the corner of my apron. 'Let's grab a table before they're all gone and have a proper catch up.'

With our paninis and drinks ordered, we sat deep in conversation with our heads together, totally unaware of what was going on around us.

'I have to say,' I smiled as I admired her flawless complexion and manicured nails, 'you are looking incredibly groomed for a work day. What's the occasion?'

'Nothing,' she shrugged, a slight blush blooming. 'Are you suggesting that I normally look as unkempt as you currently are, with your hair all piled up in a nest and your mascara smudged? What's that all about? Normally I feel like the scruffy one when we're together. Have you completely let yourself go or is this just a one off?'

Fortunately I knew her well enough not to take offence, but I could have done without her drawing attention to the state I was obviously in. I always took pride in my appearance, but having felt so groggy when I got up I hadn't bothered to tidy my casual up-do before leaving the house. The smudged mascara was just an unfortunate coincidence.

'Oh God,' I frowned, grabbing a knife and using the blade of it as a makeshift mirror. 'The hair was supposed to pass for boho casual, but you're right. This look is definitely more bag lady than couture chic.'

Bea giggled and took a delicate bite of her panini.

'Anyway,' I huffed, discarding the knife and banishing my unsatisfactory reflection, 'never mind the state I'm in. You still haven't answered my question. Of course you always look gorgeous, but even I can see that you've cranked things up a notch for a Monday!'

'It's for Sam,' she murmured, blushing deeper this time. 'I want him to see just what he's missing.'

'What he's missing?' I gasped. 'Please don't tell me you've binned him off?'

'No, of course I haven't,' she said, shaking her head. 'I just don't think it will do any harm in the run up to Christmas to let him see me at my best.'

'Oh for goodness' sake,' I tutted. 'The pair of you are so perfect together you already look as if you should be decorating the top of a Christmas cake. This is all about your fantasy festive proposal, isn't it?'

'Might be,' she conceded as I rolled my eyes. 'I can't wait another bloody year!' she added testily.

I didn't say anything.

'What?' she pounced.

'Nothing,' I shrugged.

'No, come on,' she continued, 'you've clearly got some opinion on the situation . . .'

She was cut off in mid-flow as the door swung open, the bell jangling madly in protest and a blast of freezing air sweeping inside along with the two men who were responsible for practically wrenching it off the wall.

'Oh shit,' I muttered, my hands flying up to my head in a desperate attempt to smooth and tidy my mad hair.

'There,' teased Bea, sounding thoroughly satisfied. 'And you were just about to give me the "why are you going to all that trouble for a man" speech, weren't you?'

'Oh shut up,' I muttered, looking around for a quick getaway.

'Weren't you?' she said again, louder this time.

'Might have been,' I admitted. 'Oh God, help me Bea, will you? I don't want to see him today.'

'What,' she grinned, clearly enjoying watching me squirm under the weight of my own hypocrisy, 'because you haven't got your eyeliner in place? Anyway it's too late,' she hissed, 'he's heading this way.'

As I glanced up at Steve's ruddy complexion and broad grin, I realised for the second time in forty-eight hours that perhaps I wasn't quite as 'over him' as I thought I was and given the way Bea was smiling and nudging my leg under the table, she was now well aware of the fact too. She seemed to have completely forgotten that not all that long ago he had left me heartbroken and bereft.

'Hello again, Ruby,' Steve smiled down at me. 'Twice in two days. This is an honour. You never said you were back working in here,' he added, pointing at my cupcake-patterned apron.

As much as my treacherous heart would have liked me to, I simply couldn't allow myself to fall under the spell of those sparkling dark eyes and easy-going charm. I reminded myself that he had beautiful Mia tucked away somewhere, that he had dumped me and that no amount of 'cheeky chappie' banter could make up for all the hurt. These re-emerging feelings needed to be nipped in the bud before I set myself up to get my heart broken all over again.

'Hello, Sam,' I said, pretending I hadn't heard and turning to address his friend who, I noticed just a second too late, was kissing Bea deeply and whispering sweet nothings in her ear.

Bea, giggling like a silly schoolgirl, was obviously going to be no help at all.

'I'm not working here,' I said, sweeping up the empty dishes and turning my attention briefly back to Steve when it became obvious that I had heard him and that I was going to have to say something. 'Well, I sort of am,' I continued, fumbling for an explanation.

'OK,' said Steve, looking more confused by the second. 'I guess it was the fact that you're wearing a Cherry Tree apron that threw me and that now you've just picked up a handful of dirty dishes.'

I nodded and bit my lip.

'So you can't help with my lunch order then?' he frowned.

'Afraid not,' I said, heading for the sanctuary of the kitchen, 'but Angela will.'

I busied myself folding tablecloths and drying dishes until I was sure the guys had left and only resurfaced as Bea was buttoning her coat.

'So much for our catch up,' she moaned, 'why did you go running off like that?'

'I didn't go running anywhere,' I said defensively. 'And besides, I didn't think you'd even notice I'd gone to help in the kitchen, what with Sam stuck to your face. I take it the extra preening paid off then?'

'There's no need to be sarcastic,' she pouted, before gunning straight for the heart of the matter. 'Ruby, how are you going to cope working next to Steve, if you can't even stay in the same room as him?'

'Well, a little bit of loyalty from you wouldn't go amiss,' I snapped.

'What do you mean?'

'In case you'd forgotten, *he* was the one who dumped *me*,'

I reminded her. '*I* was the one who was left heartbroken and alone not all that long ago.'

'But he only did that because he needed to be here for his family,' she said compassionately. 'He was only doing what he thought was best. It was such a terrible time for everyone. You know that, Ruby.'

'Oh, I know I do,' I conceded sulkily, throwing down the tea towel I had brought through from the kitchen.

'He's a good man,' she continued, 'and he never meant to hurt you. You know that too, don't you?'

'Yes,' I said huskily. 'I suppose I do, but knowing that isn't going to make seeing him out and about with the lovely Mia and God knows who else, any easier, is it?'

Chapter 5

It came as no great surprise that Dad had chosen not to join Mum on the doorstep in the dark to wish me luck on that first morning of trading. He had barely said a word during dinner the previous evening as I chatted about the things I would be selling and I was now resigned to the fact that rather than applauding my resourcefulness, he was going to carry on ignoring my efforts because I hadn't fallen in with his plans.

As I had watched him push his food around his plate I couldn't help thinking back over what Tom had said about something going on at the council, but I hadn't dared to ask Dad if there was any truth in it because I didn't want him accusing Tom of talking about him behind his back.

'You look absolutely lovely,' said Mum as she waved me off. 'Far too smart to be working on the market, but are you sure you're going to be warm enough?'

'I'll be fine,' I insisted, 'I've got my thermals on and I'm

47

wearing so many layers I look like a Michelin man under this coat!'

I knew my black skinny jeans, grey knitted tunic and heeled boots were probably a bit over the top and a far cry from what everyone else would be wearing, but I wanted there to be no doubt that the stylish Cherry Tree image extended beyond the café, and I couldn't deny that Bea's comments about my appearance the day before had left a lasting impression. I reassured Mum that my woollen belted coat would keep me cosy and that I had left my hair loose so I could pull on a hat if the cold really started to bite.

'And try not to worry about your dad,' she said yet again when I reached the gate. 'He'll come round.'

I set off for town feeling a little sad that my excitement for my new venture was already tarnished because of his reaction. Ordinarily he welcomed any boost to the town's economy with open arms, but evidently that didn't extend to family members becoming embroiled with the market which had always been the domain of the Dempsters.

I couldn't help thinking how strange it was that my dad and Steve's dad, Chris, shared the same desire to see Wynbridge thriving and yet couldn't find it in their hearts to get along. One day I would get to the bottom of their mutual loathing but for now I had to focus on getting through the day without turning into a giant icicle.

I hadn't sold a single thing and yet I realised that I was

already looking forward to taking my share of the profits, heading to the travel agent's, getting the hell out of Wynbridge and putting some miles between myself and all the men in my life.

A little later, and beneath a reluctantly lightening sky, I was all set to start work.

'So, that's the grand tour of the site,' smiled Harriet, one of the friendlier looking stallholders who sold shrubs and plants with her partner Rachel. 'Any questions?'

'Does it get any warmer here when the sun comes up?' asked Jude hopefully as she rubbed her hands together and blew hard on her fingers, her breath streaming dragon-like ahead of her in the crisp early morning air.

Jude and Simon were running the vintage stall that Jemma had mentioned the day before. One quick glance in the back of their van confirmed that their stock was indeed as good a quality as she had suggested, and I wouldn't have been at all surprised to see Lizzie bagging the piles of pretty floral fabrics I had seen stacked in one of the wooden apple crates.

'Afraid not,' Harriet laughed. 'Not at this time of year anyway, in fact, your suggestion that the sun will come up at all is woefully optimistic.'

'I was afraid you were going to say that,' sniffed Jude, snuggling closer up to Simon. 'I knew I should have packed my extra gloves.'

'Don't you worry,' said Peter, the roasted chestnut vendor who was also new to the market. 'If you get too cold, Jude, you can always come and warm your hands around my brazier.'

'Steady on!' laughed Simon. 'I'm sure it won't come to that, mate.'

Poor Peter turned beetroot-red and Jude dug Simon sharply in the ribs.

'Don't you mind him,' she told Peter, who was easily old enough to be her father. 'He can make an innuendo out of anything. Just ignore him and with any luck he'll go away.'

'Right,' said Harriet, saving Peter from further blushes. 'Let's crack on, shall we? The sooner we all get to work, the quicker we'll warm up.'

'Now who's being woefully optimistic?' I smiled wryly as I pulled on my woolly hat.

The Cherry Tree stall was thankfully located directly opposite the café so shifting the large plastic crates of stock with a pair of sack wheels was no problem; unfortunately however the same could not be said for working out how to secure the green and white striped canopy that was supposed to offer some protection from the biting north wind which was renowned for whipping mercilessly through the town.

I could see a couple of the other vendors watching with interest as the sheet flapped around my feet and caught in my heels in an increasingly tangled muddle, but no one seemed in a rush to come over and give me a hand to sort it out. In a desperate attempt to look as if I had at least some idea about what I was supposed to be doing, I stuffed it back under the table and set about emptying a couple of the crates and arranging some of Lizzie's decorations.

'I wouldn't start displaying anything until you've got your canopy up,' said a voice behind me. 'I can help you, if you like. Don't worry about the others. No one's feeling in a very friendly mood around here at the moment.'

'Oh thank you,' I said gratefully, whilst wondering if the slump in sales really accounted for the sagging spirits and stand-offish attitude I'd encountered so far. 'I'd really appreciate that. To tell you the truth I think I've got it in a bit of a tangle . . .'

My words trailed off as I turned around and found myself face to face, well not quite, with the tiniest woman imaginable. She had a scruffy scrap of a terrier tucked under her arm and she must have been at least eighty years old.

'I'm Gwen,' she smiled kindly, 'and this is Minnie,' she added affectionately, stroking the diminutive pooch's head.

'Pleased to meet you, Gwen,' I said, stepping forward and then straight back again as Minnie flashed her sharp little teeth. 'I'm Ruby.'

'Oh, I know exactly who you are, dear,' she nodded, clamping Minnie's jaws together in a well-practised manoeuvre, 'and so does everyone else. That's no doubt why they're so supercilious this morning.'

I was just about to ask what she meant, but was interrupted by the arrival of a smart green van with the name 'Dempster & Son' painted in gold along the side. It drew to a halt at the stall next to mine and my heart sank in my chest as my fears were confirmed. Steve and I really were going to be working literally in each other's pockets for the next few weeks.

'Right,' said Gwen as I surreptitiously watched him and his dad Chris, throw open the back and side doors and begin hastily unloading packed boxes of vegetables and sprout stalks. 'Let's see if we can get this blessed canopy sorted, shall we?'

I wasn't quite sure exactly how she intended to help when the top of her head didn't even reach my shoulder, but her clever plan was soon revealed.

'Good morning, Mr Dempster,' she called to Chris in a voice that sounded far more timid than the one she had used to introduce herself and Minnie to me just seconds earlier. 'I was wondering if you and that strapping boy of yours could spare just a few seconds to help us secure this pesky canopy.'

'Of course, dear lady,' smiled Chris, readily dumping a box of cabbages on the pavement and rushing over. 'Hello Ruby, my love, long time, no see.'

'Hello,' I murmured, stepping out of his way.

'These aren't the easiest of things to get in place,' he continued, 'especially if you're on your own, but once they're up they can stay in situ. I can't understand why whoever put the frame up didn't do this as well.'

'I'm sure I could have done it myself if I had a stepladder,' I said apologetically, blushing from my toes to my fingertips as I somehow managed to get under his feet at every turn despite my best efforts not to.

'Not to worry,' he shrugged, expertly shaking out the heavy, plastic sheet in one quick movement. 'We'll have it up in a jiffy.'

'Thank you,' I said, feeling relieved.

'So,' he said, eyeing me mischievously as he quickly set about counting the clips, 'this is your stall then, is it?'

'Just until Christmas,' I nodded, taking another step back as Steve joined in and grabbed the other end of the sheet. 'I'm selling some bits and pieces for Lizzie and Jemma from the Cherry Tree.'

'Oh right,' he smirked, as they efficiently covered the frame and smoothed out the mess I'd made. 'I bet your dad must be absolutely delighted about that!'

He let out a rich, throaty laugh and I felt the colour flush my face again. There was no doubt in my mind that he knew exactly how Dad had reacted to my little venture so I didn't need to confirm his suspicions. I stood and watched as he and Steve quickly secured the last clip and then looked over it all again to check that everything was level and as it should be. The whole procedure had taken them less than two minutes.

'There now,' said Gwen with a satisfied sigh and a wink. 'I told you I'd give you a hand to get it sorted. Come and have a look at my bric-a-brac when you get the chance. It's all sold for charity, you know!'

'I will,' I called after her as she trotted back to her side of the square. 'Thank you!'

She waved a hand and carried on without looking back.

'And thank you, too,' I said, turning back to Chris and Steve.

'Dad's had to get on,' said Steve with a nod towards where his dad was retrieving the cabbages he'd abandoned. 'We're running a bit late this morning. Van trouble,' he elaborated.

'Well, in that case,' I said, looking everywhere but up at him, and feeling increasingly conscious that we had an interested audience watching our every move, 'thank you twice over for taking the time.'

'No bother,' he said, shoving his hands deep in his pockets. 'Why didn't you tell me this is what you were going to be doing when I saw you in the Cherry Tree yesterday?'

'Oh, I don't know,' I shrugged, rubbing my gloves together. 'I guess I didn't think—'

'That it had anything to do with me?' he suggested.

'Something like that,' I agreed, although that wasn't really what I meant at all.

He looked far more wounded by my confirmation than I would have expected.

'So is this going to be a long-term thing then?' he asked.

'Come on, boy!' shouted Chris. 'This van won't unload itself, you know.'

'No,' I said, 'not for me anyway, and I don't think Jemma and Lizzie have considered keeping it going beyond Christmas. They just want to help increase the footfall through the market for the next few weeks.'

'Steve!' Chris called again, drawing yet more attention to our awkward exchange.

'Well, I'd better get back before Dad busts a blood vessel,' he muttered, still staring down at the top of my head. 'Give us a shout if you need anything else, won't you?'

'Thanks,' I said, turning away and swallowing down the lump in my throat, 'I will.'

'Oh, here,' he said, reaching inside his jacket pocket, 'take these. You might start feeling the cold sooner than you expect.'

Truth be told, my feet were already beginning to feel numb.

'They'll keep your hands warm until around lunchtime.'

Gratefully I took the hot little microwaveable pouches and slipped them into my coat pockets. The warmth they emitted spread far further and deeper than I would have expected.

The weather remained far from crisp and bright and if Jude was still hoping to catch a glimpse of the sun, I thought as I gave a cursory glance at the grey blanket of cloud overhead, then she was destined to be disappointed.

However, the dull weather did have one advantage as far as the Cherry Tree stall was concerned. The strands of battery-operated warm white fairy lights I had threaded and draped between the stock and around Lizzie's eye-catching Makes and Bakes banner stood out a treat, and with the café's trademark bunting in place, the overall effect was extremely pretty. I couldn't imagine there was anyone in Wynbridge who would fail to notice that this side of the little market had something new to offer.

I had just finished putting the final touches in place when Jemma and Lizzie arrived to give my efforts their seal of approval and drop off the float along with Jemma's cellophane-bagged biscuits and bakes. I could smell the cinnamon and gingerbread before I'd even set them out and knew that if the sight of the stall didn't draw customers in, then the smell certainly would!

'Oh Ruby,' Jemma gasped, her eyes shining with happy tears. 'This is simply exquisite. I can't believe how quickly you've set it all out and made it look so attractive.'

'Oh that was nothing to do with me,' I told her, feeling flattered nonetheless, 'everything is so pretty I simply couldn't go wrong!'

'I don't believe a word of it,' she said, taking a closer look, 'you've obviously got style, Ruby Smith, because this is beautiful, and you,' she said, stepping back again and looking me up and down appraisingly, 'look absolutely stunning!'

'Well thank you,' I laughed in my best southern belle accent as I gave a little curtsy. 'And what do you think of it all, Lizzie? Do you like it?'

'It's perfect,' she confirmed, looking every bit as thrilled as Jemma. 'It's even better than I imagined it. I know I certainly wouldn't be able to walk by without taking a closer look.'

'Look at how she's pegged up the advent calendar,' Jemma said, tugging at Lizzie's sleeve. 'And she's hung the little stockings under the bunting!'

'It really is beautiful, Ruby.' Lizzie nodded. 'I hope you're feeling as proud as we are?'

'I am now,' I beamed.

'Right,' she said, steering Jemma to one side of the stall and waving her phone about. 'Now come on you two, squeeze in. This is one moment of Cherry Tree history that simply must be recorded!'

'Hang on there!' called Peter, as he rushed over to Lizzie's side. 'Can I be of assistance? Surely the three of you should be in the shot together?'

With the happy moment recorded for posterity, Jemma and Lizzie headed back to the cosy confines of the café, with the promise to come back at lunchtime with something warm and nourishing to help thaw me out.

*

I wouldn't go so far as to say the day dragged, but business was far from brisk, even though I had displayed the Cherry Tree wares as enticingly as possible. On more than one occasion I found myself wishing there were a few more customers to be had, and not once was that because I was concerned with upping my profit margin.

Not long after Jemma and Lizzie had returned to the Cherry Tree, I found my eyes beginning to repeatedly wander to the Dempster stall next door and no matter how hard I tried to rein them in, they seemed hell-bent on watching how Steve conducted his business. Like a moth to a flame, and kidding myself that I was picking up top tips on customer service, I had watched him chat easily with shoppers, help carry heavy bags to cars and coo over dribbling babies, and none of what I witnessed helped to strengthen my resolve that working alongside him wasn't going to be a problem.

'How have you got on?' asked Jude as she ventured over at the end of the day and inadvertently blocked my view of Steve helping a mum with a loaded buggy and a fractious toddler.

'How have I got on with what?' I asked, trying to look around her.

'Earth to Ruby!' Jude laughed, waving a hand in front of my face.

'Sorry,' I said, finally focusing on her and remembering my manners. 'Sorry. I think the cold has addled my brain!'

It wasn't even four o'clock, but thanks to the generous cloud cover it was already almost dark.

'Have you had a good day?' she asked again.

'Well,' I said, guessing that she wasn't referring to watching the eye candy next door, 'I haven't exactly got a lot of experience to draw on,' I frowned, peering into the rather meagre depths of my cash box, 'but in terms of how much money I've taken then I'd have to say no, not really.'

I had practically sold out of Jemma's pretty cellophane bags of biscuits, and most of the iced and cinnamon spiced buns. However, I had a feeling that was more to do with the fact that she had been giving out free samples in the café and then sending customers in my direction, rather than any unique sales technique on my part. A couple of Lizzie's Christmas decorations had also headed off to new homes, but that was it.

'How about you?' I asked, shifting my weight from one foot to the other and imagining the seductive pleasure of immersing my aching limbs in a hot Soap and Glory scented bubble bath. 'Have you had much success?'

'Not a single sale,' she told me, shaking her head.

'Nothing at all?' I gasped, the sensual delights of the bathtub quickly forgotten.

'Nope,' she said. 'Not that we expected to sell much, of course. We knew it would take a while for word to get round, but it would have been nice to mark our first day of trading in Wynbridge with just one sale, no matter how small.'

'And what about the others?' I whispered, nodding in the direction of the other stallholders, none of whom had so much as looked in my direction all day. In fact, had it not been for Gwen's kindness when I first arrived I might well have been feeling a little paranoid about their obvious lack of interest. 'How do you think they've got on?'

'Well,' she whispered back, 'according to Gordon on the hardware stall, this is about as good as it gets at the beginning of the week and Chris told Simon that his wife Marie, who has the fresh flower stall, doesn't even bother setting up until mid-week. From what I can gather she works from her storage unit as a part-time florist because she can make more money doing that.'

I had been wondering where Marie was. Mum used to buy flowers from her every week. Not that Dad knew that, of course, or where the source of his five-a-day sprang from. He would far rather Mum lined the pockets of the supermarkets than contributed to the Dempster coffers.

'I guess people must still be all shopped out after the weekend,' I said hopefully, whilst trying not to feel hurt that no one had been across to reassure me that this was what a typical Tuesday working on Wynbridge market was like.

'You're probably right,' agreed Jude. 'We've only ever traded at car boot sales on Fridays, Saturdays and Sundays before. This is our first experience of a bona fide market. Fingers crossed things will pick up tomorrow. Anyway, I'd better go and give Simon a hand. The sooner we get packed up, the sooner we can get to the pub. Do you fancy joining us for a glass of something warming?'

'No thanks,' I told her, 'not tonight. The bubble bath beckons!'

'You sure?' she asked. 'Chris and Steve have promised to pop in.'

For a moment I was almost tempted to change my mind but then, out of the corner of my eye, I spotted immaculate Mia picking her way across the pavement and flashing Steve her almost too-white smile.

'I'm sure,' I said, 'but thanks for asking. Maybe I'll come another night.'

I turned my back on Dempster and son and busied myself carefully packing away the fairy lights and Lizzie's banner along with the rest of the stock. I had almost finished when I heard someone clearing their throat behind me.

'It's Ruby, isn't it?' said a voice I instantly recognised.

'Yes,' I said, painting on my best smile and turning round. 'Hello, Mia.'

'I thought it was you,' she nodded as she gave a cursory glance over the stall. 'This is what you do, is it? You sell things on a market stall.'

I felt my spine stiffen as I noted her disparaging tone.

'At the moment,' I said, 'yes, but only until the New Year, then I'm leaving.'

'You aren't staying in town for long, then?'

I could tell she was trying to keep our exchange casual but her intentions were glaringly obvious. She had come over to mark out her territory, although why she thought she needed to was a mystery to me.

'No,' I said, unwilling to explain my future plans to a stranger. 'Not long.'

'Hey Mia!' yelled Steve. 'Are you coming or what?'

'He hates it if I'm out of his sight for more than three seconds together,' she said with a smile as she waved at him, 'he's always so attentive.'

'He's a good bloke,' I nodded.

'Oh I know,' she said over her shoulder as she walked away, 'the best. I'm very lucky to have him.'

I resisted the urge to stick out my tongue at her retreating back and finished packing away the last few of Lizzie's bits and pieces with slightly less care than I had demonstrated before. I had just finished loading up the final box as the lady herself arrived to help me carry everything back to the café stockroom. She had a carrier bag clutched in one hand and her expression was almost smug.

'What have you got there?' I asked, pointing at the bag which I guessed was the cause of her unusually self-satisfied demeanour and feeling grateful for the distraction from mulling over Mia's determination to stake her claim on Steve's heart.

'Quite literally the most divine pile of vintage floral fabrics,' she beamed, her face aglow as she held open the top of the bag for me to see. 'Simon was just loading them back in the van as I came across.'

'Oh, I saw these earlier!' I told her. 'I meant to tell you, but I forgot.'

'Not to worry,' she said happily, 'you'll never guess how much I paid for them!'

'Go on,' I winced, thinking it would be a painful amount.

'Ten pounds!'

'A tenner!'

'Yep, ten measly quid. I think Jude was keen to secure their first sale and I know it was an absolute steal so I'm going to make her something special to say thank you.'

'A padded hot water bottle cover might not be a bad idea,' I suggested, blowing on my gloves.

'I can't believe they haven't sold anything else,' she said, biting her lip. 'How have you got on?'

I explained about the baked goods and few decorations but didn't tell her about my final exchange of the day.

'Could have been worse,' she shrugged.

'It could,' I agreed, 'but from what Jude's just told me I think it's going to take a lot more than a couple of extra stalls to breathe life into this old market.'

Chapter 6

Keen to get a head start and prove to Dad that I could get out of bed when my alarm clock dictated on more than one occasion, I had the stall set up way ahead of schedule on my second day of trading and consequently had ample opportunity to watch some of the other traders arrive.

The weather was still dull and grey, but the view of Steve working just metres away was a welcome distraction and the warm glow it gave me reached almost as far as my frozen toes. I knew I was setting myself up for a fall, but I simply couldn't stop myself, especially when fate had wrapped him in a woolly jumper and scarf and plonked him right next to me. Mia might have gone out of her way to warn me off, but for the moment I was determined to enjoy the view and deal with the consequences later.

'Sorry I didn't make it across yesterday. We were rushed

off our feet. Not that I'm complaining, of course. Oh wow! Ruby, this is amazing!'

I waited patiently for Bea to draw breath, hoping she would be so enthralled by the stall that she wouldn't notice who my nearest neighbour just happened to be.

'I'm simply going to have to have one of these pretty advent thingies for work,' she gushed, fingering the little bags with affection. 'It will look perfect behind the reception desk.'

'You really want one?' I asked, momentarily thrown by the prospect of making such a lucrative sale so early in the day.

'Yes,' she said, shaking her head. 'Some bloody saleswoman you are! Come on, hurry up, will you? I have to open up this morning. And I was hoping for biscuits,' she said, poking about amongst the bags.

'Jemma will be bringing them over later,' I told her, quickly stowing away her pretty purchase in one of the Cherry Tree brown paper bags and taking her money. 'Shall I save some for you? They sold out pretty quickly yesterday.'

'Oh yes please,' she smiled, taking the bag with the calendar in.

And just when I thought I'd got away with it.

'So,' she said with a less than discreet nod in the direction of the Dempster family stall, 'how are you finding the neighbours?'

'Fine,' I shrugged, turning my attention back to tidying the display. 'To tell you the truth, I've been too busy to notice them.'

She leant further in and lowered her voice.

'Steve and Mia were in the pub last night,' she whispered, looking over my shoulder in his direction and not yet realising the impact her words were having, 'and she was all over him like a rash. I tell you, Ruby, if they do get engaged this Christmas I think I'll implode.'

'But I thought you said they weren't serious,' I shot back without thinking. 'You told me that Sam tells you all about Steve's women and her name has never come up. Not once.' I could hear the note of panic in my voice and I didn't like it one little bit. Perhaps Mia's take on her and Steve's relationship was right after all.

'Well, they looked pretty serious to me—'

She stopped mid-sentence and I spun round to find Steve heading in our direction.

'I can't stop,' he smiled, 'but I just wanted to see if by any chance you had some of Jemma's mince pies left over from yesterday? I had a sample in the café and they're all I've been able to think about.'

Given what Bea had just told me about his and Mia's antics in the pub I found that very hard to believe.

'No,' I told him, 'I'm afraid I haven't got any left, but Jemma will be bringing some more over in a bit.'

'Great,' he nodded, rocking back on his heels, 'brilliant.'

Bea shot me a quick glance. Clearly she was as confused by his continued presence as I was.

'By the way,' he said eventually, 'how did you get on with the hand warmers yesterday? Were they any good?'

'Yes thanks,' I said, fumbling in my pockets to retrieve them. 'They were brilliant. I re-heated them for you just before I left home. Here you go.'

With a hand that was less than steady I tried to pass them back and ignore how far Bea's eyebrows had shot up.

'No, you keep them,' he said kindly.

'Are you sure?'

'Absolutely,' he insisted, 'Mia gave them to me a couple of weeks ago. She's always complaining about how cold my hands are, but I can't get on with them. I guess I've worked on the market so long I don't take much notice of the weather any more.'

'See,' muttered Bea in the background, 'practically engaged.'

I had just been about to pop them back in my pocket, but the sickening image of Steve triggering goose bumps on Mia's flawless thighs and the thought that I was handling something *she* had given him, soon changed my mind.

'Do you know,' I said, practically throwing them at him, 'I'm fine. I can manage without them. You can have them back.'

'Are you sure?' he said, scrabbling to catch them.

'Positive.' I nodded. 'Now you'll have to excuse me, I need to get on.'

I turned back to the stall and refused to look at Bea who I just knew had had her sneaky suspicions confirmed about how I was really feeling.

'We'll talk about this later,' she hissed, as Steve strode away, 'when I come back for my biscuits.'

'No, we won't,' I said.

'Yes,' she said, 'we will.'

'We really won't,' I said again, 'because there is nothing to talk about.'

As I watched my friend walk across the market square I realised that my feelings during the last couple of days had become more akin to the eighteen-year-old student who had left town over three years ago, rather than the worldly-wise graduate who had returned in her place, and I needed to get a grip.

Steve had dumped me, I reminded myself, and yes, I could appreciate that he had done it for the best of intentions and that his entire life was in absolute turmoil when he made the decision, but it didn't alter the fact that he had made it, or that he had now moved on to pastures new. In fact, if what Sam had told Bea was true and I had no reason to doubt it, he had grazed quite a few new pastures since I'd left town.

In eight weeks' time, I reminded myself, less if I was lucky,

I would be staring in awe at the exotic wonders of the world, and I didn't want that exciting prospect tainted with a heart-break that should have long since healed. I needed to stop picking at the scab of this long-dead relationship and start thinking about the future. I may have not been as 'over the relationship' as I had originally thought, but Mia had already warned me off once and Steve had given no hint since our reacquaintance that he still harboured romantic feelings for me, and with those thoughts ringing in my ears I resolved to put our renewed association on track as friends who just happened to share the same workspace, nothing more. Well, that was the theory.

'Hey Marie!' I called out before I had a chance to talk myself out of doing it. 'Can I give you a hand?'

I hadn't seen Marie since I had left for university and I have to admit that when Steve and I parted company I had missed her sunny smile and warm welcome for a long time. She was a kind-hearted woman, perfect mother-in-law material, I thought grudgingly, as an image of magnificent Mia ensconced on the Dempster sofa at Christmas forced its way uncharitably into my mind.

'Well, well, well!' She laughed, reappearing from behind an armful of florists' buckets. 'It is you! Chris said you were here yesterday, but I thought he was pulling my leg.'

'No,' I smiled, 'shocking though they are, the rumours are true!'

'Gosh, you're looking well, Ruby,' she said, dispensing with her stock and pulling me into the hug I had missed, 'and you've had your hair cut.'

'Only a few inches,' I smiled, pulling the still long ponytail over my shoulder.

'So what are you doing here of all places?' she quizzed. 'I thought you had another year at university.'

Just for a second I wondered how she could have possibly known that I had decided to stay on and take my Masters, but then common sense kicked in and I remembered that life in a small town, especially Wynbridge it seemed, was very much public property and therefore fair game for multiple discussions and dissections in the pub and beyond.

I explained about my abandoned post-grad course and the Cherry Tree stall and how I had offered to help Lizzie and Jemma out for a few weeks.

'So you don't see this as a future career then?' she asked, as we carried on unloading her van together.

'No,' I smiled, choosing my words with care knowing that she and Chris had worked on the market together for the best part of thirty years. 'I'm just helping out until the New Year. To tell you the truth, I'm not even sure if Jemma and Lizzie are planning to keep the stall on beyond that. I think this is just a short-term project to try and help draw locals back to the market.'

'Well, however long you're here for,' she said thrusting

a pretty willow basket full of moss into my arms, 'and no matter what your father no doubt thinks of the idea, you're most welcome. This place could do with a few new faces and some fresh ideas.'

'You certainly look as if you've moved with the times,' I said, nodding at the containers crammed full of seasonal greenery and chrysanthemums in striking autumnal shades of orange, red and gold.

'I have,' she said proudly, 'but I'm one of the few who has. Personally my takings are far better for the changes I've made to my little business, even though trade here is quiet, but it doesn't take a genius to work out that the market as a whole is struggling.'

I looked around and acknowledged for the first time that little about the place had actually changed since I was a young girl and used to visit every Saturday with my grandmother who would stock up on fish for the week, as well as bananas from Chris and his dad.

'So what's the problem?' I asked.

'You of all people should know that,' tutted the man who ran the pet stall next to Marie.

'Oh, leave the poor girl alone, Bob,' admonished the woman with him, who I guessed was his wife. 'She can't help who her father is!'

I felt my face go crimson as Gwen's words from the morning before sprang to mind. No doubt it was my parentage

71

that she was referring to when she had acknowledged that everyone already knew who I was.

'That ruddy out of town Retail Park is half the problem,' Bob continued, pointing vaguely in the direction of the town's newest shopping experience.

'The one my dad fought so hard to get approved,' I said, the full realisation as to why the stallholders hadn't been exactly welcoming the day before finally dawning.

'That's the one,' sighed the woman. 'Ever since it opened our takings have taken a nosedive and we just can't seem to stem the flow.'

'Not that anyone has *really* tried, Shirley,' Marie interjected, an edge of frustration creeping into her voice.

'You're probably right,' she conceded. 'But we sell dog beds and kitty litter, Marie. How are we supposed to put a new spin on that, and how are we supposed to compete when folk can buy things for a quid in one of the pound stores up the road and all under one roof?'

She had a point.

'It's all right for you,' said Bob gruffly, pointing at Marie's pretty floral display. 'But beyond stocking bird nuts in winter and chick crumbs in the spring, there's not a lot we can do to diversify or change what we sell.'

'And you probably shouldn't,' I butted in.

'Excuse me?'

'You shouldn't,' I said, rather less confidently this time, as

Gordon from the hardware stall wandered across to listen. 'People expect to be able to find certain things on certain stalls all year round and of a far better quality to what a pound store can offer. Perhaps what the market needs are more regular seasonal pop-up stalls like the Cherry Tree one I'm running. By all means keep the familiar framework of the market the same,' I said, warming to my theme, 'but throw in a few seasonal extras so shoppers can always find something a bit different and stop at the regular stalls as they're browsing.'

'That's not a bad idea, Ruby,' said Marie, looking pointedly at Bob. 'How does that sound, Bob? Rather than keep moaning about what's going wrong, don't you think we should be getting our heads together and trying to come up with some new ideas? Having a few extra stalls in the run up to Christmas isn't a bad plan, but we need more than just that, don't we?'

'Perhaps,' he shrugged. 'Although I can hardly see the point when—'

'He's not much of a one for change of any sort,' Shirley quickly cut in, 'but I'll keep working on him, Marie. We might just manage a Christmas miracle yet!'

'Well, I wouldn't hold your breath,' muttered Bob morosely, as his wife pushed him back towards the pet stall.

'Why do I get the impression there was more to that

discussion than I know about?' I asked Marie as I watched the disgruntled pair walking away.

'No idea,' she said dismissively, a slight flush spreading across her face. 'Hey, you'd better get back to your stall. Look, there's Lizzie. Has she got something to drop off?'

'That'll be Jemma's fresh batch of baking,' I said, hurrying away. 'You wait until I open the box. You won't be able to resist when you get a whiff of her spicy cinnamon buns!'

Much the same as the day before, sales of Jemma's sumptuous baked goods were reasonably brisk, especially as Steve had wandered over twice to stock up on mince pies, and I'd even managed to sell a couple of Lizzie's pretty patchwork stockings and larger toy sacks to some young mums who were walking back through the town having dropped their little ones at the local nursery. I made sure I'd popped a pile of flyers in with their purchases and asked if they would mind dropping them at the nursery when they went back at lunchtime.

'You're a natural!' called Marie, who had witnessed the transaction. 'I have a feeling you're going to stir things up around here, Ruby Smith!'

She gave me a double thumbs up and I pressed my fingers to my lips, begging her not to make a fuss. The last thing I wanted to do was alienate the other traders even more. I still wasn't sure whether Bob had appreciated me jumping in and making suggestions about how to possibly improve the market's ailing fortunes beyond the Christmas season.

'Well look at all this!' said a voice I knew well. 'Isn't this something? I love the sparkly lights!'

'Hello, Mum!' I said, stepping back so she could see the whole stand in all its glory. 'Isn't it pretty? Lizzie and Jemma are so clever.'

'They are,' she agreed, 'but I bumped into Lizzie earlier and she told me that all the setting up and embellishing had been left to you, so I think you need to include yourself in how clever the Cherry Tree staff are.'

'Oh, I don't know about that,' I said with a shrug. 'But what are you doing here? I didn't expect to see you in town today.' A quick glance at my watch confirmed it was almost lunchtime. 'I don't think I'll be able to get anyone to cover at such short notice, assuming you want me to come and eat with you of course.'

'No,' she said, waving over at Marie. 'Don't worry about that, I'll bring you a sandwich and a hot drink on my way home, if you like.'

'Ready?' asked Marie, who had now passed on responsibility of her stall to Shirley and linked arms with Mum. 'I can manage a whole hour today!'

'Oh, wonderful,' said Mum, 'that's a rare treat!'

I stood with my mouth open, looking from one woman to the other.

'Oh, close your mouth,' said Mum, 'for goodness' sake.'

'Are you two going to lunch together?' I gaped.

When Steve and I had been dating, Mum and Marie had always got on well, but I hadn't realised their friendship had stuck after we split.

'We always do on a Wednesday,' said Mum, in a matter-of-fact tone.

'We have done for years,' continued Marie. 'Did you not know, Ruby?'

'No,' I frowned, 'I didn't.'

I was somewhat unnerved by this unexpected twist of events. True, I had gone out of my way to talk to Marie and get a handle on The Steve Situation, but I hadn't been expecting her and Mum to be best buds! No wonder Marie had been so up to date with my university schedule.

'No, well,' said Mum looking decidedly shifty, 'your dad doesn't either so I'd rather you didn't mention it, if you don't mind.'

'It's like Romeo and Juliet,' said Marie theatrically, 'and the two fighting families who shouldn't meet.'

'Except the hero and heroine aren't destined to be together forever,' I reminded her, my eyes wandering across to where Steve was filling a bag with apples and laughing with a customer. 'Can you drop these off for Bea, please?' I asked Mum, handing over a bag of biscuits. Suddenly I didn't feel up to analysing my feelings in minute detail.

Mum took the bag and she and Marie quickly walked away, and although I couldn't quite catch what Marie said, Mum was very definitely nodding in agreement.

That evening, when I'd finally defrosted in the bubble bath, which I felt was destined to herald the end of most days I was going to be working on the market, I decided to try and talk to Dad about the stallholders' concerns.

'Dad . . .'

'Hmm?'

'Can I talk to you for a minute?'

A warning glance from my mother who was emptying the dishwasher suggested that she knew exactly what was on my mind, probably courtesy of her cosy lunch with Marie. From what I could gather I had been the hot topic of discussion on the menu. She had already informed me that Marie had told her off for not mentioning that I was planning to return to Wynbridge in time for Christmas.

'So why hadn't you told her?' I had asked.

'Because,' she said, kissing me fondly, 'I wanted to see you for myself before I announced to the world that my baby was coming home.'

'Did you think I might change my mind then?'

She hadn't answered at the time but the expression on her

face now as she looked at Dad gave me my answer, along with the exact reason why she reckoned I might have had a change of heart.

'Talk about what?' he asked, without glancing up from his pile of papers.

'The market,' I ventured.

'What about it?'

I pulled out a chair and joined him at the table, feeling slightly encouraged that he hadn't said 'no' straightaway.

'Have you already come to your senses and decided it isn't the best vocation for someone with a first-class degree after all?'

Mum looked at me and rolled her eyes. Her expression couldn't have been more 'I told you so', if she tried.

'Forget it,' I said, standing back up.

'Oh, sit back down, for goodness' sake,' Dad smiled wryly. 'A father can dream, can't he? Besides I'm only winding you up. Whatever's happened to your sense of humour?'

I sat back down, but didn't say anything.

'So,' he said, 'what did you want to talk about? How are you finding life working next to the barrow boys?'

I ignored his silly slur on Chris's fruit and vegetable business, knowing that if I bit back I'd never get anywhere.

'I'm doing all right,' I told him, 'and Marie Dempster is really making a name for herself now there isn't a florist in the town, but some of the others are struggling. It's so quiet. The whole place is like a ghost town most of the time.'

'I'm sure you'll find it busier at the weekend,' said Dad in what I guessed he thought was a consoling tone.

'But how can you be sure?' I frowned, my temper rising because he sounded so blasé.

'What do you mean?'

'Well, have you been down there?' I asked. 'Have you witnessed at first hand the impact this new Retail Park is having on the heart of the town for yourself?'

'Did I really just hear you say "the heart of the town"?' he asked, sounding amused.

'Yes.'

'Since when have you cared about the "heart of the town"?' he laughed.

'This isn't a joke, Dad,' I scowled, 'this is people's livelihoods we're talking about, traders who have worked the market for generations. I thought you were the one who believed in keeping the old traditions alive and regenerating Wynbridge town centre.'

Dad shrugged and sighed.

'Look,' he said resignedly, 'we were under a lot of pressure about that park, especially in the planning department. We surveyed shoppers for weeks before making a decision and they almost all said they wanted what the bigger towns have to offer. You can't expect big chain stores to move into the tiny, outdated retail outlets we've got in town.'

'I appreciate that,' I said, 'but before I left for university you were doing everything you could to rejuvenate the market square. When the Cherry Tree opened up you were thrilled. You said it was going to mark a turning point in the town's fortunes.'

'Things change,' he said, 'and anyway, why should it all be down to us at the council? Aren't the traders capable of making a bit of effort themselves?'

'What's changed?' I demanded. 'When I was growing up you were always banging on about how much you loved this little town, that you loved it so much you had never even considered living anywhere else and that when you started work at the council you were determined to see it thrive like it had when you were a kid.'

Dad looked surprised that I had remembered.

'You said you would do anything to stop it from going down the pound store and charity shop route, but if you're not careful that's all it will be and the market will be lost forever. Do you really want to see your beloved Wynbridge become just another nondescript East Anglian town with no heart and even less soul?'

Dad just shook his head and tiredly rubbed his hands over his face.

'Look,' he began but then stopped. His eyes suggested that he wanted to say more but he was inexplicably guarded, cautious almost.

'What?' I quizzed, desperate to get to the bottom of what

was really going on, because I could tell something was. The demoralised, deflated father figure in front of me bore very little resemblance to the Dad I remembered.

'Never mind,' he sighed, picking up his papers again.

Mum shrugged her shoulders and I looked between the two of them in disbelief. I had no idea what had gone on but something had occurred, something monumental must have happened to change Dad's opinion of his beloved Wynbridge so dramatically. I left him sitting there and stormed up to bed. Well, if he wanted to see more action from the traders, then he'd get more action from the traders. I was determined to find a way to make sure of that.

Chapter 7

'You coming to the pub tonight then, Ruby?' asked Simon as he wandered back from the Cherry Tree carrying a much-needed tray of hot coffees the next afternoon.

'I shouldn't think so,' I said, gratefully wrapping my cold hands around the cup he offered me. 'I'm not really a pub person.' I didn't add that I wasn't a 'let's watch Mia seduce Steve' sort of person either.

'Oh, this isn't a social thing,' he continued, 'there's a meeting.'

'What sort of meeting?'

'The traders are getting together with a couple of people from the council to talk about this year's plans for Christmas. You know, turning on the lights, raising the profile of the town and hopefully the footfall through the market, that sort of thing.'

'Oh,' I said, 'right. I see.'

I had thought I'd been making headway with some of

the others. I'd especially gone out of my way to talk to Bob and Shirley and Gordon, but not one of them had so much as mentioned planning for Christmas or the meeting. Part of me began to wonder if they thought I was some sort of industrial spy, planted by my father to keep an eye on them and report back about any bitching about him or the council's beloved Retail Park.

'Did you not know?' asked Simon, sounding surprised.

'No,' I said, 'I didn't.'

'Chris told us yesterday,' he said as he began to walk away. 'Tonight, seven thirty in The Mermaid. Do you think you can make it?'

'Oh, I'll make it all right,' I called after him. 'You can count on it.'

As usual the pub was packed to the rafters and, with a fire roaring at either end of the bar, I hadn't been inside many seconds before I was peeling off my coat and craving something crisp and cool.

'Hello, Ruby love!' boomed Jim the cheerful landlord, from his station behind the bar.

I hadn't frequented the pub all that often, but I knew for a fact that he never forgot a face. Standing at well over six foot and with hands the size of hams, he always put me in mind of Little John from the tales of Robin Hood. His considerably shorter wife Evelyn however, was a far cry from the fair

Maid Marian. From what I'd heard, her bite was definitely worse than her bark!

'What can I get you?' Jim asked as I hoisted myself up on to a bar stool. 'Are you getting one in for your dad as well? As I understand it, he's due to put in an appearance here sometime tonight.'

'No,' I said firmly. 'He can sort himself out, but I'll have half a pint of cider please.'

He gave me a knowing and, I couldn't help thinking, sympathetic smile and moved a little further along the bar. I was still smarting at the fact that no one had mentioned the meeting, but perhaps they had all been thinking that as I lived with the enemy I already knew about it.

'Can I tempt you to give the new local brew a try?' said Jim, tapping what looked like a shiny new pump.

'What do you mean by local brew?' I asked. 'Not cider that's actually been fermented around here, surely?'

'Indeed it is,' he nodded enthusiastically, 'it's come straight from the orchards of Skylark Farm just up the road in Wynthorpe. It's a new venture they're trying and it's been hugely popular. In fact,' he confided, 'this latest consignment only came in a couple of weeks ago and we're almost out.'

'Oh well, in that case,' I smiled, 'half a pint of local cider please!'

'I'll get that one, Jim,' said Steve who suddenly appeared at my elbow.

'No, that's fine,' I said, my eyes still firmly fixed on Jim, 'you're all right, but thanks.'

I didn't want to sound churlish, but I was determined to keep things with Steve on an even keel and I didn't want to feel indebted to him for anything, not even half a pint of cider.

'Just stick it on my tab,' he continued nonetheless, with a nod at the glass Jim had just set down in front of me as if I hadn't uttered a word, 'and I'd better have a round for that lot,' he added, pointing to a group sitting next to one of the fires and made up of what looked like practically every trader from the market.

They were chatting and laughing noisily and sounded in fine fighting spirits, as was I now.

'I said thanks, but you're all right,' I tried again, a little louder this time.

'I know I am,' Steve grinned infuriatingly, 'I'm in perfect health, thanks.'

'You know what I mean,' I sighed. 'Thanks for the offer, but I can pay for my own drink.'

'I'm sure you can,' he said, 'but I was just trying to be friendly.'

Of course he was, and wasn't 'friendly' how I had decided to categorise our relationship now? This change of mind set was going to be harder to get used to than I first thought. Perhaps I would have been better off cutting him out of my life completely, but that would have hardly made for ideal working conditions in the season of good-will, would it?

'Are you still pissed off at me?' he quizzed just as I was about to relent.

For a second I thought he meant about dumping me all those years ago and changing the course of our lives forever. Momentarily thrown off guard, I fumbled for a response.

'About me calling you Ruby Sue?' he added helpfully when it became obvious I was struggling to understand exactly what it was that he was alluding to.

I began to feel my internal temperature rise again and it had nothing to do with the roaring fires.

'No,' I shrugged, 'why should I be? I know, probably better than anyone else here, that you've never been able to control what comes out of your mouth.'

'Well that's OK then,' he nodded, 'because Mia said it wasn't appropriate—'

'Oh well, if Mia said,' I snapped, letting myself down completely.

'Oh come on,' he said, plucking at my sleeve and nodding towards the group, 'come and prove to everyone that you've picked a side.'

'What do you mean by that?' I asked, trying to ignore the unwanted shiver the feel of his fingers aroused as he picked up his tray of drinks.

He looked over the top of my head towards the door and raised his eyebrows.

'You know exactly what I mean,' he muttered, drawing my attention to Dad and his council cronies who had just arrived. 'Are you coming, or what?'

I did know which side of the fence I was going to be sitting on, but I didn't want to make it too obvious. Dad may well have turned into one giant pain in the backside recently but he was still my father and I knew that such a public betrayal of loyalty was going to cut him to the quick. Fortunately I was saved from having to try and explain that to Steve by the timely arrival of Tom and Ben.

'Ruby, finally, how are you?' Ben grinned. 'Lizzie and Jemma have talked of nothing other than what a grand job you're making of the stall!'

'Hello, Ben!' I laughed, jumping up and giving him a quick hug. 'My God,' I gasped. 'Look at the size of your beard! I can't believe you've kept it all this time. I never had you down as a hipster type.'

I felt my shoulders relax as Steve squeezed between us, carrying the loaded tray of drinks back to the group of stallholders. Tom, who was standing just behind Ben, rolled his eyes and sighed at my hipster comment.

'What?' I asked, wide-eyed, 'I'm only teasing. You know that, don't you, Ben?'

'Hipster?' He groaned, shaking his head and sounding

thoroughly mortified. 'I don't really look like one of the tight trouser brigade, do I?'

'Of course you don't,' I laughed, waving over his head at Lizzie who had just arrived and beckoning her over.

'Wow,' she said, looking around as she unravelled her scarf, 'great turnout—' She stopped in mid-sentence when she spotted Ben's forlorn expression. 'What?' she asked, laying a hand on his arm. 'Whatever's the matter?'

'Ruby said I look like a hipster, Lizzie. It's going to have to come off.'

'Oh for goodness' sake,' she frowned, 'I thought it was something serious!'

Tom took a sharp breath and shook his head.

'Beard business is serious,' said Ben looking wounded. 'Do *you* think it makes me look like I'm trying to fit in with the young trendy lot?'

Considering I'd only been looking for a diversion from being told where to sit by Steve, I certainly seemed to have opened quite a can of worms. Fortunately, however, we were saved from further beard analysis by Jim ringing the bell behind the bar and calling the meeting to order.

'Here, Ruby!' called Marie from her position at the table of traders. 'I've saved you a seat.'

With the space so crammed it would have been impossible to try and wedge in with someone else and therefore, without daring to glance in Dad's direction, I crossed the bar, painfully aware that his eyes were on my every step, and joined my current colleagues to publicly demonstrate far sooner than I had expected to have to that I had very definitely picked a side.

The meeting got off to a lively start and it wasn't many minutes before I realised I had chosen the right place to sit, even though I had initially been reluctant about it.

'So let me get this straight,' said Bob standing up to address Dad and his two accomplices who had delivered the first blow. 'We're going to have the same old switching on of the town lights as we always do, only this year there's no money for a tree.'

It sounded ridiculous. It was ridiculous. How much did a Christmas tree cost, for goodness' sake?

'That's not entirely accurate,' said Dad in a clipped tone, 'as we have just gone to great lengths to explain, there will be a tree but not for the market. This year the town has been assigned just the one and it has been decided that it will be situated outside the council offices.'

'Decided by who?' shouted an irate voice from the back.

'And more to the point, who's going to bloody well see it if it's stuck down there?' protested someone else.

'The market square *always* has a tree!' joined in Marie. Unlike everyone else who had spoken so far, she sounded upset rather than angry.

I took a deep breath and decided it was time to show everyone where my allegiances lay.

'Why not,' I suggested a little nervously, 'take it to a vote. If there really is only enough money for one tree, then why not let those who would normally benefit from it decide where it should go? Let the traders choose between the market square and the council building. If there's going to be just the one, then shouldn't there be some discussion as to where it will be located? You shouldn't just turn up here,' I said, looking at Dad, my confidence and indignation growing with every word, 'and tell them, us, I mean.'

'Hear, hear!'

'Surely,' I continued, further encouraged by the positive response, 'everyone should have a chance to decide where the tree goes, shouldn't they?'

There was a general murmur of assent as Dad shifted uncomfortably in his seat, his jaw grinding in the familiar way it always did when he was faced with a situation he couldn't control.

'And we all know which way that vote would go!' piped up Gordon. 'Give us your tree, Robert, and let folk enjoy it as they go about Christmas shopping in the town!'

'What's left of the town!' shouted another voice from the back.

'And could we please just clarify,' said Gwen, sounding calm from her position at the front, 'who will be doing the switch-on this year?'

'The mayor,' said Dad wearily, no doubt knowing what the reaction to this little titbit would be, 'as always.'

'Why can't we have someone different for a change?' shouted Shirley.

'Yes,' joined in Bob. 'Let's have someone who people will actually *want* to turn out to see!'

'Someone off *The X Factor*!'

'Or one of the celebrities starring in the Peterborough panto,' added Chris, a wicked glint in his eye. 'Personally I wouldn't mind seeing that girl out of *EastEnders* who's playing Cinderella in the flesh!'

Everyone started to laugh.

'Hey!' admonished Marie. 'I can hear you, Chris!'

Dad stood up and banged on the table in a vain attempt to instil some sort of order as the meeting rapidly threatened to descend into further chaos.

'You all have to understand that funds are tighter than they've ever been this year,' he said, 'and that we just don't have the manpower to assign someone to organise anything different. Perhaps next year—' he began.

'It'll be too late next year, Robbie,' said Chris, beginning to sound properly angry. 'The turnout for the switch-on was pitiful last year and people won't come back for the same old rubbish, not again.'

'Especially if there isn't even a tree,' tutted Shirley. 'What are the kiddies supposed to look at?'

'Well, I'm sorry but that's as much as I know,' said Dad, clearly nettled by Chris calling him Robbie. He only ever said it to get a rise out of him.

'The tree will be going up outside the council offices and the mayor will be turning on the lights on November the twenty-sixth as usual.'

'But that's just ten days away!' said Jude, turning bright red.

'And in line with Wynbridge tradition,' retaliated Dad, looking straight at her. 'I thought you traders were keen to uphold tradition,' he added sarcastically, turning to look pointedly at me.

'Not the shitty ones!' cut in Steve.

'What if,' suggested Simon, 'what if someone else funded a tree for the square and put it up themselves, or came up with an alternative person to turn the lights on?'

'What do you mean?' one of Dad's accomplices asked. 'How would that work?'

The noise level dropped again as Simon explained.

'Well,' he went on, 'you just said the council are stretched and don't have the manpower to come up with something new, didn't you?'

'Yes,' Dad cautiously agreed.

'So how would the powers-that-be at the council feel if we came up with something ourselves?'

The noise level began to rise again.

'Hey Si,' said Chris, 'that's not a bad idea.'

'Absolutely not!' responded Dad, shouting just about louder than everyone else and completely contradicting what he had said to me about the traders making an effort to help themselves. 'There simply isn't enough time and added to that there are all sorts of health and safety implications to consider when it comes to installing trees in public areas.'

This last comment was met with a hail of 'boos'.

'As I said earlier,' Dad continued trying to drown everyone out, 'perhaps we can arrange something different for next year.'

Chaos ensued as he and his colleagues pushed their way out of the pub and everyone carried on moaning and shouting.

'You've gone very quiet, dear,' said Gwen, plonking herself in the seat next to mine that had just become vacant.

'I'm thinking,' I told her, tapping the table and staring into space.

'About what?' she asked, her bright eyes sparkling mischievously.

'That I might,' I sighed, 'be about to climb so deep into Dad's bad books that I'll never be able to pull myself out again.'

'Oh bravo!' she laughed, clapping her hands together. 'Good girl! That definitely calls for another whisky and soda!'

Chapter 8

Having firmly made up my mind that I was going to interfere in the festive plans and make this the best Christmas the
market had ever seen, I have to admit I didn't get a whole lot
of sleep that night. I had dreaded going home and facing the
weight of Dad's martyred expression and I'd consequently
spun out my time in The Mermaid making tentative plans in
my head, gossiping and somehow managing to drink more
cider in one evening than I had managed to neck during the
entirety of freshers' week.

As closing time lurched into view Tom kindly offered to
drive me home. Pleading with me not to keep giggling, he
waited patiently as I searched for my door key, then pressed
his finger to his lips and gently shoved me over the threshold
before heading off to Jemma. I needn't have worried however, because the house was dark and silent and I crept up

to bed knowing I was going to have to endure Dad's disappointment stone cold sober.

The following morning I plastered on the most defiant expression I could muster, but it was immediately obvious when I went downstairs that nothing had changed since I had been a teenager living at home and Dad and I had locked horns in some petty battle. Dad, still the definitive game player, had managed to pull the ultimate master stroke and had left ridiculously early for work, leaving me to 'stew in my own juice' and 'think about my behaviour' all day, as if I were twelve years old rather than twenty-two.

However, unlike during my tempestuous teenage years when I fought every bit as stubbornly as he did, I now found there was a tiny part of me wishing he had stayed to thrash it out. I would have liked to clear the air and put our relationship back on track, but if this was how he wanted to play the situation then so be it.

Shored up by the quarrelsome meeting and aided by the confidence boosting, not to mention group bonding effects of alcohol, everyone at the market, even Bob, was full of enthusiasm for the forthcoming battle. They were all ready to right some wrongs, set things straight and take back some control as to what should and shouldn't happen in the market square. Personally I found the sudden change, although welcome and necessary, rather daunting and did my utmost to convince myself that none of it really had anything to do with what I had said.

'Amazing what you can do when you set your mind to it, isn't it?' said Gwen, looking with fondness at them all as they bustled about, slapping one another on the back with their chests puffed out and their voices raised in cosy camaraderie.

'What do you mean?' I asked, suddenly doubting that I really had it in me to make their dramatic change of attitude worthwhile.

'All this!' she said, pointing. 'You've certainly got everyone fired up!'

'But I haven't done anything,' I said, shaking my head and certainly not wanting to acknowledge responsibility. 'Not really, not yet anyway.'

Even though I'd drunk more than my share of Skylark Scrumpy I knew I'd had the sense to keep my 'how to spice up Christmas' ideas to myself. The only suggestion I had actually vocalised was the one about the council putting the positioning of the town's solitary tree to a vote and there was nothing particularly remarkable or rebellious about that.

'Doesn't matter,' said Gwen with a knowing wink. 'You picked a side, Ruby Smith, and you told me you were going to stick to it.'

From what I could remember, I had indeed told Gwen that I was going to get involved and I suppose I did have some interesting plans kicking around in my cider-soaked brain, so what was the point in putting it off? Christmas was already almost upon us and there was so much to do. I might just as well get the ball rolling, but not until I had faced my father and explained a few things first, of course.

'I'm afraid he isn't here,' said Brenda, Dad's ultra-efficient secretary. 'He's been in meetings over at Fenditch head office all day. I can send him a message, if you like. Let him know you need to speak to him.'

'No,' I said backing away and wondering if perhaps the early morning start wasn't actually anything to do with avoiding me after all. Perhaps I had mistaken his pettiness for my own. 'You're all right, but thanks.'

'Probably just as well,' she confided, leaning across the desk. 'I know I probably shouldn't say it, but he was in a foul mood when I spoke to him earlier this morning. Foul. Made me quite glad he wasn't here, to be honest.'

'Oh dear,' I sympathised, deciding not to explain that his miserable mood could, in some part, have been my fault. 'I'll just have a quick word with Tom before I go, if that's all right?'

'And he's another one with a face on,' she warned, before turning back to her computer screen. 'He's in his office.'

I found Tom sitting behind his desk with his hands stuck in his hair, his tie skewed and a murderous look in his eye. Had he not looked up and spotted me loitering in the doorway I probably would have turned tail and put off thanking him for the lift home the night before until another day.

'What?' he snapped when he spotted me.

He sounded as unlike jovial, kind Tom as was humanly possible.

'I just wanted to say thanks for the lift,' I said already preparing to leave, 'but it'll keep.'

He pulled his hands out of his hair, which stayed sticking up in tufts, and began throwing files from one side of his desk to the other.

'This is all your bloody fault,' he said, pointing an unsteady finger in my hastily retreating direction.

'Me?' I said stopping in my tracks. 'What have I done?'

'Come in and shut the door.'

I wasn't sure I wanted to when he looked and sounded so dangerous, but I decided to risk it, as long as I could keep the desk between us and one eye on the door.

'I've just had Jemma in tears on the phone,' he said accusingly, but with rather less heat.

'And that's my fault as well, is it?' I asked in confusion.

'Yes,' he said bluntly, 'it damn well is.'

'And what exactly have I done to cause such a downturn in the usually upbeat emotions of your competent and composed wife?'

I was trying to make him smile, but it didn't work and, given the fact that he had just told me Jemma was crying, I don't suppose a few funny words would or should have made an impact.

'You've made me cancel date night.'

'Have I?'

'Yes, you bloody well have, and I wouldn't mind, but since we instigated it six months ago we've only managed three, and two of those have just been quick trips to the pub.'

He sounded thoroughly fed up, but I still couldn't feel all of the guilt he had assigned me because I didn't know what I had done to be the cause of such apparent marital disharmony.

'So,' I said, risking sitting on the very edge of the chair opposite him, 'what exactly is it that I am supposed to have done that has sent your life spiralling out of control?'

'This isn't a joke, Ruby,' he said seriously.

'I wasn't suggesting it was,' I backtracked, feeling suitably chastened.

'Jemma and I never have any time together these days. Never. And now this bloody stall means she's under even more pressure.'

'But the stall was her idea,' I said gently, 'hers and Lizzie's.'

'Oh, I know,' he said, digging his fingers into his head again, 'and it isn't that, not really.'

'So what is it then?' I said, beginning to feel impatient.

'It's Christmas,' he said dully.

'Christmas?'

'Christmas,' he repeated. 'And the tree and the lights and the market, all of it really.'

He pulled out a thick manila file from the bottom of the teetering pile and began flicking through it biting his lip.

'I'm sorry,' I said, afraid to disturb him, but curious nonetheless, 'but I still don't see what any of this has to do with me.'

'Well, you've got them all fired up, haven't you? You joined forces with the traders last night, told Gwen that you had a few ideas about how to save Christmas and now your dad's gone into meltdown mode and handed everything over to me.'

'But handed what over to you?' I asked exasperatedly. 'I was under the impression that it was going to be the same boring old stuff the town has every year, minus the tree, of course. A few phone calls, a few tradesmen to set things up and Bob's your uncle. Same as always.'

Tom shrugged and carried on flicking through the file.

'Tom, I can't honestly see what's so taxing, or have I missed something?'

To be honest I was surprised that Dad had let someone else even look at the Christmas file, let alone given the order to take it over, and rather wished Tom would hurry up and get to the point.

'No,' he shrugged, 'no, you haven't missed anything at all, Ruby. Like you just said; Christmas is going to be happening, just the same as always.'

'So what's the problem then?'

'The problem is,' he sighed, 'that *I'm* now the one making those phone calls, emailing those tradesmen and of course fielding all the extra visits and calls from irate traders who your dad has told that I am their point of contact if they need to get in touch with the council. Give it a day or two and I'm going to be bombarded with all manner of suggestions that I have neither the time to think about or the funds to approve!'

'Oh,' I said, the full implication of the situation finally beginning to dawn, 'so it isn't just the usual stuff to sort out, is it? And because there's the potential that the situation will get out of hand,' which I had seen for myself all day down at the market, 'Dad's opted to pass the buck.'

'Well and truly and,' he added bitterly, 'if the traders stay as unhappy as they were last night, then I'm the one who's going to get all the flak, but apparently none of the support to try and make it better.'

'Oh,' I said again, 'I see. Sorry.'

'I've got more than enough on my plate right now,' he sighed, indicating the stacks of files and papers, 'and now I've got all this to contend with as well as a very unhappy wife.'

Now I was feeling suitably guilty but, bubbling away just under the surface, I was feeling excited too.

'Can I make a suggestion?' I said, leaning across the desk.

'Here we go!'

'No,' I insisted, 'it's nothing bad.'

'Go on, then.'

'Will you let me help you?'

'How can you possibly help?'

'Well, as I'm being tarred and labelled as the one who has stirred things up, although I still don't really understand how, given that I hardly opened my mouth . . .'

'Because the traders hate your dad,' Tom explained candidly, 'and, whatever you really feel about him, you've made it look as if you have an issue with him too.'

I chose to ignore this alarming thought for the time being. I had known sitting with them and speaking up in the pub was going to have consequences but this was already way beyond anything I had expected.

'In that case, why not make *me* the point of contact for the traders, then. If they have an issue or plan worth passing on I'll let you know, and in the meantime I can think about some cheap and cheerful ideas to placate them and in the process make you look good. I could act as a sort of go-between and only trouble you with the worthwhile suggestions.'

'No,' he said, shaking his head and looking mildly terrified at the thought, 'I don't think your dad . . .'

'We won't tell Dad,' I said, cutting him off. 'We won't tell anyone other than the stallholders that we're working together. If they despise Dad as much as you say they do then they'll more than happily go along with the idea, won't they?'

'But—'

'No buts,' I insisted, 'if Dad really has passed the buck and washed his hands of all this then so be it. You deal with getting the lights up and leave the rest to me.'

'I don't know . . .'

'The lights go on in just over one week,' I reminded him. 'Give me a few days, and if I can't come up with someone more exciting than the mayor to turn them on again, then I'll hand the whole project back to you for the rest of the season. At least let me come up with some suggestions and please,' I begged, 'call your beautiful wife and tell her date night is back on. You'll work so much better tomorrow with a spring in your step!'

I didn't wait for him to answer, but rushed back down to my car to begin jotting down the ideas I'd had swimming around in my head all day. It wasn't going to be easy with just one week left before the lights went on, but it wasn't impossible either. Top of the list, the number one priority, simply had to be sourcing a tree for the market square.

I pushed all thoughts of how angry Dad would be if he knew I'd interfered to the back of my mind, consoling myself with the justification that I had tried to talk to him and instead imagined myself leaving town for a warmer clime in the New Year amid a flurry of congratulations and thanks.

I was so engrossed in my list and daydreaming that I didn't hear the passenger door open.

'What are you up to?' Steve quizzed, jumping into the empty seat and scaring me witless in the process. 'You look positively furtive.'

'Jesus!' I shouted, dropping my notepad and grasping my chest. 'What the hell? You can't just go around jumping into people's cars!'

'But you're not people,' he laughed. 'You're Ruby Sue.'

'I thought Mia said you shouldn't call me that,' I reminded him, quickly grabbing the notebook and stuffing it out of sight in my bag.

'Come to make up with your dad, have you?'

'No,' I snapped, still angry that he had made me jump and struggling to find any 'friendly feelings' as a result. 'Not that it's any of your business. What are you doing here?'

'None of your business,' he mimicked, giving me a playful nudge.

'If you don't mind,' I said, turning the engine over and staring straight ahead, 'I need to go.'

'Is he here, then?'

'Who?'

'Your dad.'

'No,' I said, 'he isn't actually. He's at Fenditch head office, has been all day. What do you want him for anyway?'

Steve turned to look at me properly and I focused my attention on the indicator column.

'To tell him Mum and Dad are going to donate a tree

for the market. Two trees actually, one for either end of the square and new lights so they both look the same.'

'Really?' I said, smiling in spite of myself and feeling delighted that I could already tick the first major conundrum off the Christmas list. 'That's very generous of them.'

'Well, it's your fault really,' he chuckled, 'speaking up in the pub like that last night. You've got everyone so fired up.'

For a second or two I wondered if my fleeting suggestion about moving the tree was going to be worth the potential long-term fall-out with my father, but then I imagined the market square aglow with two trees and how happy the local youngsters would be and considered it was worth the risk.

'Well, whatever the reason behind the gesture, it really is very kind,' I told him, 'and you don't need to tell Dad.'

'No?'

'No, it's Tom you're going to want. He's the one in charge of Christmas planning this year.'

'Since when?' Steve asked, sounding amazed.

'Since Dad decided the heat was going to be too much and that he was going to end up with egg on his face.'

The words were out before I could check them and I was grateful that Steve didn't seem to take on board how scathing they were.

'Oh, that's a stroke of luck,' he said, pointing across the car park as Tom rushed over to his car. 'There's Tom now. I'll just grab a quick word with him.'

'No, don't,' I said, reaching across to stop him. 'It'll keep. Tell him tomorrow.'

'Well, he does look as if he's in a hurry,' Steve laughed as Tom reversed out of his parking spot at full speed.

'He is,' I told him, 'he has a hot date.'

'Lucky Tom,' said Steve, smiling down at my hand which was still resting on his arm.

Chapter 9

My first Saturday of trading finally dawned, and although Dad hadn't directly mentioned my contribution to the meeting I could tell by the lengthy silences and lip chewing that he was tolerating my presence in the house rather than enjoying having me home for the holidays. It was perhaps a sad reflection on just how far our relationship had recently drifted that after my conversation with Tom I hadn't felt any further inclination to explain my decision to join forces with the traders or patch things up.

I wasn't sure why it had happened or even how, but in the time I'd been home it felt as if we had gone through some strange role reversal. Suddenly I was the one working to save Wynbridge and Dad was the one who looked as if he didn't care about it at all. The switch was unnerving but real nonetheless.

I pushed our argument to the back of my mind and focused

on looking forward to what I hoped would be my first really brisk day of sales, and getting together with everyone else that evening to discuss what they had discovered customers *really* wanted to see in the town in the run up to Christmas.

A simple gathering of information had been the first idea I had suggested to the others after my conversation with Tom and as a result everyone had been making an extra effort to chat to, as opposed to simply sell to, the townsfolk ever since.

The stallholders had been delighted that Tom was now in charge of Christmas and more than happy for me to act as go-between. Personally, given the rude remarks and caustic comments, I couldn't help wondering if they were actually more interested in getting one over on Dad and his council cronies than turning around the fortunes of the market, but so long as I could help play a part in providing the townsfolk of Wynbridge with a very merry Christmas, then I was just happy to go with the flow.

'How can we provide a pleasurable Christmas shopping experience and enjoyable festive events,' I said to Gwen, 'when no one has actually taken the time to ask the people who shop in the town what they would like to see and do?'

'That's a good point,' she said while surreptitiously feeding Minnie titbits of cooked chicken to stop her showing me her sharp little teeth.

'We could throw all the money in the world at December,' I rushed enthusiastically on, 'but if it isn't being put into giving people what they actually want to see or are interested in taking part in, then what's the point? If people don't turn out then the market won't see any upturn in its fortunes, will it?'

'Quite right,' she said. 'Not that we have all the money in the world, of course, or time, for that matter.'

Both facts had been the cause of restless nights since the meeting in the pub, but I was still convinced in my heart that if everyone pulled together then we could make some sort of a difference in the short amount of time we had available. All we needed was a little bit of luck.

'Well, at least we have a tree for the market now,' I reminded Gwen, keen to dismiss all thoughts of the money and time we were lacking.

'Two trees,' she corrected, 'thanks to the generosity of the Dempster family, and that's a first for this town. Young Steve was telling me that Tom has already arranged for them to go up next Friday and the lights will be in place early Saturday morning ready for the big switch-on that night.'

'That's cutting it fine,' I frowned. 'What if the lights don't work or the trees won't stand straight?'

'Oh, you needn't worry about things like that,' she said confidently, 'the guys responsible know what they're doing. It'll all happen, you mark my words, and have you heard about the rest of the town lights?'

'No,' I said. I had been trying not to pester Tom too

much, but Steve had obviously been maintaining contact and passing information on and given that his family had made such a generous contribution I couldn't sulk about it. 'What about them?'

'Apparently there's going to be more emphasis on packing them together to light the square and the bridge rather than having the few spindly strands petering out on the outskirts of town.'

'Now that is a good idea,' I agreed. I'd always thought the lights were spread too thinly around the town to make a really impressive show. 'So who decided that?' I asked, already guessing the answer.

'Tom, of course,' Gwen chuckled. 'From what Steve's told me, it sounds like he's really taken the bull by the horns and put his foot down about it.'

'Well good for him,' I said, 'I don't blame him for making the most out of the situation. If he plays his cards right he'll come up smelling of roses by Christmas Eve! I bet he hasn't breathed a word about any of the changes he's putting in place to Dad.'

'Of course he hasn't,' Gwen tittered on. 'Can you imagine the look on your old man's face when the mayor flicks the switch and sees the illuminations all jostling together in one spot?'

'No,' I laughed, 'I can't.'

It really was going to be a picture, but I still couldn't help wishing we had someone other than the mayor lined up for the big day.

Much to my relief, trading that Saturday was brisk and I took more money in that one day than I'd taken in three earlier that week. Lizzie's pretty advent calendars had completely sold out and stocks of her festive bunting were running dangerously low. Thanks to the presence of so many children out shopping with their parents and grandparents there had been a run on Jemma's delicious gingerbread families and Steve had soon mopped up any mince pies that were lingering towards the end of the day. Consequently I had no worries about having to gorge myself on leftover stock that couldn't be carried over until Monday.

'So will you be coming back for the big switch-on next Friday?'

It had been my stock question to customers all day and responses had been mixed, but not particularly favourable.

'We might be,' said the mum of the young family who was tucking into the last bag of biscuits, 'but only if it's going to be a bit more exciting than last year.'

'The lights are always all right,' agreed her husband, 'but after the countdown there's never much to do and you notice it all the more when you've got children with you. All the shops were already shut last year, apart from the café, and even the stalls were packed up.'

'It was hardly great Saturday night entertainment,' grumbled the woman. 'Personally I would have rather stayed at home and watched *Strictly*!'

Unfortunately their responses echoed many I had heard that day.

'Well,' I said, keen to send them away feeling slightly more willing to give the switch-on another chance, 'I can't make any promises, but I know for a fact that things are going to look a little different this year, and keep an eye on the local press because I'm fairly certain there will be more going on, things just need to be finalised.'

'Well, we'll keep it in mind,' said the man as he took the pushchair handles from his wife, 'but if last year's efforts are anything to go by, we won't hold our breath.'

I watched them walk away, my mind already trying to come up with possible entertainment options that would extend the celebration beyond the ten-second countdown that usually heralded the beginning of the festive season in Wynbridge.

The Mermaid was now officially the market traders' designated meeting spot, and by the time I arrived that evening, 'Operation Christmas' was in full swing. Everyone had a similarly depressing tale to tell as we discussed customer responses to last year's event. Tom's arrival with some exciting news couldn't have been better timed, as I noticed a couple of heads had started to drop at the thought of another lacklustre start to December.

'So,' he said, standing amongst us with the spring, I couldn't help noticing, very firmly back in his step, 'as you all know by now, I've been put in charge of festive planning for Wynbridge town centre this year, and I've already managed to make some changes to how the lights are going to be displayed.'

'And that was fast work, my boy,' shouted Chris, raising his pint glass in appreciation of Tom's efforts. 'Hats off to you!'

'Yes, well,' Tom continued, looking proud, 'time really is of the essence. This time next week the lights will hopefully be on and the celebration in full swing and with that thought in mind, I have a little extra news to share.'

'I've already told them about the trees and new lights!' yelled Chris.

'Of course,' said Tom, clearly embarrassed for not mentioning them first. 'Thank you Chris and Marie. Your contribution is *hugely* appreciated, but this is something else I've been working on.'

'Even better!' Chris called out again, not feeling at all put out. 'Go on then, lad, put us out of our misery!'

Tom took a deep breath.

'Mr Bradshaw,' he began enthusiastically then stopped to explain who the man was, 'for those of you who don't know him, he's the chap who organises the fireworks display at the council offices every Guy Fawkes Night.'

'Oh, we know old Billy,' nodded Gordon and some of the others. 'Most of us went to school with him!'

'Well,' Tom continued, 'he's offered to donate and set up a small display for next Saturday. We aren't quite sure how it will work just yet, but he seems to think that if we move the mayor's platform to the front of the old town hall then he'll be able to set up there. What do you all think? Fireworks should give the event an extra bit of sparkle and excitement, shouldn't they?'

'Oh yes, that's an excellent idea!' called out Marie. 'I've lost count of the number of mums and dads who have been moaning about there not being enough for the kiddies to look at once the lights are on!'

'Hear, hear!' chorused some of the others.

'Well, that's settled then,' said Tom, looking well pleased.

'I was wondering if the market could stay open?' I shouted as loud as I dared, determined to sound out the idea while everyone was gathered together. 'I know most of the shops will be shut, but if we all stay open and perhaps string up some more lights like the ones I'm using on the Cherry Tree stall, people would be bound to stay and look around for a bit longer.'

'I could fire up my old candyfloss machine and sell it alongside the chestnuts,' offered Peter. 'I've still got the machine packed away at home. Kids love candyfloss!'

'And I could make some mulled wine for the grown-ups,' chimed in Marie, 'and perhaps someone else could put together a lucky dip or some simple games for people to play.'

'Perhaps every stall could offer something,' joined in Tom. 'How about pin the red nose on Rudolph?'

Everyone began to chatter at once, each trying to claim Tom's festive game idea for their own.

'And we could have some music!' shouted Ben from his spot at the bar with Lizzie.

Tom looked at me and winked, clearly delighted that everyone was so keen to get involved.

'But we still need someone better than the bloody mayor for the switch-on,' Chris's voice boomed out again.

'I'm working on it, Chris,' nodded Tom, 'I'm working on it.'

Once the excitement had died down and everyone had decided what their stall was going to be offering I pulled up a seat next to Bea who had just arrived, and settled down for a chat. We hadn't been talking for many minutes when a hand reached between us and half a pint of cider was plonked on the table alongside our other glasses.

'I probably owe you more than that,' said Jemma, planting a kiss on my cheek, 'but Jim says stocks are running low and apparently you can down a pint in a heartbeat!'

'The cheeky bugger!' I laughed twisting round to face her.

'But seriously,' she said, 'thanks, hon.'

'What's she done now?' asked Bea, with a nod to the glass. 'I've only been out of the loop for a couple of days and I've come here tonight and found the town and the traders in uproar. I'm guessing this has something to do with you?' she asked, cocking an eyebrow in my direction.

'She's saved my sanity,' explained Jemma, 'and put the smile back on my husband's face.'

Bea raised her eyebrows even further and looked from one of us to the other.

'Oh, I know what I mean,' Jemma giggled, as she patted my shoulder. 'She made him reinstate date night,' she told Bea, 'and offered to help out with this whole Christmas nightmare that landed on his desk a couple of days ago.'

'But I thought your dad dealt with Christmas, Ruby?' said Bea, looking just as shocked as everyone else had been when they discovered that Dad had handed everything over to Tom. 'I thought Wynbridge seasonal cheer was his responsibility and his alone.'

'It was,' I said, taking a sip of cider and thinking not for the first time how out of character Dad's decision actually was, before remembering the reason as to why he'd made it, 'until it looked like the natives were going feral and demanding that steps were taken to save the ailing fortunes of the market of course, then he decided to give Tom the opportunity to manage the fall-out.'

'Oh, that was generous of him,' laughed Bea, looking

around and taking in the air of renewed optimism and excitement with fresh understanding, 'and I'm guessing that accounts for why everyone has joined forces and are in such high spirits. I get it now.'

'No,' said Chris who happened to be walking back to the bar and must have been privy to our conversation. 'You really don't.'

'What do you mean?' I frowned.

'Well, let's put it this way,' he said, stumbling slightly as he came closer. 'It's going to take a whole lot more than a bloody Christmas tree and a few sodding fireworks to save this market.'

'Well, we're doing what we can . . .' I began.

'And you,' he said, his tone suddenly more menacing than merry, 'you need to look a bit closer to home, Ruby Smith! If you had half the wits you think you have then you'd see what was happening right under your pretty little nose and realise that this Christmas shenanigans is little more than an elaborate farewell!'

His voice had risen to almost a shout and everyone in the pub was staring. I had no idea what he was talking about and even though he was more than a little tipsy, the sight of him standing over the table waving his finger in my face was somewhat intimidating to say the least. I swallowed hard and felt sharp tears stinging the back of my eyes. I couldn't believe the change that had come over him and wondered if perhaps Dad's dislike of him had sprung from an encounter with this previously unknown ugly side of his personality.

'What exactly are you talking about?' I croaked.

'Ignore him,' said Steve, suddenly appearing and pulling his father away by the arm. 'He's drunk.'

'No,' I said, feeling slightly more confident now that Steve was there to restrain the menace that alcohol had unleashed, 'I want to know what he meant.'

'What I meant—' Chris started again.

'It's nothing,' Steve insisted, pulling harder, 'he meant nothing. He's drunk more than his fill and he's just mouthing off. He's worried about the market. Like we all are.'

He might have thought he could convince me that he was speaking the truth, but I had known Steve Dempster long enough to know a lie when it fell out of his mouth.

Chapter 10

'I know you probably can't, and I'll more than understand if you have to say no, but I was wondering if I could ask a favour.'

'What,' I laughed, 'another one! You want to be careful, Tom. Folk will talk.'

'Oh, pack it in,' he tutted, 'can you do it or not?'

'Well, that would depend on what *it* is, wouldn't it?' I teased, cradling my mobile against my ear as I rearranged some bags of iced and spiced buns that Angela had just delivered from the café.

'I need to get some paperwork over to Skylark Farm,' he explained, 'but I haven't got time to take it and your dad is watching me like a hawk. I think he's got wind that something's up. He keeps asking how the switch-on plans are coming on. I've managed to fob him off so far, but I don't want to blow it.'

'No problem,' I told him. I was especially keen to help if it meant keeping Dad off-track for a bit longer. 'If you can get the papers to the café I'll take them later this afternoon.'

'Are you sure?'

'Absolutely,' I insisted, determined to do my bit and make Tom's life, and in turn Jemma's, as simple as possible. 'It looks like it's going to be another quiet Tuesday here so I won't be missing out if I pack up a few minutes earlier than usual. What are the papers for anyway?'

'Jake and Amber who own the farm have offered to run a hog roast on Saturday night. I just need them to fill in some forms to make it official.'

'Oh, that's fantastic!' I gasped. 'What a brilliant idea.'

'Isn't it?' agreed Tom. 'It's a new project they're trying out. They've been keeping rare breed pigs in their orchards and then selling the meat alongside the cider and now they've decided to try their hand at some occasional outdoor catering for events such as ours.'

Since I had developed a taste for Skylark Scrumpy I'd heard nothing but good things about how the couple living at the farm had turned around the fortunes of the place.

'They're keen to play a part in the community,' Tom continued, 'and from what I can gather they won't be making much of a profit. This is their way of thanking everyone for their support and advertising the newest aspect of their diversification plan.'

'Well, that all sounds amazing,' I agreed, 'very entrepreneurial, and fingers crossed they'll be making their own local apple sauce as well then,' I added.

'Oh, I hadn't thought of that,' Tom drooled, 'lovely. Make sure you ask about that, won't you? And try to stay off the cider!'

As promised, I packed up the stall a little earlier than usual and raced across to the Cherry Tree to drop off the stock and collect the paperwork. I had almost made it back through the door when Chris appeared, blocking my escape and looking extremely sheepish. I swore under my breath, annoyed to find myself cornered when I'd so successfully managed to avoid everyone in the Dempster family since the one-sided showdown in the pub.

A couple of days had passed and I was still none the wiser as to what he had worked himself up into such a lather about and no one at the market had been in a rush to tell me either. Even Steve had dramatically cut down on consumption of his beloved mince pies and I had my suspicions that I was being avoided just as much as I was the one doing the avoiding.

'Excuse me,' I mumbled when he didn't budge.

'Can I just say something before I let you pass?' he asked, his brows knitted together and his hands twisting his cap into a tight ball. 'I think I need to apologise, don't I?'

'If you think you've got something to apologise for,' I shrugged, pretending I didn't care either way.

'Of course I bloody have,' he said, turning red. 'I should never have spoken to you in the pub like that, Ruby. You of all people.'

'It's all right,' I said, my heart softening as I took in his genuine tone and humble expression. 'You'd had a lot to drink and you're scared that the market might close. I get that.'

'I had,' he sighed, 'and I am.'

'But,' I added, hoping he might feel inclined to say a little more now he was sober and Steve wasn't there to stop him, 'I can't help thinking there was more behind what you said than I know about. There's something else going on with the market, isn't there?'

He looked at me for a second and I could tell there was something he wanted to say, it was right on the tip of his tongue, but he swallowed it down and stepped aside to let me pass.

'Steve's been like a different lad since you came back,' he blurted out, just as I drew level with him. 'I know it's not my place to say, but he was broken-hearted when you left.'

'So was I,' I said, forcing down the slab of heartache which determinedly made its presence felt whenever his name was mentioned these days.

'He should never have let you go,' Chris continued. His voice was full of sadness and regret.

I didn't know what to say. He had caught me completely off guard and this was the last thing I expected him to be telling me. Steve had Mia now so as far as I was concerned his heartbreak had healed and whether or not he should have let me go was irrelevant.

'They were tough times,' I croaked, 'for everyone. He did what he had to do. I understand that. I don't hate him,' I said, finally daring to look up at him.

'Well that's something,' he nodded. 'At least you can still be friends.'

'Of course,' I agreed, 'we can be friends.'

I can't honestly say I can remember much of the journey to Skylark Farm. My mind was awash not only with trying to work out what this extra information about the market everyone was keeping from me might be, but also Chris's admission that Steve had been so heartbroken when I left town.

I pulled into the farmyard, parked next to an incredibly sleek Mercedes which I couldn't help thinking looked totally out of place, grabbed the pile of papers and rushed over to the house, determined not to let Chris's words distract me from the job in hand. A cacophony of barking and shouting broke out as I raised the knocker and I took a step back, wondering if I should just leave the papers in the porch and head for home.

'Sorry!' called a woman's voice above the din. 'Just give me a sec!'

The door was eventually tugged open and a brace of Labradors raced out, their tails wagging ninety to the dozen, to see who had disturbed their peaceful afternoon.

'Don't mind them,' said the woman, jiggling a pretty dark-haired little girl on her hip, 'come in, please. You must be Ruby? Tom said you'd be coming.'

'Yes,' I smiled, pushing my way between the dogs that seemed more determined to lick me to death than maul me. 'I've got the paperwork for the hog roast you're going to be running on Saturday night.'

'Excellent.' She beamed, transferring the little girl to her other hip. 'I'm Amber, by the way,' she added by way of introduction, 'and this is my daughter, Honey. Come and have a seat and I'll make us some tea.'

'No, it's fine,' I said, 'you're obviously busy.'

'Oh, I'm always busy!' she laughed. 'Come on. Jake will be here in a minute. We can probably get these papers signed off and you can take them straight back with you. As long as you don't mind, of course?'

'No,' I said, pulling out a chair. 'That makes perfect sense.'

We settled at the table and were soon discussing the overwhelming success of Skylark Scrumpy and the merits of homemade apple sauce versus shop-bought. Honey was happily installed in her high chair and squeezing slices of bread and butter between her fingers, when the house door was suddenly flung open and a man rushed in, clearly intent on making quite an entrance.

'Jake said to tell you he'll be back in a bit, Amber,' he announced, reaching between us for a plate and a slice of cake which he then began to scrutinise. 'He said something about frozen pipes. I don't honestly know if I'm going to be able to cope with this "life in the sticks" malarkey. Oh, hello,' he smiled at me, the sulky tone instantly banished. 'You didn't say we were expecting company, Amber, and such pretty company at that.'

Not usually prone to reacting to such cheesy lines I was surprised to feel my cheeks redden under the man's twinkling blue gaze, but given who I thought he might be I considered my behaviour was somewhat justified. Rather than return his intense stare I distractedly began crumbling the remains of my cake on my plate and developed a sudden fascination with the pattern on my teacup.

Amber let out a long slow breath and rolled her eyes.

'Well, aren't you going to introduce us?' demanded the man as he abandoned his plate and flung his coat across the armchair in front of the Aga with a flourish.

His diva-like behaviour confirmed my suspicions regarding who I thought he was.

Amber stared at the coat and then at the man wearing an expression my mum would have said, could have 'curdled milk'.

'Sorry,' he said sheepishly, retrieving the coat and hanging it on a peg next to the door. 'Forgot where I was for a moment there. Now, about that introduction—'

Personally I didn't need one. I had already worked out that I was in the presence of Paul Thompson, celebrity caterer to the stars and host of the most controversial cookery show currently topping the TV ratings, but I had no idea what he was doing in the Skylark Farm kitchen!

'Actually I think I know who you are,' I said, finally finding my voice as I smoothed my hair behind my ears, 'you're Paul Thompson, aren't you, the celebrity caterer off the TV?'

'Notorious bad boy and outrageous flirt, more like,' Amber put in with a snort. 'Whatever you do, Ruby, don't salve his ego and certainly don't believe a word he says!'

'Hey,' pouted Paul, running a manicured hand through his thick blond hair and looking mortally wounded, 'I have to say I think that's a little harsh.'

'Given what some of my colleagues were reading about you in the newspaper this morning, I think Amber is spot on!' I laughed, feeling rather less star-struck.

'See,' said Amber, retrieving Honey's bread from the floor before the dogs found it. 'I told you, you were all over the red tops this morning and before you say it, I know you can't believe everything you read in the papers, but mud sticks, my friend.'

Paul bit his lip and was momentarily chastened into silence.

'Forgive me for asking,' I said, feeling more than ever as if I'd fallen into some sort of surreal dream, 'but what exactly are you doing here? According to the newspapers you were supposed to be jetting off to somewhere hot and exotic for a break before you finish filming the current series.'

'That little fabrication was his agent's idea,' Amber explained. 'Paul needed a bolthole and so I offered him our holiday cottage for a few days. He's supposed to be keeping a low profile,' she added pointedly.

'Well, you can't expect me to stay down there with no water or heating,' he retaliated, 'it's absolutely freezing.'

'But what I really meant,' I laughed, 'is why are you *here*? How do you two know each other?'

'Oh, Amber and I go way back,' Paul began, echoing what Steve had said to Mia about us, but Amber soon cut him off, obviously keen that I should hear the truth behind their acquaintance rather than the twisted version Paul was no doubt about to try and spin.

'Before I moved here,' she explained, 'I worked for a high profile corporate hospitality firm in London. Paul was one of our top caterers and when I left the city, for some strange reason, I decided to keep in touch. That was before the media beckoned to him, of course. He was far less arrogant and affected before the cameras found him and the curse of celebrity beckoned to the man who used to just feed the celebrities!'

'Hey,' protested Paul. 'Carry on like that and I won't be stocking my restaurant freezers with so much as a single joint of your delectable pork!'

'He also happens to be Honey's godfather,' Amber frowned, 'although I'm beginning to have my doubts about his suitability for the role now.'

'So you're in hiding then?' I gasped, feeling slightly dazzled by the glamour and cloak and dagger of it all, 'from the paparazzi!'

'Sort of,' he shrugged, as if it was an everyday occurrence, which to him I suppose it was.

'Until the latest bedroom scandal dies down at least,' Amber added scathingly.

'You didn't have to invite me,' he said mildly.

'Oh I know, but left to your own devices on a sunny beach somewhere you were bound to get yourself into even more trouble when what you *really* need to be doing is building a few bridges.'

'What do you mean?'

'Well, it wouldn't hurt to do something nice for someone for a change, would it? Give the papers something positive to report and get yourself back in the public's good books. I can't help thinking that if you keep behaving like the proverbial bad boy, a role for which you really are becoming a little long in the tooth by the way, then that blessed show of yours will be axed rather than recommissioned.'

'You've probably got a point there,' said Paul thoughtfully. 'Although I happen to think I'm wearing rather well for my age.'

Amber rolled her eyes again.

'But where around here,' he yawned, 'in the middle of nowhere am I going to find an opportunity to do something like that?'

Needless to say I didn't give either him or Amber time to draw breath.

'As luck would have it, I happen to know of the perfect opportunity!' I rushed in, clapping my hands together in unchecked excitement. 'If you really do want to do something that will boost your tarnished profile, then you could do a lot worse than offering to come and turn on our Christmas lights!'

'What, in Peterborough, you mean?' said Paul, looking mildly intrigued.

'No,' I said, shaking my head, 'not Peterborough, Wynbridge! Come and host the start of our countdown to Christmas event in the town this Saturday.'

Paul now looked utterly perplexed, but I could see that Amber understood.

'But from what I saw when I drove through there yesterday it's a piddling little place,' he frowned. 'Who on earth is going to know, or even care, that I turned on some lights round here?'

'God, you really are dense,' scolded Amber. 'How can you not see?'

'See what?'

'The fact that Wynbridge is so small, and out of the way, actually makes it all the more perfect!'

'Does it?'

'Yes!'

'How?'

'Well, if you turned up in some city, like Peterborough for example, then it would look as though you were court-ing attention and hoping to get picked up by the papers, wouldn't it?'

'But I am, aren't I?'

'Yes,' I interrupted, 'but you need to be a bit discreet about it. If you're simply stepping in at the last minute and just helping out a friend, like Amber here, who happens to live in a small struggling market town and you insist on keeping a reasonably low profile, then ...'

'It really will look like an act of kindness?'

'Bingo!' laughed Amber, 'I do believe he's finally got it!'

'And you never know,' I smiled, 'you might actually end up really enjoying yourself.'

Chapter 11

Once Paul had taken a moment to digest the wisdom behind my suggestion, and assimilate Amber's insistence that helping out with the Wynbridge switch-on was just the kind of low key event that could send his ratings soaring again, he didn't take much convincing to commit to taking part. In fact, he didn't take any convincing at all, and within the hour we had swapped mobile numbers and I was heading back to town with the hog roast paperwork completed, three bottles of Skylark Scrumpy tucked in the passenger footwell and a solemn promise from Paul himself that he would help put Wynbridge and its ailing little market back on the regional map in time for Christmas.

'Leave it all to me, lovely lady,' he had said as I was getting ready to leave. 'This sort of philanthropic venture happens to be just my field of expertise.'

'I thought you hadn't done anything like this before,' commented Amber.

'Well, I'm a fast learner,' said Paul, 'and I rather fancy myself in the role of caring celebrity chef who swoops in and saves the struggling small town from imminent disaster!'

'Oh good grief,' said Jake as he handed over the papers, 'are you sure about that, Paul? Honestly, girls, what have you unleashed? Poor Wynbridge won't know what's hit it!'

Personally I couldn't help thinking that was no bad thing. It was about time the town experienced a bit of a shake-up, and I couldn't wait to tell Tom the exciting news.

'Oh my God, you aren't serious?' squealed Jemma the second I finished relaying what had happened. 'What, *the* Paul Thompson? The actual real life Paul Thompson?'

I knew she was genuinely excited because both the children were asleep upstairs and she wasn't even trying to keep her voice down. Tom stood open-mouthed and speechless, looking from his star struck wife to me and back again.

'Yes,' I laughed, slapping down the envelope of paperwork on the table and basking in the glory. 'The one and only real life living and breathing Paul Thompson.'

Still Tom said nothing.

'But when?' gasped Jemma. 'How?'

'He's hiding out down at Skylark Farm,' I continued. 'He's an old acquaintance of Amber's apparently and fortunately for us, he needs to bag himself some positive media attention to get back in the public's good books. Turning on the

Christmas lights in a struggling little market town is a gift from the gods of public relations he said, or something very much like it.'

'Tom!' shouted Jemma in exasperation at her husband's reaction, or in this case, lack of reaction. 'Have you heard a single word of what Ruby has said?'

'Of course I have,' he croaked, sounding worryingly breathless.

For a moment I began to panic that I'd overstepped the mark and that rather than solving a problem I'd somehow landed him with an even bigger one, but the spell was quickly broken as he pulled me into a hug, grinning from ear to ear.

'Finally,' laughed Jemma. 'A response!'

'I take it you are pleased, then?' I gasped, as he hugged a little tighter and squeezed the last tiny bit of air out of my lungs. 'I have done the right thing, haven't I?' I spluttered.

'Abso-bloody-lutely!' he beamed, finally releasing me, 'I can't believe it!'

'I know,' I laughed, trying to catch my breath, 'talk about a stroke of luck.'

'Wow,' said Jemma, swaying dreamily from side to side and looking every inch like she was thoroughly enjoying her fan-girl moment. 'Do you think I've got time to get my hair done before Saturday?'

'This is just perfect,' Tom carried on, shaking his head in disbelief.

Apparently he wasn't at all perturbed that his wife was swooning over the A list celebrity she would be meeting in a few days' time.

'Jemma,' I said with a nod to Tom. 'Have you no shame? Your poor overworked husband is standing right in front of you.'

'Oh, don't worry about me,' said the man himself.

'But don't you care that your wife is all set for an evening of flirtation and frolics with the nation's number one celebrity chef and all round bad boy?' I teased. '*And* planning to look her very best for the occasion to boot!'

'No,' he grinned, 'and I'll tell you why,' he went on, 'because if this,' he said pointing at Jemma who carried on giggling, 'is the reaction of just one woman, can you imagine what the turnout is going to be like when word gets around? This is going to be the best festive turn-on ever!'

'Not half!' snorted Jemma, collapsing on to a chair.

Tom's prediction was absolutely spot-on. The traders' meeting in The Mermaid erupted when he made the announcement and word spread like wildfire through the town. Some said it wasn't true, others were keeping their fingers crossed that it was, but all were demanding a glimpse of the man himself as proof that the mayor had been officially upstaged. Fortunately Tom and I had had the sense to keep Paul's whereabouts a secret; in fact, we didn't tell anyone that he was staying locally for fear the place would be overrun with fans. So much for keeping a lid on the situation!

There was only one person who looked disappointed about the prospect of welcoming the 'baking bad boy', as some had dubbed him, and that was Chris.

'He was holding out for that girl from *EastEnders* who's in the panto,' sniggered Marie. 'He's really quite put out that us ladies are going to be having all the fun! What does your dad think of it all?' she asked. 'Is he as angry as I imagine he is?'

The news that the mayor's services were no longer required soon reached Dad's ears, but the only reaction from him that I'd been privy to was a disbelieving shake of the head accompanied by a bit of a moan.

'I had no idea people round here were so gullible,' he said. 'You'd think they'd have a bit more sense than to believe that someone like chef Thompson would be bothered with the likes of a little town like Wynbridge.'

I hadn't contradicted him or told him of my involvement with the scheme, as I was sure he'd hear that titbit of information soon enough. When I relayed his reaction to Marie she laughed all the harder, as did Gwen who happened, as always, to be in the vicinity.

'You were right about those bad books of his,' she quipped, 'there's no way out for you now, my girl!'

*

The afternoon before the big day I found myself sitting in the back seat of Paul's sleek black Mercedes and being driven over to Peterborough for a promotional spot on Fenland Radio. The initial plan to keep the whole event relatively low key had pretty much gone out of the window since Paul's agents had discovered what he was up to and, although Fenland Radio didn't have anywhere near as large an audience as the local BBC station, it was obvious that word would spread even further over the airwaves and as a result the event would be even busier than we could have hoped.

I was absolutely delighted that everything was coming together so well, but as with most situations in life, there was a fly in the ointment and he was sitting in the passenger seat next to Paul.

Ever since Chris had told me that Steve had been heartbroken when I left town I had been trying to avoid him for fear of developing even deeper feelings. Consequently, he was the last person I wanted to see sitting in the front of the car preparing to make his radio debut alongside me, and I dreaded to think what Mia would make of the situation when she found out.

Trying not to look at the way his hair curled as it touched his collar and how his broad shoulders filled the back of the seat, I could no longer deny that because of how our relationship had ended we were still unfinished business, but I also knew that my short stay in Wynbridge didn't need the added complication of trying to revive an old love affair and risking Steve's relationship with his current other half.

To my mind, when Dad discovered that I had played a very real part in toppling the mayor from his festive plinth I was going to be caught up in enough emotional turmoil to last me a lifetime! No, my mind was made up; come the end of December I was destined for a warmer clime and I would definitely be travelling alone. All I had to do was resist the temptation to try and rekindle our romance, and give the mistletoe a very wide berth.

'So, Steve,' I said, leaning forward between the seats and trying not to breathe in the waft of Hugo Boss that met me, 'why are you coming with us? I'm only here because Tom couldn't be, but I don't see why you had to tag along and anyway, don't you have rugby practice on a Friday?'

Steve twisted round to look at me.

'We train on Thursdays now,' he said, with a grin that sent my heartrate soaring, 'although I'm flattered you remembered.'

'I didn't,' I lied, quickly trying to cover my tracks, 'Bea just happened to mention that Sam is on the town team now so it was already on my mind.'

'You'll have to come and watch a match,' he smiled, seemingly unperturbed by my swift denial, 'it took me ages to get used to you not standing on the try line.'

'But what about Mia?' I shot back. 'Isn't she your current

cheerleader? And anyway, if you've got used to me not being there, I'd hate to set you back. Might impact on your game.'

Steve didn't say anything, but turned to face the front again and I slumped back in my seat, annoyed to have sounded so petty. I really was going to have to be more careful. He wasn't an idiot and if I always responded to every mention of Mia so truculently he would soon work out why.

'Is there something I should know about you two?' asked Paul with a sly grin. 'My radar is telling me there's some history between you.'

'Never mind your radar,' I said quickly.

'Yep,' he teased, 'there was definitely something once upon a time.'

'Anyway, Steve,' I said, determined not to further feed Paul's vivid imagination, 'you didn't answer my question. Why are you coming with us?'

'I'm coming with you because Tom thought it would be good to have someone local on hand to talk about the town and offer some background knowledge and facts about the market.'

'But I'm local,' I reminded him. 'I'm from the town.'

'Yes, but I'm part of the only remaining family who has worked the market since it opened.'

'Touché!' laughed Paul.

*

It was unbearably hot inside the little studio and wedged between Paul, who was trying to flirt, but not getting far, with Jennie Jackson the presenter, and Steve, who had produced a selection of index cards and was feverishly flicking through them as if he were cramming for an exam, I felt my temperature escalating beyond all reason.

'We've got almost a minute before we're on-air,' said Jennie with a nod towards the coat stand in the corner of the studio, 'why don't you take your jacket off? You'll be far more comfortable.'

'Right,' I silently mouthed, 'thanks.'

I didn't dare say anything for fear the massive microphone that had been plonked in front of me would pick it up and share it with the nation. Well, the few hundred listeners who I hoped were tuned in anyway!

'OK, folks,' began Jennie as soon as my bottom touched the seat again, 'this afternoon we are joined by celebrity chef, or should I say chef to the celebrities, Paul Thompson. Welcome to Fenland Radio, Paul.'

'Hello, Jennie,' said Paul in a sultry voice.

He sounded totally unflustered and I marvelled at his relaxed demeanour and attitude.

'So Paul, tell me, what are you doing in East Anglia when rumour has it you've been spotted on a beach in South Africa?'

Paul quickly laughed this off and explained, with many

a favourable mention of Skylark Farm free-range pork and cider, that he was in fact taking a break and staying with the owners who happened to be friends, while sampling and sourcing new local produce for his restaurants. Steve and I looked at one another and rolled our eyes. That was Paul's cover well and truly blown.

'So if you're just taking a breather and staying with friends as you suggest,' said Jennie suspiciously, 'then how have you become embroiled in turning on the town's Christmas lights?'

I felt Steve tense up on the seat next to me, but Paul didn't miss a beat.

'Well,' he laughed, 'I'm not sure I would say "embroiled" is an accurate description, but I admit this isn't the sort of event I usually get involved in.'

'It certainly isn't,' Jennie went ruthlessly on. 'I would have thought turning on the lights in Oxford Street would have been more your thing.'

'But Oxford Street isn't struggling to swell the Christmas coffers, is it?' said Paul, suddenly snapping into a more serious mode. 'Oxford Street is doing just fine, whereas little rural towns like Wynbridge need all the help they can get to compete with the big cities and online retail outlets, especially at this time of year.'

'So your involvement with the event is in no way a means of getting back in the public's good books after your recent run of bad behaviour?' Jennie tried again.

'Absolutely not,' he insisted, 'in fact, I'm disappointed that you would even suggest it. There was very little truth behind those allegations and even though I personally have no idea why folk would want to turn out to see me turn on their lovely lights, I have nonetheless been asked to help and I will. Keeping the market alive is the sole focus of the festivities in Wynbridge this year and the lovely Ruby and Steve here, can tell you all about what will be happening in the town between tomorrow and Christmas Eve.'

'So,' said Jennie, finally turning her attention to us, 'welcome Ruby and Steve. It's lovely to have you with us.'

'It's lovely to be here,' said Steve and I together, then pulled a face at each other while trying not to giggle because we had talked over each other.

'So what can you tell me about Wynbridge and the market and what you have planned for tomorrow night?'

Somehow between us we got through the next few minutes, eventually getting the hang of not talking at the same time, and we had almost made it to the end of the interview before disaster struck.

'OK,' smiled Jennie with a wink, 'thank you all for joining us. I hope you have a great time turning on the lights in Wynbridge tomorrow night, Paul.'

'I'm sure I will,' he said, 'I might even lend a hand serving some of the delicious hog roast and mulled wine.'

'You heard it here first, folks,' laughed Jennie. 'Pop along to Wynbridge market tomorrow night and you might get more than you bargained for! Just before we sign off, Ruby, can I ask you a question?'

'Yes,' I said with a smile, relieved that it was finally all over, 'of course.'

'My next guest is a new tattooist who has just moved to the city and he's here to talk about the sudden upsurge in the popularity of bespoke body art. I couldn't help noticing you have a small tattoo on your back. What inspired you to get it done and do you have any more hidden away anywhere?'

'Oh well,' I stammered, my heart hammering in my chest and my words tripping over themselves. 'I was very young when I had it done, I'd just turned eighteen. I can't imagine I'll have another one, so I'm no expert on bespoke body art.' I was clearly floundering.

'I have one that matches,' Steve blurted out, 'but mine is on my leg.'

'Oh really,' said Jennie, 'how sweet, matching tattoos. So are you two a couple then?'

'We used to be,' Steve mumbled, before looking at me apologetically and mouthing 'sorry'.

'Well, there we have it folks,' Jennie said, tidily rounding up her tenuous link, 'perhaps this pair could stick around and ask our next guest about some cover-up options!'

Steve and I forced a laugh as she handed over to the newsreader.

'God, I'm so sorry,' she said, her radio persona completely abandoned the second her microphone was turned off, 'I thought it would make a good link. I should have asked you before we went on-air.'

'No harm done,' I insisted, but knowing full well that someone would have told Dad about the radio spot. Not only did he now know of my involvement with the switch-on, he also knew I had a tattoo. He was going to hit the roof.

I might have been well over the age of consent but Dad was certainly not a fan of tattoos, piercings or even slightly bold hair dye for that matter and I just knew I was in for another 'while you are under my roof' lecture as soon as I got home. This latest debacle certainly wasn't going to help heal the rifts that had become even deeper since I arrived home.

'Well played, Mr Thompson,' said Jennie, turning to Paul who bent to give her a brief kiss on the cheek, 'I think you might have played a blinder there.'

'Time will tell,' he said, helping me back into my coat, 'time will tell.'

'Well I hope so,' said Jennie, 'for your ratings' sake.'

'No,' said Paul firmly, 'for the town's sake actually.'

There were a dozen or so people crowded around the door as we tried to leave the building and walk back to the car.

'What did you have to go and say that for?' I hissed at Steve while we waited patiently for Paul to sign a few autographs and take some self-indulgent selfies.

'I don't know,' said Steve, running a hand through his hair, 'I could see how mortified you were and thought I should try and say something to help.'

I tutted loudly and rifled through my pockets for my phone which I could hear pinging away. I hoped it was going to be a text from Tom congratulating us on a job well done, but it wasn't.

'Well there you go,' I said, tossing Steve my phone when I had finished with it. 'Have a read of that and promise me that if you feel like helping me out in the future, you'll resist the urge.'

To soften the blow of the text from my dad and to celebrate the overall success Paul was convinced the radio spot had been, he insisted that we ended the afternoon with a bottle of champagne.

'Ordinarily I'd have a chauffeur to ferry me about, but as I'm designated driver today I obviously won't indulge,' he said regretfully.

'Me neither,' I insisted, 'thanks but no thanks.'

'Oh come on,' he laughed, 'you two really look as if you could do with a drop of fizz to put the spring back in your step!'

'Oh come on, Ruby,' said Steve, plucking at my coat sleeve. 'I was only trying to help. Please don't make me feel worse than I do already!'

I looked from Paul's pout to Steve's hopeful, wide-eyed smile.

'Oh, go on then,' I finally relented, not wanting to be a party pooper.

'Yes!' said Steve, playfully punching my arm.

I ignored him and carried on talking to Paul.

'But I don't know where you'll find an off-licence around here.'

'An off-licence,' he laughed. 'I don't need an off-licence! Steve, would you please be so kind as to fetch the bottle and glasses from the chiller in the boot?'

'You aren't serious!' I laughed.

'Of course I am,' Paul winked, 'what sort of celebrity would I be if I left home without the obligatory bottle of Cristal?'

Steve and I, ensconced in the back of the car, managed to drink the whole bottle between us on the journey home and consequently fell to chatting about old times and some of the mischief we had got into that last summer before our cosy little world came crashing down around our ears.

'Do you remember,' he laughed, as he topped up my glass, 'that ridiculous seaside inflatable I used to keep in the back of the van?'

'Of course I do,' I hiccupped. 'It was our one concession to comfort, wasn't it?'

'Until it went bang,' he reminded me. 'An air bed really would have been a more practical option.'

'But a rather obvious one,' I giggled. 'I'm fairly certain your dad would have worked out what you wanted it for.'

'So you really think he had no idea why I insisted on driving around with a giant plastic crocodile on top of the carrots and onions?'

'Oh don't.' I cringed, mortified to think that our clandestine trysts had been so glaringly obvious. 'And anyway, the poor old croc wouldn't have gone bang had you not . . .'

'You two all right back there?' called Paul from the front.

'Uh huh,' we chorused and burst out laughing again.

Although reluctant to walk me to the house door when we arrived back in Wynbridge, Steve didn't have much choice as I was little unsteady on my feet and ridiculously giggly.

'I'd forgotten how funny you are when you're drunk,' he said, taking the opportunity to slip an arm around my waist as he helped me out of the car.

'I'm not drunk,' I said, leaning towards him and instantly moulding into the sorely missed contours of his toned rugby physique, 'just a little tipsy from all those bubbles.'

'Well, you should stay a little tipsy,' he said looking down at me. 'I like you tipsy. You're much more like the old you when you're tipsy.'

'Now don't start all that,' I said, poking him in the chest.

'All what?' he laughed, looking down at me.

'Ruby!' shouted Dad, suddenly appearing at the front door. 'Oh for goodness' sake, are you drunk?'

'No,' called Steve, 'she isn't drunk, Mr Smith. Just a little tipsy.'

146

Crippled with laughter I clumsily tried to push Steve away and Dad, after scanning the road to see how many neighbours were twitching their curtains, disappeared back inside.

'You,' said Steve, when we finally reached the door, 'are in serious trouble.'

'I know,' I giggled, thinking of more than the impending showdown with Dad, 'I know.'

'See you tomorrow, Ruby Sue,' he smiled down at me.

'See you tomorrow,' I hiccupped again.

Chapter 12

By the time I'd managed to struggle free of my jacket, pull off my boots and make it into the kitchen for a glass of water, Dad had had the benefit of an extra few minutes in which to think over exactly how many things I'd done in the last few days to upset him and it was immediately obvious that he wanted to 'talk' to me about quite a few of them.

'Oh Ruby,' he said, his tone loaded with pent-up frustration, 'a tattoo, and right where everyone can see it. I can't deny I'm sorely disappointed.'

I took a deep breath to quell the bristling sensation in the back of my neck and promised myself I would remain as calm as was humanly possible with a system which now felt pumped full of top shelf champagne.

'Yes, Dad,' I sighed, 'a tattoo, but no, not on public display and actually only really visible if I'm on the beach and wearing a bikini, so not particularly likely to cause a local scandal. It really is no big deal.'

'It's what's commonly known as a "tramp stamp", isn't it?' he said with a sniff, as if the whole thing was something unsavoury and certainly not for the likes of him, 'and I suppose it's got Steve Dempster's name written all over it.'

Having taken a moment to calculate that I had drunk perhaps a little more than half of the bottle of Cristal on the journey home, I was suddenly beginning to feel considerably bolder and not at all inclined to wait quietly until Dad had finished ranting. I didn't know whether the water I had drunk had fired the fizz around my veins or whether I'd simply had enough of being spoken to like a child, but I was determined to give him back just as good as he was determined to throw at me. All those high hopes for our happy reconciliation seemed but a distant memory. Every conciliatory move I'd made had been met with him taking a step back and I'd had enough.

'A tramp stamp,' I began serenely, as if imparting great wisdom, 'is a derogatory term used to describe a tattoo which sits below the waist but above the backside and is clearly visible whenever clothes part while bending over or stretching up. As my tattoo is situated more towards my hip than my spine and is really rather tiny, it cannot be described as a tramp stamp and no, it certainly does not have Steve's name emblazoned all over it, or love or hate or mother for that matter!'

'But he said he has the same one,' Dad said, his tone beginning to sound more weary than wound up. 'Live on air, Steve Dempster said that you both have the same tattoo.'

'We do,' I shrugged, trying not to think back to the secretive planning and heady excitement that had engulfed the day we had travelled to Norwich to get them done, 'but unless you were going to view them side by side, which I admit would be a fun position to get into given where they are,' I added, just to fuel the fire a bit more, 'you would never know they were a matching pair.'

As the seconds ticked by I could feel my temper beginning to bubble almost beyond my control. I was just as angry that my productive afternoon had been spoilt as I was by Dad's attitude towards something so private that actually at the end of the day had nothing to do with him.

'Where did you go to get them done?' he asked, tactfully choosing to ignore my Kama Sutra-like suggestion.

'Why?'

'Because not all these places are clean, Ruby,' he said with a sigh. 'Most of them don't follow the hygiene rules and regulations, you know.'

'And how would you know that?' I laughed. 'When did you become an expert?'

'Oh, for pity's sake,' groaned Mum as she walked into the kitchen. 'Will you give it a rest, Robert? It's done, end of, and as Ruby is a young woman well over the age of consent and not your little girl any more, there really is nothing you can do about it!'

I knew Mum must have heard enough from him by that point because she would never usually say a word when Dad went off on one. Ordinarily she would let him run out of steam in his own time, but clearly she had reached saturation point, as had I.

'But she knows how much I hate them,' Dad continued, as if my actions were a personal affront.

Mum was having no more of it.

'Oh, we all know how much you hate them,' she snapped, her voice rising, 'which is why you haven't got any.'

I couldn't suppress the little hiccup that escaped as I thought of Dad pinned in a chair having Mum's name in script tattooed next to his heart.

'Now,' said Mum, turning to me, 'I am going to put the kettle on and you are going to tell me all about how this business with Paul Thompson *really* started. The phone hasn't stopped ringing, has it, Robert?'

'No,' Dad confirmed, wearily pulling out a chair and sitting at the table, 'it hasn't.'

I braced myself for the next barrage of insults and accusations, but thankfully none were forthcoming. I stole a quick glance as he rubbed his hands over his face and stifled a yawn. He looked tired, resigned almost, and had I been completely sober I would have perhaps had the heart to feel concerned, but as it was I simply took his demeanour as defeated. Finally I had clocked up a victory.

'Even the mayor has been on the phone!' Mum laughed.

'Oh really,' I said, turning back to her, 'and what did the mayor have to say? Was he annoyed by the sudden change in events?'

'Absolutely not,' laughed Mum with a nod towards Dad, 'couldn't be more delighted. Huge fan apparently! Can't wait to meet the man himself!'

The very last thing I needed on Saturday, November the twenty-sixth was a hangover, but I had one and I no doubt deserved it. Fortunately the extra adrenaline pumping through my veins kept the worst of it at bay, and with the market and town so busy and a couple of last-minute errands to run for Tom, I didn't have time to dwell on my aching head and just focused on applying myself to the jobs in hand.

The weather was cold and crisp but clear, perfect for the evening's entertainment, and I couldn't wait for everything to get started so we could see if our combined efforts had been worth all the hours we had been putting in.

'How's your head?' called Steve, as he finished stringing up an extra set of twinkling fairy lights and some more bunting on Gwen's stall.

'Not the best,' I admitted, tossing him his daily dose of

mince pies, 'I'm trying not to think about it to be honest. What about you?'

'Surprisingly clear,' he said, wandering over with his toolbox and tearing into the bag of pies, 'but then I didn't have to face the wrath of your dad, did I?' he added, before cramming his mouth full of crumbly sweet pastry.

'Quite,' I said, stamping my feet on the cobbles in an attempt to get the blood flowing back to my frozen toes. 'But he wasn't all that bad, to be honest,' I added, thinking back over everything that had been said.

'Really?' Steve gaped, showering me with crumbs. 'Sorry.'

'He probably would have been,' I explained, passing him a serviette, 'but he didn't get the chance to really launch off. Mum soon shut him up when she'd heard enough.'

'Good for your mum,' he laughed.

I watched as he polished off the second pie and finished re-packing the bits and pieces he had used to secure Gwen's lights and bunting and when he looked back up he was bright red.

'All that talk yesterday got me thinking about us, Ruby; our trip to Norwich and the day we went and got the tattoos done in particular,' he said, with a small smile.

'Me too,' I admitted.

'I've still got those silly photos we had taken in that booth in the mall afterwards.'

'Me too,' I said again.

'They were happy times, weren't they?'

'Yes,' I said, because they were. 'They were the best.'

We looked at one another for a second and I could have been eighteen years old again. Part of me wished I was. With every conversation and fleeting glance it was becoming increasingly (and painfully) obvious that I was never going to stop wishing for what we could have had. If only I could turn off my heart, I thought, then perhaps I'd stop finding him such a turn-on.

'You know I only did what I thought was for the best back then, Ruby, don't you?'

'Of course I do,' I sighed, struggling to fight down the desire to fling my arms around him and tell him how I still felt about him. How I had always felt. 'I probably didn't at the time, but I do now.'

'But if I could turn the clock back . . .'

'If you could turn back time,' I cut in as Mia came striding into view, looking every inch the pristine snow queen and making my heart sink like a deflated balloon, 'you'd be a millionaire.'

'That's not what I meant.'

'I know what you meant,' I said, looking over his shoulder, pointing in Mia's direction and therefore effectively drawing a line under the conversation. 'I think you're wanted.'

'Oh God,' he sighed, muttering under his breath as he went to meet her, 'she wasn't impressed with my radio performance at all.'

Given what had been discussed live on-air, I could hardly say I blamed her.

Fortunately as the market was still heaving and time was so tight to get everything finished I didn't have the opportunity to dwell on my regrets and disappointments. In fact, with the benefit of hindsight, and the added vision of Mia wandering about looking saintly and desirable, I couldn't help thinking that it was probably best that I hadn't said anything after all. I mean, what would have been the point in stirring it all up again? If he was still single I might have felt differently but given he had Mia in tow, he was hardly pining away for me.

Just because he was feeling a bit guilty about the way we'd parted didn't mean that he wanted us to actually get back together again. Had I not arrived in Wynbridge when I did I dare say he wouldn't have given me a second thought. These fresh feelings were simply the result of my unexpected return and a timely bottle of champagne, nothing more.

Ordinarily by four in the afternoon, especially during the winter, Wynbridge town centre would be pretty much deserted and the market ready to call it a day, but on this particular Saturday there were people crammed everywhere and the air was bristling with a palpable air of excitement and heady anticipation for what was to come.

All the stalls were now prettily lit with extra sets of lights and Pete had already fired up the candyfloss machine which lent its own sickly sweet scent to the air in stark contrast to the mouth-watering smell of the pork that Amber and Jake had had on the spit all afternoon. Tom had even managed to trace the dozen or so small braziers that had been made to mark the millennium and dotted them around the place, and with an adult to keep each one blazing away and safe, the little market square looked every inch as jolly and inviting as it sounded.

'What do you think of my Rudolph?' asked Lizzie, as she staggered over from the Cherry Tree with a large plywood reindeer tucked under her arm. 'Shirley and Bob asked me to help them paint him so the kids can play pin the tail on the reindeer and look, Bob's even rigged up a little red light bulb so his nose actually glows!'

'Oh, he's precious,' I laughed, 'he looks like a proper old-fashioned Rudolph to me.'

'Yes,' she mused, admiring her creation at arm's length, 'he is. I rather like this vintage style so I based him on a design from an old snow globe. You know, I might get Ben to lend me his tools so I can make a stencil and cut out some smaller ones to paint and sell on the stall. What do you think?'

'I think that sounds like a wonderful idea!' laughed Jude as she walked by with an armful of presents for her and Simon's lucky dip. 'I'd buy one,' she winked, 'and a matching jolly old Santa would make the set complete, assuming of course that you can find one.'

'You know what,' said Lizzie seriously as Jude carried

on her way, 'she might be on to something there. I was hoping to add some extra stock as the week's countdown to Christmas and these,' she added, shifting the cumbersome Rudolph from one arm to another, 'if carefully scaled down, might be just the thing.'

By six o'clock the market square was packed to full capacity and I even noticed a few eager press photographers amongst the throng, all no doubt keen to catch a glimpse of our celebrity chef. As the town hall clock finished chiming the hour, the man himself, who had somehow managed to remain incognito until that very moment, stepped up on to the raised platform and the crowd gave an almighty cheer. I was relieved to see that no one actually fainted, but when Jemma turned round to give me the thumbs up, her cheeks were positively glowing.

'My goodness,' laughed Paul into the microphone, 'what a welcome.'

The shouts and claps triggered by his first few words meant that he had to wait almost a full minute before he could carry on.

'Thank you,' he laughed, 'thank you all for making me feel so welcome in your pretty little town.' This was met with more cheers and whistling. He then went on, sounding more serious than I would have expected. 'Before we get down to the business in hand,' he said, 'and turn on these spectacular lights, I want to say just a few words, if that's all right with you?'

More shouting.

157

'These few days around Wynbridge have been my first in the Fens,' he explained, 'but they certainly won't be my last! Don't get me wrong,' he raced quickly on before the crowd erupted again, 'life in a city is all very well. It is busy and exciting and constantly changing but here, and I know there are places just like Wynbridge up and down the country,' he continued, 'life beats to a slightly different pulse, a calmer pace, and it's communities pulling together to support one another that makes events like this happen.'

The crowd fell almost silent and began to listen more intently.

'The fun and games here tonight haven't been organised by some think tank or some suits sitting around in a board-room and having planning meetings for the last six months. This is grass roots stuff, people pulling together, people who care enough to give their time to make a difference and we should applaud that.'

'Yes!' roared Chris from his position at the back of the crowd.

'Treasure your community, folks,' Paul continued, 'support one another and never lose sight of the fact that even though the town of Wynbridge may be smaller than some, it has a strong heart, an important history and a warm welcome for any wayward traveller such as myself!'

Everyone started to applaud and eventually the count-down began.

'Here you are,' said Bea, suddenly appearing at my side and linking arms, 'I've been looking all over for you.'

'I didn't want to get too near the front,' I admitted, 'I wouldn't put it past Paul to try and pull me on to the stage!'

'Oh, I see,' said Bea, looking at him with interest. 'He really is the bad boy the papers suggest then!'

'You know what,' I laughed, 'I was beginning to think so, but having just heard his rousing little speech I'm inclined to think he has hidden depths! Come on, let's count down together.'

'Three, two, one!' everyone shouted in unison and Paul, making a great show of the moment, pressed the button with an elaborate flourish.

No one beyond the stallholders, Tom and I knew that there were going to be fireworks as well as the stirring sound of the Salvation Army band, and as the rockets and Catherine wheels began to launch at exactly the same moment as the lights came on, the crowds stood open-mouthed, their faces aglow in the light of the spectacular display. It was beautiful, rousing and exactly the kind of festive debut the town deserved.

It wasn't until the final fireworks fell that everyone could really appreciate the dazzling light display in all its glory. The trees supplied by Chris and Marie were huge, and Tom's insistence on keeping the lights all together in the market square made for a thoroughly impressive and spectacular show. I only had to listen to the gasps of the adults and the 'wows' of the children to know that everyone was mightily mesmerised.

The mayor, looking completely overwhelmed by the whole spectacle and blushing profusely, stepped up to the microphone to thank Paul for playing his part and then called Dad to the stage.

'Well, Mr Smith,' he said, shaking his head, 'you have absolutely surpassed yourself this year! I don't think I've ever seen the town looking so ready for Christmas!'

I was relieved to hear Dad cut in before the mayor really got into his stride.

'I can't actually take any of the credit this year,' he said, clearing his throat. I couldn't help thinking that he sounded far happier than he was probably feeling. 'Not all that many days ago I passed the task of festive planning over to my deputy Tom and between him and the market traders they have produced this spectacular show. I think we should all,' he said, trying to sound cheerful, 'give Tom and the traders, especially Chris and Marie Dempster, who as I understand it donated both of these beautiful trees, a warm round of applause.'

Everyone clapped, whistled, stamped and cheered but no amount of cajoling would get Tom up on to the stage, and so without further ado Paul grabbed the microphone and insisted that everyone should make the most of the fun and games on offer and make at least one stop at the hog roast where he would personally be serving customers and offering extra crackling to whoever took the best selfies and uploaded them to social media.

'Gosh,' I said when I eventually found myself at the front of the queue, 'this is very generous of you, Paul. You're going to be here all night. Won't your face ache from all this smiling?'

'Absolutely not,' he insisted, 'I'm having far too much fun and besides, I'm taking a leaf out of old Swifty's book.'

'What?' I frowned. 'Who on earth is old Swifty?'

'Taylor Swift,' he said impatiently. 'I don't want the press guys making a fortune out of snapping me at the right moment and selling the shot on, so I'm flooding the market myself. That's what she and her friend did with their bikini shots.'

'Did they really?' I gasped. 'But why should you care if the paps make a few quid?'

'Because,' he said, bending to give me a swift peck on the cheek, 'like I said, I'm thoroughly enjoying myself and I won't have the press twisting the situation and saying that I did all this for any other reason than helping you guys out. I know you and Amber said it would be good PR, but right now I don't actually care about any of that!' he shouted. 'I'm having too much fun! Now, who wants more crackling?'

Chapter 13

Paul did indeed continue, along with everyone else who had braved the rapidly dropping temperature, to have fun for the rest of the evening. Offering the games and extra food and drink turned out to be the perfect inducement to keep the money rolling in and stop the townsfolk heading home. From what I could make out, all of the stalls, including mine, had a steady flow of customers all night, but it was the old-fashioned children's games, such as Lizzie's clever Rudolph and Simon and Jude's lucky dip, that drew the biggest queues.

'Well, you weren't wrong, were you?' said one young mum as the crowd finally began to thin out a little.

'Sorry?'

'You told my husband and I earlier in the week that things would be better this year. Don't you remember?'

'Oh yes,' I smiled, 'of course. Has it been better than another Saturday night in front of the television then?' I asked the little girl who was holding the woman's hand and making short work of her sticky tangle of candyfloss.

'Heaps,' she grinned. 'I've had a lovely time, but Daddy was totally rubbish at pinning on Rudolph's tail!'

'Oh dear!' I laughed. 'Perhaps he'll have better luck next year.'

'Assuming this is all here next year, of course,' said her mum, looking round with a sigh.

'What makes you think it wouldn't be?' I frowned, shocked by her sudden change of tone.

'Well,' she said, shrugging her shoulders, 'you know how folk talk.'

'Are you gossiping again?' tutted her husband as he wandered up with the pushchair.

I could just make out the sleepy face of a very drowsy little girl inside. She was cosily wrapped in a fleecy blanket and, given how cold my toes were, I wouldn't have minded swapping places with her at all.

'No,' said the woman, looking sheepish, 'just chatting.'

'What about?'

'Whether or not the market will still be here next Christmas.'

'There,' he said smugly, 'I knew it, gossiping.'

'Oh, you don't have to worry about this place,' I said quickly, 'as long as people keep using it on a regular basis, the market won't be going anywhere.'

'But what about the site?' whispered the woman, 'I heard—'

'Never mind what you heard,' cut in her husband, 'probably just a load of old rubbish being bandied about at the school gate.'

His wife shrugged again, forbore to expand on the intriguing titbit she had let slip and turned her attention to the little girl in the pushchair who had started to wriggle.

'Well, we'd better get off home,' said her husband as he took his daughter's hand, 'it's way after your bedtime.'

'I'm not tired,' she said, stifling the biggest yawn, 'not at all.'

'Well, I am,' he laughed. 'Come on. Let's go home.'

'I hope you've got lots of other things planned,' said his wife. 'It would be lovely to come into town and do something a bit different for a change, especially in the run up to Christmas.'

'Leave it to me,' I told them as they walked away, 'and I'll see what I can do!'

After they had gone I looked at the little stock I'd got left and decided it was time to start packing away. I'd completely sold out of Jemma's bakes and biscuits and with the frosty air really beginning to bite, a warm fireside beckoned. I stowed everything away in record time and then went to see if Gwen needed a hand.

'All done,' she beamed when she spotted me heading over, 'you're too late!'

'Well, that was fast work,' I laughed. 'Last time I looked over at you, you were still swamped with customers.'

'Well,' she admitted with a wink, 'I did have a bit of help.'

She pointed across the square to where I could see Sam walking Minnie. Well, when I say walking, I mean he was holding her lead at arm's length and Bea, by his side, was looking absolutely terrified.

'Sam and Bea very kindly offered to help,' said Gwen, apparently unaware of the sheer panic and fear on her poor assistants' faces. 'They're a lovely couple,' she mused. 'I hope he doesn't keep her waiting much longer.'

'Waiting for what?'

'You know what,' chuckled Gwen, clicking her tongue. 'Don't play the innocent with me, Ruby Smith. I bet it's all you girls talk about!'

'Look out,' I hissed, as the pair headed back in our direction.

Gwen looked smug as Sam quickly handed back Minnie's lead and I had everything crossed that she wouldn't say anything. Bea would have been mortified if she knew anyone thought she was holding out for a proposal, or a leap year for that matter.

'Gwen,' said Sam, 'some of the others have decided to finish off the evening in the pub. Do you fancy it?'

'Oh my dear boy,' she giggled, 'that's the best proposal I've had in a while!'

I wouldn't swear to it, but I'm sure she winked at me as she said it.

'But no,' she continued, 'not tonight. I think I'll be heading home. I've had enough excitement for one day.'

'In that case,' suggested Bea, 'let Sam drive you home. Gwen and Ruby and I will wait for him in The Mermaid.'

'Well, only if you're sure,' said Gwen, keen as ever not to be a nuisance to anyone.

'Absolutely,' agreed Sam.

'That is really most kind,' smiled Gwen, quickly tucking Minnie under her arm and taking Sam's hand, 'I'll see you both on Monday.'

With Ella and Noah tucked up for the night at Angela's house, Tom, Jemma, Lizzie and Ben, along with practically everyone from the market, were already settled in the pub when Bea and I arrived.

'Can you believe it?' said Tom, his eyes shining as he dragged over a couple of extra chairs to where the gang were sitting around the fire. 'Can you *really* believe that was the Wynbridge we know and love?'

'Tom, I know exactly what you mean!' laughed Bea. 'Who would have ever thought the sleepy little place could be so transformed, and so quickly!'

'And it's all down to Ruby,' he said, sitting back down next to Jemma and taking a pull at his pint. 'She's the one who really made it all happen.'

'She certainly is not,' I hastily put in, although I couldn't

166

help thinking Dad might have acknowledged at least some of the effort I had put in during his little speech. I wasn't expecting to be carried through town on the May Queen's throne or anything, but a quick mention wouldn't have gone amiss. 'Anything that I had a hand in helping along was down to sheer good luck,' I said, trying to sound generous. 'If you hadn't sent me to Skylark Farm, for example, Tom, you would have had to go yourself, wouldn't you?'

'I suppose so,' he shrugged.

'And you would have asked the lovely Mr Thompson to help out you when you realised who he was, wouldn't you?'

'No way,' he gasped, 'absolutely not. I wouldn't have dared!'

'Really?' I said, laughing at his shocked expression.

'Really,' confirmed Jemma, as she leant in and planted a kiss on his cheek. 'He would have been far too shy, wouldn't you, my lovely?'

'Don't tease,' said Tom, 'I can't help it if I like to stick to colouring in the background, can I? But if you really are so unwilling to take all the credit, Ruby, how about we split it? We'll call the whole evening a combined effort and unmit-igated victory for both of us.'

'Fair enough,' I heartily agreed, 'sounds good to me, and talking of Mr T, where is he? I rather thought he'd be in here, holding court and regaling tales from his most recent misadventures!'

'He's already gone back to the farm,' explained Lizzie. 'Amber had to leave a little earlier to relieve the babysitter for Honey so Paul stayed on and helped Jake finish up and they headed back together.'

'Crikey,' said Bea, 'he's full of surprises, isn't he?'

She bent her head so only I could hear her and nodded towards the bar where Sam had just arrived and was ordering our drinks.

'I wonder if he could give my man there a few tips before he leaves for London,' she whispered with a frown, 'I'm beginning to think Sam's never going to surprise me.'

'Oh, I'm sure he will,' I soothed, while wondering if Sam had any idea that his dearly beloved was on tenterhooks.

Eventually he came and joined us around the fire, bringing with him a tray loaded with snacks and crisps as well as glasses.

'How can you possibly *still* be hungry?' moaned Bea as she helped him pass around the glasses. 'I saw you go back to the hog roast at least twice!'

'They aren't all for me,' he said, sounding really rather put out that she had commented. 'God, Bea, you sound like a nagging wife.'

'Chance would be a fine thing,' she muttered under her breath.

Given Sam's change of mood I couldn't help but wonder whether the temptation had proved too much for Gwen and she had said something about him dragging his heels after all.

'Thanks, Sam,' I said, raising my glass to toast him.

'I know it isn't really your preferred current tipple,' he said with a wink, 'but it's the best I can do.'

I wasn't sure if he was referring to my recently acquired taste for Skylark Scrumpy or something else, but I didn't much like the thought that I had already developed a reputation for draining the pub's resources dry. Fortunately he didn't give me many seconds to ponder.

'Steve tells me champagne, Cristal no less, is really more up your street these days.'

'Oh,' I said, my temperature rising as I thought of our giggly journey home from the radio station in the back of Paul's car.

'What's all this?' demanded Bea.

She was clearly put out that she'd missed out and that Sam knew something she didn't. I ignored her.

'And where is Steve?' I asked Sam. 'Is he still packing up? I thought I saw Chris and Marie in the snug.'

'No, he's having a meal next door,' said Ben with a nod to the pub's restaurant, 'I saw him before you got here.'

'He's no doubt with the magnificent Mia then,' I said under my breath.

'No,' smiled Ben, 'he's on his own actually.'

'Ruby,' frowned Sam, leaning forward in his seat, 'I think you've got the wrong idea about him and Mia.'

'Oh well,' I said, jumping up and grabbing what I guessed

was Steve's pint. 'I'll take this through to him and head home, I think. I can't wait to hear what Dad has to say about the switch-on.'

I said my good-nights and went through to the restaurant. Just as Ben had said, Steve was dining alone and not looking as if he was enjoying the solitary experience all that much. I knew he would be loving the food, but he really wasn't the type to relish his own company.

'Ruby,' he said, quickly standing up when he spotted me, his knees clashing with the underside of the table. 'I think congratulations are in order!'

'They are,' I readily agreed, 'congratulations all round. Your mum and dad's trees and Tom's changes to the lighting plans made all the difference, as did everyone's efforts with the games and things. I wish the evening had been as much fun when we were younger!'

'From what I can remember,' he smiled, 'we used to make our own entertainment. Do you remember that one night in the bandstand?'

'Anyway,' I quickly cut in, setting down the pint glass, 'Sam got you this. I said I'd deliver it as I'm now on my way out the door.'

'You're not leaving already,' he said, my heart lurching a little when I realised how disappointed he sounded. 'Oh crikey,' he added, as he checked his watch, 'I had no idea it was so late.'

'I know,' I said, taking a step back. 'The day has really flown by, hasn't it?'

'Don't go just yet,' he wheedled, pointing at the glass of cider in my hand that I still hadn't finished. 'At least stay long enough to finish your drink. You'll make fast work of it, I'm sure.'

'Hey!' I said, 'I'm not at all impressed with this growing reputation I seem to have somehow developed as the town lush.'

Before he could deny he had played a part in starting it, Evelyn bustled over with a large bowl of steamed sponge pudding and custard.

'There you go,' she smiled, setting it down in front of him. 'Sure you can manage it?'

'Not really,' he said, passing her his empty plate, 'perhaps you could bring us another spoon, Evelyn. I'm going to see if I can tempt Ruby to soak up some of that alcohol she keeps drinking by sharing my pudding!'

I knew it wasn't the wisest move in the world given the fact that I was still, and probably always would be, hopelessly in love with him, but I plonked myself in the seat opposite and took the spoon Evelyn hastily offered nonetheless.

'So,' I said, plunging into the soft sticky sponge and throwing caution to the wind, 'what's the deal? How come you're dining alone when you usually have the magnificent Mia hanging on your every word?'

'You make her sound like a magician!' Steve laughed.

'Well, she might as well be,' I muttered. 'She always seems to manage to appear when you least expect her.'

'You do know that we aren't a couple, don't you, Ruby?' he frowned.

This was unexpected news indeed and I'm ashamed to admit that even after everything she'd said and after everything I'd witnessed between them suggesting the opposite was in fact the case, my heart gave an extra quick thump in the hope that he was telling the truth. Suddenly I was back to dreaming about what I had been trying to deny myself ever since I clapped eyes on him in the churchyard.

If there really was an open spot in Steve's heart then perhaps I should consider taking up residence again and this time for good. I had no idea how rekindling our romance would fit with my plans to travel, but perhaps Chris and Marie would be willing to let him come with me for a while, given that he was such a loyal and dutiful son. Perhaps we should just give in to the inevitable; perhaps we should try again. Our journey home in Paul's car was proof enough that there really was still a spark between us and that it wasn't just burning in my heart.

'You look like a couple,' I said, wanting to be completely sure I had all the proof I needed before I let my guard down and showed my hand, 'and given what she told me and the way she drapes herself around you and buys you goodies to keep your hands warm, I'm sure everyone else thinks you look like a couple too!'

'Well, we aren't,' he said firmly. 'I don't know what she told you and even though I'm sure she'd love it if we were together, we're not and we never will be for that matter. I'm just not interested.'

'So what's the deal,' I cajoled, 'more of a friends with benefits set-up, is it? Because if it is, you should really make sure she understands that, you know. It's only fair she knows that she'll never be anything more than another notch on the Steve Dempster bedpost. Assuming that is what she is, of course?'

'If you'd asked me that a couple of weeks ago I probably would have said yes because it was certainly heading that way, but not now. I don't know why I'm telling you, of all people, but I haven't even tried to get her into bed.'

'Don't tell me you don't find her attractive!' I laughed.

That really would be unbelievable.

'I wouldn't say that exactly,' he smiled, 'I'm not blind.'

'Then what?' I pushed, trying to keep the conversation flowing and convince myself that I was about to do the right thing rather than make a complete fool of myself.

'Like I said, I'm just not interested in her,' he shrugged. 'Things have changed.'

'Why?' I asked. 'What's changed?'

'You've come back,' he said huskily.

My heart gave an extra hard thud in my chest.

'And what difference has that made?' I swallowed, desperate not to let him see the impact those three little words had made.

He took a deep breath and reached across the table for my hand.

'It's made me not want to put another single notch on my bedpost for a start,' he smiled.

'I'm not awfully sure,' I said, finally daring to look up and lose myself in his gaze, 'if that's a compliment or not.'

'Oh, you know what I mean,' he said. 'I've never been good with finding the right words; you of all people know that better than anyone.'

I smiled, but didn't say anything.

'But now of course it's complicated,' he said, entwining his fingers with mine and sending shivers coursing deep through my stomach and beyond, 'even more complicated than before.'

'It doesn't have to be,' I said, finally feeling brave enough to give him the first real indication that I felt the same way. 'If we really want it to be, it could be so easy.'

'No,' he said, slowly taking back his hand, 'it couldn't, because this isn't just about the two of us and what we want any more, Ruby. It's bigger than us, much bigger and runs far deeper than our relationship.'

I had no idea what he was talking about. It didn't make any sense.

'We aren't kids any more,' I reminded him. 'If we want to pick up where we were forced to leave off, then who can stop us? Who cares if our dads don't get on? Whatever has happened between them in the past has nothing to do with us. Things are totally different now.'

'Yes,' he said, sitting back in his chair, 'things are very different indeed and up until you just said it,' he added sadly, 'I wasn't sure you still had feelings for me at all.'

'Well I do,' I told him, finally daring to look at him properly, 'I always have. I thought I'd moved on,' I rushed blindly on, 'but I knew as soon as I saw you in the churchyard that I'd been kidding myself.'

Steve let out a long slow breath and pushed his dessert bowl to one side.

'I really don't see what the problem is,' I frowned, 'if you still have feelings for me and I still have feelings for you then there's nothing that can alter that.'

I stopped talking, suddenly aware that his expression had completely changed and not for the better. For a moment I felt as if I had been duped. I'd finally admitted how I was feeling and now I was going to end up looking like a fool.

'My God, Ruby,' he said, running his hands through his hair. 'You really don't know, do you?'

'Know what?'

'About what's going to happen to the market.'

'No,' I said, feeling frustrated. 'I have no idea.'

What was the point in this outpouring of emotion if he was only going to immediately throw a spanner in the works which, guessing by his change in demeanour, I imagined he was about to.

'And anyway, what has the market got to do with us?'

'The site is up for sale,' he said sadly.

I sat back in my chair, unable to think of anything constructive to say.

'And if we got back together,' he said, in a tone which did nothing to quell my fears, 'and the sale of the site goes through, we'd be under immense pressure, what with our fathers already hating the sight of one another . . .'

'Hang on,' I cut in, feeling even more muddled. 'Are you seriously telling me that the site the market stands on, has always stood on, is actually up for sale?'

'Yes, your dad and some of his council friends are planning to sell it.'

'*What*?' I demanded. 'But that's ridiculous. I can't believe it. If the site was for sale someone would have told me before now!'

'Of course they wouldn't,' said Steve, shaking his head. 'Have you forgotten who your father actually is?'

'Are you saying that no one trusts me, even now, after everything I've done?'

Steve shrugged.

'All I know,' he sighed, 'is that come the New Year we're

either going to be relocated to somewhere entirely inaccessible or closed down completely.'

'But that's not possible,' I shot back, my mind reeling. 'I've never heard of anything so absurd in all my life. I don't believe you.'

I tried to push the words of the woman I had spoken to earlier in the evening to the back of my mind.

'Dad might have got himself in a muddle over Christmas this year, but he loves this town,' I said, determined to defend him in spite of our differences. 'And he would never do anything to jeopardise the future of the market!'

'What, like rushing through the planning approval for the Retail Park you mean?'

He sounded suddenly more cross than conciliatory.

'He thought that was what people wanted,' I insisted, 'and it wasn't all down to him. Everyone in town was asked to express an opinion. He didn't make the final decision on his own, did he?'

'But he had a brand new car as soon as the first footings were dug, didn't he?'

Instantly I felt bile rising as I realised what he was suggesting.

'Yes,' I said as calmly as I could manage, 'he did and all paid for with money his mother left him in her will, not that that's any of your business! Look, Steve,' I said throwing down my spoon and pushing back my chair, 'I don't know what the gossips around here are saying or what it is you're *really* insinuating . . .'

'I'm just trying to point out that, given the current circumstances, us getting back together wouldn't be easy,' he said sensibly. 'Though not impossible . . .'

'No,' I choked. 'Forget it. Because what you've just accused my dad of does make it impossible. You know, I never really believed I would ever be able to say this, but we are now, very definitely, completely and utterly over!'

Chapter 14

I couldn't wait to get out of the pub and head for home. I wanted to put as much distance between myself and Steve Dempster and all the other town traders as I could, and in the quickest time possible. In something of a daze I walked back through to the bar, shakily drained my glass and put it down. I still couldn't really believe what had just happened.

'Time for another?' pounced Jim, as he rushed over to the Skylark pump and patted it affectionately. 'I'm sure there's still a pint or two left in here somewhere.'

'No thanks,' I sniffed, pulling on my coat and yanking my gloves out of the pockets.

'You can't really be off already, Ruby,' he frowned, 'you've only just arrived.'

'I'm ready for my bed, Jim,' I told him, 'and besides, your clientele leaves a bit to be desired tonight.'

'You all right, love?' he said, walking back to face me.

His gentle face was full of concern.

'Yes,' I said huskily, willing myself not to make the situation even worse by crying. 'Can I leave my car parked round the back tonight, Jim, please?'

'But you've only had a half,' he reminded me, picking up my glass. 'You aren't anywhere near the limit. You'll be fine to drive.'

'I could do with the walk,' I told him, my cheeks burning. 'I need to clear my head.'

'Fair enough then, love,' he said softly. 'Yes, by all means leave it where it is.'

'Thanks. I'll pick it up tomorrow or Monday if that's OK.'

'Whenever suits,' he said kindly. 'Are you sure you're all right?'

'Yes,' I mumbled, fiddling with my coat buttons, 'honestly I'm fine.'

'Hmm,' he said, eyeing me astutely, 'I've been married long enough to know that "fine" means anything but. Why don't you wait for Bea or some of the others? I don't like the thought of you walking home alone.'

'I'll be OK,' I insisted, heading over to the door as another group came in, 'I'll see you later.'

The wind, which was an all too common feature of Wynbridge in winter, had picked up, and cruelly dragged the bitter 'real feel' temperature even lower. I pulled my hat down over my ears, blinked back the stinging tears I could only partly blame on the weather and set off along the icy pavements towards home. All I wanted to do was to crawl under the duvet and forget, even if just for a few hours, about everything that Steve, the man I had thought I was still in love with, had said.

How was it even possible that such a special day and such a memorable and monumental evening, could be turned on its head in just a few fleeting minutes? Had he not just accused my father of corruption and goodness knows what else, we would probably have still been sitting together with our fingers entwined as we celebrated our happy ever after! But what would have happened beyond that? Surely his suspicions would have surfaced at some point and that would have been undoubtedly worse, wouldn't it?

As I slipped and tripped towards my longed-for bed I found myself wishing I'd never agreed to take on the Cherry Tree stall or become entangled with saving the town's Christmas celebrations. Not only had my involvement landed me in trouble at home, it had also put my heart in the firing line all over again. And, added to all of that, of course, there was now the horrible realisation that even after everything I'd helped achieve in the last few days, my fellow stallholders still had doubts about me because of who my father happened to be. I had thought I was part of the gang now, but if that was the case then surely they would have told me about their fears for the future of the market site, wouldn't they?

As I turned down the road to home I threw up a little prayer in the hope that Mum and Dad would have already gone to bed and I wouldn't have to face either of them just yet. I had everything crossed that a good night's sleep would give me some perspective and hope because the last thing I wanted was another row with Dad. I just knew that an argument would inevitably lead to me blurting out everything that Steve had accused him of.

This time around I needed a calm and clear head and time to think things through before I even considered whether these upsetting accusations bore any weight and were worth an airing. Surely they couldn't be. It just wasn't possible. Steve must have been listening to his dad bleating on when he'd had one too many and got the wrong end of the stick.

Fortunately, luck was with me and I crept into the house, slipped upstairs and threw myself on the bed, letting sleep take me.

'Finally!' said Mum as I poked my head in the sitting room late the next morning. 'We thought you were never going to get up!'

'Did you go to the pub last night?' asked Dad, turning off the news channel and twisting round to look at me.

'Yeah,' I said, 'everyone did, apart from Gwen.'

'Well, you certainly had some celebrating to do!' laughed Mum. 'The entire evening was an absolute triumph!'

'Everyone certainly seemed to have a good time,' I agreed, 'and plenty of people turned out.'

'And stayed out,' gushed Mum. 'The market was still heaving when we came home and we didn't leave early.'

'Yes, congratulations, love,' said Dad with an unexpected smile. 'You and Tom really pulled it off. I know we've had our differences of late, especially during the last couple of weeks and I admit I was upset when you got involved with it all, but last night you made me proud, Ruby, really proud.'

'Thank you.' I swallowed, feeling relieved that our disagreement over my tattoo had been forgotten, for the time being at least.

I couldn't help wondering if I was actually still asleep and had drifted down the stairs in a dream. I had assumed Dad would still be smarting because he had had to tell the entire town that he'd had no part in putting the event together, but he seemed genuinely pleased about it all.

'I thought you might think it was all a bit over the top,' I said cautiously, hoping not to break the spell, 'what with all the fireworks and everything.'

'Absolutely not,' he said, 'it was perfect. Just the change the town needed. People will be talking about last night for a long time and I can't wait to see what the local rag makes of it! They might even have something positive to say for once.'

I felt a tight knot forming in my stomach as I thought

about what they would have to say about Dad if Steve's allegations made their way to the editors' ears. Dad had dedicated endless hours to criticising and correcting their journalistic efforts and I could well imagine they'd love the opportunity to get their own back. They'd eat him alive.

'You all right?' asked Mum. 'You look a bit peaky.'

'I'm OK,' I said, 'just a bit tired.'

'Well I'm not surprised.' She smiled. 'Why don't you go back up to bed?'

'Best not. I left my car at the pub. I should go and get it really. I think you're right about last night, Dad. I'm sure people will remember it for a long time, and that was actually just the start. This is certainly going to be one Christmas the town won't forget in a hurry.'

I hoped that by making the suggestion he might say something that would give me a clue as to whether or not the market still had a future or whether perhaps he would instead acknowledge that what Tom and I were trying to achieve was a fitting swansong, but he didn't bite.

'Oh goodie!' said Mum.

'What do you mean "just the start"?' he asked.

'Well, it would be silly not to capitalise on the situation and offer some more entertainment, wouldn't it?' I added.

'Well, there's the tree auction on the tenth,' he reminded me. 'That always pulls a decent crowd. Do you remember when you were growing up we used to go together? You always managed to have the final word over which tree we'd be bidding for.'

'I do remember, Dad,' I nodded, my already fragile emotional state taking another knock courtesy of his happy reminiscing, 'but I think we can do even better than the auction this year,' I told him. 'In fact, we've already been making plans.'

OK, so that was a bit of a fabrication, but I didn't want him to be in any doubt that I was going to carry on helping out with the town events between now and when I left in the New Year.

'Well, I suppose that's no bad thing,' he shrugged amiably. 'And I hope the success of last night and all these extra plans has made you have a good, long think about everything,' he added.

'What things?'

'This market stall business for a start,' he began, 'you only have to think about what a triumph last night was, Ruby, to know that your talents and skills are being wasted.'

'Oh Dad!' I groaned. I had really begun to think that we were going to make it through an entire conversation without him twisting the situation to suit him, but my reckoning was obviously a little premature.

'Well I'm sorry,' he said, 'but you're wasting your time working these ridiculous hours and standing about in the freezing cold catching your death. Surely all your hard work at university means more to you than that.'

'I don't believe this,' sighed Mum.

'We've had this conversation a hundred times already,' I reminded him. 'I'm helping Lizzie and Jemma out for just a few weeks. It isn't a career strategy!'

'Well, I'm glad to hear it.'

'I'm going for a shower.'

'Oh I'm sorry,' Dad said wearily, 'but just wait, Ruby. Hear me out.'

'I've heard it all before, Dad!'

Unfortunately he was still determined to have his say.

'How about you come and volunteer at the council as the Christmas events co-ordinator perhaps? You could work in the office next to Tom and I'd pay you, out of my own pocket, twenty per cent more than you'd expect to earn on the market, just to make sure you don't end up missing out on adding to your travel funds.'

'Because she doesn't want to . . .' Mum tried to explain.

'Office hours,' Dad cajoled, 'central heating, no surly traders to deal with or heavy stock to lug about.'

As hard as I tried not to be, I was almost tempted. The thought of warm toes and a working day that didn't involve thermal vests, frostbite and the continual risk of running into the Dempster clan at every turn was seriously seductive, but there at the back of my mind was the niggling thought that Dad seemed suddenly even more keen to get me away from the market. He was now actually offering to pay me to leave.

'Look,' I sighed, 'thanks, Dad, but I can find my own way. It's fun doing something a bit different and I wouldn't dream of letting Jemma and Lizzie down.'

Dad shrugged his shoulders in what I hoped was resignation.

'Oh, and if by any chance,' I added to hammer home my point, 'your suggestion has anything to do with keeping me away from Steve Dempster then I can tell you right here and now that you needn't worry.'

'No?'

'No,' I said firmly, 'because the further I can keep away from him from now on, the better.'

I couldn't read Dad's expression but Mum looked genuinely upset. I could easily imagine that she and Marie had been bustling about in the background secretly hoping that we would get back together and planning mother-of-the-bride and groom outfits that wouldn't clash.

'So,' said Dad. 'You're sticking with the stall.'

'Yes,' I said, 'I'm sticking with the stall and nothing you can say or do will make me change my mind.'

'I can't believe you turned down your mum's Sunday lunch,' sighed Bea from the cosy confines of the snuggly cushion nest she had made for herself on her sofa. 'Things with your dad must have been *really* bad.'

'They were somewhat strained,' I said, as I felt yet another

187

wave of disappointment wash over me. The conversation that had started so well had soon begun to freefall downhill. 'By the time I'd had a shower he'd upped his offer to twenty-five per cent and poor Mum was practically frantic. Lunch or no lunch, I had to get out.'

'Well, I'm glad you knew you'd be welcome here,' Bea smiled, 'and I'm even gladder that you came with supplies!'

The floor of her little sitting room was littered with packets, crumbs and empty plates and even just the thought of how much sugar we had ingested in the last hour was enough to make me feel queasy, and that was before my mind played over Steve's unsavoury insinuations again. I hadn't breathed a word about what he'd said to Bea. My request to use her place as a bolthole was being solely blamed on Dad's nagging and I was in no hurry to tell her any different.

'There's one Oreo left,' she said, shaking out the packet. 'Want to split it?'

'Oh, go on then,' I tutted, 'you've twisted my arm, and while you're at it, pass me the remote, will you? It's like living on the set of *Jeremy Kyle* at home right now so I certainly don't need to be watching a Sunday marathon of it!'

'But it's a DNA special,' she pouted, reluctantly nudging the remote towards me with her foot so she didn't have to get up. 'I only watch it to make me feel better about my own life.'

'You live a charmed life,' I reminded her. 'You're just

sulking because Sam's holding out on you. You know full well he's going to propose one day.'

'I don't actually,' she sniffed.

'Oh you do,'

'No,' she said doubtfully, 'I'm really not so sure any more, I know he loves me, but—'

'Well, you should think yourself lucky,' I scolded, flicking through the channels and feeling uncharacteristically unsympathetic, 'if I were you I'd give him a break. Let him do things in his own time otherwise you'll end up pushing him away, and believe me, it's no fun being a singleton at this time of year.'

'I thought you still had your eye on Steve.'

'Oh that's worn off,' I said, purposefully focusing on the TV. 'I thought I had feelings for him when I first came back, but now he's with Mia all the time and I've got my travel plans to figure out, I can't say I'm fussed.'

'Well that figures,' said Bea, fortunately none the wiser. 'It had been a while since you'd seen him and the way the relationship ended meant there were bound to be loose ends.'

'Exactly.'

We sat in silence for a few seconds.

'Sam wouldn't dare dump me,' she said eventually, her tone militant. 'Not after all the effort I've put into this relationship but perhaps you're right. Maybe it wouldn't hurt to back off a bit.'

'A bit!' I snorted. 'If I were you I'd dial it right down. Go out and have a bit of fun like you used to when you were first going out and do not, under any circumstances, keep manipulating every conversation so you end up talking about bridal favours and babies!'

Bea did at least have the grace to blush.

'I suppose I have been a bit OTT lately, haven't I?'

I thought it best not to answer and threw the remote back over to her.

'Here we go,' I said, snuggling back down, 'perfect.'

Bea glanced up at the screen.

'The cheesy Christmas channel,' she groaned in disgust. 'You've got to be kidding me? Haven't we had enough sugar-coated crap for one day?'

'Look,' I told her, 'I have no relationship, a father who can't stop nagging and no Sunday lunch. The least you can do is let me wallow on your sofa and lose myself in a sickly seasonal made-for-TV shocker!'

'OK, OK,' she said, holding up her hands in surrender. 'Don't get your knickers in a knot.' She sat up and threw off the cushions she had surrounded herself with. 'I'll go and put the kettle on and you never know. If you're really lucky, your mum might have put a plate in the microwave!'

As luck would have it, vegging out on Bea's sofa that afternoon turned out to be highly productive. Not that anyone would have believed it, had they been watching me consume my bodyweight in chocolate biscuits.

However, by the time I wandered to the pub to collect my car I had phase two of the Wynbridge Christmas festivities all planned out in my head and hopefully, if I could convince Tom and the rest of the stallholders that I wasn't one of the baddies and that it was a good idea, I'd have enough on my plate to stop me brooding over Steve Dempster and his offensive accusations almost up until Christmas Day.

Chapter 15

On Monday morning I was back at the market earlier than ever with a spring in my step and a steely determination to ignore Steve and start looking forward rather than back.

'What have you got there?' asked Gwen, as she wandered over to see what I was pinning up on the back of the stall. 'It isn't something cut out of the papers about the switch-on, is it?'

'No,' I said, 'afraid not. I don't think we even made it into the papers, Gwen, but Simon has just popped over to the newsagent's to check.'

'And there was I hoping to be front page news again,' she sighed wistfully.

'Again!' I pounced, quickly turning around to see if she was pulling my leg. Given the impish grin she flashed me I knew instantly that she wasn't. 'When exactly were you front page news?'

'Never you mind,' she giggled. 'Fortunately there aren't many folk left who can remember now, so my secret's reasonably safe.'

'Oh Gwen, you tease!'

'We made it into three!' yelled Simon as he raced back to the square with an armful of papers. 'All red tops and all more interested in Paul than Wynbridge, but two of them actually managed to spell the town name right and they've included some cracking photos of the lights.'

Everyone crowded around to have a closer look at the photographs as Simon read out what had been written. All of the reports suggested the set-up was a publicity stunt but on the whole they were complimentary and none of them contained anything damaging.

'Not bad at all,' nodded Chris, winking at me. 'Well done, Ruby.'

'Well done everyone,' I said quickly, 'we all played a part.'

'But it was you who had the sense to pin down Paul Thompson when you saw him.'

'I wouldn't mind pinning him down!' shouted Shirley.

'Well, I'm just pleased the evening was a success,' I said, building myself up to say something more. I took a deep breath and dived in before they all went back to their own stalls. 'I know some of you doubted me when I first showed up,' I began, my face feeling a good ten degrees warmer already, 'but I had hoped that by helping out last week you'd see that I am every bit as determined as you lot to see the market thriving again.'

I could just about make out the top of Steve's head above everyone else, but I didn't care. I needed to have my say if I was going to carry on working on the market and helping out in the run up to Christmas.

'You can't choose your family,' laughed Chris, no doubt trying to lighten the mood and make everyone else feel less awkward.

'No,' I said, 'you can't, which is actually more of a shame for some of you than it is for me.'

No one was laughing now.

'What did she mean by that?' muttered Jude.

'We all know you picked a side, Ruby,' said Gwen, laying a hand on my arm, 'and the town is very grateful that you did, as are we all. Aren't we, folks?'

'Yes!' shouted some. 'Not half!' joined in the others.

'Well, I appreciate that,' I nodded, 'I really do, but I have also discovered that there are rumours running roughshod through the town and they are all suggesting that there's much more going on here than I originally thought and I have to admit that I'm a little sad, not to say embarrassed, that no one saw fit to tell me the truth sooner.'

An awkward hush descended.

'All I can say is,' I sighed, 'that I don't know anything about the market being closed or the site being up for sale.

This time next year, next month even, I'll be long gone, but I promise you that in the meantime I will do everything I can to make this a very merry Christmas for everyone and I would be really grateful if you could all find it in your hearts to see me as myself, Ruby Smith, Wynbridge stallholder, and not just the daughter of Robert Smith, the council planning manager.'

All I could do now was hope that at least some of my words had hit their mark and given the chastened expressions on some of the faces looking back at me I was reasonably hopeful. Steve, of course, had kept his distance, so I had no chance to gauge how he had taken my little speech, but really it was about time I stopped caring about whether or not anything I said or did had any impact on him.

'There's another meeting in the pub tomorrow night,' said Bob. 'It's about the tree auction. I only mention it because I wasn't sure if anyone else had. It would be good if you could come.'

'Thanks, Bob,' I smiled, 'I'll be there. In fact, I've already had a bit of a think about that particular event and I might just have a new idea to bring to the table.'

'Marvellous,' he chuckled, 'I had a feeling you might. We'll see you there then. The more the merrier, as always! Oh and by the way,' he added, 'Shirley and I had a think about what you said about selling seasonal stuff.'

'Oh yes?'

'And we've decided to give some new festive stock a try.'

'What have you found?'

'Christmas stockings for cats and dogs,' he said shaking his head as if he couldn't believe such things existed. 'Some are already filled with treats and others are empty. We're going to offer an extra deal if customers fill them with stock from the stall.'

'Well, that's great,' I told him. 'Just the sort of thing I had in mind. People really love to pamper their pets.'

'Shirley has even found some Christmas jumpers for dogs online, but I've drawn the line at those.'

'I've ordered three!' Shirley shouted, much to her husband's consternation. 'All on sale or return. We'll see how they go.'

'*If* they go, you mean,' tutted Bob.

'Well good luck with it all,' I said, 'I'll mention the cat stockings to Bea. She would probably love one of those for her mum's pampered puss!'

Everyone had gone back to their stalls except Gwen who I found having another closer look at the picture I had been pinning up before Simon arrived back with the papers.

'What's all this about then?' she frowned. 'Are you trying to keep warm by taking a crafty glance at somewhere hot and exotic every now and then?'

'No,' I laughed, 'of course not.'

'Well, that is a relief,' she sighed. 'I thought for a minute there that you were losing your marbles. The cold can do funny things to the brain if you aren't used to it. So where is that place then?' she said, pointing at the pristine beach in the photograph with her sheepskin-clad fingers.

'It's in India,' I told her, smoothing down the paper and imagining the hot sand between my toes. 'I've put it up as a little reminder as to why I'm out in the cold all day and trying to earn a bit extra.'

'Oh,' she said, 'are you saving for a holiday, my dear?'

'Sort of,' I explained. 'All the money I earn from running the stall is going into funding my travel plans.'

'How exciting!' she gasped, her eyes lighting up at the 'T' word. 'And when are you planning on setting off?'

'In the New Year,' I said, rubbing my hands together and stamping my feet to stave off the cold, 'possibly even before that if I can manage it. I've had all my jabs and my passport's poised for action, so as soon as I've banked some funds I'll be off!'

'Oh,' she frowned, 'I had no idea we were going to lose you, and so soon!'

'If I do go before Christmas the stall will stay, assuming Jemma and Lizzie can find someone else to run it,' I reassured her, 'so you'll only be losing me really, not another stall.'

'I know,' she said sadly, 'I realise that, but what a pity for us. The market will miss you sorely, Ruby, as well as all your wonderful ideas, but I do understand. When the old wander-lust strikes, it's best to answer the siren call.'

'Have you travelled much, Gwen?' I asked, suddenly curious to know more about the life she had led before she bowled through her seventies.

'Oh yes,' she smiled, 'when I was a young thing I travelled all over the globe. Footloose and fancy free!'

'And was that when you made headline news?' I asked, hoping to catch her off guard.

'Never you mind about that,' she said again with a giggle, 'never you mind!'

For a Monday, the market certainly seemed busier and plenty of customers told me how much they had enjoyed the switch-on and that they were hoping the council and traders were planning more events in the run up to the big day. I was encouraged by their enthusiasm but couldn't help wishing a few more mentioned Tom by name, rather than just lumping him in with the council crowd. He was working ridiculously hard to manage his extra workload and improve the Wynbridge festivities, and in turn I was determined that before I left town I would see his efforts properly acknowledged.

'A little something for the young lady with expensive taste,' whispered a voice close to my ear.

'Oh my goodness,' I laughed, taking the prettily wrapped box from the man standing beside me. 'Paul! I didn't expect to see you again.'

'Well keep your voice down,' he said, pulling the hood of his sweatshirt down a little further, 'I don't want a fuss so I'm incognito, but I couldn't leave town without saying goodbye, could I?'

'Of course you could,' I told him, 'I'm sure everyone thinks you've left already. You could have just slipped away.'

'Not really my style, dear lady,' he said in a silly voice, 'and besides I like this cloak and dagger stuff. I bet you anything you like there's still a pap or two hanging around here somewhere. You can't beat the thrill of the chase! Anyway I digress, what I wanted to say was thank you, Ruby.'

'But I'm the one who should be thanking you,' I told him. Paul wouldn't hear of it.

'You know what,' he said, sidling closer. 'I think we both did each other a good turn. How about we call it even?'

'Even it is then.'

'Thank you for getting my career back on track,' he said, stooping to lightly kiss my cheek.

'And thank you for lighting up the town,' I said, kissing him back and managing only a slight blush.

'Well, you and everyone else are most welcome,' he said, and then catching sight of the picture behind me, he began to smile. 'Oh hello,' he said, stepping around me to take a closer look. 'I recognise that place.'

'Do you?' I asked, spinning round so we were both staring at it.

'Yes,' he said, 'it's Agonda beach in Goa, isn't it?'

'Yes,' I nodded, amazed that he recognised it.

'I happen to know a couple who run a rather special bespoke little hotel just a stone's throw up the coast from that very spot.'

'You never do!' I gasped, completely forgetting my manners.

'I certainly do,' he laughed.

'Oh wow,' I said dreamily, almost swooning at his feet. 'That beach happens to be my number one dream travel destination.'

'Are you planning a trip, Ruby?'

'I am.'

'Well in that case, you should look them up. The views are simply divine and the food isn't bad either.'

'Oh well, that's quite something coming from the country's number one celebrity chef!' I laughed, happy to massage his ego under the circumstances. 'But I'm afraid staying in your friends' hotel or anywhere like it will be quite out of the question. Totally out of my league I'm sorry to say. I'll be slumming it you see, I'm going to try and work my way around the world. No seven-star luxury for me!'

'Well, they're always looking for staff,' he said, rummaging in his jeans pocket for his wallet. 'Here,' he said, passing me a rather smart business card. 'Drop me a line when you know you'll be there and I'll help get some work lined up for you in advance.'

'Oh I couldn't,' I said, shaking my head and trying to hand back the card.

'Of course you could!' he laughed, 'it's the least I can do.'

'Wow, thank you.' I grinned, my excitement cranking up a gear. 'I have to say that really puts rather a different complexion on the whole trip.'

'Ruby,' he said, looking down at me, 'I know people everywhere. You only have to drop me a line and I'll help get you sorted.'

'That really is incredibly generous of you.'

'One good turn deserves another,' he smiled, 'now, I'd better be off,' he added, nodding in Steve's direction, 'before I'm rumbled.'

I looked over at the Dempster stall. Steve couldn't take his eyes off us.

'OK,' I said, tucking his card into my pocket and standing on tiptoe to kiss him goodbye, 'and thank you again.'

'Enjoy the Cristal!' he yelled, pulling off his hood as he jogged over to where he had parked his car. 'I know how much you enjoy a drop of the good stuff!'

Chapter 16

The town's annual Christmas tree auction had been a part of Wynbridge history for far longer than I could remember. It happened every second Saturday in December and drew visitors from the furthest reaches of the county and beyond. Generations of families travelled to pick out their trees and a percentage of the profits from the sale were ploughed back into local charities and projects. As well as Christmas trees, mistletoe and holly, in fact anything green and growing and associated with Yule, was included in the auction and consequently far more people were involved in its planning than just the town market traders.

On entering The Mermaid for the meeting that Tuesday night it was immediately obvious that the popularity of the switch-on had had quite an impact, and practically everyone who was involved with the auction had turned out to see what could be done to liven up the tree sale as well.

'Crikey,' said Tom, puffing out his cheeks as he and Jemma joined me at the bar. 'What a turnout!'

'Pretty impressive, isn't it?' said Jemma. 'At this rate you're going to need another venue for these meetings, Tom.'

'Don't even think about it!' piped up Evelyn, from her spot behind the pumps. 'A night or two like this every year does our profit margin no end of good! We can pack everyone in, Jemma, don't you worry about that.'

'No sign of your dad tonight, Ruby,' said Chris as he ambled over. He towered above practically everyone there and could take in who was and wasn't present with one quick sweeping glance.

I felt my face redden and my mouth go dry as I thought of Dad sat in front of the fire at home, with his newspaper and highlighter poised for an evening of heady drama and excitement.

'No need,' butted in Tom, thankfully saving me from having to grapple for a response, 'he's handed all this over to me now, Chris, so he doesn't have to be here and besides, he's heading over to Huntingdon for a meeting early tomorrow and needs to prepare for that.'

Chris nodded, but didn't say anything. He was obviously disappointed that his old sparring partner had bowed out and that he couldn't get a rise out of his youthful replacement. Noting his frustration, I made a mental note to try and get to the bottom of his and Dad's mutual loathing before I left town. Previously I had hoped that I might be able to help them move on if not make friends, but now, given everything that had passed between me and Steve, I didn't much care whether they liked or loathed each other.

'Let me buy you a drink,' I said to Tom once Chris was out of earshot, 'and you, Jemma. You should be celebrating the fact that you've made it out of the house and it isn't even date night!'

'I know,' she laughed, 'it was very kind of Lizzie and Ben to offer to babysit. Not that the kids are much bother any more. In fact,' she added, 'Ella even suggested she could stay home alone and watch Noah all by herself. Can you imagine?'

I shuddered at the thought.

'I wonder what you would have gone home to!'

'Carnage,' said Tom, 'and a gargantuan phone bill. That would doubtless be Ella's revenge because we won't let her have a mobile phone.'

'But she's only nine!'

'I know,' he sighed, 'but apparently absolutely everyone in her class has one and she feels left out.'

'Everyone?' I gasped.

'*Everyone*!' said Jemma, mimicking her daughter's theatrical American accent. 'The latest cell is the new accessory!'

'Oh good grief,' I gaped, relieved that I didn't have

children to worry about who were growing up too fast. 'Come on, Tom,' I said, 'shouldn't you be making a start? I'll get the drinks in while you kick things off.'

It soon became obvious that although everyone had thoroughly enjoyed the Christmas switch-on this year they had all turned up to hear what was in line next, rather than come up with any ideas themselves.

Almost an hour later and the only new attractions that had been suggested and confirmed were carols sung by the local choral society members, who would be dressed in Victorian costumes borrowed from the theatre group, and more mulled wine which Marie agreed to take responsibility for once she had finished bidding on the greenery she wanted from the auction for her floristry business.

My own little idea was buzzing about in my head and as no one else had suggested anything like it I was itching to share, but didn't want to put myself forward in case anyone thought I was being pushy. Had I thought the thing through properly, I would have handed it over to Bea to suggest as she was with me when inspiration had struck. Unfortunately, however, she hadn't even made it to the meeting so that was now completely out of the question.

With the discussion drying up and the silences becoming longer, Tom suggested a twenty-minute break to give everyone the opportunity to refill their glasses and in the process hopefully also plunder their creative wells for some fresh designs as to how to make the auction even more appealing.

Everyone quickly headed over to the packed bar and I found myself standing in line next to Bob.

'I thought you said you'd come up with something,' he said, waving a twenty-pound note over the bar to try and attract Jim's attention. 'When we spoke before you said you'd been giving it some thought.'

'I have,' I told him. 'I have got an idea, but I don't want to come across as pushy and anyway it probably won't even work. It isn't exactly a simple set-up. It isn't like the fun and games we had on the stalls at the switch-on last week.'

'Well, whatever it is, if you don't give it an airing we'll never know, will we?' he said wisely. 'And I wouldn't worry about how you come across. To be honest, I think people will be grateful for whatever you can suggest.'

'Let's see how the rest of the meeting goes,' I said. 'Someone might come up with an absolute gem now they've had a break and a bit longer to think.'

They didn't, and Bob, knowing I had something up my sleeve, was not prepared to let the meeting drag on a second longer without plonking me very definitely back in the limelight.

'Ruby Smith has an idea!' he shouted out, causing everyone to stare in my direction. 'She told me earlier in the week, but she's too shy to speak up.'

'Have you, Ruby?' asked Tom.

'I have thought of something,' I mumbled. 'But as I haven't had time to run it by you, I thought . . .'

'Never mind that,' ushered Tom, 'let's just hear it now because time is pushing on.'

Reluctantly I stood up, took a deep breath and tried to think how to explain as simply as possible exactly what I had in mind.

'OK,' I began, 'this will probably sound a bit bizarre and nothing like we've had in town before, so please just go with it and hear me out.'

'Stand at the front next to Tom!' yelled someone behind me. 'We can't hear you back here.'

I eased my way through the crowd to where Tom was standing and glared at Bob who gave me the thumbs up en route.

'Right,' I said, raising my voice a little and wondering where I should begin. 'This isn't exactly a new idea,' I admitted, 'but it would definitely be something new for Wynbridge.'

I looked around the pub at the sea of expectant faces, Steve's included, and decided to just go for it. I would explain what I had in mind and then let Tom deal with the response, assuming there was one of course.

'Last Sunday,' I began, 'the day after the switch-on, I was feeling pretty tired.'

'I still am!' put in Bob, in what he no doubt thought was a positive tone.

'So,' I continued, 'I went round to a friend's house and spent the day on the sofa watching cheesy American made-for-TV Christmas films.'

I didn't mention all the chocolate and biscuits we had waded through as well.

'Oh, I love those films,' said Jude wistfully, 'they're always full of single parents looking for love or some hardworking soul looking to save Christmas.'

'Exactly,' I said, encouraged that at least one person might know what I was talking about, 'just like we are, and they are also full of great ideas. The one I enjoyed most was all about,' I paused to take a breath, 'a community bake sale.'

Silence.

'And I was wondering if it would be possible to run one here in the town at the same time as the tree auction.'

'Where?' asked Chris.

'Well,' I said, 'I thought, if we could get the local schools on board and maybe even the WI ladies and the church, we could ask for donations of seasonal cakes and bakes to sell in the town hall and I know the hall has a decent catering kitchen installed, so I was wondering if it would be feasible to run some on-site baking sessions that day for anyone who was interested, but particularly for the local children.'

A slight murmur broke out.

'The tree auction itself is lovely of course and an important Wynbridge tradition,' I said quickly, 'but there's nothing going on to keep the young ones entertained after they've chosen their tree and if we opened up the hall, and sold teas and coffees along with the cakes and things, then there would be plenty on offer to keep people in town a bit longer.'

'Perhaps Lizzie would be able to offer a couple of kids' crafting sessions,' said Jemma shyly, 'even if it was just some glue and glitter colouring sheets or something, and I'd love to get involved with the baking element, assuming of course everyone else thinks it's a good idea.'

'So,' said Tom, furiously scribbling away on his notepad, 'you're suggesting the tree auction goes ahead in the market square as always, Ruby, but that we open up the town hall for another auction of cakes and things and with some baking sessions and sales of refreshments happening at the same time.'

'Yes,' I said, relieved that he had got the gist of what I was suggesting, 'it would be lovely to have things that *everyone* could be involved in, whether that would mean they baked a cake or served teas or just came along for a chat. I admit the film I watched was a bit cheesy, but the crux of the idea and the possibility to bring all generations of a community together was really lovely, and more important than ever at Christmas time.'

'OK,' said Tom as the noise level began to pick up, 'I rather like the sound of this. Let's have another break and then come back and put the idea to a vote. If there are enough votes in favour of the idea and enough offers of help to run it, then I'll go back to the council tomorrow and put it forward as a formal suggestion.'

The noise level erupted as everyone began talking at once and from what I could make out no one thought I'd gone completely mad. Granted, we probably wouldn't have a town covered in sparkling snow that Saturday and the heroine would certainly not be riding off with her heart's desire in a horse-drawn sleigh, but in essence the suggestion was a good one and I hoped there were enough votes, and time, of course, to push it through for council approval.

'Nice one,' said Steve, as he walked over to where I was standing, 'it's a really good idea, Ruby.'

I looked at him, wondering why he thought, after all that had been said between us just days before, I would care if he had an opinion either way.

'Perhaps we should tell everyone it was down to you really.'

'What do you mean?'

'Well,' I said, 'had you not accused Dad of extortion I wouldn't have ended up feeling rotten on Bea's sofa flicking through the TV channels and found the film that inspired the idea, would I?'

'Look,' he said, trying to reach for my hand, 'about that. I was just trying to point out—'

'Forget it,' I said, snatching my fingers out of his reach and taking a step back.

'I can't.'

'Well try,' I said, 'because I have. This time next month I'll be gone and you and Wynbridge will be just a distant memory.'

'Don't say that,' he sighed.

'Why not?' I shrugged. 'It's the truth, although to be fair, I'll probably give more thought to the town than you.'

He looked deep into my eyes and for the first time since I'd been back I felt nothing. Not so much as a flicker. My stomach didn't flip, my heart didn't race, my palms stayed dry. I couldn't believe it.

'OK, folks!' shouted Tom. 'Let's put this idea to a vote!'

'I have to go,' I said, looking right back at him. 'I'll see you around.'

It came as quite a shock to acknowledge that the candle with Steve Dempster's name on it that had been burning in my heart for so long, had been well and truly snuffed out, but truth be told, it was also a relief. This time when I left the town I would be going free from all the emotional baggage that had tethered me during my time at university and stopped me moving on. Now the world was my oyster, and with Paul's business card tucked away in my purse, it was looking like I might have bagged myself an even bigger pearl.

'Right,' said Tom as he looked at the sea of hands that had shot into the air when he asked who was in favour of the bake sale idea. 'From what I can see that looks almost unanimous to me. Would anyone who isn't in favour now raise their hands please?'

There were only three and one of those was lowered when nudged into submission by its nearest neighbour.

'Great,' said Tom, beaming over at me. 'Now who would be willing to help out with serving teas and things and keep an eye on everything in the town hall?'

Again there were a great many hands in the air, although not quite as many as before, because lots of locals would be running their stalls or helping out at the tree auction.

'I'm sure lots of mums will come forward if I ask to put some posters up at school,' said Jemma.

'And the WI ladies will be out in full force,' added Gwen. 'I'll make sure of that.'

I couldn't imagine that anyone would get away with staying at home if Gwen had anything to do with it.

'Well, that's great,' said Tom, 'I think Ruby's idea is an excellent one and I will certainly put forward the suggestion first thing in the morning so we can hopefully get the ball rolling. There isn't all that long until December the tenth.'

'I shouldn't worry about that,' shouted Jim, 'you only had about a week to sort out the switch-on and look at the success that was!'

'Very true,' agreed Tom, 'but we're going to be relying on everyone pulling together for this one, folks, so if you do have any ideas to add, or any doubts that you won't be able to help out, do come and see me.'

'There is just one thing I've thought of,' I said, 'and I'm sorry to put a spanner in the works as it was my idea.'

'Go on,' said Tom.

'How are we going to fund the baking sessions?'

'And the crafts?' added Jemma.

'Don't worry about that,' said Tom, 'leave it with me. I know Amber and Jake offered to donate their profits from the hog roast last week to future community events. I'm sure we'll be able to utilise their generous contribution and per-haps we could approach some local businesses for a donation as well.'

I was relieved that he didn't think the funding would be a problem.

'Right,' he said, 'I'm closing the meeting, but do come and see me if there's anything you'd like to say before I approach the council in the morning.'

Everyone began to pull on their coats, drain their glasses and head off into the frosty night.

'Thanks, Bob!' I called over to him and Shirley who were

just about to leave. 'I probably wouldn't have said anything if it wasn't for you.'

'No, thank *you*, love,' he said, 'for another cracking idea.'

His eyes were shining and I was a little surprised that he looked so thoroughly thrilled at the prospect of a town bake sale.

'I bet you'd never guess,' he explained, 'but there's nothing I like better than a spot of baking on a Sunday afternoon, so I'll definitely be contributing.'

That night, as I walked home beneath a sky laden with stars, I couldn't get the image of Bob in a flowery apron out of my mind. At least that was one thing you could say for life in a small town; it was always full of surprises! I was delighted that the bake sale was going ahead and hoped helping to organise and run it would keep me occupied and out of the house for even longer than usual. Now Steve had seen to it that he no longer had a hold on my heart, I was hoping that my argument with Dad could be settled too, but in order to achieve that we needed to let the dust settle for a bit longer yet.

Chapter 17

By Saturday the bake sale had the council seal of approval, the planning and promotion for it were in full swing and it was all change on the market.

'Are you really sure you're up for this, Angela?' I frowned, as together we finished setting up. 'It might not feel too cold now, but when you've been standing about for a couple of hours you might feel a bit differently about the idea.'

'I'll be fine,' she said, bobbing down behind the stall and popping back up again with a hot water bottle and a thermos flask. 'See, I'm all prepared.'

Personally I couldn't help thinking it was going to take a whole lot more than a few cups of not quite hot tea and a rubber bottle of water to keep her warm, but she was quite determined.

'You've been looking forward to this all week,' she reminded me, 'and to tell you the truth, so have I.'

I looked at her doubtfully.

'Don't get me wrong,' she smiled, having successfully read my mind, 'I love the café and I love working with Lizzie and Jemma, but even I could do with the occasional change of scene.'

'Well, all right then,' I said, handing over the money belt which held the stall float, 'but if you change your mind or find the cold too much, just send someone over and we'll swap places. I've got my market coat and my boots in the car so it would be no bother.'

'Oh stop fussing,' she said, shooing me away, 'go and get yourself over there otherwise you'll be late.'

The thought of spending the day cocooned inside the coffee and cinnamon scented Cherry Tree Café was certainly one to relish and I rushed across the square looking forward to a few hours in the warm.

Although delighted that the bake sale had been approved, and that everyone had embraced the preparations so whole-heartedly, I had been feeling increasingly forlorn. The atmosphere at home when Dad and I were in the same room together was still far frostier than most early starts on the market, and although Steve had successfully quashed any desire to rekindle our romance, I wasn't at all happy about the way things had ended between us. His accusations had tainted everything and although no longer preoccupied with his presence at the market and thoughts of whether or not we would end up back together, I had now become increasingly suspicious and watchful of everyone.

I took a deep breath and pushed open the door to the café, hoping that my day indoors would warm my heart as well as my hands and set me back on track.

'Here you are,' beamed Lizzie, throwing me my apron the second she heard the little bell announcing my arrival. 'You all set then?'

'You have no idea how ready I am for this,' I told her.

I quickly tied my apron in place, looked up again and then stood open-mouthed, all thoughts of what I had been going to say next quickly forgotten. I spun around on the spot trying to take in the magical transformation that had somehow happened overnight.

'Oh, wow,' I breathed, 'wow!'

The entire café had been decorated for Christmas in keeping with the vintage style that Lizzie loved so much, but with such finesse that it looked more like a Cath Kidston inspired set for a festive photo shoot than a real business. Paper chains in pretty pastel shades decked the ceilings and doorframes, along with pictures and napkins featuring the little Rudolph that Lizzie had scaled down from the one she painted for the game at the switch-on. The crowning glory however, was her collection of vintage snow globes which she had arranged along the shelves in the crafting area and festooned with old-fashioned cotton wool snow, glitter and fairy lights.

The entire café looked like a very grown-up grotto and I couldn't wait to welcome the customers and listen to what they had to say about it.

'It's cute, isn't it?' said Lizzie, her own outfit cleverly matching the décor. 'Every year I say it, but I don't think this place can get any prettier!'

'It's gorgeous,' I beamed, 'absolutely beautiful.'

'Well thank you,' she blushed, 'and in about half an hour it's going to be heaving, so let's get everything ready.'

Rather than just waiting on tables I was going to be helping out with the first festive crafting session of the season. A dozen keen crafters had signed up almost as soon as the details of the event had been made available and they were going to be making bespoke Christmas crackers. In the crafting area Lizzie already had everything organised and arranged neatly in boxes, much as I had expected, and beyond setting everything out, there was actually very little left to do.

'We're only going to have three tables that aren't set up for crafters today,' said Jemma as she rushed through with a basket of cutlery, 'and I can easily manage to wait on those myself so don't worry about spreading yourself thin, Ruby. Just stick to helping with the crafting. Everyone has already ordered from a set menu so when we get to lunchtime it will just be a case of serving and then clearing away.'

'What's on the menu?' I asked, my mouth already watering in anticipation.

'I've kept it quite simple,' said Jemma, 'let's see. Well, there are a couple of quiche choices.'

'The triple cheese is to die for,' cut in Lizzie.

'Avocado and walnut salad,' Jemma continued, 'spiced butternut and sweet potato soup, fresh, warm rolls ...'

'Oh Jemma, stop,' I said, 'stop! I've been looking forward to today all week. I don't want to wish the morning away just so I can get to lunch!'

Jemma was clearly delighted by my reaction.

'How very clever you are,' I said, thinking back to how differently things were run when the café first opened. 'A set menu is such a good idea.'

'Oh, we weren't always this efficient,' laughed Lizzie, 'were we, Jemma?'

'Definitely not,' she said with a sigh. 'Well, you know that, Ruby, you were with us in the early days! Do you remember that one time ...'

There was no time to hear what she was going to say as the little bell sang out and the first of the crafters arrived, their noses pinched and red and their fingers blue, desperate for a steaming mug to warm them up and return them to a healthier hue.

'Oh, girls!' cried one, as she took in the pretty scene before her. 'This all looks simply adorable!'

'Lizzie, you clever thing,' joined in her friend as she hung up her coat, 'I wish you'd come and decorate my house for Christmas and perhaps Jemma could supply the eats!'

'Now there's a thought,' said another, eyeing Lizzie in an evidently new light, 'have you thought about offering your combined services beyond the café?'

'Well, I have decorated a few of the wedding marquees at Skylark Farm,' said Lizzie thoughtfully, 'and Jemma has baked her blissful cakes for each of those but beyond that no, I can't say we've considered expanding further.'

'You could do dinner parties,' someone suggested, 'and tea parties!'

'You could give the hosts' homes your clever vintage twist, Lizzie, and Jemma could seduce the guests with her delectable baking.'

'Hello everyone!' laughed Jemma, appearing from the kitchen. 'Are you all ready for a day of crafting indulgence?'

'Absolutely,' the friendly little trio chorused.

'Well,' Jemma continued, 'before you all say another word, I've been listening to your expansion plans while I was preparing your teas and coffees, and as wonderful as the ideas sound, I'm afraid that unless Lizzie and I can successfully clone ourselves two or three times over, then your ideas are out of the question. There simply aren't enough hours in the day!'

'Oh now that is a shame.'

'I know,' said Jemma, 'but there's only so much that can

be done in twenty-four hours and only so many nights a girl can neglect her husband because she's batch baking!'

I couldn't help noticing that Lizzie had been very quiet while her business partner and best friend had been fielding everyone's Cherry Tree expansion ideas.

'Don't you agree, Lizzie?' said Jemma, clearly looking for support. 'Lizzie?'

'You know what,' said Lizzie, clearly unperturbed by the thought of working even longer hours, 'it might be worth considering.'

'Says the woman who doesn't have to get the kids bathed every night and rucksacks ready every morning,' laughed Jemma.

'Oh, I know,' said Lizzie, rushing over to give her friend a hug, 'I'm sorry. Maybe this is something we'll consider in a few years' time, ladies. Run it by us again in twenty twenty.'

'Or maybe you could just take on some extra staff now and strike while the iron's hot?'

'I'd book you right now,' jumped in the woman who had first come up with the idea. 'My mum's sixty-five in the New Year and a bespoke catered tea party at home would be just the thing!'

'Right,' I said, stepping forward in an attempt to get the session started. 'Why don't you all find a seat and I'll help Jemma with the drinks.'

Half an hour later and almost every seat in the café was

filled, the chatter had risen above the level of the Christmas CD which was playing in the background, and all thoughts of expanding the Cherry Tree empire had been forgotten, for the time being at least.

Looking through the supplies and equipment, I could see that Lizzie had cleverly chosen a huge variety of papers in all sorts of colours and patterns for the main body of the crackers. My personal favourites were the pretty pastel floral and polka dot sheets which matched the café décor along with the more traditional rolls which were patterned with holly, ivy and mistletoe. There were ribbons and bows to match all options along with the obligatory snaps, paper hats and cardboard innards.

Some of the group, I noticed, had decided not to use the novelties and jokes supplied and came prepared with treats and trinkets of their own which they spread out on the table for everyone to admire. These bespoke crackers were going to be given their own matching labels with the recipient's name written in Lizzie's neatest handwriting so the right people were guaranteed to receive the right gift.

Once everyone had had a trial run and refined their technique, they settled down and the chatter gradually quietened as they focused on their work. The crackers didn't take all that long to put together and once packed inside the beautiful matching boxes Lizzie had sourced and tied up with ribbon they looked extremely smart. I particularly liked the sets which had the ends of the paper shaped by dextrous use of some clever scallop-bladed scissors Lizzie had presented with a flourish at the start of the session. Most of the boxes held six crackers altogether, but practically everyone was making multiple boxes and I guessed that a lot were going to be given away as gifts.

I spent the morning wandering between the tables, holding bows and ribbons in place and trying to avoid the warmer attentions of the glue guns. At lunchtime the tables were cleared and everyone, including Jemma, Lizzie and I settled down to eat together.

Just as I had hoped, the hours spent in the soothing embrace of the cosy Cherry Tree Café had proved a calming balm for my troubled mind, and watching Jemma zip about with her competent skill set and efficient organisation made me realise that with her at the helm in the town hall kitchen, the bake sale was bound to be a success. In fact, by the time I helped clear away the empty plates and bowls, I was really beginning to look forward to it.

'What's the deal with this table?' I asked Lizzie as she helped me tidy away the last of the dishes. 'It hasn't been used at all.'

'I know,' she said, 'the couple who booked did warn me they might not be able to make it until this afternoon. In fact,' she said, lowering her voice to a whisper, 'I'm rather hoping that what you said on the phone before you moved back still holds, because . . .'

Whatever she was going to say next was lost as the café door opened, bringing with it a rush of cold air and Sam and Steve poised on the threshold, looking like fish out of water.

'I take it this is the "couple" you were referring to,' I muttered, my recently restored spirit suddenly taking a nose dive. 'I didn't have either of them down as the crafting kind.'

'Me neither,' shrugged Lizzie, 'but they're paying customers so who am I to argue? Come in, guys, and shut the door,' she called over to the dynamic duo. 'I've saved you the best table in the house!'

Needless to say, I avoided having anything to do with Steve and the 'best table' and focused my attention squarely on the rest of the group.

'What are you putting in this one, Alice?' I asked. 'You certainly seem to be taking your time over it.'

'She's sending it overseas,' butted in her neighbour, 'it's a *very* special delivery, isn't it Ali?'

Poor Alice turned beetroot red and I got the feeling that when they left, her friend was in for an absolute ear bashing.

'Well, it's a very pretty shade of pink you've picked,' I said, 'and I love the floral ribbon, very girly.' I stood up to move on to someone else and save her from further blushes, but she tugged on my sleeve and pulled me back down.

'That's because it is a girl,' she whispered, sliding a piece of paper across the table. 'My husband is currently working abroad and he won't be back for Christmas. We thought I might be pregnant before he left, but we've had so many false alarms that I didn't want to tell him until I was absolutely sure and a little further on. That,' she said, pointing at the paper I could now see was a scan photograph, 'is one of my most recent scan pictures.'

I could feel a lump forming in my throat as I thought of her husband in some far-flung hotel pulling his cracker on Christmas morning and being presented with the very first image of his baby daughter.

'But surely it won't get to him in time?' I said, trying to keep the panic out of my voice as I imagined all her efforts coming to nothing.

'Yes it will,' she said, 'he has a colleague who happens to be heading out to work with him next week and he's taking it with him. I can't put the snap in of course, but given the circumstances I don't think my other half will mind.'

'Well, congratulations, my lovely,' I said, blinking back my tears and feeling somewhat taken aback by my unusually emotional reaction, 'I'm absolutely thrilled for you.'

'Thank you,' she said shyly as she tenderly tucked the precious photograph inside the cracker. 'We're Skyping every day, but I can't wait to have him home.'

'I can imagine,' I said, passing her the ribbon she had picked out to secure the ends.

'Oh well,' said Lizzie, 'that's two down.'

I looked through to the café area and was surprised to see that Sam and Steve had already left.

'Did they change their minds?'

'No,' said Lizzie, with a shrug, 'they've taken all the bits and pieces with them and Sam said they'd make the crackers up at his flat.'

'That's a bit odd,' I frowned. 'Why bother going to the trouble of booking a space and then not using it?'

'I think they lost their bottle when they realised the place was filled with festive-feeling females!'

Personally I had my doubts. I thought it was considerably more likely that Steve had decided, now I had spelled it out for him that I wouldn't be joining him under the mistletoe, to give in to Mia's many and varied charms and was putting together something special for her. Either that or he simply couldn't stand the thought of being in the same room as me.

'You all right?' asked Lizzie when I didn't say anything.

'Fine,' I shrugged, 'just a bit tired, that's all.'

I didn't much care for the way she was looking at me and knew that she was thinking that I'd been finding Steve's close proximity hard to cope with after all.

'You have to remember that up until a few weeks ago I was a student,' I said airily. 'I didn't see daylight until lunchtime most days!'

She still didn't look convinced.

'Hello, hello!' said Bea, sweeping in and saving me from further scrutiny. 'How's it going?'

'Super,' I said, 'great, although you'll never guess who was just in here?'

'Who?' she said, keen as ever for a snippet of hot gossip.

'Paul Thompson!' cut in Lizzie.

'No!' said Bea, her eyes like saucers. 'Not really!'

'No,' said Lizzie, 'not really. Although rumour has it he did make one stop in town before heading back to his celebrity-filled flat in the city.'

'Did he now?' said Bea, looking intrigued.

Again, I didn't say anything.

'And talking of things all sweetness and light, how do you fancy a lovely cherry-topped cupcake to celebrate the weekend?'

'Oh, go on then,' said Bea. 'You've twisted my arm.'

With Bea distracted by the luscious cherry and frosting combo, I made a beeline for Lizzie.

'Why didn't you let me tell her Sam had been in?' I hissed.

'Stick around until Christmas,' she said pointedly, 'and you'll find out for yourself. And stop being so suspicious,' she added, 'you really haven't been yourself this afternoon. Whatever's the matter?'

'She needs a break,' said Jemma, as she waved off two more happy crafters with their brown paper bags brimming with boxes full of crackers. 'We all do.'

'How about,' said Bea, tuning into the conversation as she speedily polished off her last sweet mouthful, 'we bunk off on Monday?'

'Bunk off!' laughed Jemma.

'Yes,' she said, daintily dabbing her lips with the corner of the Rudolph-printed napkin. 'Close the café, dismantle the stall, cancel the clients and head a little further afield for a girly day out.'

'Oh, I don't know,' said Jemma.

'Monday is the quietest day of the week, Jem,' Lizzie reminded her, 'and the stall takings aren't so great that we would miss them either.'

'And I only have one client and she's messed my appointment book about so much I wouldn't mind losing her for good!' added Bea. 'What do you think, Ruby?'

'I don't know,' I shrugged, 'but I guess it might be fun and it would be nice to get out of Wynbridge for a few hours.'

'That settles it then,' said Bea, 'Miss Smith's obvious enthusiasm and sunny disposition is proof enough in itself that we girls could all do with a break and I have just the thing in mind!'

Chapter 18

Never one to let the grass grow, Bea had the whole trip
planned out by the end of the day, and when Jemma twitched
the café sign from 'Open' to 'Closed' we all let out a sigh
of relief. The prospect of a day away from Wynbridge, and
all its current complications, was a cheering prospect indeed
and I found myself in the rare position of almost wishing my
Sunday sleep-in away!

'So, Angela,' I said, as we finished counting out the day's
takings from the stall. 'How did you find life as a town
trader?'

'Pretty hectic,' she nodded, blowing her nose, 'and shock-
ingly cold, but I don't need to tell you that, do I?'

'Not an experience you'd want to repeat, then?' I ventured.

'Oh well, I wouldn't say that,' she smiled. 'No, I'd love
to do it again, actually. The stallholders are such a friendly
bunch and I really enjoyed watching them work.'

'Well, I'm glad you had fun,' I told her, thinking she must have fitted in far more quickly than I did, 'and I really appreciate you swapping places with me at such short notice.'

'So you've had a good time in here then?' she asked.

'I've had a blissful day,' I told her, 'tiring, but wonderful.'

'Lizzie, have you told Angela our news?' asked Jemma as she came through from the kitchen and set about pulling down the blinds.

'Oh,' said Angela, 'what have I missed?'

'How do you fancy an extra day off next week?' asked Lizzie as she finished turning off the twinkling fairy lights in the crafting area and joined us at the table.

'An extra day off?' Angela frowned.

'We've decided not to open on Monday!' said Jemma, her words tumbling out in a rush and her face and neck actually flushing at the prospect of two days in a row away from the café.

'What?' Angela gasped, her own complexion instantly matching Jemma's, but more down to shock than excitement. 'Well I never!'

'I know,' giggled Jemma. 'I probably shouldn't be quite so excited about missing out on a day's trading, but I actually can't wait!'

'Can't wait for what?' asked Tom as he rushed in out of the cold and caught the tail-end of the conversation.

'Monday,' said Jemma.

'Monday!' laughed Tom, wrapping his arms around his hardworking wife. 'But you hate Mondays!'

'Not this Monday,' smiled Jemma, planting a kiss on his cheek. 'Gosh you're cold. What have you done with the children?'

'They're at home with Ben. He's very kindly volunteered to keep an eye on dinner as well as the kids so we better get back before it needs stirring. He's been a complete whizz at helping me stack the log pile this afternoon, but his culinary skills are definitely wanting.'

Lizzie nodded in agreement, but forbore to comment.

'Anyway,' said Tom, 'what's all this about Monday?'

'The café's going to be closed,' explained Angela. She still sounded aghast.

'We're having a girls' day out,' I added, 'Lizzie, Jemma and I are bunking off with Bea. She's organising it all, but won't tell us where we're going.'

'Well that sounds like a wonderful idea,' Angela readily agreed now she had all the information.

'I just need to think about what to do with the kids,' said Jemma, sounding suddenly less enthusiastic, 'and then I'm on board.'

'Don't worry about the kids,' said Tom straightaway, 'I've been telling you for ages to take a proper day off.'

'We all have!' put in Angela.

'So I'll sort out the troops,' Tom continued.

'And I'll help,' added Angela.

'But it's your day off as well,' Jemma reminded her. 'I was hoping you'd come with us.'

'Do you know,' she said, 'I don't think I particularly want one. I think I might treat myself to another day running the stall!'

'She's mad,' laughed Lizzie.

'Totally!' I agreed.

'But at least I have tonight and tomorrow to thaw out,' pointed out Angela, determined to have the last word.

Our girly day of rest and relaxation didn't get off to the most leisurely of starts, but as it turned out to be totally worth it, I didn't much mind setting the alarm for six and clambering into Bea's dad's car not all that long after.

'So,' said Bea, twisting around in the front seat and smiling at Jemma, Lizzie and me who were squeezed in the back like the three monkeys, though perhaps not quite so wise. 'I've taken the money we agreed to spend, booked us a couple of treats and a nice table for lunch. All you have to do is pay to get there and for any little extras you see as we go along. Agreed?'

'Agreed,' we all nodded in unison.

'And Jemma,' Bea quickly added, 'before you say another word, you'll be home in time to tuck Ella and Noah up in bed.'

'And Angela phoned me last night,' I added for good

measure, 'to say she's decided to pack the stall up mid-afternoon and spend the rest of the day baking so you can hit the ground running tomorrow, rather than tearing about trying to catch up and wishing that today had never happened.'

'Oh bless her,' sniffed Jemma. 'Everyone has been so kind and helpful.'

'Because we all want you to take a break,' said Lizzie reaching for her friend's hand, 'even if it is just for one day.'

'But you work just as hard as I do,' pointed out Jemma, 'the café is your baby just as much as it is mine.'

'I know,' agreed Lizzie, 'but when I get home at the end of the day I don't have more babies to look after, do I? Unless of course you include Ben, but when I close the door, pour myself a glass of wine and pick up a magazine, I'm done. You on the other hand, have to start all over again!'

'I suppose you're right,' shrugged Jemma.

'I am right,' said Lizzie firmly.

'So come on, Bea,' I demanded, staring through the steamed-up window at the reluctantly lightening sky and far-reaching Fenland landscape and trying to get my bearings. 'Where *exactly* are you taking us?'

'All in good time,' she teased, turning back to face the front. 'You'll guess soon enough.'

The train the four of us boarded, after thanking Bea's dad for the early morning lift, was bound for Norwich, after the obligatory change at Ely of course, and we were all delighted with Bea's choice of destination. A day out in the fine city of Norwich, with its ornate cathedral and cavernous castle which had ruled the skyline for centuries, was always a treat and we couldn't wait to amble through the cobbled lanes and look for bargains amid the permanent market which dominated the city centre and made our market in Wynbridge look Lilliputian by comparison.

'Come on,' said Bea, marshalling us all together and leading us from the grand domed station and towards the taxi rank the second the train stopped moving, 'our first appointment is in half an hour.'

'She doesn't sound very relaxed,' Lizzie whispered in my ear as Bea gave our driver some very specific instructions.

'Oh she is,' I laughed, 'believe me. This is bliss to Bea. She loves playing Mother Goose!'

Forty minutes later we found ourselves cosily cosseted inside the city's premier independent beauty salon and settling down to enjoy one of their specially tailored manicure and pedicure packages. The tiny exclusive salon, situated in the very heart of the Lanes, had a much-envied reputation and was notoriously difficult to book into. Clearly Bea had friends in very high places and had somehow secured the perfect treat to prepare us for some post-pampering boutique browsing.

'Hello, ladies,' smiled Felicity, the salon owner, 'it's so lovely to see you again, Bea.'

'And you, my lovely,' Bea smiled back, 'thank you for squeezing us in. I know you wouldn't normally be open quite this early so we really appreciate it, don't we, girls?'

'Oh yes,' we all chorused.

I couldn't help but wonder why Felicity and her staff had gone to so much effort for us, but I didn't like to ask. I would save my interrogation for later.

'So how are you finding your treatments?' Felicity asked as she walked between us inspecting her technicians' work.

'Heaven,' sighed Jemma, wriggling her toes.

'Exquisite,' smiled Lizzie.

'Divine,' I added beatifically.

'Excellent,' smiled Felicity, 'we've found that this is the ideal combination for ladies who haven't got endless hours at their disposal. We call it the "in no time at all" beauty package and we still use the same products of course, but the treatments themselves are much speedier.'

'I thought it would be just the thing to start our day,' said Bea. 'As soon as I spotted it as a new addition on the website I knew it would be ideal for us.'

'Well, you weren't wrong,' said Jemma dreamily as she settled herself back in her chair, closed her eyes and succumbed to the ministrations of her manicurist. 'Can't we just stay here all day?' she pleaded.

'Absolutely not,' said Bea, sounding momentarily outraged, 'we're on a very tight schedule!'

'What did I tell you?' I said with a nod to Lizzie. 'She's going to be herding us together all day!'

After our hour of pampering we headed to a café to top up on coffee and croissants and prepare ourselves for some serious shopping.

My nails had never looked so pristine and I couldn't help admiring them. My hands were beautifully soft too and I felt rather guilty that I had been neglecting them and leaving them to face the rigours of the Wynbridge winter wind unprotected.

'Can you imagine,' I said, spreading an unnecessary spoonful of jam on to my already calorific croissant, 'how wonderful it would be if Felicity really did open a branch of her salon in Wynbridge?'

'I know,' said Bea, her eyes shining at the thought.

Felicity had mentioned she was planning to expand her business in the next couple of years and that our hometown was actually on her preliminary list of places to consider. I had to admit I was somewhat surprised that she had even entertained it but she assured me that her business analyst had insisted that the town would soon be on the up again.

'My hands always have to look good for work,' Bea continued, 'and it costs a fortune in time and travelling to have my nails done in Peterborough every few weeks. Having a specialist salon in the town would save me a fortune and of course, Felicity is familiar with Wynbridge so I don't think she would have mentioned the potential new set-up on a whim.'

'I didn't realise she was so familiar with the town?' I remarked, only just remembering that I had planned to ask how she and Bea knew one another. 'How come?'

'Oh well,' said Bea, 'I can't go into specific details, client confidentiality and all that, but she came to us for some treatment a while back and rather liked our little outpost in the Fens. We've kept in touch ever since.'

So that explained how Felicity had discovered Wynbridge. I have to admit I sometimes forgot just how popular and successful Bea's family business was. I couldn't help noticing that Lizzie had been looking doubtfully at my best friend ever since she mentioned the possibility of saving money if Felicity opened a local salon.

'What?' frowned Bea, having also noticed her suspicious expression.

'I'm not sure you'd save any money,' Lizzie smiled wryly as she flicked through the glossy brochure she had picked up as she left, 'these facials look amazing. I bet you'd end up spending a fortune, Bea! You'd never be out of the place.'

'I like to look my best,' said Bea, sounding slightly nettled, 'there's no harm in that.'

'Of course there isn't,' I soothed, 'and come on, ladies, look at the man she's bagged herself as a result! A hundred girls had their eyes firmly fixed on Fireman Sam, but our Bea captured his heart.'

'Yes,' agreed Jemma, biting her lip. 'And he certainly is hot stuff.'

'Definitely calendar material,' added Lizzie, 'I'd even go so far as to stick a kitten up a tree just to see him rescue it!'

We all burst out laughing as Lizzie turned bright red and began crumbling the remains of her croissant on her plate.

'And the pair of you married women!' I admonished. 'I'm seriously shocked!'

'I'm not married,' Lizzie piped up, 'so surely I'm allowed to have a little look around, aren't I?'

'I think I've got more cause than you,' said Jemma, 'don't forget, I'm tethered for life!'

'And loving it,' I reminded her.

'True!' she beamed.

Bea, I noticed, had gone very quiet.

'You do know we're only messing about, don't you?' said Lizzie, also picking up on our friend's sudden silence.

'Oh I know,' said Bea, looking alarmingly tearful, 'I'm a very lucky girl. Now come on, drink up. We have shops to peruse before lunch and a bit of culture lined up for this afternoon.'

Rather than shop for Christmas presents, we had all decided during the train journey that we would only buy things for ourselves and breaking out her credit cards soon put the spring back in Bea's step. The cost of what we chose was irrelevant, but it had to be something to treasure, a little trinket that would become a reminder of our indulgent day.

Keen not to dip too far into my savings, I didn't spend as much as the other three, but I found exactly what I was hoping for, courtesy of the Lisa Angel shop which was dressed to look like a veritable winter wonderland. The reflective surfaces shone with colour and light and I noticed Jemma quickly bagged herself some of the copper-coloured cookie cutter fairy lights for the café. I found my heart's desire nestled among the trays and displays of delicate necklaces and pretty pendants.

I picked out a rose gold chain, just the right length, which had a tiny postcard pendant attached. The colour would look even better when I had worked on my tan a little and I knew it would be the perfect travel companion and a subtle reminder to keep in touch with everyone back home.

A plethora of shops explored and our purchases complete, we headed to The Forum for yet more eats.

'I know its only pizza,' said Bea as we scanned the menu, 'but in my opinion there's nowhere else in Norwich to rival that view.'

She was right, of course. The colourful striped canopies of the market stalls, and the solid presence of the castle stamped firmly on the skyline ensured we spent as much time gazing at the panorama and admiring the landscape as we did chatting and eating. Eventually however, and somewhat predictably, our talk turned back to the men in our lives.

'You and Ben have been together a while now, Lizzie, haven't you?' Bea began.

'Years,' confirmed Lizzie with a nod. 'In fact, I'm fast reaching the point when I can't remember life without him.'

I knew exactly where Bea was trying to steer the conversation, but to my eyes she looked a little unsure of herself so, for better or worse, I decided to help her out.

'Any sound of wedding bells on the horizon?' I asked on her behalf.

It was Jemma who shook her head and sighed.

'Oh yes,' she said sadly, 'they're chiming away, aren't they, Lizzie, but always a little too far over the horizon for my liking!'

'Oh please,' sighed Lizzie, rolling her eyes, 'not this again.'

'Have I put my foot in it?' I winced, inwardly cursing Bea and her contagious one-track mind.

'No,' said Lizzie, taking a long sip of wine, 'not really.'

'Ben keeps asking her,' cut in Jemma without a care for whether or not her best friend was happy for us to be privy to such personal information, 'but she won't commit.'

'Thanks for that, Jem,' said Lizzie.

'Why ever not?' gasped Bea, with as little tact and diplomacy as Jemma.

'Because I just don't need it,' answered Lizzie with a shrug,

'I couldn't possibly be more in love or more committed to the relationship. A ring and a piece of paper certainly won't change how I feel, so why go to all the bother and expense?'

'Well,' I said, 'I'm shocked.'

'Why?' laughed Lizzie.

'Because, I always imagined you and Ben would have the perfect wedding. Something the rest of the world would aspire to. Something simple but unique, a bit quirky and eccentric, you know?'

'Exactly,' cut in Jemma crossly. 'This is one wedding I've been looking forward to helping plan for years, but she just won't have it!'

'It's typical, isn't it?' said Bea, shaking her head and looking wistfully out at the view. 'All I want is a proposal and I haven't had one, and all Lizzie wants is to keep things as they are and yet Ben trails about behind her on bended knee!'

'Yes,' sighed Lizzie, with a little smile. 'It is rather ironic, but cheer up, Bea, I'm sure there's plenty of time for us to both get our happy ever after.'

'You probably think I'm shallow, wanting the bother and expense of a wedding as you put it,' sniffed Bea, 'but it's what I've always dreamt of.'

'Not at all,' said Lizzie, reaching for her hand, 'everyone's different. The world would be a boring place if we all wanted the same thing, wouldn't it?'

'And what about you, Ruby?' asked Jemma, focusing

everyone's attention on me. 'Do you think there's any chance that you and Steve will find your way back to one another?'

'God, no,' I said with a little shudder, 'absolutely not and I'm not even going to bore you with the ins and outs as to why. The only relationship I want right now,' I said firmly, raising my glass and encouraging the girls to do the same, 'is with a one-way plane ticket out of Wynbridge.'

Bea didn't look as if she believed a single word but for once, thankfully, decided not to contradict me.

Our afternoon of culture, after a leisurely look around the market, where Jemma picked up an excellent idea for Christmas baking kits we could sell on the stall, involved a trip to the Castle Museum's special exhibition. I was delighted that the old mechanical knight, a firm favourite with school trips, was still in situ outside the gift shop. After a quick scrabble for coins, we were able to see him and his little doggy companion spring into life before we headed back to the station to catch the train back to Wynbridge.

'I can't believe we crammed so much into one day,' laughed Lizzie as the train bore us back towards the Fens.

'It feels like we've been away far longer,' agreed Jemma. 'Thank you, Bea, this is just what I needed. I feel more than ready to face the Christmas chaos now.'

Bea didn't say anything and when we all turned to look at her we found her fast asleep, no doubt dreaming of her perfect proposal and dream wedding.

Chapter 19

Two mornings later and with our day trip already feeling more like light years away than mere days, Jemma presented me with a batch of bespoke Kilner jars, not dissimilar to those we had seen for sale on Norwich market.

'What do you reckon?' she asked. 'I think they'll sell like hot cakes, especially ahead of the bake sale on Saturday, but for some reason Lizzie isn't quite so sure.'

'Oh, come on,' I said, holding one of the jars up to the light to admire the cleverly layered contents, 'these are gorgeous. Of course they'll sell.'

Every jar contained the correct measure of dry ingredients to make a batch of Christmas cookies, gingerbread men or Jemma's trademark seasonal biscuits. Lizzie had added her own flourish by attaching pixie-sized cookie cutters tied on with a festive ribbon decorated with presents, snowflakes or plain red gingham. Each jar also came with its own holly-shaped instruction label so baking success was pretty much guaranteed!

'With the bake sale just days away I can't imagine we'll have any left by Friday,' I told her.

'Well, I hope you're right,' said Jemma, 'I thought we were on to a winner, but Lizzie has made me doubt the idea. Anyway, I've kept a couple back in the café for customers to see and Tom has taken some to work and school, so hopefully word will soon get round and we won't have too many left over.'

'Oh, what have you got there?' asked Jude, rushing over to have a look. 'I thought I spied some new stock.'

Jemma explained what was inside the pretty jars and Jude's face lit up.

'Can you put aside one of each for me, please?' she asked.

'One of each!' laughed Jemma, quickly passing me three to stash under the stall.

'Absolutely,' confirmed Jude. 'I'm pants in the kitchen, but Simon's mother is a baking queen. If I can pull these off she might actually think I'm not starving her son after all!'

Jemma and I giggled as Jude walked back over to her stall.

'Actually,' she called over her shoulder, 'can you save another three?'

'What, six in total?' I called after her.

'Yes,' she nodded, 'three for me and three to give away. They're so pretty, they'll make perfect presents.'

'What did I tell you?' I said, turning back to Jemma. 'They're a hit already!'

Sales of everything began to pick up that week and the Kilner jars were an unmitigated success. In fact, as I looked around the market I could see that everyone was busier. Hanging up and opening a few doors on the advent calendars had clearly had quite an impact and galvanised the population of Wynbridge, along with the rest of the world it seemed, into a present buying and gift wrapping frenzy.

I also couldn't help but notice that along with the increased footfall through the market, lots of the stallholders were now offering more festive items and Bob and Shirley's 'presents for pets' range was proving hugely popular. I hoped the sea change was, at least in part, down to the suggestions I had made when I first arrived in town.

'You all set, then?' asked Lizzie, as she joined me early on Saturday morning ahead of the tree auction and bake sale.

'I think so,' I told her, handing over the money belt. 'I hope you've got your thermals on under that coat.'

'Oh I have,' she said, 'and Angela's going to swap places with me at ten so I'll have a chance to thaw out when I'm crafting with the kids.'

'And where's Ben?' I asked, 'I thought he was going to help you out.'

'Um,' she frowned, 'he was, but he's come over all lumberjack at the sight of all the trees and has decided to help Tom with the fetching and carrying instead.'

Jemma had decided earlier in the week that as she was going to be baking in the town hall and Lizzie would be running the crafting sessions for the children, it would be better all-round to close the café again. It was an incredibly generous gesture, especially given how busy the town was going to be, but she was thrilled to be able to 'give something back' to the townsfolk who had supported her and Lizzie ever since the Cherry Tree opened its doors.

'So,' I said, 'let me get this straight. 'The café's closed, you and Angela are juggling the stall between you, Jemma's baking and Tom and Ben are helping out with the tree auction. Is that right?'

'Yes,' Lizzie nodded. 'And Noah and Ella are with my mum and dad. They're playing the role of token grandchildren as I have yet to provide them with any of their own.'

'Oh,' I said, 'I see.'

'Yep,' she smiled grimly, 'bring on the guilt!'

Perhaps I wasn't the only daughter in town who had family issues after all, and talking of which . . .

'I think you're wanted at the town hall,' said Dad, 'some of the WI ladies would like a word before they open the doors.'

I had spotted him a little earlier, skulking about and having a discreet look at everything. With his collar turned up and his hat pulled down it was obvious that he was going out of his way to make sure he wasn't noticed.

'OK,' I said, 'thanks.'

Our brief conversations had been chillier than the weather since he had tried to convince me to leave the market and I couldn't imagine the situation was likely to thaw before I left town now.

'I saw some of these on the tables in the hall just now,' he said, picking up one of the Kilner jars and examining the contents. 'They're a rather good idea, aren't they? And these are lovely too,' he added, pointing at Lizzie's collection of Christmas stockings.

I stood rigid with shock rather than the cold and unable to form a coherent response.

'Thank you, Mr Smith,' said Lizzie, 'I made those myself.'

'Wonderful,' Dad nodded.

He took a step back and looked about him again, taking in the predominantly testosterone-fuelled group striding about amongst the diverse collection of trees that had been delivered for sale and then at the much-enhanced market and light display.

'This is how I remember it,' he said wistfully. 'Granted the stalls might be a bit different, but when I was a boy the town was always as busy as this, even on a week day.'

'Well this is what we've been working towards, Dad,' I said, finally finding my voice, 'this is what we were hoping to do for the traders and the town in time for Christmas.'

'You'd better get to the hall,' he said croakily, 'time's pushing on.'

I didn't have time to dissect his comments and reaction, but even without pulling it all apart I knew something was seriously wrong. When we had spoken about the market at home he had been almost scathing, but faced with our efforts and the reality of it all there was a definite warmth and fondness for all he saw and it just didn't add up.

I rushed over to the town hall and the scene that met my eyes as I crossed the threshold was breathtakingly beautiful and enough to make me forget all about Dad's moment of nostalgia. Ordinarily the building was reserved for monthly auctions and the odd civic reception, but today it was full of noise and colour and excitement. Marie had kindly supplied huge displays of festive foliage and hung tendrils of ivy from the snowy cloth-covered tables that were gradually filling up with plates full of festive bakes and treats.

There were iced and decorated cakes in abundance, gingerbread houses with stained-glass sweetie windows and, my favourite of all, a table at the end of the hall which had been set aside for the playgroup and schools contributions. This particular table was packed and I knew that some poor soul was going to be responsible for judging the wonky-eyed Santas and clumsily decorated trees. I didn't envy whoever was going to be given that particular task at all.

Lizzie's crafting corner was filled with Christmas-themed

templates, brightly coloured card, glitter in every available colour and pots and pots of sequins, snowflakes and googly eyes. All in all, the scene looked set for a truly wonderful day and I was relieved that my afternoon on Bea's sofa watching cheesy films had turned out to be worthwhile after all.

'Miss Smith!' called one of the WI ladies from the doorway of the kitchen. 'Could we just have a quick word?'

'Of course,' I said, joining her, 'but please call me Ruby.'

The kitchen was packed full of women from the WI and had I not seen the scene with my own eyes I would have considered any description of it as extremely exaggerated, but it wasn't and I couldn't help but smile as I imagined this sort of thing being played out in town and village halls up and down the country.

'We just wanted to say,' said the woman who had called me over, 'that we all think this is going to be a great day for the town.'

'Well I hope so,' I said, the colour of my face turning from flushed to seriously scarlet.

'And that we're very grateful that you came up with the idea,' piped up someone else.

'Well,' I said, staring at my shoes.

'We all know that it was you who got Paul Thompson to turn the lights on,' said another, 'and that's made all the difference to the town.'

'Well everyone's pulled together,' I said, hating every second of their praise and just wanting to melt into the background. 'But thank you for your kind words,' I added as they each bustled back to their tasks. 'I really appreciate it.'

'How about that then?' said Mum with a smile as she pulled on her apron and set about gathering ingredients for the morning session. 'You are honoured if the WI ladies have taken note of your efforts!'

'Here,' said Jemma, passing me my Cherry Tree apron and bringing me back down to earth with a bump, 'can you come and give us a hand? We've had about thirty families sign up to bake altogether so there's a fair bit to get ready.'

'As many families as that,' I gasped. 'Wow, I had no idea!'

'I know,' she grinned, 'but that means it's going to be heaving. The WI and church ladies are going to be serving teas and coffees from the urns in the corner of the hall for health and safety reasons as much as anything else, and that will free up all this space for us to bake in.'

'But it's still going to be an awful squeeze,' I said looking around and trying to imagine thirty families crammed into the kitchen.

'They aren't all going to be baking at once!' Mum laughed. 'We've split them into smaller groups, given everyone a timed slot and allowed a few minutes either side for washing up.'

'And the biscuit and fairy cake decorating will be happening out in the hall,' Jemma said pointedly, 'when they've cooled down a little, of course.'

'Of course,' I nodded, feeling foolish for imagining that

she would be anything other than meticulously organised. She even had regimented rows of name badges and matching Post-its so everyone would know who had baked what.

'Is this what you imagined?' she asked. 'When you came up with the idea, is this how you imagined it would happen?'

'No,' I said truthfully, 'not really. I just thought we would bake with a few children, the locals would contribute cakes and there would be a sale, much like what's happening in the square with the trees. This is way and above what I hoped for.'

'Well that's good,' she smiled. 'There's nothing so satisfying as when a plan comes together!'

She had of course spoken about ten seconds too soon. Just as I looked up and spotted Steve hovering awkwardly in the doorway there was an almighty crash and a collective cry of what sounded like about a thousand women's voices.

'I told you that shelf wasn't strong enough!' shouted one.

'We've lost the lot!' cried another.

'What are we going to do now?' contributed the majority.

The upshot of the situation was that someone had filled a tiny table with what looked like every egg that had been laid in the land during the last week and above it, on a less than sturdy shelf, were balanced the bags of caster sugar and flour. When the shelf inevitably collapsed the bags landed on top of the eggs, smashing practically every one and the entire scene was now covered with clouds of the snowy contents which billowed far and wide.

'Oh no,' groaned Jemma, 'this is a disaster. We've only got an hour until the first bakers arrive.'

'It'll be fine,' said Steve, rushing in, 'honestly, we'll sort it. Ruby, you come with me. We'll go and buy more supplies while you lot scrape up the mess and dry the floor.'

Abandoning my apron as I went, I begrudgingly followed Steve out of the town hall and back to the market.

'Let's try John the butcher first,' he called over his shoulder as he set off at a pace, 'he always has trays of eggs.'

'Right,' I said sulkily, trailing behind in his wake.

'Look,' he said, suddenly stopping dead and spinning around so quickly that I almost walked straight into him, 'I know you hate me and I dare say you've got every right to, but this is a genuine crisis, yes?'

'Yes,' I agreed, looking everywhere but up at him.

'And between us we can sort it, yes?'

'Oh all right, yes,' I said, trying to forcibly turn him back round, 'point taken, now can we please just get on?'

For the next sixty minutes we raced between the market, the shops and the town hall, depositing supplies and feeling ever more grateful that we had been anywhere other than on our hands and knees in the kitchen trying to clear up the sticky mess that didn't seem to want to shift at all.

As the first bakers arrived and with the smell of disinfectant hanging in the air and the floor still drying, we offloaded the last few boxes and bags and threw ourselves down at a table to catch our breath.

'I only came over to see if everything was good to go,' panted Steve, 'and that you'd all got everything you needed.'

'Well,' I puffed, 'to be fair, when you arrived, we did have.'

'True,' he smiled, 'at least the rugby coach can't moan that I've missed out on training today,' he added. 'He was already fed up I'm missing the match.'

'Why aren't you playing?' I asked.

'Because of the auction,' he explained, 'I always spend the day helping out shifting the trees.'

'Of course,' I said, 'I remember.'

I didn't particularly want to, given our last bitter exchange in the pub and the realisation that he wasn't part of my life any more, but I couldn't help thinking what a genuinely good bloke Steve was. He was always on hand to help out, and he loved Wynbridge just as much as he loved his family. It was guys like Steve who were the heart of the town, families like his who were the lifeblood and heartbeat of the place. Had he been anyone else's son I was sure my father would have considered him ideal son-in-law potential and welcomed him with open arms. But then of course, a loyal son-in-law wouldn't go around accusing his in-laws of fraud, conspiracy and extortion, I reminded myself, quickly hardening my heart before it had a chance to be touched again.

'I'd better get on,' I said, standing back up. 'I'll see you later.'

There were moments during that day when I wished I was back outside manning the stall rather than having to cope with the searing heat the ovens emitted as a result of being turned on all day. The money raised in the sale along with the smiles on the families' faces and the delightfully wonky biscuit decorations and slightly insane frosted Santa cupcakes made up for it, though.

'You should see the size of the tree Daddy's got tied to the car roof,' Ella confided as she helped me check that every plate had been given a rosette. Whoever had judged had cleverly awarded 'special mentions' to everyone who hadn't been placed first, second or third and therefore avoided upset and heartbreak. 'It's massive.'

'Is it?'

'Huge,' she grinned. 'Mummy's going to go nuts when she sees it and there's no chance of getting the fairy on the top.'

'She's right,' said Lizzie's mum, who was pushing Noah around in his pushchair in the hope that he would fall asleep, 'it's vast.'

I couldn't help but giggle.

'What is it with men and Christmas?' she mused. 'In my experience when it comes to trees they always go over the top.'

'Perhaps it's the hunter-gatherer in them,' I suggested.

'Either that or some kind of phallic representation,' she laughed.

'What does phallic mean?' asked Ella.

'Never you mind,' she said, 'now come along with me and we'll see if Mummy and Daddy will let you stay at our house for the night.'

'Yes,' said Ella, thrusting the last of the rosettes back into my hands. 'See you later, Ruby!'

When the hall was eventually tidied, the plates of cakes and biscuits collected and the money counted, I made my way back to the square to discover that the tree sale had been equally as successful and the market had been heaving. The only trees left were a straggly little collection of about half a dozen that were destined for the chipper, or would have been had Gwen not come to their rescue and insisted on buying the lot.

'I'll pay to have them delivered, of course,' she said, happily inspecting her puny purchases, 'I can't bear the thought of them not seeing out their true destiny.'

'I'll drop them round tomorrow,' offered Chris, 'no charge. I can bring them in the van.'

Here was another Dempster man who knew the true meaning of community spirit. It was no secret where Steve got his willingness to pitch in and his desire to help out from.

'Oh thank you, dear man,' said Gwen. 'Now, who fancies a trip to the pub to round off the day?'

Chapter 20

It was beginning to feel as if an event or celebration of any kind in Wynbridge simply wasn't complete unless it ended with a trip to The Mermaid, but I wasn't complaining. I might have been almost asleep on my feet, but just the thought of a restorative glass of Skylark Scrumpy or three was enough to revive my flagging senses.

As I hung up my coat and let the smoky warmth from the fire wrap around me I began to wonder how I was going to cope on my travels without the cosy embrace of the pub and its regenerating brew. Somehow a beachside cocktail at sunset didn't seem to have quite the same appeal, but at that very moment someone opened the door and let in a sharp blast of bitterly cold air and I realised I was still prepared to give it a shot nonetheless.

'Half a pint of cider please, Jim,' I smiled when I had finally pushed my way through to the bar.

'I understand congratulations are in order,' he boomed as he reached for a glass, 'Evelyn tells me the bake sale was a huge success.'

'As was the tree auction,' I nodded, 'I think we might have come up with a winning combination there. I hope whoever finds themselves responsible for the town festivities sees fit to repeat the whole thing again next year.'

'As do I,' said Steve, suddenly appearing at my side, 'although perhaps the baking could happen without breaking quite so many eggs!'

'Oh, I almost forgot,' I tutted, the sudden remembrance taking the sting out of having to talk to him again, 'you paid for all those extra ingredients out of your own pocket! Make sure you put in a bill for them, won't you?'

'Absolutely not,' he insisted, 'let's just call it my contribution to Christmas.'

'Well, that's very generous of you,' I told him, thinking the gesture deserved some acknowledgement, 'what with you practically single-handedly funding the bake sale and your mum and dad supplying the trees and lights, and not forgetting the beautiful foliage arrangements today, I think we should have some signs up declaring that this Christmas has been sponsored by Dempsters of Wynbridge.'

'Oh, don't even joke about it,' said Steve rolling his eyes, 'Dad would love that! Crikey, we'd never hear the last of it! Come on,' he laughed, giving me a nudge and making it increasingly difficult to stay cross with him, 'let me buy you a drink, although given today's unexpected expenditure I can't run to champagne, I'm afraid.'

I might have been just about capable of engaging in a civil conversation with him, but this was taking things too far. There was no way I was going to let him buy me another drink.

'No,' I said, 'it's kind of you to offer but I'll pass, if it's all the same to you.'

'Oh well,' he shrugged, 'if you insist. I'll just have a pint of bitter then please, Jim.'

It was only as Jim finished filling my cider glass that I remembered I hadn't got my bag with me, or my purse. That morning I'd left home with just my phone and car keys tucked in my jeans pocket so I didn't have to spend the day wondering where I'd put things.

'You aren't serious,' laughed Steve as he watched me go through the motions of patting my pockets and making a fine show of delving up my sleeves for loose change. 'Here, Jim,' he said, handing over a crisp ten-pound note.

'No,' I said, shaking my head, 'it's fine. I'll sort it.'

'How?'

He sounded annoyingly amused and I felt increasingly cornered.

'I'll pay you back,' I told him, biting my lip and wishing the floor would open up and swallow me whole.

'I know you will,' he said, then added with a mischievous twinkle, 'Oh, look what Evelyn's just hung above the door.'

It was the biggest bunch of mistletoe I'd ever seen.

With practically the entire town crammed inside the pub I had rather hoped staying out of Steve's way would be easy, but it didn't seem to matter where I went or who I spoke to, somehow he managed to nudge his way into the conversation or at the very least into my eye line.

I don't know what on earth had made him think that I was fair game or that I'd forgotten about his unsavoury accusation from a few days before, but the way he puckered up when I so much as glanced in his direction left me in no doubt that he wasn't quite as prepared to be as 'over us' as I was. By ten o'clock I was ready to head home, but I knew I wouldn't make it out of the door without being kissed and Bea was being no help at all.

'Just do it,' she kept hissing in my ear, 'at least if you kiss him you'll know for certain whether you still have feelings for him or not.'

'I already know,' I hissed back venomously, wishing I'd told her the whole story.

'Well there's no harm in testing the theory,' she winked.

'You aren't thinking of leaving are you?' said Steve, sidling up as Bea melted away.

'No,' I said, 'not yet, but my decision to stay has nothing

to do with the mistletoe and besides I think you'd have more success making out with Mia under it than me, don't you? I thought you might have changed your mind about hooking up with her as nothing's going to happen between us.'

'Absolutely not,' he said crossly. 'I've already told you I'm not interested in Mia and I've no plans to change my mind.'

'Anyway, where is she?' I said, standing on tiptoe and scanning the crowd. Her glossy head was nowhere to be seen.

'She's not been around for a few days now,' Steve shrugged.

'Why not?'

'Because I took your advice and told her the truth.'

I didn't know whether to believe him or not, but thinking back, I hadn't clapped eyes on her fine form for quite some time.

'I told her everything,' he said, 'just like you said I should and she decided to move on to pastures new.'

I wasn't sure if this new piece of information made me feel better or worse. Surely if Steve really had given Mia the heave-ho that was because he couldn't put his feelings for me to one side and I didn't want to have to deal with that, especially after everything else that had happened, and not forgetting that I didn't love him any more, of course.

'Well good for her,' I said, tossing my hair over my shoulder, 'I can't say I blame her. I'd never let a man mess me about like that.'

Steve looked at me and shook his head.

'What?'

'Well, aren't you forgetting something?'

'What?' I said again.

'You're the reason why I ended up treating her like that.'

'Oh thanks,' I said, 'how convenient for you to be able to pass the blame on to me.'

I can't deny I felt a slight flicker as we sparred and it only began to burn a little brighter when our skin touched.

'Oh come on, Ruby,' he said, making a grab for my hand, 'are you going to let me kiss you or not?'

'Not,' I swallowed, snatching my hand away as it began to tingle and before he had a chance to pull me towards the gargantuan bunch of mistletoe, 'of course not. I still can't stop thinking about what you said about Dad taking bribes and the market being up for sale. In fact,' I added, forcing myself to call time on our little frisson, 'I still can't believe it is up for sale or that you could have such a low opinion of a man, irrespective of who he is, who has lived his entire life in the town and has made his career out of trying to improve it.'

'But have you asked him about it?' Steve frowned.

'Oh don't be so ridiculous!' I laughed derisively, 'of course I haven't.'

I had been tempted, of course, but how could I possibly begin that conversation without causing the biggest family rift ever? I'd even thought about stealing into the office at home and looking through Dad's private papers, but every time I came close I just ended up resenting Steve a little bit more for even putting such an underhand thought into my head.

'Have you talked to anyone about it?' Steve demanded.

I really couldn't see the point in dragging this absurd conversation on any longer. We were just going round in circles.

'Hey, Ruby,' called Jake, as he and Amber pushed their way through the crowd towards me. 'Congratulations on the bake sale!'

'From what I can gather,' added Amber, 'the auction made a small fortune. I put in two Christmas cakes and they made a packet. Rumour has it,' she said proudly, 'one of them is destined for the Wynthorpe Hall dining table, although I'm not sure which one.'

'Well, thank you for contributing,' I said, 'it was very short notice for actual Christmas cakes and puddings.'

'It was,' she nodded, 'but some friends and I had recently got together for a marathon baking session and I had a couple left over.'

'That sounds like fun.'

'It was great,' she said, then added in a whisper, 'I've been feeling a bit isolated since Honey was born but getting everyone together and eating cake was the perfect tonic.'

I thought about the farm's location and guessed that life there could be a little on the quiet side.

'It's amazing how often cake really is the answer, isn't it?' I smiled.

'You have no idea,' she laughed. 'We're already planning to do it again in the spring. There are quite a few mums living out in the Fens and it can be very lonely.'

'I can imagine,' I nodded, 'some of those drove roads seem to go on forever and you only find two or three houses dotted along them. To be honest, I can't say I've ever given much thought as to who actually lives in them.'

'Well now you know,' smiled Amber, 'we'll have to come up with a name for ourselves, won't we?'

'Fenland Foodies or something,' I suggested.

'Oh yes,' said Jake, 'and talking of foodies, I understand that you and Paul are thinking of jetting off to India together in the New Year!'

'What?'

'Excuse me,' said Steve, pointing towards the bar, 'I need to grab Mum before she leaves.'

'See you later, mate,' said Jake, 'now come on, Ruby, spill the beans!'

I explained to him and Amber about the day Paul left town and how he had recognised the beach in the photograph I had pinned up on the stall.

'But we have absolutely no plans to travel together!' I insisted. 'In fact, we haven't even been in touch since he left. I said I'd contact him before I fly out and see if he can arrange some work for me while I'm there, but that's all there is to it.'

'God, he's such an old flirt,' laughed Amber, 'you'd think

after all these scandals he would have learnt his lesson, wouldn't you?'

'I wouldn't be surprised,' joined in Jake, 'if you find yourself turning down his bed when you get there, Ruby. He'll probably fly out to surprise you!'

'Of course he won't,' I gasped. 'Crikey, I don't know if I want to phone him at all now.'

'No, you must,' said Amber seriously, 'he's a good bloke at heart and his contacts are second to none. Knowing him could put a totally different complexion on your travels.'

'Well, if you're sure.'

'I am,' she said, 'absolutely. Do not even book your flight without having spoken to him first.'

'All right,' I told her, 'but if I find myself being seduced in a foreign climate, I'm holding you responsible.'

'Fair enough,' she shrugged, 'but given all the things I've heard about him over the years I don't think you'll be complaining!'

'Right,' said Jake, taking her by the arm, 'that's quite enough of that talk, thank you very much. Come on, I need another drink.'

'And I need to go,' I said, looking furtively about me to try and pinpoint Steve before I made a dash for the door.

'You sure?' asked Amber.

'Yes,' I said, 'I have a completely lazy day planned for tomorrow and I'd hate to sleep through it!'

Stealthily I crossed the bar, lifted the latch on the door, felt a bitter blast of freezing air and was just about to cross the threshold, when another hand appeared from nowhere covering mine and Steve pulled me around and into a close embrace.

'What on earth do you think you're doing?' I spluttered, trying to pull away as my traitorous body melted and settled into the familiar contours of his.

'You didn't really think I was going to let you get away that easily,' he whispered, smiling down at me. 'Did you?'

'This is sexual harassment. I never had any intention of paying you for that drink in kind,' I seethed, but annoyingly loving the electricity flowing between us. 'Now let me go,' I insisted, trying to wriggle free before he realised, 'or I'll have to shout for help!'

I opened my mouth to protest but found my lips covered with his, his arms wrapped around my back and a thousand butterflies and fireworks fighting for the upper hand in my stomach. It felt so right, so familiar and as I felt his tongue dip into my mouth to meet mine I realised that I hadn't been kissed like that since I left Wynbridge four years before. No one in the world could make me feel like he could and I knew, had we been anywhere other than a packed pub, I would have been ripping the shirt off his back and quenching my desire without a second thought.

'This is ridiculous,' I said, my hands pummelling his chest as I tried to push him away. 'What are you doing? Let me go!'

He pulled away slightly and loosened his grip, but I didn't move.

'Do you really want me to?' he said seriously.

His pupils were enormous and the way he licked his full, soft lips made my insides melt.

'Yes,' I squeaked, 'yes please.'

He took a step away and I poured every ounce of strength I had left into forcing my knees not to buckle.

'Sorry,' he said. 'I just thought a kiss might help you remember how good we were together and to be honest,' he added pointing to the mistletoe, 'I've been looking for an excuse to take you in my arms ever since the very first moment I caught sight of you again.'

'Well, you had no right,' I said, retrieving my coat from the row of pegs behind the door and wishing he'd never accused Dad of anything more damning than being a pain in the backside. 'And I don't remember anything about how good we were together, so you've got it all wrong, haven't you?'

'I don't think so,' he said huskily.

I looked at him for a second and shook my head. 'I just don't understand you,' I said.

He shoved his hands deep in his pockets and didn't reply.

'Just a few days ago you were telling me that getting back together wasn't an option because of all the complications with the market. You broke my heart when you said those things about my dad . . .'

'I'm sorry,' he said, 'but I just can't help it. Everything I said about the market is true and I do still have my doubts about your dad, but I can't deny my heart. I can't pretend my insides don't fall through the floor whenever I see you, Ruby.'

I couldn't believe what I was hearing.

'Well you're just going to have to try,' I said, 'otherwise we're both going to end up in big trouble, aren't we?'

I didn't wait around to hear his answer. I knew there was simply no way he wouldn't have noticed how my body had behaved in his arms and I couldn't bear to see that knowing look in his eyes.

'I'm sorry, Ruby Sue!' he shouted after me as I finally made my escape and headed for home.

Chapter 21

'You all right, my love?' asked Mum as she peeped around the bedroom door. 'I didn't hear you come in last night, but you did say to wake you if you slept after nine and it's now quarter past.'

'I'm fine,' I yawned, feeling anything but.

Truth be told, I felt as if I'd only climbed into my bed a few minutes before.

'Do you want me to open your curtains?' she offered, stepping into the room.

'No,' I said, sitting up far too quickly and making my head spin. 'I'll do them. I'll be down in a minute.'

'All right,' she said. 'Dad's got all the boxes down so we can make a start whenever you like.'

'Can't wait,' I smiled.

I knew she was looking forward to putting the Christmas decorations up together and I couldn't deny that the smell of the tree they had picked out at the auction was enough to send my excitement soaring to the same level as Ella's, even if I was feeling a little worse for wear. It had been years since I had decorated the house and I was looking forward to doing it every inch as much as Mum was.

'I thought I might put the slow cooker on and make a stew for lunch,' she added, 'with herby dumplings.'

'Perfect,' I sighed.

She slipped back out, quietly closing the door behind her and I thanked my lucky stars that she hadn't noticed the floor behind the door.

Steve and his stupid, unwanted, electrifying, awe-inspiring kiss had set my pulse racing and my brain whirring and I'd spent far too much of the night looking through the memory box I'd kept hidden and which was crammed full of cringe-worthy photographs and receipts, Valentine's cards and diaries. The last thing I had put inside before I left for university was the order of service booklet from his brother's funeral.

Sean's untimely death up at Hecate's Rest had stopped more hearts beating than his own and although I knew it was no one's fault I couldn't help wishing I could have just had a glimpse of how things might have been had his bike made it around that corner.

'Sorry,' I said, looking at the photograph of him smiling back at me as I packed everything away again, 'I know it's selfish of me to blame you, but sometimes I just can't help it because I know you would have loved working alongside your mum and dad and I know your brother would have loved life at university.'

I had just finished hiding the box at the back of the wardrobe when Mum called up the stairs.

'I'm coming,' I shouted back. 'Just give me two minutes.'

After the speediest shower ever and with the smell of Mum's delicious steak and red wine stew in the slow cooker beginning to mingle with the pine from the tree, we settled down to make a start on the decorations.

'Do you mind the music?' Mum asked.

'Of course not,' I told her, reaching for the remote and turning the volume up a little.

'We can change it if you like,' she frowned.

'Decorating the house without the sound of your *Carols from King's* CD in the background would be like your roast dinner without the gravy,' I insisted, 'it would just be wrong, all wrong.'

Mum looked suitably soothed as Dad came through from the kitchen with a tray loaded with sherry and mince pies.

'I know we aren't quite over the yardarm,' he smiled, 'but you can't do the decorations without the traditional accompaniments.'

'It's a great tree this year, Dad,' I said as I helped him find a place for the tray amongst the boxes.

'Yes,' he agreed, 'I'm rather pleased with it. I think they were all better quality this year and from what I can gather they all sold.'

'They did,' I confirmed. 'Gwen took the last few stragglers.'

'Oh, now there's a surprise,' laughed Mum, 'and I dare say Chris Dempster offered to deliver them free of charge.'

'He did, actually,' I said, wondering how she knew and whether she had just slipped up and revealed a little more about her association with the family than she had intended.

'Happens every year,' she tutted, with a meaningful look in my direction, 'you take a trip along Gwen's road between tomorrow and the New Year and you'll find those trees lined up in her garden and bedecked in a collection of interior decorations she has kept outside for years.'

'She is certainly one of life's eccentrics, isn't she?' I laughed, shaking my head.

'She is that,' agreed Dad, as he passed around the glasses, 'but you won't find a more community-minded resident in this town.'

It was on the tip of my tongue to suggest that the Dempster clan could probably give her a run for her money but decided to keep the thought to myself.

'And talking of community spirit,' I ventured, 'I was pleased that you thought the town was looking good yesterday.'

I thought it best not to specifically mention the stall. Not when the morning was going so well.

'It all looked wonderful,' he conceded. 'You and Tom certainly seem to have everything under control.'

'Not just us,' I reminded him, 'everyone at the market is making a huge effort in the run up to Christmas and it seems to be working. You said yourself that the town looked like it did when you were a boy yesterday, didn't you?'

'Yes,' he said, taking a gulp of sherry, 'but of course, one good day doesn't mean a return to the glory days. It would take a lot more than that.'

'They'll get there,' I said firmly, 'if they get the chance.'

'What do you mean?' Dad asked.

I swallowed hard and ignored Mum who was determinedly trying to steer our attention towards the plate of mince pies she was proffering.

'Well,' I swallowed, 'I heard this rumour . . .'

'Oh another rumour,' cut in Dad. 'What is it this time? I'm planning to bulldoze the church to make way for a cash-and-carry, or am I in line for another new car courtesy of the council tax pot?'

I bit my lip thinking it was ironic that he'd mentioned another car as that was what Steve was convinced the Retail Park had bought and paid for.

'There's talk that the market site is up for sale,' I said, deciding not to back down, 'and that the stalls will either go straightaway or be relocated to somewhere so inaccessible that it won't be long before the holders give up of their own accord.'

'And who exactly,' said Dad, picking up one of the mince pies, 'is spreading this rumour?'

I shrugged, determined not to mention Steve's name. But in fact, thinking back to the day at the market when I'd made my rousing little speech to the traders about treating me as *me*, rather than as Dad's daughter, not one of them had stepped up and mentioned that the site was up for sale. The only talk that I'd heard of it had come from Steve's own lips, the very same lips that he had forced on to mine when he kissed me the night before and I actually had no proof that he was right or justified on either front.

'Oh forget it,' I shrugged, 'I probably got the wrong end of the stick. If it's any consolation, I did defend you to the person who told me.'

'And how did Steve Dempster feel about that?' Dad asked, as he took a bite of the pie.

Fortunately I was saved from grappling for an answer as he began to cough and splutter and spat his mouthful of mince pie into his napkin.

'Where the hell did these come from?' he cringed, draining his glass of sherry in one big gulp.

'The bake sale,' Mum shrugged. 'Some of the children from the playgroup helped make them. Are they not nice?'

'Not nice,' Dad groaned, 'that's something of an under-statement! They're full of salt!'

Mum and I tried to suppress our giggles until he was out of earshot but I'm not sure we succeeded.

'I wish I knew what's really going on with him,' I sighed as we began unpacking the boxes.

'You and me both,' said Mum, as she began carefully unwrapping the coloured glass baubles that had once belonged to her grandmother. 'He was fine up until a few months ago and no matter how hard I try, I can't pinpoint anything that happened to put him out of sorts.'

'Nothing at all comes to mind?'

'Not a single thing,' she said, setting aside the baubles to help me unravel the string of lights Dad had carefully wrapped around a cardboard tube to avoid tangling the flex. 'I know he's under an awful lot of pressure at work.'

'But so is Tom and yet I haven't noticed that he's had a dramatic change of personality.'

Spotting the look on Mum's face I decided to drop the subject. She'd been looking forward to our day of decorating ever since I got back and I had no intention of ruining it by making her even more worried about what was going on with Dad.

'There,' she said, standing on tip-toe to reach the top of the tree when we'd finally finished. 'Every year I tell myself to put the angel on first and I always forget!'

This particular angel wasn't a vintage beauty such as the one Simon and Jude had for sale on their stall. No, this was a pipe cleaner and paper doily glitter-fest fright, crafted by my own fair hands when I was about six. Every time she unwrapped it I begged Mum to buy a replacement but she was adamant that the cross-eyed creation should have pride of place during the festive season.

'I'd better go and stir the stew,' she said as she stepped back and took a final quick look around the room, 'it's almost time to make the dumplings.'

Right on cue my stomach gave a loud rolling groan and I remembered I hadn't bothered with breakfast.

'It all looks lovely, Mum,' I told her, pulling her in for a hug. 'I'm so pleased we got to do it together.'

'So am I,' she said, kissing my cheek, 'who knows where you'll be next year, or where I'll be for that matter.'

'What do you mean by that?' I asked as she disentangled herself and I followed her into the kitchen.

'Well,' she said, wafting the oven gloves to disperse the steam that poured out of the slow cooker as she lifted off the lid, 'I'm not supposed to say anything, but your father has said he's taking us on a cruise for our anniversary next year!'

'A cruise?'

'I know!' she smiled, giving the stew a stir. 'How exciting is that? I can't decide if I want to go somewhere hot like the Caribbean or cold like the Norwegian fjords, either way it's my choice so I need to hurry up. I imagine these things, especially the really exclusive ones, book up pretty fast, don't you?'

My mind was whizzing and there was a tight little knot of pain in the pit of my stomach that had nothing to do with the fact that I'd missed my breakfast.

'Ruby?' said Mum.

'Sorry, what?'

'I said,' she laughed, 'I hope you aren't jealous that you won't be the only Smith travelling the world next year.'

'No,' I said, 'of course not. It sounds wonderful.'

'But . . .?' asked Mum. 'I know you, Ruby Smith, I can tell there's a "but" coming somewhere.'

'Well, cruises don't come cheap, Mum,' I began, then stopped myself.

'And silver wedding anniversaries only happen once in a lifetime,' she said in a tone that suggested she had heard more than enough out of me. 'Come and give me a hand with these dumplings.'

Mum's cooking was an absolute joy as always. The beef was tender, the dumplings were plump and comforting and the red wine gravy was rich and fragrant, filling the house with its wonderful aroma. Weekends in my student digs were spent dreaming about meals like this, but this time around it was spoiled. The taste was divine but the consumption of it was shrouded in an unsavoury feeling that, no matter how hard I tried, I couldn't shake off.

'Did you enjoy that?' asked Mum as I passed her my almost empty plate.

'It was delicious,' I told her, 'every bit as wonderful as I remember and if Dad wasn't so averse to the idea,' I added with a smile, 'I would have licked the plate clean!'

To my surprise, Dad didn't say a word. He just continued to stare into space, his jaw grinding and a frown fixed firmly in place.

'Did you hear what Ruby said, Robert?' Mum asked.

'Yes,' he said, finally tuning back in. 'Yes. It was delicious.'

Mum and I exchanged worried glances.

'Why don't you both go and turn the tree lights on?' she suggested. 'I'll load the dishwasher and put the kettle on.'

Dad got up from the table and headed off towards the lounge leaving Mum and I shaking our heads, our concern for him and whatever was on his mind cranking up another notch.

Chapter 22

My head was still abuzz after the weekend and Dad was beginning to look as if all the fight had been knocked out of him. I found it somewhat disconcerting that he had made no further attempt to tempt me behind a desk at the council and I was curious as to how he was going to finance this anniversary cruise that Mum was so excited about. Even though I hadn't been around for all that long, the niggles and upsets that came with moving home had sucked me in and I was far more preoccupied with the woes at Wynbridge than I wanted to be.

Life in the small town was beginning to close in around me and as I watched my fellow traders (but not Steve, of course) at work that week, I tried my best to remind myself that actually none of what was going to happen here next year was my problem. In just a few short weeks I would be long gone, protecting myself from nothing more demanding than the searing heat of the sun and quite possibly the attentions of one very handsome celebrity chef.

Trying to convince myself that was all that mattered didn't work, of course, because I had fallen into the trap, the caring trap and not just about my dad. No matter how hard I tried to persuade myself otherwise, I genuinely cared about what was going to happen to this little square and the people who made their living in it. I tossed and turned at night as I imagined the lights being switched off and the stalls being rebuilt miles from the centre of town down some back alley that was impossible to reach and where no one wanted to go. Don't get me wrong, I had no intention of changing my plans, but I was still concerned for everyone who would be living through what I imagined would be a tumultuous few months.

Again I smoothed down the picture of the beach I had pinned to the stall and tried to imagine myself there, thousands of miles away from the market and those ridiculously soft yet firm lips of Steve's that had sent my resolve flying out of the door on the coat tails of the Wynbridge wind.

'Not long now,' said a voice behind me, 'have you booked your ticket yet?'

It was Tom.

'No,' I said, 'not yet. I'm waiting to see how far I can get on the money I've saved before I decide where I'm heading for first.'

He took a step closer and sighed wistfully as he took in the pristine beach and cerulean sky.

'That looks like a pretty good starting point to me,' he said with another sigh. 'What I wouldn't give for a week or two somewhere like that with Jemma.'

'Still no plans for a break just yet then?'

'We can probably stretch to a wet weekend in Maidstone,' he said, 'with the kids, of course, but there's always date night,' he added stoically.

'I'm pleased you're keeping up with it,' I smiled. 'You and Jemma deserve some time alone together. You both work so hard.'

'We do,' he sighed, 'you're right, but,' he added, waving around the clipboard he had tucked under his arm, 'I don't think we'll be going anywhere this week. Not with Santa visiting town on Thursday night.'

'Oh, of course,' I said, 'I'd forgotten about that. It's late night shopping on Thursday, isn't it?'

'Yep,' said Tom, 'it's yet another new venture for the town and we're only trying it for a couple of weeks, but if it's popular then next year we'll encourage the stallholders and shopkeepers to stay open late every Thursday from the switch-on. Not everyone can or wants to get into the cities, but they still like to have a look at some lights while they fill their stockings with their festive haul so I'm hopeful it'll work.'

'Well everything has so far,' I reminded him, 'although I have to say I'm rather looking forward to taking a back seat on this one. You never know, I might even get a bit of my own Christmas shopping done instead of helping everyone else with theirs!'

'But what about the stall?' said Tom, looking dismayed. 'Jemma and Lizzie said it would be open along with everyone else's. You will be able to run it, won't you?'

'Of course I will,' I reassured him. 'Don't panic. My mum and Angela have agreed to juggle it after Jemma closes the café, leaving you two free to take Ella and Noah to see Father Christmas. So there will be plenty of time for me to get the few things I need. I've done most of it anyway, thanks to Lizzie's clever crafting!'

'What's your dad going to say about that?'

'What, Mum running the stall, you mean?'

'Um . . .'

'No idea,' I shrugged, thinking of Dad's apparent distance to everything that was going on around him, 'but if last weekend is anything to go by, I don't think he'll be saying anything to be honest.'

'Oh,' said Tom, biting his lip. 'I'm guessing he's as inattentive at home as he is in the office at the moment then?'

'Just a bit,' I sighed. 'Tom, can I ask you something?'

'Of course.'

'About the market . . .'

'Ask away.'

I took a deep breath and was just about to take the plunge when Chris's deep bass rang out across the square.

'Hey, Tom!' he hollered. 'Come and have a look at these cables. Will they have to be taped up again for Thursday night?'

'Sorry, Ruby,' he said, 'I'd better go. Will it keep or do you want me to come back?'

'Oh it'll keep,' I shrugged, 'don't worry about it. In fact,' I added, waving him away, 'forget I said anything.'

'Has anyone seen Santa?'

Had the situation not been quite so dire, it would have been hilarious, but as it was, that Thursday evening, the market square was filling up with families, the horses tethered to the sleigh were getting frisky and Tom's puce complexion suggested he was heading for an embolism or a nervous breakdown or possibly even both.

'Any joy?' puffed Steve as we arrived back at the sleigh at the same time.

'No,' I panted, bending over to massage the stitch in my side, 'not so much as a sleigh bell.'

Somehow the pair of us had been roped in to help track down the elusive special guest, but with the minutes ticking by and panic beginning to set in I had no time for an attack of the vapours or more reminiscing about our awe-inspiring last kiss.

Mum had told me that Steve had rung the house a couple of times during the week and I had been doing everything I could to stay out of his way on the market, but when Tom came looking for help when Santa's absence was first noticed, ironically it was us two who answered his siren call.

'Would you look at that,' smiled Bea knowingly, and to my mind a little too smugly, as she took the money belt for the stall, 'fate seems determined to keep blowing you two back together, doesn't it?'

Steve rocked back on his heels and didn't say anything and I gave her what I hoped was a look that would have turned a lesser mortal to stone. The last thing I needed in the middle of this crisis was to be thinking about fate, any of the things Steve had said in the pub or whether his insides really did 'fall through the floor', whenever we were in the same vicinity.

'Just watch the stall until I get back would you, please?' I scowled. 'And don't go eating any more biscuits!'

She stuck out her tongue at me as we hurried off.

'Well, this is just bloody brilliant!' shouted Tom as he began pulling his hair so it stuck up in his trademark tufts and clumps. 'What the fuck are we supposed to do now?'

'I think we may have lost the Elf as well,' admitted Steve.

He caught my eye and for a split second I could have sworn

he was going to laugh, but I quickly turned away so I didn't succumb. It wasn't funny, it really wasn't.

'Well, that's it!' hollered Tom, throwing his hands up in the air and unsettling the already skittish horses again. 'I might as well hand my notice in right now.'

'Shhh,' said Steve, holding up a hand, 'listen.'

'To what?' said Tom, sounding increasingly manic, 'the sound of children crying or their parents braying for my blood?'

'Shut up,' said Steve, 'seriously mate, just shut up for a second.'

I cocked my head to one side and listened.

'What is it?' I whispered.

'I dunno,' he said, shaking his head, 'but it's coming from over there.'

We crept over to the trade bins which I guessed, assuming I had my bearings right, were at the back of The Mermaid and there, with an empty bottle of whisky and a greasy chip carton balancing on his gargantuan belly, was one snoring Santa and cuddled up at his side was his worse for wear Elf.

'What the hell's gone on here?' muttered Steve under his breath.

'Oh thank God,' said Tom, smiling broadly as his shoulders dropped back to where they should be rather than up around his ears, 'that is a relief.'

'A relief!' frowned Steve. 'Mate, I can smell him from here. You can't send him, or her for that matter, out there. He's pissed and he stinks.'

'Tough,' shrugged Tom, 'it's too late to do anything else. Ruby, just grab his other arm, will you? We need to wake him up.'

'I'm not touching him,' I said, taking a step back.

'So what am I going to do?' Tom shouted, his desperation escalating again. 'We can't say Santa hasn't come. The kids will be mortified and I'll be driven out of town.'

We stood staring at the unsavoury slumbering duo. Had I been a parent, I certainly wouldn't have wanted either of them anywhere near my offspring.

'You do it,' said Steve, pointing at Tom. 'You dress up as Santa.'

'I can't,' said Tom.

He sounded so frantic I thought he was going to cry.

'My kids are out there! They'll know it's me.'

'He's got a point,' I said, biting my lip as the seriousness of the situation began to knock the edge off the farcical hilarity.

This really was fast becoming more of an unmitigated disaster rather than a comic catastrophe.

'Oh for fuck's sake!' shouted Steve, sounding far from happy. 'Here, help me get his suit off. I'll have to do it.'

I turned away so he wouldn't see me laughing.

'And I don't see what you're finding so funny,' he said, 'you're going to have to be the bloody Elf!'

*

I don't ever want to have to think again about how absolutely horrid it was to be pulling on clothes, including tights, that were still warm because someone else had just been wearing them. It was vile, worse than vile, but at least the outfit was a decent fit.

A green dress, red stripy tights, a pointy hat and ears, and shoes with bells on, made up the ensemble and thanks to the red lipstick I had in my jeans pocket I even managed to supply Steve and myself with a pair of rosy cheeks apiece. Not that he needed them, mind you, having caught an eyeful of me dithering in my undies on the pavement, he looked hot enough already. I was furious with myself for feeling so pleased that I happened to be wearing matching underwear that day and burgundy lace at that. If there was any chance that he had forgotten what my body looked like in the last four years he was now certainly back up to speed, not that I cared of course.

The couple who had supplied the horses for the sleigh had remained remarkably professional throughout the whole stripping and re-dressing debacle and the man in charge, Philip, offered to stay with the staggering, partially dressed Santa and his sidekick until Tom could find someone to take them home.

'God help that bloody agency tomorrow,' said Tom, wiping his sweaty brow, 'I should have stuck to my guns and asked someone local to do it.'

'Just shut up moaning,' said Steve, 'you've got someone local now, haven't you? Come and give us a leg up, I can't quite reach the sleigh step. These trousers are a little on the snug side around the crotch.'

With Steve in situ and me precariously balanced at his side we made our slow way towards the market square where we managed one lingering lap around the perimeter, thanks to the horses being led at a snail's pace by their second trainer, before coming to a halt in the middle of the market to greet the children and get on with handing out the presents.

Whether or not any of the adults guessed that there had been a change of plan I couldn't be sure, but Steve played his part admirably and towards the end I was pretty sure he was actually beginning to enjoy standing up and 'shaking his belly like a bowlful of jelly'.

The only moment that I had been slightly panicked by was when it was Ella's turn to come up to the sleigh with Jemma and Noah. She had been eyeing me suspiciously from her position in the queue and I knew she had guessed something was amiss.

'I know it's you,' she said as I bent down to give her a present from Santa's sack marked 'G' and I felt my heart sink. 'But I also know how these things work. Father Christmas is a very busy guy,' she said sagely, 'and he can't be everywhere at once. Not at this time of year anyway. I won't tell,' she added, giving me a secret little smile and doubtless feeling delighted that she was above her younger comrades in the queue and 'in' on the big secret.

'Merry Christmas, clever girl,' I whispered in her ear.

'Oh my God,' said Jemma who was right behind her, holding a very wriggly Noah. 'Tom said I'd have a surprise when I got up here!'

'I know,' I smiled, trying to maintain as elfish a demeanour as possible, 'just close your mouth, Jemma, before you give the game away completely and don't ask, just don't ask.'

By the time she got to Steve she was laughing uncontrollably and Ella, now back with Tom, was looking at her witheringly.

'Why is Mummy kissing Santa Claus?' She frowned up at her father who also started to laugh as he watched his wife peck Steve on the cheek.

By the end of our session on the sleigh my face was frozen rigid. My smile felt as though it would be permanently set for the rest of time and I imagined myself going to my grave with rosy cheeks and a grin that didn't in any way match the expression in my eyes.

'I think we did it the wrong way round,' said Steve as he gingerly climbed down and rearranged himself in the uncomfortable trouser department.

'What do you mean?' I frowned.

'Well, the kids are supposed to see Santa *before* they get a present, aren't they?'

'Oh yes,' I said, 'you're right.'

'Did anyone say anything?'

'No,' he shrugged, 'I guess they all thought that the kids around here are all so well behaved and polite that they were guaranteed to get a present and actually,' he said, reaching so deep inside his trouser pocket I began to blush, 'I got a couple of presents myself!'

With a flourish he pulled two crumpled-up pieces of paper out from the depths.

'What have you got there?'

'Phone numbers,' he said, smoothing out the creases.

'Phone numbers?' I frowned, not really understanding.

'Yes,' he said, 'look. This one's from a woman called Jane. She's written her name and number on the back of a till receipt.'

'I don't believe you!' I tutted, snatching the paper from his grasp. 'Oh my God. "I'm Jane, call me",' I read. I turned the paper over and laughed even harder. 'She's written it on the back of a receipt from the chemist's for Canesten duo.'

'What's Canesten duo?' Steve asked innocently.

'Thrush cream,' I said bluntly.

'Oh,' he said, 'nice. You can bin that one then and you might want to wash your hands.'

'What about that one?' I said, passing back Jane's seductive love letter and wiping my hands down my Elf outfit. 'Any luck there?'

'Not really,' he said. 'This one was from a lady who was escorting her grandchildren.'

'What's she written?'

'It says, "Hi, I'm Sandra. I'm looking for a larger man to light up my life", and she's put her number as well.'

'You aren't serious.' This one really was too much.

Steve handed it to me as proof that he was undoubtedly irresistible to the older local ladies.

'When did she write this?' I frowned. 'The ink isn't even smudged.'

'I have a horrible feeling,' said Steve with a little shudder, 'that she already had it with her.'

'Well, well, well,' I laughed, trying to pretend that I really didn't care that even though Mia was out of the picture more women were already queuing up to take her place, 'Steve Claus, you really are a magnet, aren't you?'

I handed him back the second note which he crumpled up with the first and shoved back in the trouser pocket.

'Are you not feeling guilty that I'm trying to get over you with anyone who throws themselves at me?' he said, sounding almost hopeful. 'Are you not even the tiniest bit jealous?' he added.

'Oh absolutely,' I said, turning away as he began to strip off again and my heart sank in my chest, 'I'll be sobbing into my pillow tonight when I think of you out partying with Jane and Sandra. You can guarantee it!'

Chapter 23

Whether it was down to the skimpy Elf outfit or the fact that I was feeling rundown as a result of all the freezing early morning starts, I couldn't be sure but by the middle of the following week, when I really needed to be on top of my game at the market, I had been blessed with the cold from hell and a nose that could have rivalled Rudolph himself.

'You sure you're all right to be out here?' frowned Steve as he wandered over for a closer look. 'You look awful, Ruby, really awful.'

'Thanks for that,' I choked, my voice catching in my throat as I began to splutter and cough inelegantly. 'I bet you're relieved I didn't drag you back under Evelyn's mistletoe now, aren't you?'

After our Santa special we had ended up in the pub again and I had even managed to remember my purse, however, rather than another round of flirting and soul baring which resulted in a return match of tonsil hockey we'd ended up calmly talking through Steve's suspicions about Dad's potentially dodgy dealings and, given Mum's recent revelation about the possible anniversary cruise, I'd had the sense to just listen this time, rather than retaliate.

It was with a heavy heart that I had inwardly accepted that everything Steve suggested made uncomfortable, but nonetheless perfect sense. Dad *had* indulged in a brand new car when the Retail Park planning application was approved and now, with Steve's fears that the market square was up for sale ringing in my ears, there was talk in the Smith household of a global trip of a lifetime. I hadn't, of course, mentioned that to Steve, but facts were facts and I was beginning to wonder if there could possibly be an element of truth in at least some of what he said.

'Actually,' he said now as he dithered on the cobbles in front of me, 'I've been thinking about that whole debacle and I want to say that I'm sorry.'

'What do you mean?'

'For kissing you in the pub like that.' He winced, looking far less like his usual confident self and more like someone riddled with regret, 'and telling you that I still have feelings for you. I had no excuse, especially as you so rightly pointed out, I had already gone out of my way to tell you that starting up again would be too complicated given everything else that's going on.'

I could see his cheeks were beginning to redden in spite of the cold.

'I accept now that we can't be a couple again, Ruby, and I'm sorry I tried to use a silly kiss to convince you otherwise.'

It had been far from a silly kiss for me.

'So why didn't you say anything in the pub last night?' I asked.

'Because you looked as if you had enough to think about and I didn't want to put my foot in it again,' he said, scuffing the pavement with the toe of his boot. 'I wanted to be absolutely sure and last night as I lay awake going over it all I realised that even if I couldn't have you back properly, I couldn't bear it if we weren't at least be friends.'

I wasn't sure what I had been expecting him to say but it wasn't this. Part of me had been hoping that he would try to kiss me again. I had fully expected him to pull out all the stops to tempt me back into his arms, but I'd read the situation wrong and now I really had lost my chance with him again. Steve Dempster was offering to do the honourable thing. He wanted us to be mates.

'And I don't want you thinking this is some kind of trick on my part,' he carried on when I didn't say anything. 'I still like you, you still like me. I get that, but we can cope with settling for friends, can't we?'

I nodded and blew my nose.

'So please don't worry,' he insisted. 'I won't be trying

to kiss you again, because we're over, aren't we? Properly over.'

'Yes,' I nodded numbly, 'I suppose we are.'

'No more kissing or flirting,' he reeled off, 'and definitely no more fighting to win you back. You'll be gone again in a few weeks anyway, so there's no point in trying to convince you to stick around when you've got your sights set on sunnier climes, is there?'

'No,' I croaked. 'There isn't.'

So much for wasting endless hours worrying that he had noticed how my body reacted to his when he held me close; so much for thinking that the sight of my shivering body in my best matching undies had driven him wild with desire, cranked up his feelings and been the cause of the snug-fitting Santa trousers!

Now he'd kissed me again *and* seen me practically naked, he was retracting his previous declaration and offering to settle for 'friends'.

'Well,' I said, with a gargantuan sniff. 'I'm pleased we've got that straight.'

'Me too,' he said, unexpectedly pulling me into a platonic brotherly hug and kissing the top of my head. 'No hard feelings.'

'Of course not,' I said, forcing my heart to believe that what he had said was right.

In a few weeks' time I would be pulling on my backpack

and boarding a plane and I certainly didn't need to be heading off with a broken heart in tow. Not again.

'And if you're really lucky,' I told him, reluctantly pulling myself free from his arms, 'I'll even send you a postcard.'

'I'd like that,' he smiled, 'I'd like that a lot.'

'So have you made up your mind then?'

'I have,' I sniffed, blowing my nose for what felt like the hundredth time that hour, 'I'm heading straight for that beach.'

'I thought you might say that and with that in mind, I have good news.'

Had it not been for Steve's insistence that we were 'properly over' and always would be, I probably wouldn't have got my backside in gear that afternoon and headed home to trawl through the online travel agents. Neither would I have found the courage to message Paul Thompson and arrange the Skype call I was now taking, so really I should have been feeling grateful for Steve's timely apology and attraction retraction, but actually, all things considered, I was feeling pretty miserable.

'Oh,' I sniffed, pinching the end of my nose to delay the sneeze I could feel brewing, 'that sounds promising.'

'Yes,' frowned Paul, quickly taking what looked remarkably like a giant step away from his phone camera.

'Don't worry,' I told him, 'I'm fairly certain you can't catch a cold over the internet. Now, what's this news? I could do with cheering up.'

Paul took a tiny step closer again and began to relay the exciting update.

'The couple, Tanya and Mike, who own the hotel up the road from your dream beach . . .'

'Yes,' I nodded, 'I remember.'

'They're going to be looking for more staff in the New Year and I've put your name forward.'

'Really?' I gasped.

'Of course,' he tutted, evidently annoyed that I had doubted him, 'I told you I would.'

'Sorry,' I mouthed, feeling suitably chastened.

'Now, they're looking for one person to work in the hotel, just domestic stuff I'm afraid, and someone else to maintain the grounds.'

'Well, I can strip a bed,' I told him, my head already filled with the scents and sounds of an Indian summer, 'and I can work on my towel folding skills!'

'It's long hours, though,' he said, 'and only one full day off a week, so not all that much time for sight-seeing.'

He was clearly intent on reminding me that I was going to be working for a living and that if I didn't pull my weight it would be his head on the block.

'No problem,' I reassured him, 'after all the early hours working in Wynbridge in winter I'm sure I'll be able to manage.'

'That's what I thought,' he smiled, sounding mollified. 'They would like it if you could commit to working for eight to twelve weeks to begin with, living on site, of course, with all meals provided. The wages are more like pin money really and the work will be hard but it's as good a starting point as any.'

'It certainly is,' I told him, 'just the sort of thing I was hoping for, although until I met you, of course, I had no idea how to go about finding it!'

'Well,' he grinned, sounding flattered, 'one good turn and all that.'

'Don't forget,' I laughed, 'that it was *your* good turn that got *us* out of a pickle when you were here.'

'That's as maybe,' he shrugged, 'but the good publicity has helped get my career back on track and actually helped me get other things into perspective on a far more personal level.'

'Really?'

'Really,' he said, 'I've got great plans for a couple more community-based projects and events, so watch this space, Ruby Smith.'

'Oh I will,' I told him, 'I will.'

'Right,' he said, running his hands through his hair, 'I have to go. These celebrity customers won't feed themselves. I'll email you Tanya and Mike's details and you can contact them directly, but please keep me in the loop.'

'Will do,' I nodded, fighting back the sneeze again, 'and

thank you, Paul. I just know this trip is going to be the start of big things for me!'

When I said that, I really, really deep down believed it, but by the end of the week, with the cold still firmly in situ in my poor blocked sinuses I was beginning to doubt I would ever be well again, let alone have the energy to pursue the 'big things' I had been hoping for.

'Right,' said Mum, looking at me with a fierceness I'd never seen before, 'that's it.'

'What?' I croaked.

'You are staying here.'

'What are you talking about?' I coughed, pulling myself upright in my sweat-soaked bed, 'I need to get to the stall.'

'No, you don't,' said Mum, deftly flicking off my alarm clock and pushing me back under the duvet. 'I'm running the stall today.'

I opened my mouth to protest, but she didn't give me a chance.

'Tom's helping me set up this morning and then Ben's coming along later. I had a great time the night you were playing Santa's little helper, but Angela wouldn't let me do much. Well, today she's serving in the Cherry Tree all day, so it's my turn to get stuck in.'

'But,' I protested. 'there's only one Saturday left before Christmas. The market's going to be heaving!'

'Good,' said Mum, 'you know I can't stand twiddling my thumbs.'

'I can't just stay here and do nothing!' I protested.

She took a step towards the door and shook her head. 'Jemma said you'd react like this,' she tutted, 'so we've come up with a back-up plan.'

'A back-up plan?' I sneezed.

'Yes,' said Mum, looking at her watch. 'We reckon you're probably past the contagious stage but you certainly can't go spluttering about in the café. If you feel up to it, and not for a few hours yet, mind, you can join Marie and Lizzie in the town hall and help out with the wreath-making session they're running today.'

With my life deftly organised I collapsed back on to the pillows and slept through the best lie-in I'd had in weeks.

I wouldn't go so far as to say that the three or four undisturbed hours of sleep had cured me of the common cold, but when I joined Lizzie and Marie in the town hall that afternoon my head was feeling a lot clearer, even if my mood was still refusing to reach the giddy heights that Paul's help, and timely organisation, deserved.

Inside the cavernous hall the floor was awash with greenery and the level of chatter and laughter reached the lofty ceiling, competing with and easily beating the dulcet tones of Bing Crosby whose familiar voice was belting out of the little CD player and its inadequate speakers. Lots of townsfolk had already completed their wreaths and left them displayed in rows on the trestle tables we had used earlier in the month for the bake sale, and no doubt they would be back to collect them later when they had finished their shopping.

Even my still blocked nose could smell the luscious seasonal scents emanating from the clove-studded oranges and cinnamon sticks, and as I picked my way through the ruby-studded holly and trailing lengths of ivy I found myself wishing I had had the opportunity to sign up for one of the sought-after spots.

'Hello, Ruby,' said Marie, as she bustled past with a pair of pretty candles standing in a bed of mistletoe and laurel and carefully added them to the already burgeoning display. 'How are you feeling?'

'Better, I think,' I shrugged, 'although to be honest, it's hard to tell.'

'Well, at least it's warm in here, love, and out of that miserable wind.'

'Yes,' I said, thinking of Mum shivering outside, 'I suppose I better—'

'If you're even thinking of swapping places with your mum,' she interrupted, 'forget it. I'm under strict instructions to keep you in here.'

'Fair enough,' I smiled back, thinking I should have

known that Mum and Marie would have already had their heads together. 'Where's Lizzie?'

'In the back,' said Marie, 'helping out with the teas.'

'I'll go and give her a hand,' I said, making a beeline for the kitchen. 'I won't touch anything,' I said over my shoulder, 'I'll just carry the trays out and let people take the mugs and cups themselves!'

The kitchen was a buzz of activity and along with the hot beverages there were all manner of cakes and mince pies and some of Jemma's iced and spiced buns, plated up and ready to pass around to the wreath makers.

'How are you feeling?' asked Lizzie, echoing Marie's words. 'You know Steve was in earlier and he has a stinking cold as well. There isn't anything . . .'

'No,' I cut in sharply, guessing where her supposition was heading, 'there isn't. Shall I make a start with these?'

Poor Lizzie didn't deserve being snapped at like that, but I hated the way everyone jumped to conclusions. Simon, I had noticed the day before, was also sounding decidedly snivelly but no one had suggested that I had been going around kissing him.

'I'm sorry if I upset you earlier,' said Lizzie a little while later, as I helped her stash the crockery ready for washing. 'I didn't mean to, you know.'

'Oh I know,' I said, 'just ignore me. Blame it on the cold. It seems to have sent my usually sunny self heading for the door.'

'Even so,' said Lizzie, giving me a quick hug, 'I know this whole business about working next to Steve every day has taken its toll.'

'Has it?' I frowned, feeling instantly defensive again.

I could feel myself bristling even though I didn't want to.

'Why don't you go and make something for your mum?' she suggested, clearly aware that she'd overstepped the mark. 'It's quietened down out there now and I'm sure she'd appreciate it.'

'That sounds like a great idea.'

It seemed to take me an age to twist and bend the willow base into any kind of shape and in the end I decided to make one of the pillar candleholders that I'd seen Marie carrying about earlier.

'Not as easy as it looks, is it?' she smiled, passing me some lengths of ivy which I hoped would hold everything in place.

'No,' I puffed, 'it isn't.'

Carefully I began to weave the tendrils through and between the basic circle and it wasn't long before I was brave enough to let go and see if it would keep its shape and stand flat. Fortunately it did, which was just as well because considering the silly mood that had descended I might have otherwise been tempted to launch it across the town hall in true Noah tantrum fashion.

'These are pretty,' said Marie, handing me some of the

cinnamon sticks which had already been threaded on to wires so they could just be twisted into place.

'Perfect,' I said, spinning around the base and looking for the best spot to put them, 'are there any of the oranges left? I rather liked those too.'

'Just these small ones,' she said, 'although actually, they'd be perfect for a holder that size.'

Eventually I was finished and I was rather pleased with the result.

'You always make it look so easy,' I said to Marie, whom I had watched making simple displays and arrangements with alarming speed on her stall on the market. 'And you do it so quickly!'

'Practice,' she said, tapping the side of her nose, 'and a few tricks of the trade.'

Her jeans pocket began to vibrate to the tune of jingle bells and she pulled out her phone and groaned.

'Steve's had to go home early,' she tutted, 'that's not like him at all. He needs the love of a good woman to keep him warm and happy. I'm beginning to wonder if he's picked up flu rather than just a cold,' she added, looking pointedly in my direction.

I couldn't help thinking that after his searing kisses in The Mermaid he had very nearly had one.

'He's feeling rotten,' she continued, when I didn't say anything.

'Good,' I said childishly.

I was of course hoping he was feeling rotten about sending my emotions and mind off on a reminiscent roller-coaster but Marie didn't know that and her head snapped up, pinning me with a fierce expression which would have been worthy of any mother bear who had just found her cub in dire circumstances.

'I didn't mean . . .' I began, but she didn't give me a chance to finish.

'I know what you meant,' she retorted. 'I know it must be hard for you to forgive him for breaking up with you.'

'No,' I said shaking my head. Now it was my turn to cut in and explain that we'd worked things out between us. 'No, I do understand. I always have . . .' but she was having none of it and talked right over me.

'But before you go around thinking Steve was the villain of the piece, you want to look a bit closer to home.'

'Marie!' said Lizzie, rushing in from the kitchen and looking ashen.

'What do you mean?' I frowned.

'Marie!' shouted Lizzie again.

'Have a chat with your dad,' she said, turning to walk away, 'see what he has to say for himself before you keep on blaming my boy!'

I was dumbstruck, absolutely dumbstruck. I'd never known Marie to raise her voice, let alone have a cross word with anyone. Not even with Chris, and his behaviour after a session in the pub was enough to test the patience of a saint. No, whatever she was getting at about Dad wasn't going to be good news or easy listening.

Chapter 24

It seemed to me that the only day the Smith family found ourselves alone together at home was on a Sunday, and Sundays, rather than being about bonding, rest and recuperation, were fast becoming more of a weekly flashpoint and the opportunity for arguments and accusations. Two Sundays before Christmas, thanks to Marie's timely outburst, was no exception.

The comforting smell and warmth of yet another of Mum's legendary meals was gently wafting up the stairs as I ventured out of my bedroom and drew myself up to my full height (all five foot four of it), ready to go into battle. At exactly that very moment I discovered Dad backing quietly out of his office, locking the door, checking it twice and pocketing the key. Furtive would be the best word to describe his behaviour.

'What are you doing?' I demanded. 'Why are you locking the door?'

'Ruby!' he gasped, spinning around and clutching his chest while at the same time trying not to topple over the banister. 'What are *you* doing, sneaking about up here like that?'

'Sneaking!' I reacted, sounding far more like Gollum than I intended. 'I've literally just walked out of my bedroom and found you locking the office. You never lock the office. What have you got in there? Enough secret paperwork to topple the top brass or were you browsing through the cruise catalogues looking for the best one to surprise Mum with?'

Rather than bite back he just stood there looking tired and careworn.

'Are you all right?' I asked, my attitude well and truly kicked into touch.

'No, of course I'm not all right,' he shot back, 'you just scared me half to death!'

'Well, I'm sorry,' I said, stomping down the stairs, 'but whatever you were up to, I'm glad you're here.'

'Where else would I be at this time on a Sunday morning?'

'Because,' I said, ignoring his question, 'I want to talk to you. It's important.'

Watching Dad competently slice and neatly plate up the roast pork while Mum haphazardly added piles of crispy potatoes and spoonfuls of scattering peas only served to make me acknowledge yet again just how very different to each other my parents actually were.

Dad would always sigh as Mum noisily flung pots and pans around the sink rather than stacking them tidily next to the dishwasher, but their relationship had always worked. Dad's fastidiousness and Mum's more devil-may-care attitude normally balanced out perfectly, but something was certainly awry now. Dad sounded more exasperated than amused by her antics with the veg and Mum was clearly right to feel worried about what was going on.

'So what did you want to talk about?' Dad asked once he had finished stirring the gravy and checking it met up to his exacting standards.

It didn't matter how I put it or where I chose to start from, the conversation was all about the Dempster family so I fathomed I might just as well dive in and get on with it.

'At the wreath making yesterday—' I began as we took our places around the table.

'I can't believe you found the time to make this,' Mum butted in, 'it's actually very good, you know.'

She had given my first attempt at foliage arrangement pride of place on the dining table where it stood with only the tiniest of wobbles as we ate our delicious dinners.

'Marie helped,' I explained, grateful for the easy way of easing into the conversation.

Dad shifted in his seat a little and let out a long, slow breath.

'Well, she's the expert,' smiled Mum, her eyes flicking to Dad for the briefest second.

'She certainly is,' I pressed on, 'the wreaths she made were stunning and I've no idea how they managed it, but between her and Lizzie everyone who attended went away with something to be proud of.'

'As did you,' said Mum with a quick nod to Dad who was concentrating on his plate as if his life depended on it. 'Now, what was it you wanted to talk about, my love?'

I had to feel sorry for her really. She no doubt thought she was steering the conversation into safer waters when what she was actually doing was releasing the piranhas!

'It was about Marie, actually,' I said, spearing a potato and now keeping my eyes firmly fixed on my plate.

'Oh,' said Mum, a slight waver in her voice.

Dad said nothing.

'And Steve,' I added.

Still no reaction from Dad.

'And me and Steve,' I said finally, my voice rising.

'What about you and him?' Dad eventually asked, an edge of frustration already noticeable in his tone.

I swallowed hard, amazed that he still couldn't bring himself to mention Steve's name in the same breath as mine.

'Marie seemed to think,' I said tentatively, hardly believing that I was about to pick the potentially biggest bout I'd had with Dad since my move back to Wynbridge.

'It's a dangerous occupation that,' he said. 'Thinking can get you into all kinds of trouble.'

'Marie seemed to think,' I tried again with a sigh, 'she seemed to think, that you had something to do with the way Steve and I—' I faltered, not quite sure of the label to stick on the situation.

'How you and him what?' Dad frowned.

'How Steve and I ended up before I left for university.' I swallowed. 'How we broke up.'

There, I'd said it, and probably made it sound like some silly pre-teen melodrama, but who cared. I'd said it.

'If you're suggesting,' said Dad, 'that I was in some way responsible for him ending your relationship—'

'Well,' I swallowed again, 'I wouldn't perhaps go that far . . .'

'Then you'd be right.'

'What?' Mum and I chorused.

'I was,' he said, carefully laying down his cutlery.

'Robert!' gasped Mum, her fork frozen in mid-air. 'Whatever are you saying?'

'I'm saying,' said Dad, turning redder than Santa's suit, 'that it was me. I was the one responsible, I told Steve to end the relationship before Ruby went to university.'

'But when?' I said, numb with shock. 'Why?'

'Does it matter?' he said, sounding almost impatient. As if we were going over old ground rather than a brand new discovery. 'Does any of it matter now?'

'Of course it does!' I bawled, slamming down my knife and fork.

'Ruby, love,' said Mum, reaching for my hand.

'No!' I shouted, snatching it away. 'Before you even say it, Mum, I will not calm down. I need to hear this. I want to know the whole truth!'

For a split second I couldn't make out the expression on Dad's face and then I realised, it was shock.

'Do you still love him?' he asked incredulously, his voice barely more than a whisper.

'Of course I do,' I yelled, surprising myself that I hadn't even taken a moment to think about it. 'I always will.'

I pushed back my chair ready to see through the threat forming in my muddled mind.

'If you don't tell me the truth then I will pack my bags,' I told him as calmly as I could, 'leave this house and never set foot in it again.'

Mum sobbed into her napkin, but Dad didn't move a muscle.

'Don't think I won't do it,' I seethed, 'don't think for one second that I'm bluffing.'

I put my hands on the edge of the table and levered myself upright out of the chair.

'Robert!' cried Mum. 'For pity's sake.'

Dad took a deep breath and sat back in his chair, then took off his glasses and began to clean them on his napkin. I registered the tell-tale sign that he was feeling increasingly uncomfortable and stood my ground.

'It was right after his brother's funeral,' he finally began, 'that very afternoon actually. He came here looking for you, Ruby, but you'd gone back to his parents' house. You'd come here for your overnight bag and gone back. You must have missed one another by seconds.'

I flopped back down in my chair again.

'He didn't want to come in,' Dad continued, 'but I insisted. For once.'

'You never made him welcome,' I whispered, my voice catching in my throat in a way that had nothing to do with my retreating cold, 'you never made any of them welcome.'

'He came into the kitchen,' Dad went on, 'and I poured us both a brandy. Given the circumstances,' he swallowed, 'I thought we both deserved one. It had been a long time since the town had buried such a young lad. I hope I never have to live through such a day again. I hope none of us do.'

He shuddered at the thought and I tried to push the memory of the horrid time we had all been forced to live through away.

'But what does this have to do with what happened to us?' I urged, ignoring the compassionate way he spoke of that despicable day. 'What does any of this have to do with Steve dumping me?'

'I asked him what his plans were, whether he'd even had time to consider what he was going to do?'

'And what did he say?'

'Well, he already had it all worked out,' Dad explained, with an approving nod, 'a lad like that with a strong sense of duty and an understanding of what being part of a family actually meant wouldn't do anything else. He said he was going to stay and support his mum and dad.'

I couldn't make any sense of what Dad was saying. The way he was talking about Steve and the decision he had made, made him sound in awe, impressed even, when actually he was always anything but when he spoke about any of the Dempster family as a rule.

'But surely you supported his decision then?' sniffed Mum. 'He'd done exactly what you would have considered the right thing, hadn't he?'

'Oh yes,' said Dad, 'totally the right thing. The only thing he could have done, given the terrible circumstances.'

'But then I don't understand . . .'

'When I asked him if he'd talked to you about his decision, Ruby, he said no, he hadn't known how to. He said he couldn't face it until after the funeral. He planned to talk to you that very weekend and work out how you could juggle things, the physical distance there was going to be between you, for a start. He was still determined to make the relationship work, even though he knew you were going to be disappointed to go alone.'

'We did talk that weekend,' I said numbly, 'but that was when he told me he was breaking it off. I was the

313

one who suggested juggling things,' I added, 'but he said it would be too much of a strain. He said he was worried that a long-distance relationship would hold me back and stop me getting stuck into life away from Wynbridge. I told him I didn't want to get stuck into anything without him, but he was adamant. I really don't think you were the problem, Dad.'

'I was,' he said, shaking his head. 'I was, love. It was me who put all that in his head. I was the one who said he'd be holding you back. I told him that if he loved you, he should let you go.'

'But why did you do that?' Mum burst out, before I had a chance to ask the question myself and making me jump. 'What right did you think you had to interfere?'

Dad ignored her and kept his eyes firmly fixed on me.

'I was only thinking of you, Ruby, and how hard you'd worked to secure that university offer. You had every opportunity to do what I had never managed; to rise above the mediocre and really make something of your life. I couldn't just stand by and watch you throw away the best opportunity you were ever likely to have because you were tethered to a boy who would never be able to equal your academic aspirations.'

'But it was my life, Dad,' I reminded him, 'my hard work, my choices and ultimately it should have been my decision, mine and Steve's. You put those ideas in his head when he was vulnerable; you manipulated the situation to suit your own twisted ends. Have you ever actually stopped for a second and thought just how wrong that was?'

Dad didn't say anything.

'But you must be able to see now just how much Steve loved you, Ruby?' Mum said, desperately trying to smooth over the cracks.

'What do you mean?'

'He loved you enough to let you go,' she tried to say. 'He saw what was for the best—'

'No,' I interrupted, 'no. If he had really loved me he never would have done this. He would have fought for me, for us. He would have done anything to keep us together.'

Mum was having none of it.

'He just did what he thought was for the best, what he thought would help everyone in the long run.'

Given the way my knees had buckled when he kissed me in the pub, given the way my body yielded and moulded to fit his, I couldn't believe that any of what had happened had been 'for the best'.

'And as for you,' said Mum, turning to face Dad. 'I don't think I even know who you are any more. When I was working on that stall yesterday, Robert—'

I saw Dad flinch, but he didn't comment.

'You'd be amazed by the things I heard. The rumours that are circulating through town about the future of our little market and how they all revolved around you, was unbeliev-able. Or so I thought.'

Still Dad sat in silence.

'And I defended you,' said Mum. 'I stood amongst those people and defended every decision you have ever made. I just hope to God that you haven't made as big a fool of me as you have of yourself.'

As shocked as I was by everything I had just discovered, I have to admit that the ball of pain twisting in the pit of my gut had just as much to do with the fact that the stallholders had opened up to Mum when they had never said anything to me as it did with Dad's shocking revelation.

Needless to say I couldn't possibly stay at home after that. To be honest, had it not been for the stall and the thought of letting down Lizzie, Jemma and everyone else who was working so hard to turn around the fortunes of the market, I probably wouldn't have even stayed in the country.

'Can I crash at yours tonight?' I had asked Bea when she fortuitously phoned just a couple of minutes after Mum's aborted Sunday dinner.

'Of course,' she said, without a moment's hesitation.

'I could just do with a change of scene,' I added, feeling obliged to offer some sort of explanation for the unexpected request. We were, after all, getting a little long in the tooth for girly sleepovers.

'No problem,' she said, no doubt catching on that life at home was getting to me, even though she didn't know the reason why. 'I already happen to have a bottle of wine chilling in the fridge,' then she added, 'and you really are in luck because tubs of Ben and Jerry's were on offer this week!'

I decided to walk round and in the process grab myself some mind-clearing fresh air. And if that didn't work I could always tot up the alcohol units in an attempt to blot out the unpalatable details of what I had just been told. I packed my warmest market apparel for Monday and a spare pair of pants in case I still couldn't face going home the day after.

'You know why I'm going, don't you, Mum?' I sniffed as she gave me a hug as I was about to leave. 'You do understand.'

'Of course I do,' she smiled grimly. 'Given half the chance I'd be gone myself. Let him stew for a couple of days and think about what he's done. You do know that I didn't know anything about all this, don't you?'

I couldn't believe she'd asked.

'Yes,' I said, 'absolutely.'

'I still can't get my head around the fact that Marie never told me,' she tutted, shaking her head. 'I'm not altogether sure I'm going to be able to forgive her for that.'

'Oh, now don't you two go falling out as well,' I told her sternly and really meaning it. 'What would be the point in that?'

*

The weather reports were all warning of snow in the East for the forthcoming week and ordinarily I wouldn't have minded a spot of Christmas shopping in the town when the white stuff was on the ground, but I wasn't sure my lingering head cold would be too impressed with the further down-turn in working conditions. Eight hours outside in the bleak midwinter working next to someone who should by rights still have been mine, suddenly seemed far less appealing than when I had accepted the job.

As I set off towards Bea's wrapped in my winter coat and with my overnight bag flung over my shoulder, my thoughts turned naturally enough to how my life would have panned out had Dad not seen fit to interfere in it.

Had I been privy to everything that had happened during my last few weeks before I left for university, I might well have been more inclined to agree with Steve and his idea that fate had blown us back together and that we should pick up the pieces and start again. Had I known that the only reason he'd let me go in the first place was because Dad had manip-ulated him into believing it was the right thing to do, then I would have been far more willing to admit how I felt after that kiss under the mistletoe, how I still felt. Unfortunately I hadn't of course, and now Steve had apologised for the kiss, admitted that he had made a mistake and reiterated in no uncertain terms that he had got the message that we were well and truly over. Talk about shitty timing.

I pulled my coat tighter around me in a feeble attempt to dismiss the wind, bent my head low and carried on towards where Bea was waiting with the vital components which would, I hoped, go some way to soothing my sore heart, for a little while at least.

I had just passed the rugby ground when I heard someone hollering my name.

'Hey, Ruby! Wait up. I want to talk to you!'

'Steve,' I whispered.

For a second I thought I'd dreamt him up but no, there he was, suddenly in front of me, bent double and panting, having just run what I guessed was the length of the pitch to reach me.

'Just give me a minute,' he said, cradling his side.

His face was glowing and his hair was plastered to his head. His thighs looked red raw and I could imagine how cold the taut skin would feel to the touch. I stuffed my hands in my pockets out of harm's way just in case they were tempted to test out the theory.

'Jesus,' he puffed, still panting, 'I'm built for strength not speed.'

'So why have you just sprinted across the pitch?' I frowned. 'And what are you doing here today anyway?'

'Extra training,' he wheezed, finally standing upright. 'But never mind that. I need to talk to you.'

'What about?' I swallowed.

'Yesterday,' he said, shaking his head. 'At the town hall wreath making thingy.'

'What about it?'

'What about it?' he laughed. 'What the hell happened? Mum's been like a bear with a sore head ever since she came back, but everyone I've talked to has said the day was a resounding success.'

'It was,' I confirmed, feeling my face go red, 'everyone had a great time. Your mum was amazing.'

'But something must have happened,' he went relentlessly on, 'I can't believe it was the short journey home that put her in such a foul mood.'

'I don't know,' I shrugged. 'Why are you asking me anyway?'

'Because you were there,' he said. 'You must have noticed something.'

It was suddenly right on the tip of my tongue to tell him, to let it all come spilling out but really, what would have been the point? The calendar back in my bedroom was proof enough that it was almost time for me to begin planning my travels in earnest. I'd be gone soon and this whole sorry muddle could be put to bed once and for all.

'Have you asked her?' I suggested.

'What do you think?' he laughed. 'I wouldn't dare. She snapped Dad's head off this morning when he asked if there was any chance of a roast dinner.'

'You should send him round to my mum,' I said, thinking of the leftovers filling the fridge.

'Why?'

'Never mind,' I muttered, hoisting my bag higher on to my shoulder. 'I have to go.'

'Where are you off to?'

'I'm staying with Bea for a couple of days,' I explained, thinking I'd told enough half-truths in the last ninety seconds.

'God help us,' said Steve, shaking his head. 'A girls' night in, hey. No man will be safe from scrutiny.'

'Oh, I shouldn't worry about it,' I said with a shrug, 'we aren't fifteen. We do have better things to talk about than you lot, you know.'

He looked at me and wriggled his eyebrows.

'Oh all right,' I admitted, willing myself not to smile and rolling my eyes, 'you should probably expect your ears to be burning in an hour or so.'

'Interesting,' he quipped, eyeing me with an expression that in no way suggested we were completely finished business. 'If you can hang on five minutes I'll give you a lift if you like.'

'No,' I said, stepping around him, 'thanks, but no. I could do with the walk.'

'Are you sure?' he asked. 'Surely it's only fair that you give me a chance to do you a good turn before you start gossiping about me with your best friend.'

'No, honestly,' I said, turning away and thinking I'd still like him to do me a good something. 'I'll see you tomorrow.'

'Fair enough,' he smiled, 'but if you do happen to think of what might be up with Mum let me know, would you?' he called after me.

'Yes,' I shouted over my shoulder, 'of course, I'll text you!' I added, knowing I never would.

Chapter 25

'You have got to be kidding me?' gasped Bea, her mouth hanging open and her eyes wide. 'Ruby, please tell me you're having me on.'

'No,' I said shaking my head and plunging the spoon back into the tub of cookie dough she had presented me with at the front door. 'I'm afraid not.'

'Your dad is the reason why Steve dumped you?'

'Yes,' I said again, 'I told you. Now can you please stop saying it? I'm struggling to keep my ice cream down.'

'And you really think that there's a chance the market is going to close?' she carried on, ignoring my request.

'There could be,' I said carefully. 'Dad's definitely up to something and if I could find a way of breaking into the office at home I bet I could find out what.'

Bea whistled under her breath and topped up my half-empty glass with more fizz.

'Does anyone else know?' she ventured. 'About the market, I mean.'

I thought about what Mum had said earlier.

'I think everyone has their suspicions, but no one other than Steve has spoken to me about them directly.'

I still felt rather upset by the thought that even after I'd said my bit in the pub some of the traders still viewed me with what I thought was suspicion rather than as part of the team.

'Poor Steve,' said Bea sadly, 'I do feel for him, you know.'

'Poor Steve,' I spluttered, choking on the bubbles from my Prosecco, 'what do you mean, poor Steve?'

Bea looked at me and bit her lip. The reaction was a dead giveaway. I'd known her long enough to recognise when she was holding something back and chewing on her lip was her trademark way of trying to keep quiet.

'What?' I demanded.

She plonked herself down on the chair opposite and reached for her own half-empty tub of ice cream.

'What?' I said again, more sharply this time.

'When you left,' she began, her eyes firmly focused on the chunks of chocolate chip.

'What about when I left?'

'Oh, I don't know,' she said, abandoning the tub again and picking up her glass, 'I just always thought there was more to the situation than met the eye, but it was so hard to tell.'

'What do you mean?'

'With Steve,' she continued. 'I always thought there was more to him calling time on your relationship than he let on, but what with losing Sean and having to step in to help with the stall I could never be sure. Losing his brother like that was bound to have a massive impact, it was obviously going to change him but I always thought that hanging on to you and what the pair of you had would have helped him through it. His decision to break things off and then not changing his mind when everything began to settle down again, well it shocked me, it shocked a lot of people.'

'How do you mean?' I quizzed. 'Did you think he was going to come after me, then?'

'Not exactly,' she said, 'but let's put it this way, I did think that by the time you came back for Christmas that first year he would have seen sense. I thought he would have sought you out and tried to put things back together but he didn't, did he? Even though he was utterly miserable he kept his distance. Now having heard the part your dad played in the situation, it all makes sense. I dare say Steve was desperate to get in touch but your dad had done such a good job convincing him that you were better off without him he thought better of it and left you alone.'

I didn't like the sound of it one little bit, but I could understand what she was getting at. Dad could be very persuasive when he set his heart on something. He was used to getting his own way and a young man, grieving for his older brother and trying to fill the gaping great gap he left, had no doubt been the easiest person in the world to manipulate.

'Why didn't you ever say anything?' I said, trying to keep the accusatory tone at bay, 'why didn't you ever tell me that you had these suspicions?'

'Because I couldn't be sure,' she said, her tone beseeching me to understand. 'You were miles away and you were hurting. I didn't want to make the situation even worse so I just kept quiet. When you came back that Christmas you seemed resigned to the situation, you were making yourself a new life and you had new friends. I didn't see the point in dragging it all up again.'

'Did anyone else know?' I asked, suddenly remembering the look on Lizzie's face when she had tried to stop Marie the day before. 'Did anyone else think the same thing as you?'

Bea started chewing her lip again.

'Lizzie did, didn't she?' I said to help her out. 'Lizzie had her suspicions.'

'Yes,' sighed Bea, 'and so did Jemma. After a few weeks, when Steve had made no effort to build any bridges, we all began to think that something was amiss. Of course, if we'd known that your dad was behind it all we would have stepped in and tried to help, but we didn't have a clue.'

I knew it wasn't Bea's, Lizzie's or Jemma's fault that my dad had acted like a prize rat. Deep down I knew it wasn't Steve's fault either, although I couldn't help wishing that he had had the strength to stand up and fight for us, but given the circumstances I don't know where I would have expected him to find that strength from.

'What are you going to do now?' asked Bea when she realised we had been sitting in silence for well over a minute.

'What do you mean?'

'Well, are you going to tell Steve that you've found out about what your dad did?'

'No,' I sighed.

'Are you going to tell him that you're still in love with him then?'

'Oh look,' I said, jumping up and rushing to the window. The weather had saved me from having to answer. 'It's snowing,' I said. 'Would you look at the size of these flakes!'

The snow continued to fall for the rest of the day and thanks to the plummeting temperature that night it was a slippery but picturesque walk to work the next morning. The market square had been totally transformed and had I just been passing through, I would have no doubt considered it picture postcard pretty, but the thought of stamping my feet and blowing on my gloves for eight hours straight was daunting to say the least.

'Have you heard?' asked Jude, rushing over the second she spotted me and almost losing her footing in the process.

'About what?' I asked cautiously as I carried on knocking

the snow from the stall canopy before I went to the café to collect the stock.

I braced myself for whatever she was going to say, hoping that it wasn't more bad news. Given the rosy glow and broad smile I thought I was going to be safe, but given the shocking revelations of the last couple of days I wasn't counting my chickens.

'I can't believe it,' she giggled, tugging on my sleeve and almost putting us both in the firing line for a covering of dislodged snow in the process.

'Believe what?' I asked, quickly dodging out of the way.

'OK,' she said, taking a deep breath and trying to compose her features into a slightly more businesslike expression. 'Yesterday afternoon Simon and I went and had a look around the empty shop next to the Cherry Tree.'

'The old shoe shop you mean?'

'That's the one,' she beamed, 'and we've decided we're going to take on the lease. We're planning to open a vintage store in the spring.'

'Oh wow!' I said, pulling her into a hug and feeling relieved that it was good news after all. 'Congratulations, that's fantastic!'

'I know,' she said. 'I can't wait. The unit has been empty for ages so we've managed to get it for a song really and we've only had to commit to six months, just so we can see how it goes before deciding if we want it for any longer. Isn't it fantastic?' she gushed, 'our own shop! It's what we've always dreamed of, and,' she added, lowering her voice, 'if the worst comes to the worst and the market does close, we'll have got out in time and we won't have to go back to working the car boots. We're actually going to be able to turn this into a proper business, Ruby!'

'Uh huh,' I nodded, that horrible knot of pain in the pit of my stomach was making its presence felt again. I had thought I'd feel better if people were open about the potential problems on the market's horizon, but if my rolling insides were anything to go by I was obviously wrong.

'And we'll be able to sell much bigger things,' Jude carried on. 'We've got loads of furniture and fabrics but we can't put it out on the stall in this weather. A shop will give us much more scope.'

'Of course it will,' I agreed. 'I'm thrilled for you. I really am. The town could do with a new shop or two to pull the shoppers in and next to the Cherry Tree is the perfect spot.'

'Funnily enough,' she said, as she rushed back to help Simon unload the van, 'that's exactly what your dad said when he arrived with the shop owner to show us around.'

The time was pushing on and I didn't have time to stand about with my mouth open. As dumbstruck as I was, I had to get the stall set up and keep moving if I didn't want to become frozen to the spot. I had just finished arranging more of Jemma's Kilner jar baking kits and some new strings of

Lizzie's stocking-shaped bunting when Marie arrived to add her own layer of confusion to my already muddled thoughts.

'Ruby,' she said, hopping from one foot to the other.

'Marie,' I nodded, 'I didn't expect to see you today. What are you doing here on a Monday?'

I had been hoping to avoid her for a few days, at least until I'd come to terms with the devastating revelations her comments in the town hall on Saturday had unleashed.

'You aren't setting up today, are you?'

'No,' she said, 'but we start our Christmas delivery service this week. Chris and Steve are going to be run off their feet packing orders and taking out the van so I'm helping with the stall. I mostly just sell bundles of holly and mistletoe from now until the twenty-fourth anyway and I can easily do that from their stall.'

'Oh,' I said, 'right.'

'Anyway,' she said, 'that's not what I came over to talk about.'

I turned back to the stall and began fiddling with the chilly bags of biscuits and buns.

'Ruby,' she said again.

'What?'

'I want to tell you that I'm sorry, love.'

'For what?'

I had absolutely no desire to make things easy for her.

'You know what,' she tutted, 'I spoke to your mum

last night. She said you had it out with your dad yesterday and he told you that he was the one responsible for Steve's decision.'

'To ditch me,' I jumped in.

'To let you go,' she said softly.

'And?'

'Well,' she sighed, 'I just wanted to say that I'm sorry.'

'Why are you sorry?'

'Because you shouldn't have found out like that, that's why. Because it probably would have been best all round if you hadn't found out at all.'

'What, you mean you would have been happy for me to go on blaming Steve for everything, when all the time it was actually my dad who was behind what happened?'

'But you never did really blame Steve, did you?' she pointed out. 'You always knew deep inside that he was only doing what he thought was for the best, irrespective of what your dad might or might not have said.'

'I suppose so,' I shrugged. 'Anyway what does it matter? It's done now.'

'And have you told Steve that you know?'

'Of course I haven't,' I snapped. 'What would be the point in that? We've already had one near miss since I came back and after that I made it very clear that I wasn't interested in starting again.'

I had, hadn't I?

'He knows how I feel and I know how he feels. We've laid our cards on the table and I think it would be best all round if everyone just left us alone. I'll be gone in a couple of weeks anyway and to be honest I don't know now if I'll ever want to come back.'

It probably sounded dramatic, but it was the truth. At some point in the future Steve would fall in love with someone else. They would get married and have a dozen little Dempster sprogs and I had no desire to see him playing happy families with someone else who could so easily have been me, were it not for an out of control motorbike and my father's interference.

'But if Steve knew that you now know why he let you go in the first place . . .'

'But he doesn't,' I said firmly, 'and I don't want him to. Had I known coming back to Wynbridge was going to start all this back up again I never would have agreed to take the stall on.'

'But now you're here,' Marie tried again.

'I can't wait to leave,' I told her. 'Now, if you'll excuse me, I need to see to my customers.'

Now the local schools had broken up for the holidays, the market was much busier and the addition of the currently pristine snow seemed to encourage everyone to grab their wellies and sledges and enjoy the picturesque scene. Snow in

Wynbridge usually arrived in February from what I could remember, so its presence in the run up to Christmas was, for now anyway, most welcome.

'I feel about eight years old again,' Gwen told me as she came tottering over later that afternoon. 'Isn't it wonderful?'

I wished I had the enthusiasm and exuberance to match her, but as the day had already begun to darken and the cold was penetrating my very marrow I was feeling increasingly less than delighted with the snowy situation.

'It's brilliant,' said a voice behind me.

'Steve,' Gwen beamed. 'We've missed you today. Where have you been?'

'Making Christmas deliveries,' he explained, 'I've got yours in the van, Gwen.'

'My what, dear?'

'Your delivery.'

'But I haven't ordered anything,' she said, looking confused.

'Well, I have a box in the back with your name on it,' he said seriously, giving me the merest wink. 'Dad made it up earlier. There's enough fruit and veg in there to see you through the next couple of weeks and he's added a couple of extra treats: those dates you love so much, as well as a big bunch of mistletoe to hang above your back door.'

'Oh well,' she faltered, 'I'm not sure about that.'

'It's all paid for,' Steve continued, 'I told Dad you've been keeping me in kisses all year and he said it was the least we could do.'

'Oh you naughty boy,' she giggled, turning scarlet.

'And I'll run you home tonight,' he insisted, 'so I can help you unpack it.'

'And hang the mistletoe?' she smiled.

'Of course!' he laughed. 'I won't be going anywhere until that's up and we've tested it out!'

I turned back to face my stall.

'Are you all right, Ruby?' Steve asked.

Yes,' I nodded, as I struggled to swallow down the lump in my throat and blink away the tears, 'it's this wretched cold,' I sniffed, determinedly keeping my back to both of them. 'Can you watch the stall for a minute?'

I didn't know why that little exchange had had such an impact but it felt as if someone had reached inside my chest and given my heart a jolly hard squeeze. I had always known that Steve Dempster really was the very best of men and for a moment I couldn't swallow away the raw pain of heartbreak that came with the acknowledgement he was no longer mine all over again.

Chapter 26

After two nights of hiding out at Bea's and with less than a week to go before Christmas, I decided the only way I was going to survive seeing out my time in the town was by immersing myself in my work on the stall, so that was what I did. I had spoken briefly to Jemma about what she estimated my earnings were going to be from the profit we had made and, assuming we had a great few days in the run up to the twenty-fifth, my plane ticket to India and a few extra pennies were guaranteed.

Emails between Paul, myself, Tanya and Mike had been flying to and fro and everything was all arranged. In less than two weeks I would be working on the other side of the world and the whole situation with Steve and my dad and my worries for the future of Wynbridge market would be behind me.

I know it was probably selfish to even think it, but I was

fast reaching the point where I'd had enough. Not of the place so much, or the people (apart from Dad, of course), but one thing my few weeks of living at home had taught me was that you can never go back to a situation, especially one with such painful memories, and expect it not to leave an imprint on your heart. At that moment my heart was feeling trodden on all over again.

'So,' smiled Harriet, 'how has living the life of a Wynbridge town trader been suiting you, Ruby? I know your mum had a great time last Saturday while you were helping out with the wreath making, and Angela from the café has loved it too.'

I took a moment to think back over everything that had happened during the last few weeks and, not factoring in the Steve scenario of course, I was pretty overwhelmed by just what I had managed to be a part of.

'You know what,' I told her, 'it's been pretty phenomenal actually.'

'I thought you might say that,' she laughed, 'it's not as if you've just been working on the stall either, is it?'

'No,' I agreed, 'I guess not.'

'Everyone is so happy about the way you've got stuck in and shaken things up.'

'Really?' I asked, suddenly feeling grateful that only Bea, Mum and Marie had known about everything else I'd been trying to cope with.

'Absolutely,' she nodded, 'we're all aware that the switch-on and bake sale were a success thanks to you, not to mention how you stepped in to play Head Elf last week! And we've now had three enquiries from potential new stallholders who want to join our happy band in the New Year.'

I was delighted that she felt my suggestions and efforts had made such an impact, of course, but I still wasn't convinced that the market was out of the woods just yet. That knot of pain in my gut had stubbornly refused to leave and I couldn't help feeling there was some drama looming on the horizon that was still to be played out before I left town.

'That's great,' I smiled, 'really good news. I don't think I really appreciated how important a part the market played in the town before. I guess I just always took it for granted when I was growing up.'

'I think we all did,' said Rachel, Harriet's partner, who had wandered over to join us, 'and that's been a big part of the problem.'

'A little town like Wynbridge can't just rely on the same old stalls year in year out any more,' added Harriet. 'The way people shop and where they shop has changed so dramatically over the last few years and unfortunately it's taken the traders a while to catch up and realise that.'

'Well,' I said looking around, 'I think they've got the idea now.'

'Yes,' said Rachel, 'I think you're right.'

Practically every stall in sight was now offering something a little different, something a little more tailored to the season and, judging by the number of shoppers milling around, it had all been worth the effort. The addition of three more stalls in the New Year could well make all the difference when it came to keeping the momentum going.

'But what about you two,' I asked, 'I've hardly seen your stall set up at all since I arrived?'

'A lot of the plants we sell are rather lacking in kerb appeal at this time of year,' Harriet explained. 'Most of our business is mail order during the winter as the bulk of the stock looks like sticks in pots!'

'Exactly,' laughed Rachel, 'just sticks, or pots of compost waiting to burst into life in the spring! We certainly don't have much in the way of eye candy at the moment but we'll be back in the New Year with the bulbs and things.'

'Do you know what Lizzie and Jemma are planning to do with the Cherry Tree stall after Christmas?' asked Harriet.

'No,' I told them, my eyes taking in the pretty Christmas makes and bakes that had proved so popular, 'I don't.'

'I dare say there won't be much scope for carrying on in January,' sighed Rachel.

'Oh, I wouldn't say that,' I frowned, 'think of all the fabulous things they could sell for Valentine's Day and then of course you've got Easter not long after. Bunnies and baskets in abundance,' I mused, 'not to mention the fabulous potential of a Wynbridge market Easter egg hunt for the children and perhaps another bake sale and a proper Spring Fair with chicks and lambs.'

My mind was off and racing with all manner of ideas that could keep the community spirit of the entire town, not just the market, thriving throughout the entire year.

'Are you absolutely sure you have to leave us so soon?' wheedled Harriet. 'Wynbridge could really do with someone like you sticking around to give us all a kick up the backside when we start to get stuck in our ways and take things for granted again.'

'Don't tease,' I blushed.

'I'm not,' she said seriously, 'I really mean it. Your ideas are wonderful, Ruby! I think the wider world has this idyllic idea that everyone who lives in a country town is somehow automatically part of the rural community and vice versa, but actually, more often than not it isn't the case at all, is it?'

'Half the children round here don't see chicks or lambs from one year to the next, which is why your suggestions are so inspiring, Ruby.'

'Well,' I said, feeling secretly rather chuffed that they both liked what I was saying. 'How about I write a few things down and leave them with Lizzie when I go?'

'I think that sounds like a wonderful idea,' said Harriet.

'Really wonderful,' agreed Rachel.

'What's wonderful?' butted in Steve.

He had just arrived back in the van, having no doubt spent the morning making more bespoke Christmas veg box deliveries.

'Ruby,' said Harriet.

'I could have told you that years ago,' Steve yawned, stretching his hands above his head and giving me and the rest of the world a tantalising glimpse of his wonderfully toned torso.

'Oh dear, Steve,' laughed Harriet. 'Are we keeping you up?'

'Sorry,' he said, dropping his hands, 'I'm done in. We seem to have twice as many orders to deliver this year and if I'm not out in the van I'm at the warehouse getting them ready to go out. I blame you, Ruby.'

'Me?' I squeaked.

'Yes you,' he said, fixing me with a blatant stare. 'You and that Kirstie Allsopp woman and Nigella, you're all in it together.'

'What are you talking about?' I frowned, but feeling flattered to be in such esteemed company.

'Homespun, homemade, home grown,' he groaned, 'the world's obsessed, and if folk can't create it, make it or grow it in time for the big day then they're heading to Wynbridge market to buy it.'

'Well, don't knock it,' said Harriet, steering Rachel over towards the Cherry Tree, 'think of your healthy bottom line!'

I wished Steve would go away with them. His healthy bottom line was all I could think about since he'd stretched in my eye line.

'You all right then?' he asked when they were finally out of earshot.

'Of course.'

'Finally got rid of the cold?'

'Yes, just about. I think the snow finally saw it off, or froze it out, as it were.'

'Oh very good,' he grinned, 'ha, ha.'

It hadn't been meant as a joke.

'And we're all right, aren't we, Ruby?'

'What do you mean?'

'Oh, I don't know,' he said, tucking in his shirt and buttoning up his jacket. 'I just kind of got the impression that you've been avoiding me.'

'Of course I haven't,' I lied, 'I've just been so busy here. To tell you the truth, I haven't really seen anyone. I haven't made it to the pub once in the last few days and I can't imagine I will before Christmas now.' I stopped, horribly aware that I was gabbling on and doubtless over-gilding the lily in the process.

'Well that's all right then,' he sighed, his shoulders dropping, 'I was beginning to feel a bit paranoid.'

'About what?'

He shuffled awkwardly from one foot to the other on the icy cobbles and ran his hands through his hair.

'I thought I'd upset you,' he said, 'misread the signs.'

'What signs?'

'Well, ever since I told you that I'd finally got the message about us, you've kind of seemed offish.'

'Offish,' I frowned. 'I don't think I've seen enough of you to be "offish".'

'Exactly,' he said, 'and that's what made me think you were avoiding me. I thought perhaps you might be having regrets.'

'Of course not,' I lied again, giving the idea the eye roll it deserved, 'absolutely not. Like I said, I've just been busy and you've been making all these deliveries so it's hardly surprising our paths haven't crossed during the last few days.'

I did my best to return his stare and crossed my fingers behind my back in the hope that my pupils weren't doing their utmost to contradict me.

'And you've still got no idea what happened at the wreath making that has put my mum in such a funny mood these last few days?'

'Funny' was an interesting choice of word, but I let it pass, lest I became embroiled in one more conversation I'd really rather avoid.

'Nope,' I said, shaking my head and feeling relieved that he'd moved the conversation on, even if it wasn't into much safer territory. 'No idea.'

'OK,' he said, still staring. 'How was the sleepover at Bea's?'

'Fun,' I said, my stomach rolling at the thought of heading back home later.

I'd stayed with Bea for two nights but she had told me that morning over tea and toast that Sam would be staying over for the rest of the week and I had no desire to hear their bedroom gymnastics.

'So are you all set for your big adventure then?' he asked.

'I think so,' I said, surprised that he had mentioned it. 'What's with all the questions all of a sudden?'

'I'm just interested,' he shrugged. 'Trying to be friendly, you know, steer us away from awkward.'

It wasn't really working.

'India first, isn't it?' he went on. 'Have you had your jabs?'

'Yes,' I said, 'every last one, but how did you know?'

'There's one dead giveaway,' he said, pointing over my shoulder at the now creased dream beach picture, 'and it came up in conversation when I was talking to Paul Thompson.'

'Oh,' I said lightly, 'I didn't know you two were still in touch.'

I hoped Paul hadn't mentioned how he had been helping me out on the accommodation and work front.

'Just the odd text,' Steve shrugged. 'Nothing more.'

I couldn't help thinking that texting and talking were two very different things, but I didn't point it out.

'Excuse me love, how much are the big stockings?'

343

'Well, I'd better let you get on,' said Steve, backing towards the van again.

'They're twelve pounds fifty,' I said, painting on my jolliest smile and giving the customer my full attention. 'Would you like me to unfold it so you can get an idea of the full size?'

'See you around, Ruby Sue!' Steve called before jumping back in the van and driving off again.

Chapter 27

I really needn't have worried about life back at home with Dad being awkward because I hardly saw him for the next two days. Evidently we were both making an effort to stay out of each other's way and Mum had cleverly managed to separate herself from the situation by plunging into Christmas overdrive.

The house, continually filled with smells of her delicious baking, could have easily rivalled those Jemma had been concocting at the Cherry Tree and I couldn't make it through either the kitchen at home or the café without pausing to grab a sausage roll, mince pie or slice of Yule log. Something told me, as my jeans began to feel a little tighter than I would have liked, that I wouldn't be in any hurry to send back bikini selfies from my dream beach destination when I finally got there.

'Are you going up to bed already?' asked Mum, when she

spotted me heading for the stairs that Wednesday evening. 'It's not even nine.'

'It's late night shopping tomorrow,' I reminded her, 'the last one before Christmas. Something tells me I'm going to need to be on my toes to face the clamouring hordes.'

At the time I had no idea just how prophetic those few words were going to turn out to be.

It didn't matter how hard I hit my alarm clock the next morning or how many buttons I tried to press, I couldn't stop the noise that had dragged me from the depths of a sleep that I could have happily indulged in for a few more hours at the very least. Eventually I gave in, opened one eye and squinted at the clock next to my bed. Four forty-five. There was no way on earth that I would have set my alarm for four forty-five, even with the hectic day I knew I had ahead of me. In a befuddled daze I smacked the buttons again and it finally dawned on my fuzzy brain that the noise wasn't coming from my clock or my phone, but from downstairs.

'What the hell?' I groaned, pulling myself upright as Dad came rushing into the room and over to the window. 'Will someone kindly tell me what on earth is going on?' I demanded as he peeped through the tiniest crack in the curtains and down into the garden below. 'Dad!'

'Shush,' he said, waving one hand behind his back. 'Be quiet, Ruby. If we can just stay quiet they might go away.'

'Who might go away and why have we got to keep quiet?'

'Meet me in the dining room in ten minutes,' he whispered urgently as he rushed back across the room, 'and do not, under any circumstances, turn on any lights or open the curtains.' He disappeared out of sight for a second and then just his head reappeared around the door, 'or flush the toilet.'

Ever since I'd arrived back in town I'd known he was going to lose it, and given everything I had just seen and heard I guessed it had finally happened. Shame it was on what I had been hoping was going to be the busiest day of my time on the market, but at least I was still in the country and would be on hand to help Mum get him to the doctor's, committed or otherwise.

'Will someone please tell me what is going on?' I yawned, as I padded down the stairs, tying my dressing gown more securely around me.

Whoever was hammering on the front door and rattling the letterbox was pretty persistent and I was half tempted to yank it open and remind them of the ungodly hour.

'In here,' hissed Mum, who was clearly in on whatever was going on, as she pulled me into the dining room.

'Change of plan,' said Dad, crashing into us and landing with his full weight on my right foot. 'They're in the garden. I think we better go back up.'

With him leading the way like Captain Mainwaring in

stealth mode, Mum and I followed up the rear and into their bedroom which was located at the back of the house.

'Close the door,' said Mum. 'I've already made a flask and I packed a few of these mince pies, just in case.' She fished a bag up from next to the bed and began arranging the strange breakfast picnic on the duvet.

'Just in case of what? And why on earth would I want to be eating breakfast at this time?' I said exasperatedly. 'And I know I've already asked, but will one of you please tell me why we're being held hostage in our own bloody home?'

Mum started to sniff into her dressing gown sleeve and Dad left his station by the window and plonked himself on the bed next to her.

'I'm afraid,' he said, running his hands through his hair in a way that reminded me of Tom in full-blown crisis mode, 'I've made a bit of a fool of myself, Ruby.'

'A bit!' said Mum, letting out a strangled sob.

Dad reached out and grabbed her hand.

'All right,' he admitted, 'I've made a total prat of myself.'

I was beginning to panic. Not only had he let my cursing pass without admonishment, he'd now also added his own.

'That's almost right,' said Mum with a disgruntled snort and uncustomary toss of her head. 'Personally I would have added a few fruitier expletives just to really hammer home the point, but you're the one doing the explaining.'

'Explaining what exactly?' I asked for what felt like the

hundredth time, as the increasingly familiar knot of pain began to twist and writhe in the pit of my stomach again.

Dad let out a long slow breath and resignedly shook his head.

'You'd better read this,' he said, reaching under his pillow and pulling out a copy of the local paper. 'This is hot off the press,' he added. 'An early copy. It was shoved through the letterbox about an hour ago and will be on the doormat of practically every household in Wynbridge by breakfast.'

'Who delivered it?' I frowned, picking it up.

'Could have been any number of people,' stated Mum. 'Your father has managed to offend and upset practically everyone in this town at some point or other during his career with the council.'

I saw Dad wince but he didn't contradict her.

'My guess is the editor,' he admitted. 'According to your mother I've given him enough reason to want to get his own back and a pretty nasty spin he's put on the whole thing.'

'Well, you can hardly blame him,' Mum tutted, 'always pointing out all those mistakes. I told you no good would come of it, didn't I? Didn't I always try and warn you what would happen one day? And now it has.'

'But my reasoning for always pointing out those mistakes was that they should never have been there in the first place,' Dad insisted.

'Your problem is you've never known when to stop,' Mum carried on, 'until now.'

Gingerly I picked up the paper, only just noticing that the majority of the front page was filled with Dad's face and it certainly wasn't the most flattering of close-ups.

'They snapped that as I was leaving their offices,' Dad tutted. 'The fellow with the camera couldn't have got any further up my left nostril if he tried.'

'You don't look very happy,' I said, not really thinking. 'What were you doing at the newspaper offices?'

'For heaven's sake, just read it, Ruby,' said Mum, wringing her hands.

The unpalatable truth, I discovered as I skimmed the column inches, was that Steve had been right. Not the part about the new car being paid for with a Retail Park planning approval bribe, the car had very definitely been financed by Dad's inheritance pot, but the part about the future of the market was bang on.

'So who exactly is this Mr Monroe?' I frowned, trying to make some sense of the words that were swimming in front of my eyes.

'He's a property developer from Manchester,' Dad said quietly.

'And what was his interest in the market square exactly?'

'To be honest, I don't really know,' said Dad, looking embarrassed. 'All I can say for sure is that he just wanted to get his hands on the site.'

'And according to this,' I said, pointing at the paper, 'he

was prepared to pay you a pretty penny for helping him get it.'

'I still can't believe it,' sobbed Mum. 'Whatever came over you, Robert?'

'I don't know,' he said, his head now in his hands and his voice barely audible, 'I just got swept along with it all. One of the councillors at Fenditch introduced us and before I knew it I was in it up to my neck. To begin with all I could think about was our retirement fund and how it would swell the coffers and by the time I'd come to my senses and realised how wrong it all was, it was too late.'

'So how has all this come about?' I said, with another nod to the paper. 'Who spilled the beans? Was it you?' I frowned, the penny finally dropping. 'Is that what you were doing at the newspaper offices when the guy snapped the photo?'

'Yes,' said Dad, 'and that's why they're all down there,' he added with a cursory look towards the stairs, 'no doubt baying for my blood and hoping for another scoop.'

'Just stick to the facts, Robert,' Mum said grimly. 'We can do without the drama.'

'Sorry,' he sighed and then carried on, 'by the end of last weekend I'd had enough. I realised I've made enough of a balls-up of the things in my life that really mattered and I couldn't have this hanging over me as well. It was time to come clean and put an end to it all.'

I swallowed hard, guessing that he was talking about the

little heart-to-heart we'd had about mine and Steve's relationship, but I didn't say anything.

'By Monday I'd made up my mind. I was going to the paper and I was going to tell them everything, well, almost everything. There are certain things I've held back on, but it will all come out in the end. I'm just relieved I saw sense before I had any of the money.'

'And what was it exactly that made you see sense, Dad?' I asked, still unable to equate what the paper was saying he had almost done with the man who resembled my honest, loyal and sometimes ever so slightly superior dad.

'It was you actually, love,' he said, looking right at me.

'Me?'

'Yes,' he smiled, looking more like the affable man I remembered, 'you, Ruby.'

'But how,' I gawped, 'what have I done?'

'You made me believe in the importance of the market again,' he explained, 'and the entire town, for that matter. You've only been here a few weeks but in that time you've achieved so much and it made me realise that Wynbridge and the people who live in and around it are worth a whole lot more than a few grand deposited into my bank account. In short, you managed to open my eyes and see how wonderful it is all over again.'

I couldn't help wondering if this new-found attitude explained why he had decided to help show Simon and Jude around the empty unit and whether his recently rediscovered feelings for the community would extend as far as shaking hands with the Dempster family.

'I'm just so pleased you decided to come back,' he sniffed, 'and I'm even more pleased that you took on the market stall. I dread to think what might have happened if I'd been left to my own devices.'

'But what about your job?' asked Mum. 'What about your position at the council?'

'Oh that's all gone,' said Dad, sounding almost blasé about the situation, 'I'm retiring on a shoestring before they have a chance to sack me, but at least my conscience is clear.'

'But you love your job!' I burst out. 'What are you going to do now?'

'I *did* love my job,' he said with emphasis, 'but I blew it. There's no way back for me there now. We'll probably have to sell the house and downsize a bit, but we won't be going far.'

'And how do you feel about that, Mum?'

'I don't know,' she said, but she didn't sound as upset as I would have expected. 'I haven't had long to think about it but I suppose it does seem a bit silly to have all this space with just the two of us rattling around in it. Perhaps we could buy somewhere smaller out of town.'

'You could have those chickens you've always wanted,' Dad smiled, leaning across the bed to give her a kiss.

'Jeez,' I whistled, under my breath, 'and there was me thinking I was coming home for a quiet Christmas.'

'So far it's been anything but, hasn't it, love?'

'You can say that again,' I nodded.

No matter how hard I tried to squash them down I couldn't stop my feelings for Steve, and what our relationship might have been, forcing their way up to the surface again. If only Dad had had a timely prod from his conscience all those years ago then things might have been very different for us. I still couldn't forgive him for interfering and I knew that if Steve and I had been left to steer our own course then things would have been very different indeed.

But that wasn't the only thing on my mind. I watched Dad as he re-read the newspaper headline and shook his head at the unflattering photograph. Although pleased that he had said that I was the one responsible for making him see sense, I still couldn't *really* believe that any of what I had heard or read was true. I couldn't imagine my dad ever being the kind of man to take bribes, no matter how tempting. He had worked too hard to simply sacrifice his career or become embroiled in some unknown developer's dodgy dealings. No, none of it rang true to me. None of it had anything to do with my dad.

He looked up from the paper and caught me staring, trying to puzzle the situation out. I could see straightaway from the look he gave me that it didn't add up. I opened my mouth to ask him to explain it all again but a sudden extra hard thud on the door and assault on the doorbell brought us all out of our reverie and snatched the moment from my grasp.

'Come on!' bawled an all too familiar voice through the letterbox. 'I know you're in there, you silly old bugger, and I'm not leaving until you let me in.'

There was a moment's silence before Chris shouted again.

'I know that didn't make any bloody sense, but you know what I meant. Now, open this damn door.'

I still have no idea what Chris said to the journalists hanging around the front door and hiding in the shrubbery, but by the time Dad gave me the go-ahead to let him in the back door, they had all scarpered, no doubt taking with them an unsavoury soundbite or two courtesy of Mr Dempster.

'What the hell's going on, Robert?' Chris demanded the second the door was closed behind him, 'I've only just seen the paper. Is it all true?'

Mum and I stood there open-mouthed and numb with shock, firstly that Dad had even allowed Chris to cross the threshold and secondly that Chris had just called Dad 'Robert' rather than 'Robbie'.

'You better sit down,' said Dad, pulling out a chair at the kitchen table. 'Put the kettle on, would you, Ruby, please?'

'And don't worry about the milk,' said Chris producing a bottle of whisky from the inside of his jacket and thumping it down, 'I've brought my own.'

Once the pot had been filled and mugs distributed we sat together around the table and Mum and I listened again as Dad relayed the whole sorry story to Chris. Throughout Dad's explanation our visitor sat silent and grave, the occasional nod or shake of his head the only indication that he was taking it all in.

When Dad eventually finished, Chris unscrewed the bottle and gave Dad and himself a generous quota of 'milk' before reaching for the teapot.

'You daft old bugger,' he said under his breath, 'whatever were you thinking?'

'I don't know,' said Dad, running his hands through his hair.

I took a long sideways glance at him and couldn't help thinking that even though I had just listened to the seedy little story again I still didn't believe a word of it.

'Well, I don't envy you,' said Chris, raising his mug to Dad and knocking back his brew in one gigantic slurp. 'Not this time around, anyway. Pour us another, would you, Ruby?'

'I'll refill the kettle,' said Mum jumping up as Dad began to chuckle and likewise knock back his drink.

'Am I missing something?' I couldn't help asking because personally I couldn't see a funny side to the situation, no matter how hard I looked for it.

'You are,' said Chris, slapping Dad on the back and making him wheeze, 'but don't worry about it.'

I got up to help Mum with the fresh tea.

'I've never really understood why those two don't get on,' I muttered to Mum, 'but this is a total bolt out of the blue.'

'We've never got on,' said Chris, demonstrating there was nothing in the world wrong with his hearing, 'because your dad was always the blue-eyed boy around here and I was as jealous as hell.'

'What do you mean?' I frowned, rejoining them at the table.

'Oh it doesn't matter,' said Dad, 'it's all in the past now.'

'No, come on,' I said, hoping that whatever the cause of Chris's jealousy was it wasn't going to be as awkward to listen to as Dad's former revelations, 'I really want to know.'

'Well,' said Chris, a slight smirk playing around his lips, 'when your dad was a young lad, he was, now let me see ... How can I put it?'

Dad shrugged and sat back in his chair.

'Oh, I know,' Chris nodded. 'He was a spoilt little sod who never wanted for anything.'

'And he,' said Dad, jerking his thumb at his old rival, 'was from a hard-working family who didn't have to resort to using material crap to show how much they loved their kids.'

'Not that I realised that at the time,' shrugged Chris, slopping more whisky into their mugs, 'all I knew was that your dad had everything I ever wanted and I had no means of getting it.'

'Do you remember the bike?' sniggered Dad as he slapped Chris's arm.

'Do I remember it?' shouted Chris. 'My backside still bears the belt marks my dad gave me when he found out what I'd done!'

'What bike?' I urged, totally drawn into the explanation that evidently accounted for so much. 'What did you do?'

'One Christmas,' Chris continued, shaking his head, 'your dad had the bike everyone wanted, and I mean everyone.'

'It was lovely,' agreed Dad.

'I can't believe he's saying that,' said Chris to Mum, 'you were only interested in the damn thing for a few days and then you left it lying on the pavement and went on to play with something else you'd no doubt just mentioned in passing you wouldn't mind.'

'That still didn't give you any right to liberate it!' Dad retaliated, good-naturedly.

'What did you do?' I laughed.

'Took it for a spin,' said Chris, 'thought I'd give it the ride it deserved.'

'But not the respect,' chuckled Dad. 'Tell her what happened.'

'I was so busy looking down at the shiny new frame and glittering wheel spokes that I didn't notice the row of parked cars in front of me and rear-ended the damn thing, front wheel first!'

'When I went back outside to pick it up,' said Dad, picking up where Chris had stopped, 'the whole thing was buckled, bent and twisted.'

'I'd scarpered,' Chris cut in.

'But what he didn't know,' said Dad, 'was that I'd seen him ride away on it and bring it back. As soon as your grandfather came home from work, Ruby, I told him what had happened and he went and paid a call to Chris's dad.'

'Who then gave me a leathering I'll never forget,' said Chris shaking his head, 'but I know I deserved it.'

'So let me get this straight,' I said, looking from one to the other. 'You two have always hated each other because you,' and here I pointed at Chris, 'trashed a bike, that you,' now pointing at Dad, 'never even wanted.'

The two men looked at each other and then at me.

'Sort of,' said Dad, looking edgy.

'There were other things,' said Chris, fiddling with the whisky bottle again.

'You might as well tell her,' said Mum, who was apparently privy to at least part of their background, 'as we're soul-baring, she might as well hear the whole thing.'

'There's more?' I laughed.

Neither man looked keen to continue, but I wasn't going to budge until I knew it all.

'As we got older,' Dad said, sounding far less jovial, 'we envied each other on a whole new scale.'

'We did that,' agreed Chris.

'Oh come on,' I encouraged, 'what was next on the agenda? Fighting over girls?'

'Yes,' said Dad and Chris together.

'Exactly that,' nodded Dad.

'Marie and her family moved to Wynbridge,' said Chris with a sheepish grin, 'and before she knew it she had the two most dedicated suitors this town has ever seen.'

'And God knows why,' said Dad, giving Chris a punch on the arm, 'but she chose this bloody buffoon and our rivalry turned into something more serious.'

'Finally I had something that *he* wanted,' said Chris returning the punch, 'and for a while I was over the moon, I still am, of course, because I love Marie to bits but eventually my maturity caught up with my years and I realised how your dad really felt. I hated seeing him so—'

'Bitter,' Dad smiled sadly. 'I was bitter and jealous. I didn't get back in the dating game for a very long time after you and Marie tied the knot.'

Suddenly the penny dropped and I began to understand the age difference between Mum and Dad. I dare say by the time he decided he wanted that someone special in his life, everyone local his own age was married off.

'I know what you're thinking,' Dad said, eyeing me astutely.

'Do you?' I blushed.

'I do,' he nodded, pulling Mum on to his lap in a show of affection that I hadn't seen in quite some time, 'but you're wrong. One day I'll tell you the love story of us, but I think I've had enough of coming clean for today!'

Intrigued as I was to hear more, I knew what he meant. I was exhausted and the day hadn't even got going.

'I'd better be off,' said Chris, leaving the half-empty bottle on the table. 'I dare say you're going to have a busy couple of days ahead of you and you'll probably want to keep your head down.'

My insides groaned at the thought of having to face the rest of the traders. Perhaps I could call in sick or run away to India a little earlier than planned.

'But I want you to promise me that you'll come to the carol service with Marie and me on Christmas Eve,' he said.

'Oh, I don't know about that,' said Mum, jumping off Dad's lap.

'Promise,' said Dad, standing up and shaking Chris's hand. 'We'll be there.'

Chapter 28

As much as I longed to, I didn't call in sick or run away that day. There were only three days of trading left before Christmas and fingers crossed, they were going to be busier than any I had experienced so far. Had I stayed hiding out in my room at home not only would I have been letting Jemma and Lizzie down, but I would have been selling myself short as well as missing out on the extra profit which I hoped would bump up the savings and equip me with the financial means to leave town as soon as possible.

There were, of course, other deeper seated reasons for wanting to get out of the house and I hoped a few hours' distraction in the ever-present biting Wynbridge breeze might help me to think through and make sense of those as well.

As heart-warming and entertaining as it was listening to Dad and Chris chronicle their early years, and the subsequent love triangle that emerged when Marie arrived on the scene, I couldn't stop myself wondering if Dad's interference with my relationship with Steve had been more to do with keeping our two families apart as opposed to worrying about me throwing away the golden, and hard fought for, opportunity that my place at university offered.

Romeo and Juliet we might not have been, but the fact that Steve and I were no longer together and weren't ever likely to be, was indeed the greatest tragedy of my young life if no one else's, and the fact that Dad and Chris's tempestuous relationship had turned such a positive corner only served to make the sad situation even more insufferable.

I kept my head down to begin with that morning as, I couldn't help noticing, did everyone else. I set the stall up in silence, my back turned away from the now familiar early morning hustle and bustle as I tried not to think about what was being said and how many columns of newsprint were being devoured. Everyone loved a good gossip and a local scandal, but I can't deny it felt incredibly uncomfortable being part of the family on the receiving end.

I had just finished setting up when I heard a heavy footfall behind me and braced myself for what I imagined would be an inevitable ear bashing and barrage of questions from my fellow traders.

'I hope that dad of yours keeps his promise.' It was Chris. 'I'm rather looking forward to Christmas this year and that's the first time in a very long time that I've been able to say that, I can tell you. It would be really lovely to go to the carol service with someone I've known for so long!'

I felt a lump, easily the size of a golf ball lodge itself at the back of my throat. He hadn't had to come over and say anything to me at all and certainly not so loudly, but I was extremely grateful that he had. As self-assigned leader of the 'trader tribe' I knew lots of the others would be watching, listening and waiting to follow Chris's example, and I could have hugged him for providing me with such a potentially easy ride.

'Oh, I'm sure he'll be there,' I eventually managed to croak, 'and I'm sure he'll make Mum and I tag along as well. If only to show some family solidarity and offer a bit of moral support.'

'You would have made a damn fine daughter-in-law, Ruby,' he said, reaching for my hand, pulling me into a quick, but rib-cracking hug. 'And I would have been proud to welcome you into our family.'

I nodded, but this time the words refused to come and not only because I couldn't breathe.

'I have to tell you, love, that I did know that your dad had a hand in parting you and my Steve,' he went on, 'and I knew it wasn't his place to, but with everything else . . .'

'Doesn't matter now,' I said, trying to sound more resigned to the situation than I really felt and to stop my bottom lip from trembling, 'it's done. Customers,' I added, with a nod towards his stall, 'you'd better go.'

I watched him walk away, willing myself not to cry or think about Dad's meddling or how much it hurt to feel that there really was no conceivable way back.

'I understand congratulations are in order!'

'Are they?' I frowned, blinking away my tears. 'Are you sure about that, Gwen?'

'Why, of course,' she beamed, rushing over and almost losing her footing in the snow in the process. 'As I understand it, your father has secured the future of our little market!'

I wasn't quite sure how she had talked herself around to putting such a positive spin on the situation or whether what she was suggesting was even right, but I was grateful for her optimistic attitude nonetheless.

'Has he?' I asked.

'Why yes!' she insisted. 'Haven't you seen the paper, my dear?'

'Of course,' I told her, feeling even more baffled by her positivity now I knew she had seen the sordid story in black and white for herself.

'And aren't you proud?' she asked, wide-eyed and evidently willing me to say yes.

'Yes, Ruby,' joined in Jude, 'you must be proud.'

'I'm not sure I would say I'm exactly proud,' I began.

'Having the guts to expose what some of his fellow

councillors were sneakily planning even though he knew it would cost him his job,' sniffed Gwen. 'I admire him. We all do! You should be proud.'

I was in no rush to remind them that for a while at least, Dad was involved in the sneaky planning as well.

'He wasn't the only one caught up in it, you know,' said Bob, ambling over to make his own contribution to the conversation. 'From what I can make out, there was definitely someone else who was in far deeper than your dad, Ruby, possibly more than one.'

'Are you sure about that?'

'Absolutely,' said Bob determinedly, 'the other person or people, if the rumours are true, and let's face it, in this sort of situation they nearly always are, were in it up to their necks and from what I've heard had been taking bribes for years.'

'But your dad didn't actually take any money, did he?' said Shirley with a grin. 'He came to his senses before he was at the point of no return.'

'Yes,' I said, because they were obviously expecting me to say something, 'he did.' Personally I was still struggling to come to terms with the thought of Dad even considering being involved in anything so dodgy, let alone going through with it. 'But I had no idea that anyone else was implicated,' I added, my brain ticking over faster than ever.

'Oh yes,' said Bob importantly as he stuck his thumbs through his braces, 'it'll all be on the news tomorrow, you mark my words. This so-called investor is part of the group who owns that damn Retail Park and from what I can make out, they planned to take the town apart piece by piece until the only option folk had was to use their poxy out of town superstore!'

'The absolute scoundrels!' scowled Gwen, sounding out-raged. Minnie, tucked as always under her arm gave an extra little growl to demonstrate that she agreed with her mistress. 'Thank goodness your dad spoke up when he did, Ruby.'

'Hear, hear!' joined in Jude. 'When he showed us around the shop I said to Simon that he looked like a man with the weight of the world on his shoulders.'

'And you were right,' said Simon, slipping his hand in Jude's, 'what a burden he must have been carrying all this time.'

I had no idea how he'd done it, or whether it actually had anything to do with something Dad had done at all, but somehow the rumour mill had launched him from zero to hero and it looked as though I was going to have the oppor-tunity to enjoy my last few days' trading, even though I knew we hadn't heard the last of the market saga just yet.

Chapter 29

Ever since I was a child I've always been acutely aware that the final few days before Christmas somehow managed to take on a surreal, almost unreal feel all of their own, and with everything that was happening in and around Wynbridge, at home, at the market, in the café and in the papers, this year was certainly no exception. With that in mind, I'd decided to give the trip to The Mermaid after late night opening a miss. Even though a sip of Skylark Scrumpy would have been most welcome, I wasn't sure my already frayed nerves could cope with hearing my family being dissected and devoured as the current talk of the town.

Just as Bob had predicted, and I had feared, we certainly hadn't heard the last of the sordid council saga and the next morning rumours were rife that another bigwig was going to fall from grace before the end of the day. The newspaper might only have been in print every Thursday but its online presence, along with the piqued interest of the local radio and television stations, meant it was all that anyone could talk about.

However, I was relieved to discover that with far bigger salaried fish to fry, Dad's name had slipped from top of the gossip-mongering list to considerably further down but I still couldn't make head or tail of his unexpectedly upbeat attitude. I kept expecting to find him in bits, but for a man who had dedicated his life to his council career and lost it, he was certainly sounding remarkably chipper.

'Can you hear him?' I said to Mum the next morning as I was getting ready to head to the market for the penultimate day's trading. 'He's actually whistling.'

'I know,' said Mum with a cursory glance up the stairs towards where the sound was coming from.

'I've never heard Dad whistle in my life, not ever,' I said. 'Something's not right.'

'Lots of things aren't right, Ruby,' Mum tutted.

'Oh, you know what I'm getting at,' I hissed, 'you know exactly what I mean.'

Mum ignored me and carried on filling my thermal cup with hot chocolate.

'You know as well as I do that there's more to this situation than he's letting on,' I persisted. 'Since when would Dad have given up his job without a fight? And what about planning a revenge assault on the newspaper? Shouldn't he be stocking up on new highlighters and forming a battle plan by now?'

Mum bit her lip.

'I have asked him,' she whispered conspiratorially, 'a hundred times, but he insists he's told us everything.'

'Well, he must be cracking up then,' I said, checking the lid on my cup was secure and not noticing how she was suddenly clearing her throat and discreetly shaking her head.

'Not just yet,' said Dad, smiling broadly as he appeared in the doorway as if by magic, 'maybe I'll give that a go at the end of the month. I wouldn't want to ruin Christmas!'

'Ha, ha,' I frowned, 'very funny. Not.'

'I thought you were always telling me to lighten up, Ruby,' he laughed, picking up my car keys. 'I hardly think it's fair that you've started complaining now that I have! Get yourself sorted and I'll go and de-ice your car.'

'See,' I said to Mum, as we listened to him crashing about in the utility room and pulling on his wellies, 'definitely not right.'

That day the footfall through the town and the market was so high I didn't have time to draw breath from the second I finished setting up until the moment I'd sold the last iced and spiced bun. The wonderful winter weather was helping to play its part as overnight the snow had continued to fall, and by day the temperature plummeted under clear, azure skies, meaning the entire town and surrounding Fens had taken on a fairy-tale winter wonderland look.

Jemma's popular bakes were barely out of the oven and bagged before they were sold and Lizzie was sewing stockings and Christmas bunting as fast as her fingers could work. If my takings and the weight of my money belt were anything to go by, the locals were definitely in the mood to celebrate and spend.

'That's it,' said Lizzie, when she slid and slipped her way across the square mid-afternoon. 'I'm done. Jemma's going to bake for tomorrow but I reckon there's just about enough of my stock left to last the day.'

'Are you sure?' I said, looking over the few bits we still had left. 'You could always pack anything away that you don't sell for next year.'

'Oh, I like your optimism,' she laughed, passing me the bag full of her pretty handiwork, 'but who could we possibly find to replace the inimitable Miss Ruby Smith, even with a whole year's notice?'

I gave her a comic little salute as she rushed back to the café. It would be a real shame if the Cherry Tree stall was packed up on Christmas Eve with no prospect of reappearing. I really had meant what I'd said to Harriet and Rachel about celebrating Valentine's Day and having a Spring Fair, complete with chirping chicks and leaping lambs.

'Have you heard?' Bob shouted over to me.

'Heard what?' I asked tentatively.

'Two more have been sacked this afternoon!'

He was clearly delighted that his earlier prediction had been right.

'Two,' I said shaking my head. 'Crikey.'

'Yep,' he said, showing Simon, who had joined him, the screen on his phone.

'Who is it?' I asked.

'Doesn't say,' shrugged Simon, 'but I'm sure we'll know soon enough.'

'Hey, Tom!' called Shirley at the top of her voice. 'Do you know who's got the chop this afternoon?'

'Afraid not,' he said, pushing Noah over in his pushchair, 'I finished for Christmas yesterday and to be honest, I'm just grateful to be out of the way.'

'Goodness knows what you must think of my dad,' I blushed. It was the first time I'd clapped eyes on Tom since the story had broken.

'I happen to have a very high opinion of your old man,' he said, grinning from ear to ear before checking himself. 'Well, I'd better get on,' he mumbled, looking guilty. 'I'm supposed to be collecting Ella from the café and cooking dinner tonight.'

I watched him walk away, feeling more convinced than ever that I still didn't know the full story.

'Pub?' asked Jude, giving me a hopeful little nudge.

'Yes,' I nodded, suddenly not caring a jot for the gossiping hordes, 'why not?'

*

I had expected the pub to be heaving by the time I finally arrived, but it was really rather quiet.

'Where is everyone, Evelyn?' I asked, hanging my coat on the hook behind the door and hopping up on a bar stool.

'We were packed last night,' she explained, 'but I dare say you'd already worked that out for yourself.'

I nodded but didn't say anything. Given what she said, I was glad I'd decided to give the place a miss. It had been hard enough trying to ignore the exchanged glances and head nods in my direction on the market. Being trapped at a table watching it all play out in front of me would have been torture. Perhaps I did care a little more than I was willing to admit after all.

'I would imagine everyone's at home making sure the cupboards are full and the presents are all wrapped up,' Evelyn continued sagely, 'but you wait until tomorrow when the reality of impending in-laws and rushing about for forgotten cranberry and carrots sets in. They'll be flooding in here in droves.'

'I guess you've seen it all before,' I sighed, reaching in to my jeans pocket for some change.

'A hundred times,' she laughed. 'The folk might change but the stories are pretty much the same!'

I couldn't help thinking that if she was right then we humans were a pretty predictable lot.

'What can I get you, love?' she smiled.

I looked around to double check I hadn't missed Jude and Simon sitting ensconced behind a table somewhere, but they were nowhere to be seen.

'If you're looking for Jude,' said Evelyn following my gaze, 'she was in here earlier but had a phone call and had to go. She said you might be expecting to see her.'

'Oh dear,' I said, 'I hope everything's all right.'

Evelyn smiled and shook her head.

'Dodgy fridge door apparently. Simon's arrived home tonight to discover the cat has got his paws on a considerable amount of smoked salmon and devoured the lot.'

'Oh no,' I sympathised, 'that's not good, is it? Better make it just half a cider for me then, please,' I added with a nod to the pump.

'Like I said,' smiled Evelyn, 'the folk on the merry-go-round might change, but the stories don't. If I had a pound for every time Minnie had got to Gwen's dinner before she had I could be on a lounger in the Bahamas right now!'

I guessed my own decision to rush off to the other side of the world was a story that had been told here many times before: the local girl who drops out of university or her job and decides to spread her wings. I shuddered at the thought of turning into a cliché. It wasn't even as if I could go all out and do something shocking before I left town because Dad had already very definitely stolen my thunder on that front.

'Crikey, it's like a morgue in here,' observed Steve as he rushed through the door with a sharp blast of Wynbridge winter air. 'You all on your lonesome, Ruby?'

'Looks like it,' I nodded, 'but according to Evelyn this is how it always is the night before Christmas Eve.'

Steve looked thoughtful for a moment, as if he was trying to think back over previous years.

'Anyway, I'm glad I've seen you,' I told him. 'I have something for you.'

'That sounds promising,' he grinned, giving up on trawling back through the memory bank and straddling the stool next to mine. 'What is it?'

'Go and have a dig about in my coat pocket,' I ordered, 'and you'll see.'

What with everything else that had happened in the last twenty-four hours, I'd completely forgotten that I had been fretting over his conversations with Paul Thompson. There were far bigger things to worry over now. He looked at me quizzically, then hopped off the stool and began rifling through the coat pockets as instructed.

'Aha!' he laughed, when his fingers met his quarry.

'I thought you might be having withdrawal symptoms,' I said, taking a sip of my cider. 'It's been a few days, hasn't it?'

'Yep,' he said, sitting back down and ripping into the bag of mince pies I had been holding back for him. 'It sure has.'

I watched as he sank his teeth into the first one and started making appreciative, but ever so slightly suggestive, yummy noises.

'You'd better make the most of them,' I insisted as he made a grab for his second, 'that will probably be the last lot you get this year.'

'Oh, what?'

'Jemma will be baking for the stall tomorrow, but given the speed I sold out today I can't guarantee a supply beyond these last few.'

Reluctantly he returned the second pie to the bag, crinkled the top together and pushed it away.

'In that case I'd better pace myself,' he tutted. 'Pint please, Evelyn.'

'Good plan,' I smiled.

'Do you think you could spare me a minute, Ruby?' he asked once he'd paid for his drink. 'Only I'd like to talk to you, if that's OK.'

'We're talking now, aren't we?' I shrugged, 'but yes, come on. Let's grab a seat by the fire. I'd like to talk to you too.'

Sitting either end of the squashy sofa in front of the roaring log fire we both took a long sip at our drinks and eyed each other over the rim of our glasses.

'If it's all right with you,' I said eventually for fear that we'd be sitting there all night if one of us didn't start talking again, 'I'd like to clear the air and say I'm sorry.'

'For what,' he frowned, 'what on earth have you got to be sorry about?'

'For not listening,' I explained, 'for snapping your head off and not really believing what you were trying to tell me about what Dad was up to for so long. I know you were only half right but you were definitely on the right track and if I'd just taken everything on-board sooner we might have been saved some of the mess from the last few days.'

Steve shook his head, put his glass down on the table and sat further back on the sofa.

'No,' he said, 'I'm the one who should be apologising. The way I went about it that first time was all wrong. I was just so convinced of it all in my own mind that I launched off without a thought for how you were going to feel about what I was saying. I'd completely disregarded that fact that I was talking about your dad and that no matter how you might feel about him at the moment, at the end of the day he's still your flesh and blood.'

I was grateful that he'd realised that.

'And anyway,' he added, leaning over, 'between you and me I think I've probably got it more than half wrong.'

'What do you mean?'

'Well, I've been thinking it all through,' he said, biting his lip and picking up his glass again, 'and it doesn't add up. None of it adds up at all.'

I was still thinking the same myself but had come no closer to discovering if my hunch was right.

'Your dad loves this town,' Steve went on, turning his attention to the flames licking up the chimney, 'and he loves his job. I know we've never exactly hit it off but even I know that he's not the sort of bloke who would throw away the things he cares most in the world about for the sake of a few quid.'

'I do have to agree with you there,' I nodded. 'And he seems so ridiculously upbeat about it all.'

'Does he?'

'Yes. He's going around smiling and whistling as if this is the best thing that's ever happened to him.'

'What does your mum have to say about it all?'

'She's suspicious as well, but she says she's asked him and he's sticking to his story. He's even planning to put the house on the market in the New Year so they can downsize and find a way of living comfortably on their reduced means.'

'I can't believe for one second that would really be a prospect he would be looking forward to!'

'I know,' I shrugged, 'me neither.'

'He's a very driven bloke, your father, a man who's used to always getting his own way.'

'That's something else I've had confirmed since I've been back,' I sighed.

Steve turned to look at me, his eyes searching my face. His cheeks were flushed from sitting too close to the fire.

'You know, don't you?' he said eventually.

'What,' I croaked, 'what do I know?'

He didn't elaborate, just carried on looking at me, silently willing me to confess.

'Oh all right,' I caved, 'yes, I know. I found out last Sunday. He said he'd done it with the best of intentions. He also said he'd only told you to let me go because he thought parting us was going to be the best thing for me in the long run.'

'As did I,' Steve swallowed, 'that was why I went along with him.'

'It's a shame neither of you thought to sit down and ask me if I had an opinion on what was best for me, wasn't it?'

'God yes,' he said, running his hands through his hair.

'I wish you had,' I said, my eyes brimming with hot tears. 'I so wish you had.'

'So do I,' said Steve, his hand reaching across the cushions towards mine, 'I wish that more than anything. What would you have said?'

I swallowed hard, my brain trying to formulate an answer that would put an end to all the wondering once and for all. Just as I was poised to begin, Bea came bursting through the door, her usually tidy hair escaping from its tight bun and her eyes furious and aflame.

'Where is he?' she demanded, banging the door shut behind her.

'Evening, Bea,' smiled Jim, as he ran a tea towel over the stack of glasses on the bar in front of him.

Steve and I sprang apart before she spotted us and I quickly blinked away my tears.

'Don't you "Evening, Bea" me,' she said, pointing an accusatory finger at the pub in general. 'Is he here?'

'I assume you're talking about Sam,' guessed Jim, 'but I don't know why you'd bother asking me. I'm just your affable landlord. No one tells me anything.'

Bea's eyes swivelled around the room and came to rest on Steve.

'Aha,' she said, marching over. 'You're the other half of the dynamic duo. What have you done with him?'

'Why don't you sit down?' I suggested, budging up a little. 'Get your breath back.'

I had worked out she was on the warpath searching for her beloved Sam but I also knew that if she carried on making such a show of herself she'd soon regret it, even though the pub was practically empty. Decorum and modesty, at least in public, were all important to a girl like Bea.

'I don't want to sit down,' she seethed. 'I just want to know where he is.'

'Well, where have you looked?' asked Steve.

And if he carried on using that tone of voice I knew he was going to get more than he bargained for when Bea worked herself up to answering him. Or was he?

'Everywhere,' she sniffed, flopping down on the chair opposite and dropping her many shopping bags in a muddled heap around her feet. 'He promised me he wasn't going to be working over Christmas and that we'd spend some proper time together, but now he's just disappeared. Vanished. I can't find him anywhere.'

'Have you tried his mobile?' I suggested.

Bea looked at me witheringly and I had the feeling that Steve wasn't the only one skating on thin ice.

'Of course I have,' she tutted, 'and his flat. It's all locked up and he's never given me a key so I can't even get inside to make sure he hasn't had an accident.'

'What an imagination you have,' chuckled Steve.

Bea turned her beady attention to him.

'So where is he then?' she demanded. 'You're his best friend. He must have said something to you. Boyfriends don't just disappear off the face of the earth the day before Christmas Eve for no reason. He's got another girl, hasn't he?' she sobbed. 'Some pert young thing he's rescued and he's got so sick of me hinting about marriage proposals he's gone off with her somewhere. Oh God, I'm going to be Miss Havisham!'

'Of course you aren't,' I soothed, 'that's a silly thing to say. Isn't it, Steve?' I scowled, looking to him for support.

'Completely silly,' he agreed with a smile.

'There,' I told her.

'Compeyson had proposed to Amelia Havisham before he buggered off, if my school memories of studying the plot are still up to speed.'

Bea started to sob into her already saturated tissue.

'Oh well done,' I said, glowering at Steve who seemed to think the whole situation was highly amusing.

'What?' he mouthed silently before draining his pint glass.

I continued to glare at him, beseeching him to say something to soothe my sad friend.

'Oh, he'll turn up,' he said, leaning forward and patting Bea's knee. 'I'm sure he hasn't gone far, but perhaps you should break into the flat just to make sure.'

'Could I do that?' asked Bea, looking up at him, wide-eyed and raring to go. 'Do you think I should?'

'Of course not,' he laughed, 'honestly, Bea. He'll be back in time to watch you open your presents, I'm sure.'

'You do know something, don't you?' she asked again.

'Nope,' he said, giving me a sly wink. 'I know absolutely nothing about anything.'

Chapter 30

Having spent the larger part of the previous evening trying to placate Bea and convince her that she was the only young, pert woman that Sam was interested in, and not thinking about what might have happened between Steve and me had she not burst in when she did, I wasn't feeling quite as ready for Christmas Eve as I would have liked. Fortunately, however, when I arrived to set up the stall for the last time, Gwen's smiling face coupled with the sheet of paper she was brandishing soon sent my seasonal spirits soaring back up to where they should have been.

'Here,' she said, thrusting the sheet into my hands, 'read this! We've all been given a copy and this one's yours.'

'What is it?' I said, smoothing it out and noting the council logo emblazoned across the top.

'Read it!' insisted Gwen. 'Just read it!'

As my eyes scanned over the paragraphs, some of the

other stallholders wandered over to join us and by the time I had finished reading everyone was chattering excitedly and looking far happier than I could ever remember seeing them.

'Looks like we're not going anywhere after all then,' boomed Chris, his face radiant and relaxed, 'Wynbridge market is here to stay!'

His voice echoing around the stalls was met with cheers from every direction.

'And this says there are plans for even more events to be scheduled next year,' I cheered, my own complexion as flushed as Chris's. 'This really is wonderful news,' I told them all, 'I'm so pleased you're all here for the duration.'

'The Smith family have had more than a small part to play in securing the future of our livelihoods these last few weeks and I for one am very grateful,' sniffed Shirley, her rough and ready tone sounding unusually softened.

'Well, I've certainly tried my best,' I said, 'not that I really knew just how at risk your future was when I started out,' I reminded them, 'and I'm still amazed that you've all so readily forgiven Dad for being swept along with this corrupt developer.'

Everyone turned to look at Chris again.

'Now, Ruby,' he said sternly, 'you know as well as I do that we still haven't heard the whole story as far as that's concerned.'

'So you don't really believe it either, then?' I asked.

'None of us do,' cut in Simon. 'Jude and I listened to your dad singing the praises of Wynbridge long enough the Sunday he showed us around the shop to know that he wasn't the type to jeopardise the town by taking a bribe, or even by being tempted to take one,' he quickly added, before I reminded him that the situation had never had a chance to get that far.

'So what do you think has gone on?' I said to Chris.

'We'll find out all in good time, I'm sure,' he said good-naturedly. 'Now come on everyone, we need to make the most of today. I suggest we pack up around three and head to The Mermaid. Everyone up for it?'

Marie lingered behind as the others went back to finish setting up.

'You all right, Ruby?' she asked, her manner not at all assured, 'I haven't had a chance to talk to you for a few days.'

'I'm OK,' I shrugged, 'still looking forward to getting away, to be honest.'

'I spoke to Steve last night,' she said, distractedly fingering the bunting I had strung up across the front of the stall. 'He told me that you talked about what your dad did.'

'Did he?'

'He seemed to think that you were going to say something else but Bea arrived looking for Sam and you didn't get the chance.'

Inwardly I cursed Steve for telling anyone, especially his

mother. I loved Marie to bits, always had, but I knew that she and Mum had already had their heads together on more than one occasion trying to decide what was to be done about us, when what they really needed to do was butt out. Mum was too discreet to say anything but Marie, with her fiery temper and forthright manner, was struggling with her position in the back seat.

'Do you know if he's turned up yet?' I asked, trying to get her to change the subject.

'Who?'

'Sam.'

'No, I don't think so. He's still off on his travels or what-ever it is he's doing, and talking of travels,' she began, 'have you booked your plane ticket yet, Ruby?'

'No,' I said, 'not yet. I'm waiting until Jemma and I have sorted out the stall money.' I don't know why I'd felt the need to explain that. It wasn't anyone else's business. 'I'll probably go to Peterborough after Boxing Day.'

'Is that the only reason why you haven't booked?'

'What do you mean?'

'You aren't holding out to see if you need to book two seats, by any chance?'

I knew exactly what she was getting at, but why she would think I would want to travel halfway around the world with an ex-boyfriend was beyond me. The sooner she and every-body else could accept that Steve and I were not getting back together the better. I was about to say as much when I realised she had pulled a handkerchief out of her pocket and her eyes were filled with tears.

'Oh, I'm sorry,' she sobbed quietly, 'I know you probably think I'm an interfering old cow.'

'I wouldn't go that far,' I smiled.

'But I just want to see one of my boys happy,' she said, wiping her eyes. 'All I want is to see my Steve living the life he wants, rather than the one he had thrust on him when we lost our Sean.'

'But why would you think that the life he wants would revolve around me any more?' I asked, in the hope that she would get the message that I was very probably not the answer to her son's dreams.

'Well, if you haven't worked that out by now,' she said stiffly, 'then you're an even bigger fool than I thought.'

By lunchtime the earlier crowds of townsfolk had started to disappear and beyond the sound of the enthusiastic carollers singing their hearts out under Chris and Marie's beautiful trees at either end of the square, there was little in the way of customers. The final few stragglers had begun to head for home, each weighed down with last-minute presents, bunches of mistletoe and the odd forgotten Christmas dinner component as predicted by Evelyn in the pub the night before.

Lizzie had been right not to worry herself over making any extra stockings as there were still a few left, hopefully for next year, but Jemma's bakes, buns and biscuits had sold out completely. Not so much as a crumb was left and from what I'd seen, lots of people had been eating them on the go. A timely sugar hit amid the general chaos.

'Well, that's it,' said Bob, as a customer left, clasping their shopping bags, 'that was the last cat Christmas stocking we had.'

I couldn't help but laugh.

'You thought I was mad when I suggested you tried selling a few seasonal things, didn't you?'

'I've thought you were mad about a lot of things,' he admitted with a chuckle, 'but I'm delighted to say you've proved me wrong on every single occasion.'

'Good,' I smiled back, trying to relax and stretch out my shivering spine, 'there's nothing as satisfying as proving people wrong! Are you packing up now?'

'Yes,' he nodded, 'I think we'll call it a day. Jude will want to get the sprouts on in about an hour,' he said with a wink.

'No she will not,' said Jude, appearing from behind a stack of boxes at the side of the stall. 'Mushy veg was more your mother's speciality than mine, thank you very much.'

I left them arguing mildly between themselves and turned back to look at the stall with its pretty sparkling fairy lights and the clever 'Makes and Bakes' banner Lizzie had painted in time for my first day of trading. It was impossible to believe that my weeks of working at the market had flashed by so quickly. It seemed like only yesterday that I was drinking cheap coffee in my student digs and accepting Lizzie and Jemma's offer with such enthusiasm.

As I began to unpin the lengths of bunting and lights, I couldn't help but wonder whether if I'd had the benefit of hindsight those few weeks ago I might have thought twice about coming back at all. I'd had no real expectation of rekindling my relationship with Steve, until the moment I'd clapped eyes on him in the churchyard of course, but nothing could have prepared me for the twists and turns we had endured, for all the near misses and not forgetting that one heart-stopping, stomach-twisting kiss under the mistletoe.

'So that's that, then,' I said a little while later as I handed Jemma the money belt and Lizzie flicked the café sign to closed and locked the door.

'Are you all right?' asked Angela, her head cocked to one side as she came through from the kitchen with four steaming mugs of tea. 'You look tired, Ruby.'

'And is it any wonder?' said Lizzie, draping a comforting arm around my shoulder. 'This girl has lived through more shock and trauma during the last few days than most people round here face in a lifetime!'

'And she's managed to keep working through it all,' added

Jemma proudly. 'Had it been me, I would have crawled under the duvet and never come out again.'

'Oh, I've had my moments when I've wanted to do exactly that,' I smiled, 'believe me.'

'But you do know this whole situation with your dad isn't for real, don't you, Ruby?' Angela insisted.

'Funnily enough, you're about the hundredth person to say that.'

'Well, it's just a smokescreen, isn't it?' she said. 'The truth will come out in the end.'

'I hope so,' I said, warming my hands around the mug Jemma passed me, 'and I hope it happens before I leave. I can't bear the thought of going away with this all still hanging in the air. I'm fairly certain Dad has something else to say about the situation but for some reason he's still holding back.'

'Perhaps he has to wait for the opportune moment,' said Angela, narrowing her eyes. 'Perhaps he has to wait to get the nod from the big boss or something.'

'Oh good grief,' laughed Lizzie, 'she's gone all Agatha Christie on us again!'

'Well, he could be,' said Angela, 'you never know. Robert Smith could be our very own 007 for all we know!'

It was a good few seconds before we all stopped laughing. I was sure Dad was holding something back, but he was definitely no Daniel Craig. Leaping out of bed he could manage, but certainly not out of a plane.

Jemma picked the money belt up off the table and gave it a little shake.

'Do you mind if we settle up later?' she asked.

'Of course not,' I nodded, 'you can leave it until after Christmas if you like, if that's easier.'

'Are you sure?'

'Absolutely,' I told her, 'I'm not planning to buy my plane ticket for a couple of days yet. There are still some details to finalise and I won't be thinking about them when I'm stuffed with Mum's delicious turkey and cranberry.'

'Well, as long as you're sure,' she said, 'that would be great. The last thing I feel like doing right now is sorting out the books. I've still got Ella's costume to finish before the service this afternoon. She's managed to pull the hem down somehow and she looks far from angelic, tripping about all over the place!'

'I'll bet,' I laughed.

'Why ever didn't you get Tom to bring it round earlier?' scolded Lizzie. 'I could have had that fixed in seconds when I had the machine out. You've more than enough still to sort without worrying about sewing.'

'I didn't think,' said Jemma, biting her lip.

'I'll come home with you and do it by hand,' insisted Lizzie, 'then we can all leave together.'

'Thanks, Lizzie,' said Jemma gratefully. 'And you'll come with us, won't you, Angela?'

'If that's all right,' she said. 'It does seem a bit silly going all the way home just to come practically straight back again.'

'Then you could have supper with us all and Tom could run you back after,' Jemma suggested. 'How does that sound?'

'Perfect,' beamed Angela. 'Thank you. Are you coming to the crib service, Ruby?'

'Yes,' I said, 'believe it or not, Chris made Dad promise that we would all go together.'

I had to laugh as the three ladies looked on, their mouths hanging open in shock.

'I know,' I said, 'don't ask. I'll tell you all about it one day, but now I'd better go home and get ready. To tell you the truth, I've got mixed feelings about going back inside the church. I haven't set foot inside it since Sean's funeral.' I felt a little shiver course through my body as I thought back to that most dreadful of days.

'Well,' said Jemma as she put the now empty mugs back on the tray, 'you couldn't have picked a nicer time to go back.'

'No,' I said, 'I suppose not.'

'Oh yes,' joined in Lizzie, 'what with tripping angels and Mary dropping Jesus all over the place, the crib service is always excellent value!'

Chapter 31

Given how uncomfortable I had been feeling about setting foot back inside St Mary's church, I was surprised (and somewhat relieved) to discover it wasn't the traumatic experience I thought it would be. The path down to the porch was lit by strings of clear, white lights and the large arched windows, illuminated by countless candles, threw out a warm and welcoming glow.

Not dissimilar to the day of Sean's funeral service, every pew was crammed, but on this occasion the place was a riot of colour, chatter and laughter. The atmosphere was thick with excitement and expectation for the start of the traditional religious celebration.

I had never been much of a church-goer but it was impossible not to be moved by the sight of the dozen or so children waiting in the wings to play their part. Mary clutched the doll assigned to the role of infant Jesus to her chest, whispering soothingly into his curly hair, while angels adjusted their itchy tinsel crowns and Ella, slightly taller than the rest and looking decidedly self-conscious, stood a little apart from the unruly group.

'Over here!' shouted a voice from one of the pews closest to the altar. 'We've saved you a seat!'

Chris was windmilling wildly and pointing at the empty spaces at his side while Marie pulled at his sleeve, imploring him to pipe down. I didn't think I could cope with being crammed next to Steve in this church of all places and urged Mum and Dad to take their seats before someone else nabbed them.

'But what about you, Ruby,' frowned Mum, 'where are you going to sit?'

'I'll squeeze in at the back,' I said, stepping awkwardly aside to avoid blocking the aisle. 'Bea just messaged to say she's coming but she still hasn't found out where Sam has disappeared to. I don't want her feeling all on her own, especially not tonight, so I'll stay here.'

Standing at the back, I could see over the heads of everyone sitting down and I had mixed feelings as I watched Mum and Dad exchanging hugs and handshakes with Chris and Marie as if they were long-lost friends. Why couldn't they have got themselves sorted out years ago and celebrated my relationship with Steve rather than sabotage it?

'No chance of a seat now, I suppose,' said a voice next to me. 'I hadn't realised how late it was until I heard the bells.'

I stared down at the little posy of Christmas roses and holly I had quickly put together before leaving home and shook my head in disbelief.

'I thought you were already at the front with your mum and dad,' I said, my gaze flicking up to the altar and the last-minute alterations to the running order being orchestrated by the vicar.

'I was supposed to be,' tutted Steve, 'but I had to go and collect Gwen. She took an age fiddling about over Minnie and checking the cottage door was locked and then when we got here I had a job getting her out of the van. I had to practically give her a fireman's lift all the way to her seat because she was afraid the path was icy!'

He bent over, rubbing his back and I couldn't help but smile at the image of him carrying Gwen into church. She really was a mischievous old rascal. But talking of firemen, where had Bea got to? My plan to avoid Steve had failed spectacularly so far. I hoped she wasn't going to let me down as well.

'Oh and by the way,' he added almost telepathically, 'Bea's not coming.'

'What?'

'She said she couldn't face it without Sam so she's gone straight to the pub to drown her sorrows.'

'Perhaps I should go and make sure she's OK,' I whispered, trying to step around him and make my escape, but he quickly put a hand out to stop me.

'It's only forty minutes,' he said quietly, 'I think she'll manage, don't you? And besides,' he added with a nod to the front, 'they're about to start.'

The service was every bit as wonderful and entertaining as Jemma and Lizzie had suggested it would be. One of the kings forgot his gift for the baby Jesus, whom Mary dropped on more than one occasion, and the front and back of the camel never did quite work out how to walk in tandem, but Ella excelled as she expertly guided her fellow charges through their few short lines.

'When I came last year,' whispered Steve, nudging my arm to get my attention and staring down at me with his unnervingly penetrating gaze, 'I wondered what it would have been like watching our kids up there.'

The admission came completely out of the blue and was a total shock. For a second I wished I had taken the seat next to Mum and Dad at the front because I wasn't sure my legs were going to keep me upright long enough to formulate a response.

'Don't you ever think about things like that?' he asked, bending closer as the organ struck up and everyone jostled to their feet.

'Not really,' I whispered.

I didn't want to just say a flat 'no' and hurt his feelings, but judging by his pained expression I already had. From the anguished look on his face I just knew my arrow had fired straight and true through his heart and that hadn't been my intention at all.

'But then, of course, I've been away, haven't I?' I quickly backtracked. 'Had I still been living here, surrounded by reminders of what could have been then I dare say I would have thought about it. A lot.'

'You don't have to say that,' he said, turning his attention back to the sheet we were sharing. 'Given everything that has happened, I probably wouldn't have given any of it a second thought either if I was you.'

'I wouldn't say that I haven't given it *any* thought,' I swallowed, 'but we're a bit young for you to have been thinking about us having kids, aren't we?'

I was trying to lighten the moment but it didn't work.

'Actually,' Steve sighed wistfully, 'I seem to remember there was a time when we'd planned our lives out entirely.'

I remembered that time too, as if it were only yesterday. Without thinking too hard about it or dissecting my intentions, I quickly slipped my hand into his and gave it a little squeeze. When I went to pull away, he wouldn't let me go and so we stood side by side, for once united, and I honestly thought my heart would break if I had to let go again.

No one was in a rush to leave when the service finally finished.

'You are coming to the pub, aren't you?' asked Steve,

reluctantly letting go of my hand before the congregation cottoned on.

'Yes,' I said, fiddling with the flowers again as the noise level of chatter and well wishes began to escalate. 'But I want to see Jemma and everyone first, and I made this for Sean,' I said shyly, holding the posy up to show him, 'I want to make sure he knows there's no hard feelings.'

'Oh, you silly sod,' smiled Steve with a shake of his head. 'I'm sure he knows that already, but the flowers are beautiful and Mum will be really touched that you've been thinking about him.'

'What did you think?' shouted Ella as she skipped down the aisle towards us. She'd already managed to pull down part of the hem I knew Lizzie had only just finished repairing. 'Did I do all right?'

'You were wonderful,' I told her, 'I don't think the little ones could have managed without you.'

'Thanks,' she beamed, giving me a twirl, 'but I don't think I'll do it next year,' she added, wrinkling her nose.

'No?'

'Nah,' she said, 'I'm getting a bit too old for all this now.'

I knew there was absolutely no point contradicting her; Ella was one young lady who certainly knew her own mind.

'Right, madam,' said Jemma, as she finally fought her way to us through the crowds, 'go and find your coat and wellies. We need to get home and get sorted for Santa, don't we?'

'Oh yes,' Ella giggled, before racing off again, 'and we don't mean you this time, Steve!'

As she skipped off to find her things I couldn't help noticing that Jemma was eyeing Steve and me speculatively and I took a cautionary sidestep to avoid her jumping to the wrong conclusion.

'So,' said Steve, as Tom carried Noah back down the aisle with Lizzie, Ben and Angela filing close behind, 'are you all set for tomorrow then?'

'I think so,' said Jemma, 'it's been tricky finding suitable hiding places for all the presents this year, not to mention finding the time to wrap them all, of course. Kids' things always seem to be in such massive boxes these days!'

'Tell me about it,' smiled Steve, 'I've been helping my cousin lug things for his two around in the van. Goodness knows how many polystyrene chips are going to be littering his lounge tomorrow morning!'

'Ordinarily we hide stuff at my parents' house,' explained Tom, 'but this year they're heading north to spend Christmas with my sister so there was no point really. We would only have had to move it all again.'

'It's going to be just the four of us this year,' sighed Jemma dreamily, 'and I can't wait.'

'And what about you two?' I asked Lizzie and Ben. 'Are you home alone as well?'

'No, not this year,' said Lizzie. 'We're eating at the pub

with my mum and dad and, from what I can make out, practically every other Wynbridge resident!'

'Snap,' said Steve, 'and if last year's celebration is anything to go by, it's going to be one hell of a party.'

'I'm not sure you should say H-E-L-L in church,' chastised Ella who had returned in record time and was pulling on her coat while stuffing her feet in her wellies.

I couldn't help smiling. Evidently she thought it was all right to spell the word, just not say it.

'And what about you, Angela?' I quickly asked before Ella had a chance to get into her stride and give anyone else a lecture.

'Just me, myself and I,' she smiled, 'but I've got a Skype call with my daughter planned for last thing.'

'Why not come to the pub?' jumped in Steve.

I knew straightaway that he was uncomfortable with the idea of Angela being home alone on Christmas Day, and I felt further endeared towards his kind and caring personality.

'There's always plenty of food and fun to go around,' he added, trying his hardest to tempt her.

'That's really very kind of you, Steve,' said Angela, 'but I'm actually looking forward to a couple of days' peace and quiet. It's all got a bit hectic in the run up to Christmas this year and I could do with a proper rest.'

'Well if you change your mind,' Steve couldn't resist adding, 'you'll know where we'll be, and if the weather puts you off I can always run you there and back in the van. I wouldn't mind.'

Mum, Dad, Chris and Marie finally made it out of their pew and I was flabbergasted when Dad told me that he and Mum had decided they would join everyone in the pub for a celebratory pre-Christmas drink.

Outside, under the watchful gaze of the constellations, we said goodbye to Jemma and the gang and Marie and I walked over to Sean's grave. Just as Steve had predicted, Marie was very touched that I had thought of him.

'These look really beautiful,' she said, caressing the soft petals of the Christmas roses, 'and you've put them together with such finesse.'

'Well, I had a good teacher,' I told her. 'I spent a long time watching you at the wreath making.'

'Oh well, I'll take that as a compliment,' nodded Marie. 'It's really very kind of you to remember Sean, especially at this busy time of year.'

'I don't think anyone will ever forget him, Marie,' I reassured her. 'He was a wonderful guy.'

As his mother, I had no doubt that Marie was well aware of how wonderful her first born had been, but I didn't know what else to say. Faced with the reality of a gravestone bearing such short dates on a bitterly cold night it was all too easy to fall into cliché and sound as if you were trotting out platitudes even if you didn't mean to.

'Come on,' she said, kindly helping me out, 'it's freezing out here. Let's catch up with the others and get to the pub.'

I set my little present at the foot of the stone with the family wreaths, told Sean I wished that he was with us and that wherever he was I hoped he knew how much he was loved, missed and thought of, and not just at Christmas time.

Chapter 32

Hot, crowded and very noisy, The Mermaid was everything Dad usually hated, but watching him throw back his head and laugh at something Chris had said, and quickly drain his first drink, I began to think that losing his job might have been the making of him after all.

'I'm getting a round in,' said Steve, as he pushed his way through the crowd to the bar, 'do you want a cider?'

'No thanks,' I called after him. I had no desire to wake with a hangover tomorrow. 'Can I have a diet Coke instead, please?'

Bea was camped out on the sofa next to the fire. She was still wearing her coat and scarf and the glass she nursed as she stared morosely at the floor, was almost full.

'I missed you at the church,' I told her as I plonked myself down next to her. 'We all did.'

'I just wasn't in the mood,' she said with a sigh, 'I thought I wanted a drink,' she added, holding up the glass, 'but I don't seem to have the taste for it now.' She dumped it on the table and tried to look a little more cheerful. 'So how was the service?'

Evidently she hadn't heard anything from Sam and as far as I knew no one else had either. His disappearance was all a bit of a mystery really and given that Bea's pleasant enquiry didn't match the miserable expression in her eyes I guessed that she didn't really give two hoots about how the crib service had gone but I told her anyway. I would have said anything to try and stop her brooding.

'No sign of lover boy, then?' said Steve as he passed my diet Coke. I frowned up at him, hoping he would get the message and change the record. 'According to one of the guys at the station he took hand luggage and his passport.'

He sat himself on the sofa opposite and took a long pull at his pint.

'What?' he frowned over at me when he had swallowed his mouthful.

'Honestly, Steve,' I scolded, 'a bloody charging rhino would make less of an impact.'

'Doesn't matter,' shrugged Bea, who had taken the news unnervingly well. 'What difference does it make where he is? If he's decided to dump me, whether he spends Christmas in Doncaster or Dubai is hardly relevant, is it?'

'I don't think you need a passport to visit Doncaster,' said Steve flippantly, 'and since when did he say anything about dumping you, Bea? I can't help thinking you've blown this situation out of all proportion.'

'Steve,' I warned, 'give her a break. Sam's buggered off just days before Christmas without so much as a word; what's she supposed to think?'

Steve shrugged and examined his glass.

'Well,' said Bea, 'wherever he is, at least we gave our relationship a try which is more than I can say for the pair of you.'

'What?' I gasped, twisting round to face her and remind her that I was an ally, not the enemy.

'You've been pussy footing around each other for weeks,' she went relentlessly on. Apparently she was immune to my best death stare. 'It's more than obvious that you're both still crazy about each other but rather than getting on with it you just keep going round in bloody circles.'

'I don't think—' I began.

'Neither of you do,' she moaned, 'it's ridiculous. These last few weeks have been your second chance but you're both too dense to realise it, or too chicken to go for it. I wish you'd just get on with it one way or another because if this whole business with Sam has taught me anything, it's made me realise life's too short to try and twist and mould relationships to your own liking. You just have to grab what you can and be bloody grateful that someone loves you!'

Speech over, Bea picked up her bag and left. I sat

open-mouthed and embarrassed and before I could think of anything to say Steve was on his feet and making for the door as well.

'I have to go,' he said over his shoulder.

And he did.

'There you are, Ruby!' called Dad as he spotted me from his position at the end of the bar. 'Let me get you another drink.'

'I'm OK, thanks,' I told him as I struggled back into my coat. 'I'm off now, actually.'

'What, going home?'

'Yes,' I said, my mind still reeling from Bea's impromptu monologue and Steve's swift departure. 'I'm shattered.'

I didn't add that I also needed some peace and quiet and a few minutes to think. Was Bea right, I wondered? Were Steve and I really still crazy about each other? His hasty exit certainly seemed to suggest otherwise, but how could I be sure?

'You can't go yet,' said Dad looking crestfallen.

'Sorry,' I muttered, 'you and Mum can find your own way home, can't you?'

I could see Mum sitting at a table with Marie. She was sipping a glass of white wine and laughing. She seemed more relaxed than I'd seen her in ages.

'No, I mean it, Ruby,' said Dad sounding suddenly serious, 'I really need you to stay, just for a few more minutes at least.'

'Why?'

'Because I have something to say.'

'Well, say it then,' I said testily. I was beginning to lose my patience. 'Just spit it out, would you. I want to go home.'

Before I could utter another word he had walked behind the bar, whispered something to Jim and was pulling with real gusto on the big brass bell. In an instant the place was in uproar and then, one by one, as everyone began to notice who was responsible for the din they slowly fell silent. Dad turned redder than I had ever seen him and I had the distinct feeling that we were all finally about to discover the whole truth behind the market square saga.

'Don't worry,' he began, his colour deepening again. 'I'm not calling time.'

'What are you doing then, you silly old sod?' called Chris from the back.

Clearly old habits died hard, but there was no malice in his tone and his thumbs up suggested that he, unlike the rest of us, knew exactly what was going on.

'I have a couple of things I want to explain,' continued Dad, addressing everyone, but his gaze lingering longest on me, 'and it'll only take a minute. It's important you all get to hear what I have to say, especially you market traders and I want you to hear it from the horse's mouth, as it were. That way there'll be no confusion.'

The pub door creaked open, bringing with it the customary rush of freezing air and the not so familiar face of the newspaper editor, John Porter who, in true Chris Dempster style, gave Dad another unexpected thumbs up and melted into the crowd at the back.

'As you all know,' said Dad, picking up the thread, 'there has been a considerable amount of upheaval and reshuffling at the council offices during the last few days and there are a few of my former colleagues who will be reassessing their CV's this Christmas.'

'You included,' shouted some comic from the sidelines.

'No,' said Dad calmly. 'Not me, actually, because that's what I want to tell you. I haven't lost my job at all.'

There were gasps all round.

'And,' he continued, 'I haven't been tempted to take any bribes or get myself caught up with dodgy investors or lose sight of the fact that I love our little Wynbridge almost as much as I love my wife and daughter.'

'What the hell?'

'I know we've all been through the mill a bit these last few days, months even.'

'You're not wrong!' said Mum who, given her pallor, evidently didn't have a clue what Dad was going to say next. 'I think you better tell us the whole story, Robert.'

Dad looked at her and nodded.

'I'm sorry, love,' he smiled across at her, 'I've gone to tell you and Ruby this a hundred times but I just couldn't take the risk.'

'It's all my fault really,' spoke up a voice from the back. 'You can blame me, Mrs Smith.'

Everyone's eyes swivelled to the back of the bar and John Porter, editor extraordinaire, stepped forward.

'I'm the one who got your husband involved in all this.'

'In all what?' demanded Mum, wringing her hands.

'I think I'd better start from the beginning,' he said, walking up to join Dad at the bar, 'but I'll keep it brief. Almost a year ago, Robert came to me with concerns he had about some of the goings-on at the council.'

'Why didn't you to talk to someone at work, Robert?' Mum asked.

'I did try,' said Dad, 'but I soon got the feeling that the folk I was talking to were probably involved as well.'

'So that was when he came to me,' cut in Mr Porter. 'I knew Robert of old, of course. Our battles over misspelling and the odd journalistic inaccuracy are well known.'

A couple of people began to laugh.

'And I too had my suspicions,' he said. 'A couple of the high ranking council employees over at Fenditch had enjoyed one too many luxury holidays for my liking and more often than not for some reason they began to refuse to take my calls. It was all very suspicious and I was desperate to investigate but I needed someone on the inside. Someone trusted and completely beyond suspicion who could find out what was really going on, if anything.'

'And that was where I came in,' Dad continued. 'I agreed to infiltrate the situation, convince the others that I wanted a slice of whatever action was occurring. I soon discovered that money was changing hands left, right and centre, with certain people already greedy for more and willing to take increasing risks.'

'We quickly realised,' said Mr Porter, 'that if we gave them enough rope—'

'They'd hang themselves.'

'Exactly.'

'But then you came home, Ruby,' said Dad, turning to look at me. 'You arrived back in Wynbridge and suddenly the whole thing was in danger of folding.'

'But what did I do?' I demanded.

'You fell in love with the place,' said Dad, his tone softer, 'you fell in love with the town, the market, the traders and their cause. You reminded me just how much I loved it along with the true value of what I trying to protect.'

'But surely that was a good thing,' said Mum, 'wasn't it?'

'It should have been,' Dad nodded, 'but when Ruby came back I lost my edge. I was terrified of getting it wrong, not knowing when to draw the line. I knew if I pulled the plug at the wrong time I was going to be jeopardising so much more than just my reputation.'

'And so we decided to call it a day before it got further out of hand,' jumped in Mr Porter. 'Fortunately we already had enough evidence to expose what had been going on and as the last few days have proved, thanks to certain folks' greediness, the whole thing was actually poised to come tumbling down like a stack of cards.'

'So you aren't the miserable, market hater you made out then?' shouted Chris. 'It's all been a deceptive façade, has it, Bob?'

'Most of it,' smiled Dad. 'You know as well as I do, Chris, that our differences used to extend way beyond the market, but for the most part, yes, I've been playing the villain in this sordid little pantomime to try and protect everything I love. I'm just glad it's all over and life can return to normal. We've finally sorted the wheat from the chaff and in the New Year the Wynbridge town regeneration project will be well and truly back on track!'

Silence lasted for about two seconds and then chatter, cheering and a barrage of questions broke out, most of them from Mum. Apparently Dad had a lot of explaining to do but for the most part I was just relieved the truth was finally out and that I had been right. Dad wasn't the town ogre he had set himself up as recently, and the town and the market were in safe hands.

I knew I should have trusted my instincts about how this situation was going to turn out. Dad would never have tried to tempt me to work with him if there was ever any real danger of him being 'on the take', but he had been such a

411

convincing actor, even making us believe that we were going to lose the house! Talk about throwing himself into the role.

I barged through to where Dad was standing and flung my arms around his neck, relieved that the version of the man who had presented himself ever since I came home wasn't my dad after all. I knew I couldn't change what he had done to sabotage my relationship with Steve all those years ago, but it was good to know that he hadn't changed beyond all recognition.

'I'm so sorry, love,' he said, kissing my hair as he hugged me tight, 'I hope you can forgive me. I know I've been a miserable old sod since you've been back, but I've been so worried about cocking everything up that I've made a complete mess of everything else.'

'It's OK,' I said, pulling back a little and wiping away my tears, 'I'm just relieved to have my old dad back. I've really missed you.'

'I was always there, Ruby,' Dad swallowed, 'I was just waiting for the right moment to put in an appearance.'

Chapter 33

I don't think it ever matters how old you are, there is always something deliciously different about waking up on the twenty-fifth of December, no matter which day of the week it falls on. I might have been a little long in the tooth for a Christmas stocking but as I nudged the bulge at the end of the bed I knew 'he'd been' and I felt that sudden upsurge of childlike excitement bubbling up in discovering that I had been good enough to be rewarded with that most longed-for of treats.

I heard feet padding along the landing, no doubt Mum heading to the kitchen to turn on the oven, and couldn't resist calling out.

'Merry Christmas!'

The feet stopped at the top of the stairs and headed back to my door.

'Merry Christmas,' said Dad, his face unexpectedly appearing around the door, 'I thought you'd be awake!'

'And I thought you were Mum,' I yawned. 'Hasn't she got the oven going yet?'

'No need,' said Dad, stepping into the room, 'she's not cooking this year.'

'What?' I gasped. 'Why? She's got a fridge full of festive goodies down there. What's going on?'

'We're having it next week instead,' Dad explained. 'Today we're going out for dinner. We're going to be eating turkey and all the trimmings at The Mermaid.'

'You're kidding.'

'No,' said Dad, grinning with childlike excitement, 'I'm not. We thought it would make a nice change, and besides Chris made us promise before we left last night.'

After Dad's amazing announcement I'd left him and Mum to it and come home to bed. My head was thick with information, not to mention the accusations Bea had flung at me and Steve. At least a hundred times I had gone to text him but I just couldn't bring myself to press Send. Although relieved to have Dad and the market situation so succinctly explained, my mind had still been abuzz with everything else and I was still awake at midnight when I heard my parents giggling and stumbling up the stairs. Evidently, from what Dad had just said, more had gone on at the pub after I left than I realised.

'You could always change your mind,' I suggested hopefully. I had been so looking forward to a quiet Christmas Day at home. 'I probably won't be here next year,' I said, sounding sulkier than I should, 'and I want to make the most of today so I have a special day to remember.'

'It will be a special day,' Dad insisted, 'just a bit different to normal, that's all, and as far as changing my mind is concerned, I don't think that's really an option.'

'Why not?'

'Because Chris said if we didn't turn up he'd come and kidnap us all anyway.'

Having seen Chris in full-blown persuasive action recently I was in no doubt that he was fully prepared to see through the threat and braced myself for what was potentially going to be the most awkward Christmas Day I had ever experienced.

'Cheer up, love,' said Dad, coming into the room and patting my leg, 'I'm going to make us all tea and then you can open your stocking on our bed. How about that?'

An hour later, stuffed full of chocolate coins, I sat cross-legged on Mum and Dad's bed, drinking tea and feeling slightly nauseous, but whether from the sickly treats or the prospect of avoiding having to pull Steve's cracker I couldn't be sure. I was just about to launch another appeal to boycott the pub when Mum spoke up.

'Do you know,' she said, stretching her hands above her head, 'I'm rather looking forward to shirking off the responsibility of producing Christmas dinner for once.'

'Really,' said Dad, sounding as surprised as I felt. 'I thought you'd be rather more reticent about the idea than this.'

'So did I,' Mum admitted, reaching for another segment of chocolate orange, 'but I could get used to this. I'll actually have the opportunity to sit down to eat feeling calm and cool rather than sweaty and exhausted!'

I'd never really thought about Christmas Day from Mum's point of view before. I'd always been so preoccupied with presents and her to-die-for pigs-in-blankets that I'd never considered all the effort and time she put into producing everything. I swallowed another coin and decided to keep quiet.

Ordinarily 'big' presents were exchanged after lunch and just before the Queen's speech but we decided to share them before leaving the house this year so we wouldn't have the worry of leaving anything behind when it was finally time to come home. Mum and Dad were delighted with their few simple gifts but I was surprised to find just one for myself under the tree this year. Ordinarily I knew exactly what I was going to be opening but the lumpy parcel under the tree was a complete mystery.

'I hope it's the right one,' said Mum. 'The chap in the shop said you can change it if needs be. I've kept the receipt.'

I tore into the pretty paper and discovered the perfect rucksack with all the features required to make the back-packing experience as painless as possible.

'It's brilliant,' I grinned. 'In fact,' I added, taking a closer look, 'this is the exact one that I'd been looking at online but didn't think my savings would run to! Thank you so much.'

I gave them both a hug and a kiss. I was delighted that Dad had finally come round to the idea that I was going to see something of the world before I decided to settle down.

'There's a little something inside,' he told me. 'You'd better have a look at that before we go.'

At the bottom of the empty bag was an envelope containing a card and a cheque that quite literally took my breath away.

'Can't have my girl travelling in the cheap seats,' laughed Dad, when I couldn't find the words to express how I felt, 'and besides, my spoils from the Retail Park planning approval covered it.'

Mum and I turned as one, our eyes on stalks.

'I'm kidding,' he laughed again, 'it was a joke.'

'Well, it's not funny,' scolded Mum, 'don't you ever let me catch you making light of that situation again.'

'Sorry,' said Dad, the smile wiped off his face.

'But hang on,' said Mum, the thought evidently only just occurring to her. 'Does this mean the cruise is off?'

I had assumed that Jim and Evelyn would be serving Christmas dinner to family groups at individual tables in the restaurant but stepping through the door my assumption was swept aside in one blink. The bar area had been completely transformed and was bedecked with balloons, streamers and gut-wrenchingly, even more bunches of mistletoe. Long tables had appeared overnight and were arranged in sinuous rows which filled the space completely and along with their festive tablecloths and crackers, the atmosphere was one of a street party, rather than a formal gathering.

Bing Crosby's dulcet tones filled the air and locals were already beginning to arrive in droves. A quick look through to the restaurant revealed a similar set-up and I had no idea how the pub kitchen could produce enough food to feed so many people; however, if the delicious smells pouring through the door every time Evelyn bustled in and out were anything to go by then there wasn't going to be a problem.

'You came!' shouted Chris as he arrived weighed down with armfuls of bags and boxes.

'Didn't have much choice, did we?' Dad laughed.

'Can we have those round the back, please?' said Evelyn briskly when she spotted the load Chris was carrying.

'I'll give you a hand,' said Dad, rushing to open the door. 'Back in a minute,' he called to Mum and was gone.

'Do you really not mind that we aren't spending Christmas Day at home?' I asked Mum as we got stuck in and helped set out the cutlery and cruets.

'No,' she said, 'I don't. I've been trying to get your dad to socialise a bit more and to be honest I wouldn't have minded what day it was if it meant we'd get out of the house and have some fun. Although,' she added, with a nod towards the door, 'not everyone looks up for a laugh.'

Bea, pretty and pristine as always, had certainly lost her sparkle even though I could tell she was trying her best not to show it. Her mum helped her out of her coat and threw me a worried glance before heading into the kitchen to assist Evelyn and the ever growing team. During the last half an hour or so it had become increasingly obvious that the colossal task of entertaining so many people was very much a combined effort but with everyone in such high festive spirits it didn't feel like work at all.

By the time I got the chance to talk to my sad friend everyone was lining up to take their seats and there was still no sign of Sam anywhere.

'He's back from wherever he's been,' said Lizzie, who had just arrived with Ben but was already folding napkins and passing around bowls brimming with cranberry jelly as if her life depended on it, 'Ben saw him getting out of a taxi this morning. I haven't said anything to Bea. I didn't think there'd be much point.'

'I'm sure you're right,' I agreed. 'Why upset her even more?'

'Exactly.'

'Merry Christmas, you!' I said in as jolly a tone as I could muster as I sat myself in the empty seat next to her.

'Merry Christmas,' she smiled back.

'Gosh, you look pretty,' I told her, only just really noticing the deep red silk dress and diamante clip in her hair.

'Thought I might as well wear it,' she sighed, 'I bought it with today in mind and couldn't bear the thought of it hanging in the wardrobe and missing out on its chance to shine. I'll probably take it to the charity shop in the New Year.'

'Right,' I said, not really taking in what she was saying as there was a commotion happening around the door, not to mention a vast amount of heat disappearing out of it.

Gwen sat herself in the seat opposite us, shoving Minnie out of sight under the table and I made a mental note to keep my feet tucked in and my ankles out of reach.

'Do you know how the seating works?' she asked me while at the same time dipping her finger into the cranberry jelly.

'Oh yes,' said Bob, who was sitting with Shirley a couple of chairs away, 'I'd forgotten how it works. Perhaps I should tell Jim to remind everyone before we start.'

'What do you mean "how the seating works"?' I asked Gwen, as Bob went in search of our landlord and I moved the cranberry out of reach.

'Well,' said Gwen, 'you can sit anywhere you like, but you have to change seats after every course. It gives everyone a chance to talk to one another and makes the folk who are on their own like me—'

'And me,' added Bea morosely.

'Not feel quite so out on a limb. Not that it's ever bothered me being on my own, of course,' she shrugged.

Out of the corner of my eye I could see Bea taking a good long look at Gwen and I wondered if she was considering her future as a long-term spinster of the parish. I was just about to try and pull her out of her stupor when someone began ringing the bar bell. I quickly looked around to make sure it wasn't Dad.

'Can everyone please make their way to the bar?' shouted Jim. 'We're almost ready to serve but before we do, there's someone here who has something to say.'

Everyone groaned and struggled to their feet and I looked about me wondering if Steve had decided to spend the day at Sam's place. I hadn't caught so much as a whiff of his after-shave or even his name on the air.

'Not again,' tutted Shirley, 'I think we've had enough shocks for one week, don't you?'

'Well, I'm not moving,' said Bea, crossly folding her arms.

It took a couple of minutes for everyone to jostle into a position that meant they were going to be able to witness the unexpected scene that was about to unfold.

'Where's Bea?' hissed Lizzie in my ear.

'Still at the table,' I hissed back, 'she won't budge.'

'Oh for goodness' sake,' she tutted.

'Right,' said a voice I instantly recognised, 'if the mountain won't come to Mohammed!'

421

The crowd parted and there was Sam looking every inch as handsome as Bea was beautiful. Finally realising that everyone was looking in her direction, she looked up, a scowl firmly etched on her pretty face.

'Where the hell have you been?' she demanded.

'New York,' said Sam, walking over to her table and pulling out the chair next to her.

'New York!' Bea snorted, clearly disgusted with the thought that her once beloved boyfriend had been on a shopping spree across the pond without her.

'Yes,' he said, 'I got you this.'

Bea looked at the cracker he held out to her and shook her head.

'You didn't get that from New York,' she said scathingly, 'it came from the Cherry Tree. I recognise the paper.'

Suddenly I spotted Steve right at the back of the crowd. He was grinning broadly. He winked when he realised I had seen him and my heart started to thunder in my chest as I guessed exactly what was about to happen, even if Bea didn't.

'Just pull it!' shouted Chris. 'Our dinner's getting ruined.'

Bea looked at the sea of expectant faces, grabbed the end of the cracker and pulled. Along with the expected snap, a small turquoise box flew through the air. Sam deftly caught it and was on bended knee before Bea could catch her breath. He opened the box and smiled up at her face.

'I know it's the one you've always wanted,' he grinned. 'You've told me often enough.'

'Oh my God,' Bea gasped.

'Unfortunately the only place I could get it was New York and I wanted to collect it myself.'

Gwen rushed forward and handed Bea the handkerchief she was in dire need of.

'Bea,' smiled Sam, carefully pulling the stunning princess cut diamond from its bespoke box, 'would you consider doing me the honour of becoming my wife?'

The cheers that erupted meant that no one actually heard her answer, but when everyone stopped jumping up and down, the happy couple were kissing passionately and Bea's left hand was sparkling and dazzling us all.

Chapter 34

I can safely say, without a shadow of a doubt that was by far the happiest Christmas Day I had ever spent. The smile on Bea's face was far brighter than all of the lights put together, but not quite as bright as the ring on her finger.

'So how does it feel,' I nudged her, as I poured rather more cream over my pudding than was really necessary, 'to finally have your dream come true?'

'I can't believe it,' she sniffed, looking from her hand to the box and back again for what must have been the five thousandth time. 'It's just amazing. The whole day has been amazing.'

'Thank goodness you wore the dress!' I teased. 'Just think if you'd turned up in sweats and left it hanging in the wardrobe, never to fulfil its Christmas destiny.'

'It doesn't bear thinking about,' she shuddered, so wrapped up in her own little world that she was completely unaware of my joshing. 'Did you know?' she asked.

'What Sam was planning to do, you mean?'

'Yes.'

'No,' I told her truthfully, 'I didn't have a clue. I had no idea where he'd gone or what he was up to. However,' I added, with a nod to where Steve was sitting talking to Bob, 'I think Steve did.'

'How do you know that?'

'Well, the way he spoke to you for a start,' I said. 'You were so worried and he was so flippant. That's not Steve at all, is it? You know what he's like. He cares about everyone, would do anything he could to make sure they were happy.'

Bea looked at me and raised her eyebrows.

'I should have twigged he knew what was going on when he teased you about the Doncaster, Dubai, passport thing.'

'But I didn't exactly give you a chance, did I?' she sighed. 'I'm sorry for what I said,' she swallowed. 'I had no right to tell you to get on with it. Even though the way you still feel about one another is ridiculously obvious.'

Now it was my turn to raise my eyebrows.

'Oh, I'm sorry,' she said, looking at her left hand again, 'I just can't seem to stop myself. I can't begin to tell you how happy I am right now and I want you to be happy too.'

'I am happy,' I told her, 'but you have to remember, Bea, that you and I don't want the same things. I don't need a ring on my finger; I don't want to settle down yet. I want to see something of the world.'

I didn't add that I would have liked someone special to see it all with. My honesty would only stretch so far.

'But you've been living away from Wynbridge for the best part of four years,' she reminded me.

'I hardly think studying at university in the country you were born in is the same as jumping on a plane to satisfy your wanderlust,' I reminded her right back. 'I need more in my life than this little town can offer right now.'

'And what about Steve?'

'What about him?'

'Well, don't you think he wants more than a fruit and veg business? Don't you think he might want to break out and go somewhere new?'

'I don't know,' I shrugged. 'I haven't asked him, but I can hardly imagine he's given it much thought. He seems so happy and so settled here. I know I won't feel like that for a long while, if ever. Besides, you gave him the ideal opportunity to say something and he just upped and left.'

'I'm not so sure you've got that right,' she said, shaking her head, the diamante clip in her hair glistening under the lights.

'What do you mean?'

'Well, you're forgetting one very important thing?'

'What's that?'

'You weren't the only one who had your life all mapped out, were you? When you left for uni, Steve stayed behind.

For all we know he could be thinking that his whole life is just one big compromise. After all, you had arranged to study and travel together, hadn't you?'

'I guess so,' I mumbled, thinking how he had so recently reminded me that we had made so many plans to do everything together and that I myself had thought about how much he would have enjoyed university life.

'So what makes you think he doesn't still crave that? How can you be so sure that he's shelved his dreams?'

'I don't know,' I told her, disliking where the conversation seemed to be heading, 'but it's nothing to do with me now, is it?'

'So you really don't think there's any chance for you and him, then? There's no way you're going to get back together?'

I had to laugh at her enthusiastic matchmaking. It was astounding what a piece of good jewellery could do for a girl!

'Look,' I said, 'when you left here last night Steve was literally two steps behind you. There's no way he wants to get back together, and besides, he knows I'm leaving in a few days and that there'd really be no point stirring something up just to abandon it again.'

'Well, as long as you're sure,' she shrugged, as Sam arrived back at the table with yet more fizz.

'I am,' I told her.

'Then perhaps you should say goodbye to him properly and resolve the situation once and for all.'

'All right,' I agreed, 'if the opportunity to do just that presents itself any time soon, I'll take it.'

'Promise?'

'Promise.'

A couple of hours later, and as if by magic, just such an opportunity did come my way and with Bea's beady gaze watching my every move I knew I had no choice but to grab it with both hands.

'Fancy a walk?' asked Steve. 'It's stifling in here and I could do with a breath of fresh air.'

'All right,' I agreed. 'To be honest, I thought you'd already gone home.'

I hadn't seen him for a while, not that I'd been looking out for him, of course, and had begun to assume that I was going to get away without having to say a proper goodbye. Evidently the Christmas gods had other ideas.

'No,' he said, 'I've just been helping sort a few things out and catching up on your dad's latest revelations.'

I imagined him listening to the latest news, his elbows in soap suds and dirty dishes and thought that was about right. I really should have done more to help clear away myself.

'Where are you planning on going?' I asked as we stepped back over the threshold, safely under the mistletoe and out into the bitter evening air. Thankfully there wasn't a breath of wind or a cloud in the sky. It was glacial but not unbearable.

'Don't know,' he shrugged, 'let's just see where our feet take us, shall we?'

I pulled my collar up a little higher and rummaged for my gloves.

'I'm sorry about what Bea said last night,' I sniffed.

'Oh,' he said, 'why?'

'Well,' I hesitated, 'it was awkward for both of us, wasn't it? I mean, she's totally got the wrong end of the stick about everything. She's so caught up in her own happy ever after that she expects what works for her will work for everyone.'

'I'm sure she was just meaning to be kind.'

'Well yes,' I said, 'I'm sure she had the best intentions really.'

We fell into step and didn't talk for a little while.

'You don't want a Tiffany engagement ring and a happy ever after then?' Steve eventually asked.

'I did once upon a time, you know I did, and you were supposed to be the one who supplied it.'

'But that's not what you want any more?'

'No,' I said, 'I don't think so. I'm not saying I'll never want to settle down, but for now I just want to enjoy living.'

'I couldn't agree more,' he nodded.

'But you're happy living here, aren't you?'

Bea's doubts were still fresh in my mind.

'I am,' he said, an edge of hesitation creeping into his tone, 'but that doesn't mean that I don't want to break out every now and again.'

I couldn't help thinking that perhaps my friend might have been right after all.

'Don't get me wrong,' he continued, 'I love Wynbridge and I love the business . . .'

'And the pub and the rugby,' I nudged, trying to make him acknowledge that the life he had been living for the last four years had been worthwhile.

'Yes,' he said, 'all of that, but you're forgetting one thing.'

'Oh?'

'I had hopes and dreams as well, didn't I? I wanted to study and travel, but here I am.' He threw out his arms indicating the park we had arrived at. 'Same old, same old.'

I was slightly taken aback that Bea had realised what I hadn't, and that he sounded so dissatisfied. I had always assumed Steve was very happy with his lot, that he had settled into the life he hadn't been expecting to live and was enjoying it.

'So what are you going to do about it?' I asked.

'I'm not sure,' he said, rubbing his gloves together, 'that depends.'

'On what?'

'You mostly,' he said, reaching for my hand which I found I had no desire to pull away.

'Oh look,' I said, 'there are lights in the bandstand.'

'I know,' he said, pulling me along, 'I put them there.'

I could hear music quietly playing as we approached and I felt my heart picking up the pace. It began to suddenly thump hard in my chest, trying to outrun my stomach which had flipped over and back again and once more for good measure.

'Can you remember,' said Steve, letting go of my hand and jumping up the steps, 'all the fun we used to have in here after dark?'

'Of course I can,' I blushed, 'every second of it.'

'And can you remember the last time we met here?' he asked, suddenly pulling me close.

'Yes,' I said, my eyes brimming with tears.

We had spent an afternoon hidden under the canopy out of the rain talking through our plans. It had been the day before Sean had died and everyone's lives had changed forever.

'Well, I've got this crazy idea, you see,' said Steve looking deep into my eyes, 'but it will only work if you agree to it.'

'What is it?'

'I'm going to turn back time,' he said seriously.

'Now we've talked about this,' I reminded him as he lowered his lips almost to mine. He was so close I could feel his warm breath on my face.

Just when I thought he was going to kiss me he lifted me off my feet and spun me around and around, faster and faster.

'Stop!' I squealed, screwing up my eyes and laughing, 'I'll throw up!'

He set me down but didn't let me go. I kept my eyes closed until everything stopped spinning.

'What do you think?' he whispered, looking around him. 'Has it worked? Do you feel eighteen?'

'I feel sick,' I laughed.

'Never mind that,' he tutted, still holding me close, 'how do you feel in your heart?'

'Like I never want to let you go again,' I whispered, the words escaping without a second thought.

'Because you think you'll fall over,' he frowned, 'or because you love me?'

'Because I love you, of course!' I giggled.

He was right. It was working. I was beginning to feel eighteen all over again.

'OK,' he said seriously, 'well, that's a start.'

'And,' I asked, 'given everything we've been through during the last few weeks, how do you feel about me?'

'Well, you've aged all right.'

'Hey,' I laughed, 'you said we'd turned back time.'

'But we haven't though, have we? Not really. Let's face it, I'm no Cher.'

He let me go and went and sat on one of the benches at the side. I didn't know what to say. I looked out at the stars thinking that we weren't going to make it after all.

'Which is just as well really,' he said, pulling me towards him, 'because I never could have found a way to afford to do this when I was eighteen.'

He pulled out a cracker from inside his coat and I felt a sense of déjà vu descending.

'Sam stole my thunder a bit with the cracker idea,' he tutted, 'but at least I've managed to get you on your own to do this.'

'Do what exactly?' I winced.

I really hoped there wasn't a little blue box destined for me waiting in the wings.

'Pull it and see,' he whispered.

I grabbed hold of the end and with a snap that ripped through the air the pretty paper split and two pieces of paper floated out.

'Plane tickets!' I gasped, bending to pick them up.

'Plane tickets,' he confirmed, pulling me back up and kissing me firmly on the lips. 'This is what I went to sort out last night. I had stuff to collect and calls to make and they all add up to me coming with you,' he laughed. 'But only if you want me to, of course.'

'But when, how?' I gabbled. 'How can you get away?'

'Dad says he can manage without me, Mum says I'd be mad to let you go again and Paul Thompson says he has the perfect job for me in India. All I need now,' he said, gazing down at me and pulling off my hat, 'is you.'

'Oh well, you can have me,' I laughed as he began to kiss me again, 'I've never been anybody's but yours!'

'But this is for ever,' he said, pulling away slightly and looking at me seriously. 'I don't know where we'll end up or when, but if we do this then we're back together for ever. You and me for always, just like we planned. Is that what you want, Ruby? Will you want me for ever?'

'Oh yes,' I said, sinking into his arms. 'For ever sounds simply perfect to me.'

Acknowledgements

It hardly seems possible that I'm already writing the acknowledgements for my third novel, yet here I am, with an even longer list of folk to thank than last time.

There are of course, the usual suspects – my wonderful family – Paul, Oliver, Amelia and Storm the cat (now used to seeing their names in print). They're all still here, waving their pompoms or rolling their eyes depending on the occasion. Thank you guys, your support means the world to me.

And it simply wouldn't be right, three books down the line, not to thank Patsy, Andrea and Christine, my work colleagues and friends, who have listened to my incessant chatter in the staff room, even before I signed my first contract, and who are still interested and enthusiastic about every twist and turn in my writing career.

No author acknowledgement would be complete without a nod to their writer chums and I am immensely lucky to have a great bunch never further than a few taps on the keyboard away. Kate Jackson, Sam Tonge, Dame (she really should be) Milly Johnson and Jenni Keer, you are all worth your weight in gold and I know there is no conundrum you cannot help me through. Thank you for your words of wisdom and, as far as Milly is concerned, refreshingly candid advice.

Behind every lucky author there is a fabulous publishing team working tirelessly behind the scenes and I am fortunate enough to be able to brag one of the best. Clare Hey, Sara-Jade Virtue, Emma Capron, Dawn Burnett and Jamie Criswell, you, and the entire Books and the City team at Simon & Schuster, have made this a truly memorable year and I love you all to bits. Thank you.

Huge thanks as always to the many, many book bloggers who work so hard to promote, review and champion my books. Your commitment to sharing your love of my work with the wider world is hugely appreciated. Whether you have signed up for a blog tour, helped reveal a cover, left a great review or offered an interview spot on your blog, it has all helped spread the word that Heidi Swain is now, finally, a published author.

And last, but by no means least, thank you, dear readers. Thank you for picking up the paperback or downloading the e-book. I hope you have enjoyed your Christmas trip to Wynbridge and I look forward to sharing a brand new story with you all next summer. May your bookshelves, be they virtual or real, always be filled with fabulous fiction!

H x

Curl up with Heidi Swain for cupcakes, crafting and love at *The Cherry Tree Café*.

Lizzie Dixon's life feels as though it's fallen apart. Instead of the marriage proposal she was hoping for from her boyfriend, she is unceremoniously dumped, and her job is about to go the same way. So, there's only one option: to go back home to the village she grew up in and try to start again.

Her best friend Jemma is delighted Lizzie has come back home. She has just bought a little café and needs help in getting it ready for the grand opening. And Lizzie's sewing skills are just what she needs.

With a new venture and a new home, things are looking much brighter for Lizzie. But can she get over her broken heart, and will an old flame reignite a love from long ago . . .?

'Fans of Jenny Colgan and Carole Matthews will enjoy this warm and gently funny story of reinvention, romance, and second chances – you'll devour it in one sitting'
Katie Oliver, author of the bestselling 'Marrying Mr Darcy' series

Available now in eBook